What readers say about Blue

Absolutely brilliant! —Bridget, Readaholic b

a thoroughly engrossing time travel story that promises to continue as vividly as it started. —Nan Hawthorne, *An Involuntary King*

a delightfully intricate tale of time travel, life lessons, challenges of faith, and redemption...moving, witty, and captivating...a page-turner...I highly recommend this novel. —Jennifer, Rundpinne.com

Vosika spins a captivating tale.... The pacing flows from a measured cadence...and builds to a climatic crescendo reminiscent of Ravel's Bolero. I become invested in the characters. Both Shawn and Niall are fully fleshed and I could imagine having a conversation with each. Write faster, Laura. I want to read more.
—Joan Szechtman, *This Time*

fast-paced, well-written, witty...Captivating! —Stephanie Derhak, *White Pines*

Ms. Vosika wove these aspects...together in a very masterful way that...kept me spellbound. I could hardly put it down. —Thea Nillson, *A Shunned Man*

Original & intelligently written. I couldn't turn the pages fast enough.
—Dorsi Miller, reader

Ms. Vosika spins the web so well you are a part of all the action. If you love history, romance, music and the believable unbelievable...this book is for you. I couldn't put it down until I closed the cover on an ending I never expected.
—Kat Yares, *Journeys Into the Velvet Darkness*

...best time travel book I have ever read. Fantastic descriptive detail and a sweet love story are combined beautifully. —Amazon reviewer

some of the best writing it has been my pleasure to read....
—JR Jackson, *Reilley's Sting, Reilley's War,* and *The Ancient Mariner Tells All.*

a very exciting tale.... —Ross Tarry, *Eye of the Serpent,* and other mysteries

Vosika is a master at creating engaging characters...a riveting plot, well-drawn cast, and the beautiful imagery of Scotland.
—Genny Zak Kieley, *Hot Pants and Green Stamps*

I love books on time travel, but this is so much more. The characters come to life in your heart and mind. —Jeryl Struble, singer/songwriter, *Journey to Joy*

One of the most intriguing stories of Scottish history I have ever read...riveting.
—Pam Borum, Minneapolis, MN

I found myself still thinking about the characters after finishing the book.
—Goodreads reviewer

In memory of Mark

who also loved writing

Waverly Public Library
1500 West Bremer Ave.
Waverly, IA 50677

BLUE BELLS
OF
SCOTLAND

By
Laura Vosika

Gabriel's Horn Publishing
in association with
Night Writer Books
www.nightwritersbooks.com
www.bluebellstrilogy.com

copyright © 2009 by Laura Vosika and Gabriel's Horn Publishing
2nd edition 2010

All rights reserved. No portion of this book may be reproduced, stored in retrieval system, or transmitted in any form or by any means— electronic, mechanical, photocopy, recording, scanning, or other— except for brief quotations in reviews or articles, without the prior written permission of the author and publisher.
Contact at laura@bluebellstrilogy.com

Published in Minneapolis, Minnesota by Gabriel's Horn Publishing

Publisher's Note: This novel is a work of fiction. Names, characters, places, and incidents are either products of the author's imagination or used fictitiously. All characters are fictional, and any similarity to people living or dead is purely coincidental.

First printing September 2009
Printed in the United States of America

For sales, please visit www.bluebellstrilogy.com
Available for e-readers and for the blind through www.bookshare.org

ISBN-13: 978-0-9842151-0-2
ISBN-10: 0-9842151-0-7

Acknowledgments

Writing a book, despite the name on the cover, involves many people. I would like to thank Andrew for his support in seeing that I have the time to write, buying me a multitude of books and DVDs on all things Scotland and medieval, driving me all over the Highlands and following me up and down the hills Shawn, Allene, and Niall would have climbed.

My thanks and love to my children for their patience: Karl, Caoimhe, Kian, Cara, Michael, Matthew, Connor, Liam, and John Paul. They have listened to many a story of Robert the Bruce, Bannockburn, and Scottish and medieval history.

My thanks and appreciation to the Night Writers of Maple Grove who have been both enthusiastic and full of good advice: Ross, Judy, Genny, Judd, Jack, Janet, Jerry, Lyn, Larry, Linda, Brin, Inna, Will, Stephanie, and Sue. You are all a great blessing in my life.

Thank you to my parents and sister Linda for making my trip to Scotland possible.

My thanks to the many helpful people we met in Scotland, especially Judith Aitkin, Arts Education Manager at Eden Court Theatre and Joe at the Bannockburn Heritage Centre, both of whom took a great deal of time to show me around and answer my many questions. I was impressed by their knowledge, friendliness, and willingness to take the time to help a stranger, and by Joe's obvious love of his country's history.

My thanks to Chris Baty and National Novel Writing Month, www.nanowrimo.org for bringing sky-castles down to earth for so many, and to Cindy, Jeryl, Pam, Courtney, Kim, and Rita for their encouragement and support.

Historical Notes

As a musician and American, I learned many new things in researching *Blue Bells of Scotland*. I developed an incredible appreciation for Robert the Bruce and James Douglas, and their loyal friends and followers, and the amazing feat they accomplished at the Battle of Bannockburn against 'impossible' odds. I hope the reader will come away from this story with a similar appreciation for these great men. I have enjoyed every minute of research and have kept the events of the *Blue Bells Trilogy* as historically accurate as possible. 700 years later, sources often conflict, so at times, I've had to choose between sources and guess which is most reliable.

The time slips Aaron describes to Niall have been recounted in several sources. The story of the boys in Kersey, in particular, is told in Andrew MacKenzie's book *Adventures in Time: Encounters with the Past.*

Prelude

"*Shawn* means *self* and *Kleiner* means *centered!*" His girlfriend, an English major, flung it at him as an insult. Shawn plucked it from midair, polished it off, and, grinning, wore it as a badge of honor.

But Shawn surpassed mere self-centeredness. He strove also for selfishness, self-importance, and self-satisfaction. He was the center of his own existence and, the problem was, of many others', too.

His audition for second trombone, a month before completing his music degree, was legend.

He swaggered into the reception room and leaned over the secretary's desk, smiling his infectious smile and complimenting her eyes. In minutes, he had a date with her. She called her fiance to cancel dinner with his parents. Postponed it indefinitely. He drew a rose from the vase on her desk, brushed it across her lips, and took it, and her longing gaze, with him.

Strutting into the warm-up area, he sized up forty-five world-class trombonists. His eyes fell on the lone woman. He trailed the rose along her cheek and flipped his card up between two fingers. "Call me," he mouthed. Her eyes melted.

When he pulled out his trombone, seventeen musicians stopped playing to stare. Shawn had that affect. He stood six feet, strongly built. Dark chestnut hair brushed his shoulders. Deep amber eyes sparkled with confidence as he leisurely scanned his competition.

Satisfied, he drew in a deep breath. Thirteen more stopped playing. He blew one long, golden note, and fourteen more lowered their instruments. He dipped warning eyebrows at the lone holdout still prattling off scales. The man dropped his instrument and looked away.

Now it was only Shawn.

He warmed up with the triplet section of *Blue Bells of Scotland*. He played it twice as fast as anyone ever had, skipping over the hardest parts like a mountain stream bubbling downhill. His *Russian Easter* thundered out every gravitas Rimsky-Korsakov had intended. A little bluesy *Body and Soul* just for fun, at which an older gentlemen in the back of the room wiped the corner of his eye.

The door burst open. The conductor charged through, yelling for a contract. The principal trombonist dropped to second chair and Shawn ruled the trombone section.

"Are you crazy?" the concertmaster demanded, when he heard. "All we needed was a second trombone. What have you done?"

"Vision!" Conrad Schmitz pushed his face right back into the concertmaster's. "Charisma. Flair."

"It's just a trombone. Oompah, oompah, and the occasional *Valkyrie*. It's only a step above bassoon for comedic value. What were you thinking?"

"When you meet him, you'll understand! He has magnetism. Power! He could turn a tin whistle into stardom. He can do for us what James Galway did for flute, what Yo-Yo Ma did for cello. He can give us success we've only dreamed of till now!"

Within a week, inspired by Conrad's vision, the music committee had re-engineered the season's program to feature Shawn, the new centerpiece of a sagging orchestra, the man who would lead them to a brighter future.

Shawn celebrated his victory as he celebrated most days of his life: with self indulgence. He took the receptionist for steak and lobster at a restaurant heavy with silver and crystal. The chef treated him. They had fine wine, and a night at the Hilton, between red silk sheets. And the next week, with a carefree grin, Shawn allowed the orchestra to begin accompanying him on his rise to fame and wealth.

Scottish Highlands, early June, 1314

Niall gripped white knuckles in the pony's mane, leaning tight over its neck. Its hooves flashed over the moonlit moor. Beside him, raced his nephew Gilbert and best friend Iohn. Half the MacDougall clan thundered after them. "Ahead!" Iohn shouted. Two MacDougalls burst from the rise before Niall. One swung at Gilbert, doubling him over, howling. Niall whipped his sword from his back. A swipe from a MacDougall's sword knocked it from his hand. The man on his left, teeth bared in victory, grabbed Niall's reins. Niall's eyes flashed to Iohn. He, too, grinned.

Iohn's sword spun through the air, flashing sparks of moonlight. It jolted into Niall's outstretched hand, jarring his arm clear up to his shoulder. He swung at the first man, knocking him senseless, even as he tore the dirk from his belt and plunged it into the other man's chest. The man's eyes flashed wide. He dropped the reins, scrabbling at his breast.

"Go!" Niall shouted at Iohn. "Help Gil." Iohn obeyed his future laird. Niall yanked his knife. The man slid off the blade, clutching his chest, and dropped to his knees. Niall swallowed bile. But his duty to the Laird included retrieving their cattle from the thieving MacDougalls. "For Gil," he whispered, shoving the dirk in his belt. Still, he made the sign of the cross over the dying man.

Hooves rumbled behind him. MacDougalls spilled down the steep slope, onto the moor. It was Niall's job to lead them away from the cattle. With a last glance at the bodies, he kicked his mount. The pony skimmed the spongy field, shooting over clumps of heather. Niall's enemies lost ground steadily. He rose in his stirrups, driving the pony hard, grinning, and shouted over his shoulder, "Ye'll no forget the night Niall Campbell retrieved his cattle!"

And he flipped his tunic up at them, baring everything.

The thin whine of an arrow streaked across the moor.

Chapter One

Inverness, Scotland, Present

Blinding lights, pulsing drums—the timpani deep and dark—sent pulses through his body. Shawn's eyes closed, feeling the music, the slide flowing, moving, as if on its own. Behind him, he felt, before he heard, the orchestra move into the final chord: just the violins at first, almost imperceptible; a swell as violas joined, then cellos; a low rumble of basses; a soft trill of flutes, growing; more woodwinds. Shawn gulped air and poured it, liquid gold, into the instrument. Up in the balconies flanking the stage, a rank of pipers added their sound. Their drone hummed through his body.

The conductor's arms slashed down. All sound stopped.

Silence.

Shawn's eyes opened. He lowered the trombone slowly, pushed his long, dark hair from his eyes, and surveyed his minions in the crowd. Beyond the glare of lights, a sea of dark shapes heaved upward. Applause erupted into the void, pouring over him like the warm breath of life. His face broke into a huge grin. Energy surged through him as the final concert of his Scottish tour ended to thundering acclaim. A girl screamed, "Shawn, I love you, I *looove* you!"

"And I love you!" he boomed. His voice reverberated through the microphone clipped to his shirt, ricocheting from the speakers around the auditorium. "Every last one of you!" He searched the audience for the girl flailing her arms and blew a kiss. She screamed again. "You're a wonderful audience! You are truly the best of Scotland! We'll be back, right Conrad?"

The conductor, his wild white hair almost tamed for the evening, beamed and nodded, bringing on more applause.

"Thank you," Shawn said, again and again, nodding to various sections of the audience. He blew kisses to women. "The pleasure is mine. I've loved every minute!" He gestured to the kilted bagpipers lining the balconies. "The best of Scotland!" he beamed. "Show them your appreciation! I know you'll all want to buy them a drink or two afterward." The bagpipers bowed gravely. Smiles passed the lips of several at mention of a drink. The crowd cheered. Shawn swept his arm over the orchestra, who stood, as one, to bow. "They deserve a hand, don't they? They're a great, hard-working bunch." He gestured toward Conrad, stiff in his tuxedo. "Conrad Schmitz, our fearless leader! Show him you love him!" Conrad stepped down from the podium. They shook hands. Finally, with a last bow and wave to the girl still screaming his name, he stepped off stage into the black void of the wings.

"Well done, Shawn," Conrad said.

"Of course!" Shawn gave his usual cocky grin, listening to the applause. There would be curtain calls. There always were. He lifted the double tall mocha, left backstage after each concert for him, in a toast. Conrad smiled tightly, lifted his own water glass in salute, and sipped. Shawn and Conrad stepped back onstage, bowing again. They went through the routine several times. This audience was especially generous, loving both the concert's theme of traditional Scottish music, and Shawn's skillful arrangements combining bagpipes, lutes, harps, uilleann pipes, and singers with a classical orchestra.

A girl burst onstage, her hair in green spikes, and skinny legs in striped stockings. Security floundered after her. She threw herself at Shawn, pelting his face with kisses. He kissed her back with gusto, and the audience cheered. The guards dragged her away, still yelling, "I love you, Shawn!"

"I love you, too!" He blew kisses after her, much to the audience's delight.

Bows. Applause. More bows. Smiles so broad his face hurt. A wave of the hand. An encore. *Blue Bells*, of course. They never tired of it. Finally, loosening his bow tie, and removing his cummerbund, Shawn signaled with a good-natured smile that the night was really over. He pushed backstage, swaggering and slapping high fives, yanking at the buttons constricting his throat, eager for the night's real fun to begin.

Glenmirril Castle, On the Shore of Loch Ness, Scotland, 1314

Flames crackled in the great hall's fireplace. Flickering red shadows danced over gray stone walls. Voices called across the room, and laughed nearby. At the head table, one of the Laird's great, shaggy hunting hounds nudged Niall's elbow. He patted its head and tossed a bone.

"That's a greedy one, that is." Allene laughed at his side, shaking her copper hair. They watched the huge animal skitter across the rush-strewn floor after the bone, and settle down, gnawing. Allene leaned close. Her red hair tickled his cheek. "How's Gil?"

"The laddie's no well," Niall answered. He watched a juggler in multi-colored tunic spin knives in the air. "I brought him a bannock an dram, and played for him a wee bit. But the fever's no broken."

"And you?"

"I've been better." Niall leaned close and whispered with a wink, "as has my arse." He laughed at her shock and shifted uncomfortably on his thick cushion. MacDougall's arrow, by excellent aim or dumb luck, had caught his exposed parts.

It had been a nightmare ride, unable to sit, and the arrow jolting his posterior with every hoof beat, through a labyrinthine moonlit glen, following a glittering silver ribbon of stream, and circling back to the hollow where his men and cattle hid. He'd bullied a stray cow over the lip of the hollow, bellowing to his men, "You louts left one behind!"

His attempts to distract them from his growing weakness had worked all too well. When blackness swamped him, tumbling him from the pony-like hobbin he rode, they were too slow to prevent his head striking a rock.

He hurt everywhere. But they'd be telling the tale for years, how Niall Campbell, even with an arrow in his arse, turned back for one more cow. Just today, he'd heard them around the corner, regaling young boys, who had gazed with awe, when Niall limped into view.

He laughed, rubbing his posterior with an exaggerated grimace. "'Twas a small price to pay to bring home our cattle."

"And for yer own vanity in mocking the MacDougall," Allene replied. She lifted the hair at his temple, studying the vicious purple-black bruise. Her fingertips grazed rough lacerations. "Aer ye still seeing double?"

"'Tis a fine thing to see two of ye, my lady." Niall smiled, hoping she wouldn't press, for at the moment, three of her swam before his eyes, three heads of fiery curls, three freckled faces, three pairs of bright blue eyes.

"Wheesht!" spoke Lord Morrison on Niall's right, and he was glad for the interruption. "Rabbie's a-goin' to tell a story." Voices died down around the hall. Rabbie was a favorite. As the old man pulled up a stool facing the Laird, Allene and Niall fell to their meal, spearing bread, turnips, and slabs of meat from platters lining the table.

"The tale of King Herla," old Rabbie began in his ancient voice. Whispers of appreciation swept around the room from older folk who knew the story. Children fell quiet, leaning in close to hear how Herla, after a hard day's riding, rested in an ancient forest. Exciting, mysterious things always happened in ancient forests. "But as he dozed," Rabbie creaked, "a noise woke him." More children left their seats and eased into the circle at old Rabbie's feet.

"I'd wager he saw a dwarf," Niall whispered to Allene, under cover of lifting his tankard. "With cloven feet."

"And what did he see," said Rabbie, "but a dwarf. With cloven feet!" The children gasped.

"Go for your sword," muttered Niall.

Allene lowered her head, covering a smile.

"He went for his sword!" Rabbie leaned toward the children, reaching for his belt. They drew back. Older ones giggled, wrapping protective arms around younger siblings. "But the dwarf smiled and said," and Rabbie imitated the dwarf's voice, "'I've heard o' your wisdom and would feign call you friend. I'd make a bargain wi' ye. I'll attend your wedding, and ye'll attend mine.' They sealed the promise with a drink from a gilded hunting horn."

The story wove through King Herla's adventures, to his eventual marriage, attended by the dwarf king. Niall rose from his seat, unable to sit on the wound any longer, and stood behind Allene's chair. "Did the dwarf marry within the year?" he whispered, leaning close to her ear. Lord Morrison lowered dangerous eyebrows, daring him to speak again. Allene stared down into her dinner, tightening her mouth against a laugh.

"Within the year, the dwarf announced his marriage," said Rabbie. "The king and his men, carrying gifts worthy of a fellow monarch, traveled to a great cavern, where they celebrated for three days with the dwarf's people."

The sun sank, leaving velvet blue sky peering through the eastern windows, and streaks of pink and orange through the western. The loch lapped softly outside. Insects hummed. Niall rested his hands on Allene's shoulders, stifling his aches. He needed more ale.

"When the celebration ended," Rabbie said, "the dwarf king gave them gifts, including a bloodhound. 'Ye're no longer safe in your world,' the dwarf said. 'Carry the bloodhound on your saddle. Doona get off your horses until he gets down. Then will ye be safe.' The king and his warriors rode out, full of fine food and ale. Imagine their surprise when they reached their world and dinna see the forest."

Rabbie leaned down, opening his eyes wide. The children stretched forward, waiting.

"There were fields, and villages," Rabbie whispered. "King Herla rode on, seeing naught he knew. At last, they found an old man—even older than me!" Rabbie tugged at his long, white beard. The children giggled. "They asked him what had become of the forests and the Kingdom of Herla. The old man stroked his beard." Rabbie matched action to words. "And at last remembered an old legend, about a king who had disappeared. But that, the man said...." Rabbi stopped, looking from face to eager face, making them wait. "That was *three hoondred years ago!"*

The children's eyes grew round. "Could tha' really happen, Grandfaither Rabbie?" piped a little girl with straw-colored braids.

"Och, who's to say?" said the old man. "The fairy folk, they like to play tricks on us poor humans. There's many a story of fairies takin' a man to fairyland, an hoondreds o' years passin' ere he leaves."

"Fairies!" scoffed Niall.

"Do ye be careful, Niall Campbell," Allene murmured. "Ye doona want to be temptin' them."

He winked at her. "No, I doona want to be tempting the fairies."

"Niall!" roared the Laird. Niall jumped. A shock of pain crashed through his head. "Get your harp, laddie, and play for us!"

Niall nodded obediently, still smiling at Allene's concern. Taking his harp from a peg on the stone wall, he scuffled through the rushes and settled himself gingerly on Rabbie's stool. Men chuckled; women blushed. He grinned, rubbing his posterior in jest at his own foolhardiness, and began one of their favorites, a ballad of love lost. Iohn drifted to his side, harmonizing. Some people watched. Others returned to their conversations; the hum of talk swelled gently.

He liked it this way, playing in the background. A dog sniffed his knee and wandered away. A few children remained in the straw, watching. Some played games with their hands, bits of string, or marbles. The youngest slept in their mothers' arms. Sitting beside her dozing father, Allene smiled at him. His world was complete.

Inverness, Scotland, Present

The hall backstage filled with laughing musicians in concert black, drunk on a fine performance, and well-wishers from the audience. They packed the narrow passage between white-washed concrete walls, bumping tables and brushing tall wheeled crates of ballet costumes. Most strained toward Shawn. He lifted a hand to friends over the press, signed programs, called a greeting, laughed, chatted, and shook hands with ardent admirers he'd never met before.

"Where to, Shawn?" Dana called. She hugged her French horn close to her body in the crowd. Her ginger red hair shot in short spikes in all directions from her head. Several others slipped through the press of people, squeezing through the green room door.

"Shawn! Got a party going?" shouted Rob, the principal trumpet player.

"Ask Amy," Shawn called back. Amy, his girlfriend of two and a half years, would deal with it. He turned his attention back to a short, elderly man with traditional kilt and a bristling mustache. Smiles, more

Waverly Public Library

handshakes. Shawn thanked him, turned to an elderly woman spangled with diamonds, congratulated her on her son's own musical success, and edged toward the green room.

He signed a boy's program, patted his shoulder, and encouraged him in his up-coming audition; got two steps closer and greeted a young woman. His eyes lit up. He clasped her hand in both of his, stopping his pursuit of the green room.

"Beautiful playing!" she gushed. Her hand fluttered to her chest. Shawn's eyes followed. "Just beautiful!"

"Likewise," Shawn replied. His gaze slid up past auburn curls brushing her shoulders, to green eyes. "Just beautiful!" She blushed, glanced at the floor with a giggle, and returned her eyes to his with a bold gaze. "Come to my party tonight," he murmured.

"You don't even know me." She dimpled. "I'm a stranger."

"There are no strangers," Shawn crooned. "Only friends we haven't met. The Blue Bell Inn." She simpered. With a slow smile, he eased his hand, palm against palm, from hers, and turned the doorknob behind him. She'd be at his party. He didn't waste time wondering.

In the green room, he surveyed his domain. Despite the name, the walls and carpets were pale blue. Fluorescent bulbs flooded the room with light. Coffee burbled on a counter against the far wall. Bouquets of roses and mixed flowers lay between the percolator and a tray of cookies. Men and women sprawled on comfortable couches and chairs scattered around the room. Some spoke quietly. "...called my son," said the concert master, Peter, as Shawn passed. And the young man—Shawn didn't know his name—who'd just joined the violas: ".... meeting my wife at the airport."

The excitement of the hallway carried into the musicians' private quarters. A boisterous group of men in tuxedos and women in black dresses surrounded Amy. She, too, wore a flowing, black skirt, and long-sleeved black blouse that set off her cobalt eyes, long, dark lashes, and pale skin—unusually pale tonight, he thought. Thick, black hair hung to her waist. "The Blue Bell Inn," she repeated. "As soon as people get there."

Heads turned as Shawn pushed through. Cheers went up, calls of friends, hands raised in greeting. The volume rose, swallowing the irritated glances of the concert master and several others. But Shawn didn't bother about the opinions of those who didn't know how to have fun. The good cheer of the more lively crowd reached out and drew in their king with hand shakes, congratulations, and back slaps.

Shawn reached for Amy. He pulled her close, kissing her enthusiastically to catcalls from his friends. "Hey, what was with your playing tonight?" he asked, pulling back. "It was a little off."

She smiled weakly, and twisted away.

"She played great. As always," the concertmaster snapped, turning from his conversation. "Ignore him, Amy."

"You coming to my party?" Shawn asked her.

"Not tonight," she said.

"Oh, come on, Amy." Dana squeezed her shoulder. "I want my best friend there."

A couple of the men hooted. "Losing your touch, Shawn?"

He grinned at them, unfazed. But Conrad arrived, tugging at his bow tie and staying Shawn's comeback. "Fine job, as always, Shawn," he said. "We sold out all five performances. Dan suggested scheduling a Saturday matinee. Big bonuses for everyone as usual."

"I'll think about it." Shawn spared a glance after Amy and turned back to the conductor. "You coming to my party? Lots of good Scottish ale!"

"I need my sleep," Conrad answered. "Have fun. Keep the orchestra's reputation in mind this time, will you?"

Rob guffawed. "Like the fox will watch the hens!" Several men laughed.

Conrad shot Shawn a stern look. "I'd like to be welcome back."

Shawn held up a placating hand. "Just a little unwinding. I promise!"

"You promised in Edinburgh." Conrad did not look amused.

"I really, *really* promise this time." Shawn put on his most innocent face. His friends laughed. Conrad gave him a last, hard look, and turned to the concertmaster, giving a sharp nod toward the door.

Near Loch Ness, Scotland, 1314

Dark clouds scudded across the pale sliver of moon. But even a full moon would hardly have pierced the thick pine boughs sheltering the small clearing. A stiff wind sloughed through the branches high above, rustling over the night sounds of insects and loch.

He called himself Fearchar when he met MacDougall. Whether they knew better, he did not guess or care. His friend, he called Tearlach. He smiled at his own joke. Tearlach: instigator. His friend, not convinced of the wisdom of the plan, backed against the biggest pine, his shoulders hunched, hand on sword, peering this way and that.

Tearlach jumped suddenly, yelping. A large shadow hovered behind him, hand on his shoulder. A gruff laugh echoed from the wood, and MacDougall stepped into the clearing. Little more than his shape showed, a tall, bulky silhouette of flowing, fur-edged cloak and a full beard. Another, larger, shadow, emerged beside him. Tearlach made a sound somewhere between a sigh and drawn-out grunt. It might have been fear or pain. Fearchar ignored him.

"Waitin' long, were ye?" MacDougall asked.

"Not verra," Fearchar answered. These men did not scare him. He alone could provide the information they wanted. They'd scarce hurt him. And if they offered too little in exchange, he'd slide back under the protection of Glenmirril, no one the wiser. He couldn't lose.

He glanced at Tearlach. The man was a rabbit. He wouldn't tell. Fearchar stretched out a leather-booted toe to crack a twig. Tearlach jumped, with a sharp intake of breath. Fearchar laughed. "'Tis but a twig, Tearlach." He turned to MacDougall. "The Laird knows someone is taking word out."

"He doona ken who," said Tearlach.

"'Tis bad enough he knows," snapped Fearchar. "If MacDonald learns I am here, if aught should happen to me, there are those who know where to look." Dark eyebrows tightened over fierce eyes. He stared from one man to another. Tearlach fidgeted, but did not look away.

"If the MacDonald hears of it and comes after us, there are also those who know who gave him that information," said MacDougall's companion. A breeze lifted the shadow of heavy fur collar around his cloak. Tearlach looked over his shoulder at the rustle of tree limbs.

"'Tis but the wind," Fearchar said. He turned to MacDougall. "You say you can protect me, if MacDonald finds out. How do I know you're as good as your word?"

MacDougall's accomplice growled deep in his throat. Tearlach twitched and stepped backward, brushing a low-hanging tree branch. He jumped at its touch on his shoulder. "MacDougalls doona lie," MacDougall ground out. "How I can trust *you*? How do I know you speak the truth?"

The lord from the castle spread his hands. "My word, my Lord. You will see, the day after tomorrow...."

"You could be gone from the castle and I, dead with a knife in my back by then!" MacDougall's hand clenched on his sword hilt. "I want a token of confidence *now.*"

"I've naught to give!"

MacDougall jerked his head at his companion, whose cloak rustled in response. From it, he pulled a squat, round shadow, which he set on the ground amidst the four men.

MacDougall reached inside his cloak, tearing a heavy chain from his neck. He released it over the shadow; it clanked against the sides of the pot, shattering the quiet of the night. This time, even Fearchar jumped. "Careful!" he hissed. "You'll wake them!"

"An I do?" said MacDougall. He laughed. The large man beside him pulled a ring off his finger, and dropped it. It clattered, rolled, and settled. "I'm already risking all, being here on your land. Put your marker in the pot."

Fearchar glowered. "You dinna tell us this was part of the deal." Leaving proof of his complicity here ended his ability to walk away.

"Put a token in the pot," said MacDougall, "or this night may yet end in bloodshed. I must know I can trust you. We bury the pot, and we're all protected. If anyone tells, he'll be cutting his own throat, too, as the proof of this night's doing is here."

Still, Fearchar hesitated. MacDougall's hand tightened on his hilt. Eyeing the sword, Fearchar reluctantly pulled a ring from his own finger and dropped it in. He nodded to Tearlach, who fumbled at the brooch on his cloak, and tossed it in. It rolled around and around on the bottom of the pot. MacDougall stared until the brooch stopped rattling. He nodded to the other man, who produced a lid. Stooping there, just outside the circle, he began scraping at the dirt with his dagger.

"To business, then," said MacDougall, with the soft sounds of digging at his feet. "What is MacDonald's decision? My castle, my clan— I've hundreds of lives at stake."

"MacDonald supports the Bruce," Fearchar said.

MacDougall muttered an oath, and spit. "Fool! He gambles hundreds of lives. Thousands."

"He has decided," Tearlach whispered. He eyed the larger man, scraping at the dirt by the pot. "Naught we say will change his mind."

"O' course not." MacDougall's voice dripped with sarcasm. "But I wager his support means little without his men."

"And how are we to stop MacDonald's men joining Bruce? What's more, he is sending for Hugh."

MacDougall spun, wrenching his sword from its sheath. He flailed the flat against a tree. Then he stabbed it into the ground, where it quivered. "'Tis a dangerous game MacDonald plays! Can we no find Hugh?"

Fearchar eyed the quivering sword. He spoke calmly. "He's well-hidden, he and his men. We think to the east. The Trossachs or mayhap Ettrick Forest."

From where he dug in the dirt, MacDougall's companion scoffed. "'Tis half the lowlands, that is. Even if the rumors are true. Can ye tell us no more?"

"He has trusted few with his secret, perhaps only Niall."

"Och, young Niall Campbell." The large man chuckled. "And how is his arse?"

"Well enough to go for Hugh," Tearlach replied stiffly.

"Then Niall must be stopped," said MacDougall.

"You mean to kill him." Fearchar spoke flatly.

Heavy silence settled in the clearing. "What is one man's life to the good of a nation?" spoke MacDougall. "But stopping him from reaching Hugh will do." A strong wind pushed through the trees. It rustled the leaves, cracking two branches together, and lifted the smell of cow dung from the earth.

Fearchar lifted the back of his hand to his nostrils. His face gave nothing away. "You seek revenge for the death of your kinsmen, John Comyn," he said, lowering his hand. "I'll say naught to MacDonald of this meeting." He couldn't help a glance at the pot being lowered into a deep hole by MacDougall's companion. "But why should I gamble on Edward rather than on my own laird and people?"

"To save yourself!" MacDougall leaned forward, his eyes dark. "To save your people. Edward's reward to you will be great, an you serve him."

"I am already highly placed. What more can Edward give me?"

"Land. Your own castle. Look how he once lavished favor on my Lord Gaveston for naught."

His companion pushed the last of the dirt over the pot, and stood up, coughing loudly. "'Twas hardly for naught, my lord."

"I'd wager," said MacDougall, with a lewd wink, "that his name means more to him even than Lord Gaveston's company. Will he no do as much for those who restore Scotland and his name?"

"Who's to say Edward will conquer Scotland?" asked Fearchar. He bristled, moving a step forward. The clouds scuttled across the moon, and dropped a beam of silvery light through the trees, lighting his face.

MacDougall's companion laughed. "Edward's luck will turn."

"He is gathering troops from far and wide," said MacDougall. "He has cast all on this venture."

"He has raised thousands," said the larger man. "The army will stretch for miles. The earth will shake as they march."

"The Bruce cannot stand against him," said MacDougall. "You gamble nothing," he told the men from the castle, "because you cannot lose. Edward will take Stirling, and from there, all of Scotland, with or without your help. Those who oppose him will bring suffering on themselves and their families."

The man from the castle considered. The silence stretched between them. An owl hooted and glided onto a tree branch above.

"You cannot lose," MacDougall said again, softly, "unless you cast your lot with those who are ill-equipped and outnumbered."

"What is it you want from me?" Fearchar asked. He stared at the ground. His ring was in the pot. The die had been cast, the hand dealt.

MacDougall's lips curved into a smile. He had his accomplice.

"When does Campbell leave and what route does he take?"

"That has not yet been told us."

MacDougall stared pointedly at the spot where the pot had been buried. Clouds slipped back over the moon, and the copse darkened again. "Find out and send word. My men will be waiting in the forest, when Niall leaves."

Inverness, Scotland, Present

The orchestra's steering committee gathered in the conductor's suite. Apart from Shawn's own, it was the nicest the castle had to offer. Muted rose hues colored the wallpaper, carpet, and paintings. A spray of roses in a crystal vase adorned the sideboard, beside lattes and gourmet cookies. They sat on upholstered chairs around a mahogany table.

"Shawn's become a real problem." Dan, the principal French horn, spoke bluntly. His coffee sat untouched before him, his bow tie thrown beside it. "More women have complained about his leering and suggestive comments. We all know about that."

"Everyone except poor Amy," the elderly string bass player said. Muttered assents went around the table.

"We were barely able to smooth it over with the hotel in Edinburgh," Dan continued. "Sooner or later, he's going to pull something we can't handle. A lawsuit over sexual harassment or property damage."

Aaron, the young percussionist, spoke up. "With any luck, he'll get himself shot by the next husband who walks in on him." He took a forceful gulp of his black coffee and stared fiercely around the table.

"Shawn tends to be the one with the luck," Dan said dryly.

Conrad raked a hand through his wild, white hair before speaking. "I've already *done* everything short of firing him. Here's the problem." He pushed a sheet of paper, with computer-generated bar graphs, to the center of the table. They all leaned in. "If we keep him, we have growing dissatisfaction from one group. If we fire him, we have mutiny from another." His finger pinned the first bar on the graph. "We were barely holding on, financially, before he came. In fact, we weren't. Now," his finger moved to the second bar, soaring high above the first. "We are the most financially successful orchestra in the United States. Maybe the world. He's reached huge audiences, with his music, his arrangements, the big names he brings in. His on-stage persona. We have crowds. We have young people at our concerts. We're the only classical musicians with groupies! The audience loves him. Let me be clear on that: they love *him*. Have you heard the girls screaming when Shawn comes onstage?"

"Who could miss it?" Aaron glared at the polished tabletop.

Dan clapped his shoulder. "Celine will come to her senses."

"It's their money paying for all this." Conrad looked around the suite, the deep pile carpet, crystal, and mahogany, and noted the irony. "It's their money, thanks to him, paying for the room we're sitting in and the coffee we drink while we talk about how to get rid of him. When he goes, they go, and so does the money."

The men leaned back in their seats. Bill, the bassoonist, shook his head. "We're victims of his success. Our salaries have doubled since he started, plus bonuses. Do you know someone on the internet has made trading cards of our members, and Shawn's negotiated for royalties? How do we tell them," he asked Dan, "we're taking it all away?"

Dan sighed. "I understand. Likewise, how do we tell the women there's nothing we can do about his groping and grabbing? How do we tell the hotels they can expect damage when we're here? How do we handle the lawsuit that's coming any day? He's out of control. Something has to be done."

"I agree," said Conrad. The others, too, nodded.

"But the orchestra," said Bill. "Can we fire him without destroying what he's created? Is there someone else who can take his place and do what he does?"

"Amy does a lot of the work on those arrangements," Aaron said. "We'd still have her."

Conrad and Peter nodded thoughtfully. "She's good," Peter said.

"And I've done some scouting." Dan pulled a folder from his briefcase and dropped it on Conrad's charts. "These trumpet players are real possibilities. This Zach Tyler."

The men leaned back in, scanning the dossiers of two prominent musicians, pointing, questioning and talking. "We have leverage," Bill said, "if he understands he's replaceable." Nods went around the circle.

"One way or another," Conrad assured them, "this situation is going to be resolved. He's approaching his last misstep."

Inverness, Scotland, Present

Shawn met Amy in the castle's hall, still in her concert black, and pulled her through his suite, to the bedroom. "I can't get over it," she said, surveying the chamber. It could hold several of the smaller rooms. A mahogany four poster dominated everything. A bas-relief carving of a hunting scene adorned its foot board. Deep blue velvet curtains hung all around it, with a matching bedspread. Wallpaper and carpet echoed a palette of blues, a gentle contrast to the dark furniture. An intricately carved mantelpiece framed the fireplace opposite the bed. Evening sunlight poured through diamond-paned windows.

"Impressed?" He laughed. "This room belonged to the lord of the castle."

"Of course that's what they'd give you," she said. "It's incredible. And you don't even appreciate it."

"'Course I appreciate it. Look at that bed!" He gestured, an expansive sweep of his arm. "Who wouldn't appreciate that! You're welcome to join me any time. I wish you would." She glanced at the bed, twisting a ring on her finger. It flashed a spark of deep red.

"Hey, stop with the ring." Shawn took her hands, separating them. "What's wrong?"

She pulled away, walking toward the window. Evening sun streaked pink and orange across the sky, casting splendid pastels over the stone-walled gardens below. "There's so much more than that," she said.

"The bed? Yeah. I'm throwing a great party. Sure you don't want to come?" He pulled off his tuxedo jacket and started on the shirt's tiny buttons.

"I'm sure." She stared at the floor. "I'm tired. I'm going to bed."

"What's with you lately?" He shrugged off the crisp dress shirt. "You're always tired. I thought those antibiotics helped. Come on, look at me."

She twisted the ring.

He tried again. A little humor always got her. "Come on, baby, I'm here for the taking. The shirt's off." He turned, arms outspread, showing off his powerful chest, his perfect and unblemished back. "The pants are coming off. We could have our own private party before I go." He dropped his hands on her shoulders.

She edged away, and boosted herself onto the window seat under the diamond-paned windows, staring out at the gardens. "I don't feel well. I'm going to bed."

He stared at her for a moment, before turning to dig a shirt from the Victorian bureau. He'd have to find something like that for his own bedroom at home, he thought. He turned back to Amy, trying to guess what had brought this on, or when it had started.

"You upset about that girl onstage? You know it's just a show."

"You didn't have to give quite such an enthusiastic show."

"Look," he said, more subdued, "I've been neglecting you. I know these parties aren't really your thing. I'm kind of committed, you know people already coming and all, but we have the whole day off tomorrow. We could go to that castle."

"The one on the loch? Glenmirril?" Her eyes brightened a little, then dimmed. "Tomorrow's the last day with the living history actors. It'll be packed."

"We'll go at night, when everyone's gone."

"Can we do that?" She slid the ring up and down her finger.

His lips brushed her ear. "I'm Shawn Kleiner. I can do anything I want. We'll take a six pack up to the tower, look at the stars, make love."

"Why?" She met his gaze forcefully.

He glanced away, uncomfortably. "Why? Because it's fun! Making love is always fun." She continued staring at him. He wracked his brain, wondering what he'd said wrong. "Making love to *you* is fun," he added, with enthusiasm, and then, hesitantly, "I guess it would be okay with someone else. I wouldn't know. But it's great with *you!*"

"No," she snapped. "Why me? You can have anyone you want, and you've always wanted plenty of others."

"You know that's not true!" His voice took on a hurt edge.

"Don't lie to me."

"I'm not lying! There's never been anyone else, not since I first saw you and fell in love with your angelic smile, those beautiful blue eyes...."

She snorted. "Beautiful eyes are a dime a dozen. Especially for you. What is it about me?"

"Your...you...." He gestured helplessly.

"Because I'm useful? Like doing your party arrangements while you were reeling in that girl?"

"I wasn't..."

"I saw it," she said, dryly. "Have fun with her at the party. I'm going to bed." She boosted herself off the window seat, and left his suite.

"Hey, Amy...." He followed her into the hallway, still holding his shirt. "The town, the castle. Tomorrow?"

"I guess." She didn't turn around. "But you know I hate beer." Her door shut with a loud bark.

Caroline, one of the flutists, sauntered down the hall, her blond bob swaying against her jaw, her black sweater tight, her eyelids at half mast, appraising Shawn's bare chest. "Hey, how you doing?" she said. "Gonna be at your own party?"

"Wouldn't miss it!" Shawn smiled. His cares slid away like bubbles down a drain, forgotten. "Can I walk you over? In ten minutes?" His eyes trailed her appreciatively down the hall. She turned once to smile at him, swung her blond hair, and disappeared into her room. Yes, he thought, he would enjoy his party.

* * *

With Caroline clutching his arm and preening in the limelight, Shawn sauntered into the pub, swinging his trombone case, and surveying his domain: heavy wooden paneling, laughter, a trio fiddling and singing at the back, bottles reflected in the mirror behind the bar, flirtation, tables and booths jostling for space among the shoulder to shoulder crowd of good-looking men and pretty women shouting for his attention. He gave it first to the barmaid. "You have *incredibly* beautiful eyes," he murmured, accepting a beer and dropping a tip down her blouse. She laughed raucously, pushing his hand away in pretend outrage.

He sidled up to Dana at the bar, sliding an arm around her shoulder and nibbling her ear. She laughed and swatted him away.

He drank his ale with the redhead from backstage, pressing her close during a slow song, whispering things in her ear that made her giggle, blush furiously and lean back for more. He ordered a lager, crooned a mournful *Caledonia* with the band, and pulled out his trombone, playing *Blue Bells* faster and faster, with snatches of cartoon and movie themes thrown in for fun. He slid into a bluesy striptease, making eyes at Caroline while he played, to the hooting of the patrons. The beer glowed inside him, flushing him.

"Shawn, put that thing away and join us," Rob hollered, from a poker game in the corner. "Jimmy here thinks he can beat you." Dana, seated at Rob's left, nodded. Bar lights glinted in her spiky auburn hair.

Shawn laughed, already pulling the mouthpiece from the trombone. "You warned him?"

Rob grinned. "We told him about your legendary luck. He says prove it."

Shawn eyed the ruddy-faced Scot, who stared back sullenly. He grinned, packed away his instrument, and joined them. Cards slithered around the table under Jimmy's expert hands, and they settled into a routine. Caroline planted herself on Shawn's right leg, kissing him enthusiastically with each win, while the redhead spilled ample cleavage over his left shoulder, comforting him in each loss. As his money piled up, and the beer soaked his brain, he took more chances. He didn't notice Caroline's pouts as the redhead comforted him more frequently, or the groans of the crowd. Musicians and patrons pressed close.

"You're almost out of money," Caroline purred in his ear, pulling his face from the redhead's cleavage. "Where's that famous luck?"

"You're right here, baby." He kissed her soundly. "One more game."

The cards flashed around the table, bets placed, antes upped, and Dana grinned as she reached across the table, claiming his emaciated pile of bills. The redhead once again cradled his head in consolation.

"Double or nothing!" Caroline pulled his face back toward herself. "Let him play on credit, Rob."

Shawn guffawed. "Schmitz warned me to learn a lesson last time I did that."

Laughs went around the pub. The musicians remembered that peccadillo. "Schmitz isn't here." Dana winked as she passed her cards to Jimmy.

Too many beers made the decision easy. "He sure isn't," Shawn announced, his voice echoing with the effects of alcohol. The patrons cheered. They'd be talking about it for years, how he came back from nothing.

Rob looked to Jimmy, who stared hard at Shawn, while his hands shuffled the deck fluidly. Jimmy nodded. The redhead dug a notebook and pen from her purse and began scribbling IOU's. "You good for them?" she asked.

"You know I'm good, baby." He scrawled a drunken signature on each one, even as Jimmy slid cards swiftly to each player, around and around the table.

Shawn gulped a mouthful of frothing ale before scooping up his cards. Rob and Dana scanned their hands and pushed in their ante. He edged Caroline off his lap. The redhead backed up. Jimmy pushed in a large pile of bills, his eyes boring into Shawn's.

Shawn thumbed his cards aside, close to his body. Nine of spades. Jack—spades. Another spade—the queen. He kept his face still, despite the flush of liquor, and pushed aside the next card. A three of hearts. He thumbed the next one into view, hardly daring to hope. It was the ten of spades.

He didn't react. It was still a matter of extreme luck. But then, he was known for just that. Rob pushed in twenty-five pounds. The bets flew around the table, even as whispered side bets flew around the room behind him.

Rob exchanged three cards. Jimmy exchanged two, Dana three. Shawn discarded his three of hearts, drawing the six of diamonds. More bets flew around the table and around the room, the stakes climbing as Rob put in seventy-five, and Jimmy a hundred. They discarded and drew again. Shawn slid his new card up.

The eight of spades.

A corner of his mouth twitched up. He couldn't lose.

Rob put in another hundred.

"I raise you two hundred," Jimmy grunted.

Dana folded with a dramatic roll of her eyes. "Easy come, easy go," she sighed.

Shawn snapped his fingers for the redhead's pen, and put a three in front of the twenty-five on his IOU.

Jimmy's eyes narrowed. "How do I know you're good for it! Ye're

19

already playing on credit."

"Give him a marker, Shawn," somebody yelled from the crowd. "Your trombone!"

Even in his liquor-logged state, Shawn's head spun at the blasphemy. But the crowd pressed close, tingling with the drama.

"Worth a lot, your horn?" Jimmy asked. "A big name like you?"

His inner Conrad shrieked, but Jimmy's attitude rankled. "A big name like me, yeah, it's worth a year's salary to you. Bring it."

Caroline swayed like Vanna White, and the fawn-colored case moshed over the crowd, into her waiting hands. She dropped it with a flourish and a thud in the center of the table, and reached underneath to pile bills on top of it, flashing white teeth.

"An you lose, you give me the money, and you get yer horn back," Jimmy said.

The crowd cheered, like Romans at the Coliseum, demanding their excitement. Shawn glanced down at his cards. He couldn't lose. They'd be talking about it for years, how he bet his trombone against the big Scot. The crowd edged in. Body heat slicked the surface of the air. The chatter and side bets rose to a fevered pitch.

He stared sternly around the room, one eyebrow cocked. Silence dropped like a guillotine blade. He cocked the eyebrow next at Rob, who smugly laid out four aces. Shawn grinned slyly, spreading his hand for all to see. "Straight flush," he announced needlessly.

Cheers erupted. Caroline shrieked, pumping a fist in the air, and grabbed his face in both hands, kissing him and stamping her feet. He came up for air, grinning at the Scot. Someone slapped his back. His hand fell on the money covering his trombone. "Game's over, big guy." His fingers flexed on the crisp bills.

The noise diminished suddenly, sending a nervous chill down Shawn's back. He froze, looking around. "What's wrong?" His eyes fell on Rob's face; he followed Rob's gaze to where Jimmy had wordlessly laid out his own hand.

"Straight flush." Jimmy's meaty hand fell on top of Shawn's. "To the king."

Glenmirril Castle, On the Shore of Loch Ness, Scotland, 1314

Late at night, Niall leaned on the tower parapets, gazing over the dark loch, far below. Its soft murmur reached him, and an occasional splash as a fish leapt for a night insect. A rich baritone melody floated up the tower stairs. *"The Laird's own bard to war is gone."*

Niall smiled, and sang back, softly, *"His harp and sword at hand."*

20

"I thought I'd find you here." Iohn appeared in the arched doorway, crossed the small space, and rested his arms on the wall beside Niall. "Feeling better?" he asked.

"At times." The summer breeze lifted Niall's hair. He tugged his cloak closer. "Suppose it were true." He turned to Iohn. "Suppose you fell asleep and woke up hoondreds o' years on?"

"Go 'won," said Iohn. "Doona tell me ye believe in fairies!"

Niall laughed, not bothered by his ribbing. "I'll no tell ye sich. But 'tis no the only story, what Rabbie told, o' hoondreds o' years passin' when a man thinks 'tis but days or hours. Ye've heard the things Thomas the Rhymer claimed?"

"Aye." Iohn nodded. "Being whisked away by the fairy queen for three days and findin' seven years had passed. And they say there was ne'er a more honest man."

"What would it be like, d' ye think?"

"To wake up and find hoondreds of years passed?" Iohn mused, staring out at the loch, resting his arms on the tower wall beside Niall's. "Mayhap the forests would be gone, as the story says? More villages?"

"Does aught ever change?" Niall asked. "A few villages more or less. But life goes on as always, no? We fish and hunt and rescue our cattle from the thieving MacDougalls."

"Aye, the thieving bastards." Iohn spit. After a moment's silence, he asked, "Gil?"

"He'll be aw' right. Thanks be to God ye were there for him."

"Aye," said Iohn, and they fell silent for a moment before Iohn said, "William's waiting for us."

Inverness, Scotland, Present

"Of all the damned luck," Shawn shouted once more, laughing.

Spinning high and happy with several more pints inside, he and Caroline stumbled down Inverness's dark streets, under the shadow of Inverness Castle, and south along the banks of the River Ness. The moon glowed a silver crescent in its waters. They swung a metal pail stuffed with cash between them, singing *Caledonia* as they stumbled toward the castle-turned-hotel.

Shawn routinely skated to the center of thin ice, and never fell through. He hadn't this time, either. "I don't get paid for three days," he'd told Jimmy. "We're doing one more gig. Give me my trombone, and I'll pay you right after the concert. "

Jimmy scoffed. "I'll never see it. I'll be at your room tomorrow at noon. Wi' me mates." Shawn understood his meaning. The redhead followed the newly wealthy Jimmy out of the pub, while the patrons and musicians passed a deep bucket around.

"Let's make sure Shawn doesn't get beaten to a pulp before he can play the next gig," Rob encouraged them. The barmaid presented it to him, and received a passionate kiss in thanks. Caroline glared at her. She smirked at Caroline.

"Shh, shh," he whispered now, shushing their song as he and Caroline pushed in the castle's towering front door. He tripped up the broad red-carpeted stairs inside, barking his shin on the bucket. She giggled, and stumbled down a couple of stairs, retrieving the bills spilling behind them. Reaching his room, he pulled her into his suite. She looked around in drunken delight, oohing and ahhing, racing through the sitting room to the bedroom, to touch the dark blue velvet curtains hanging from the four poster bed.

"You curtains think...think curtains...." Shawn threw his head back and roared with laughter. The room spun. Caroline looked good. "You think the curtains are nice! Try the bed!" He lifted the tin bucket high, scattering money. Bills fluttered over the velvet comforter. He pulled her down, rolling in it, yanking at her clothes, and indulging in a drunken romp.

"To the king," he muttered, shaking his head when they finished. Sleep began to swallow him. "To the king. What a night. What luck. To the king." He sighed, and fell asleep.

Glenmirril, 1314

Deep in the dungeon, Niall, Iohn, and young William Darnley made their way, Niall limping, to the farthest reaches of the dank stone-walled tunnels. They'd ever been together, the three. It wasn't the first time they'd explored the dungeons, but it was the first time they'd come with MacDonald's knowledge.

Niall grinned at Iohn and William. "The Laird was impressed with how quickly I learned my way through this maze."

"'Tis your quick mind among other things that brought you to his attention," Iohn replied. With a friendly nudge in Niall's ribs, he added, "'Tis your good fortune I canna tell him 'twas *me* who taught you, or I might be the next Laird."

Niall laughed easily. "'Tis both our good fortunes we canna tell him many a thing."

"Aye, he'd no like to know you were messin' with his sackbut," William said.

Niall chuckled at his failed attempt on the instrument. By watching and listening, he could copy anything. He'd had no one to watch. "'Twas a miserable thing, anyway." He turned back to Iohn.

"Sure an' you'll be my right hand man, Iohn. As good as being the laird yourself."

"No, Niall," Iohn murmured. "'Tis not the same."

"We are like brothers," Niall replied. "What is mine is yours." Cold sweat prickled his forehead in the cool dungeon. He wiped a sleeve across his brow, raised the smoky torch, and searched the stone walls. The flame trembled, shining, off something metal. He worked his fingers into the hidden ring and tugged. A door scraped outward, revealing the chamber within, feebly lit by two torches. The lords huddled around the circle of light, their faces shadowed.

"Welcome, Niall," the Laird rumbled. The three young men pushed through the narrow opening. Niall bowed all around, and settled his torch in a bracket. It flickered on rugged gray stones and black smoke stains, and over the older men already gathered. They wore leather boots, thick tunics, and heavy surcoats. Cloaks warded off the chill. Heavy gold chains hung around their necks, and rings glinted on several fingers. Smoke crept into nostrils and stung the eyes. The walls trickled with Scotland's eternal dampness. Several men glanced toward the door, wary still of being overheard.

"The cattle are recovered," the Laird said. "They remain undisturbed?" He put his hand to his mouth, coughed forcefully, and wiped his hand on his tunic. The others glanced at him, then turned away, pretending not to notice.

"Aye, my Lord," Niall said. "Are you ill?"

"'Tis naught," grumbled MacDonald, with a heavy-browed glare around the men who might question his health and power.

"We've kept careful watch over them, William and I," Iohn offered, quickly turning the subject back. "There has been no sign of the MacDougalls."

"And Niall's wounds?" the Laird asked.

"'Tis minor," Niall assured him. "I'll not even remember it on the fortnight."

"You were seeing two of me only this morning," Lord Darnley reminded him.

"Aye, but none would object to two of your comely face," Niall said. The men laughed. "And I am seeing less of the two of you as the days go by." He rubbed his head ruefully, where the hair covered the vicious purple bruising of his fall. He didn't volunteer that the walls had swum before him during his passage through the dungeons or that even now, Iohn's face wavered, split, and re-joined.

"To other matters, then," MacDonald said. "I've had news today. Edward Bruce has made a deal with de Mowbray at Stirling Castle."

"The rumors are true, then?" asked Iohn. He turned to Niall, who arched one eyebrow significantly. They'd discussed Stirling, he and Iohn, in late night talks atop the castle tower, and the possibility of Niall being sent for Hugh. Now the future they'd feared was unfolding. Not to his liking.

"Aye." The Laird looked tired. "Edward Bruce's siege of Stirling goes poorly, but de Mowbray knows he canna hold out forever. He agreed to turn Stirling over if King Edward does not send reinforcements by Midsummer's Day."

The men stared at each other in the flickering light. The older men all bore the same bristling beards, in shades of red, gray, and black, and thick, heavy eyebrows. The young men, Conal, Niall, Iohn and William, wore their dark hair loose to the shoulders. Their backs were straight and strong, their eyes direct. Each knew what this meant: more war for Scotland.

"England is sending the largest army the world has ever seen." The Laird paused significantly, looking one by one at each of the nobles. All looked back with forceful eyes. "A hundred thousand, they say. They plan to reinforce Stirling, and crush all Scotland from there."

Lord Morrison scoffed. "Edward is not his father. He'll not take Scotland back. He couldna even keep what was left him."

"Look how easily Roxburgh and Edinburgh were taken from him," added Lord Darnley.

"A hundred thousand," MacDonald repeated, stressing each word. "Edward Bruce threw down the gauntlet. King Edward's pride is at stake. Better if young Bruce had not made that agreement. But it is done. We will send our men, and send also for all our kin, immediately."

"If he is so powerful," suggested William Darnley, "might it not be better to stand with him, that his wrath might not fall on us?"

MacDonald stared at each in turn. Their eyes reflected the flickering torches. "I will risk all," he said, "before I will let that monster take my country."

There was a long silence. A drop of water formed along a ceiling beam and fell to the stone floor with a loud *plop* in the silence.

"Will you send for Hugh?" Lord Darnley asked. "He has become strongest of us all, with his men and all their clans at his command."

"I will send word," said the Laird. Several men looked at Niall.

"Tell me where he is, my Lord," spoke the small and wizened Lord Morrison. "Niall is still recovering. I'll go."

"'Tis but a scratch," Niall said. "I will do my duty."

"No one doubts your willingness, Niall," said Lord Morrison. He rubbed his hands together for warmth. "But are you able? We must think what is best for Scotland."

"I will think on it," said the Laird. His eyes met Niall's. They held each other's gaze momentarily, the torch flames flickering reflections in their eyes.

"'Tis not good," Lord Darnley persisted, "that so few know his whereabouts. What if aught befall that one or two?"

"'Tis a matter for another day," said MacDonald. "As it is, we must send runners for all of our kin, with greatest haste and secrecy. I am not so foolish," he looked carefully at each man, "as to be unaware there are traitors in this castle who would as soon side with England."

"Who is it!" demanded Lord Darnley, staring around the circle.

"Not me, my lord," said each man in turn. The torches flickered.

"Nor I, my lord!"

Another droplet swelled and fell to the floor with a loud *plop*.

"Surely not I."

* * *

Smoky torches stood sentry at each side of the heavy wooden door, deeper yet in the dungeon than the lords had been. Flames threw eerie shadows high against the damp walls and far into the soaring roof of what had once been a cave. Shadows leapt and wound around MacDonald, demented spirits casting discouragement on him. On a rough wooden stool, he braced his hands on his knees. A fierce red beard, heavily streaked with gray and white, sprang from his jaw. Matching eyebrows bristled in perpetual anger over craggy, hooded eyes.

For another moment, his head drooped, giving in to the aching back, aching shoulders, aching arms. His muscles begged for rest. The headache, which had raged for days now, pounded at his temples, demanding a good night's sleep. He gave his head a fierce shake, stood, and arched his back. He stretched his arms over his head, flexing still-powerful muscles, and looked to the six foot crucifix hanging on one wall of the cave, back in a recess. He'd carved it himself, the year his son had been murdered by the English. It had given him strength then, and it gave him strength now.

He bent back to the work in front of him, shaping and smoothing the wood to its purpose. It resisted, testing him.

"Like a bairn, aern't ye?" He scraped the plane, curling up a thin spiral shaving. Like the oak before him, people resisted. "Niall, now," he said aloud. He rose again, inspecting his work, stooping to peer at a joint. A fine young man he'd become, just as he'd expected, the day he'd caught him kissing Allene. Capable. Intelligent. A quicker mind he'd never seen, faster than the tiny silver fish darting in the loch. A man who was loyal and inspired loyalty in return. He would make a fine laird, when his time came. "If ye dinna get yerself killed first," MacDonald muttered. Spotting a flaw, he resumed his seat, and set the plane again. His muscles tightened, holding the tool on course. But headstrong, he thought. Niall was headstrong. And overly confident. It would be his undoing. He'd warned him over and over: Trust no one.

No one.

A drop of water fell from the great wooden beam overhead, landing with a loud plop in the silence. He glanced at it. Niall had, MacDonald knew, exempted some people from the class of *no one*, without looking ugly possibilities in the eye. His confidence extended to other people, when maybe it shouldn't. He, himself, did not yet know who it might be, but a hard life had taught him that no one, ever, was exactly what they appeared. Niall had yet to learn that harsh truth.

The Laird sighed, running his hand over the smooth surface of his handiwork, and deciding on his next step. The torches filled his eyes with smoke. He wiped the back of his hand against them, and thought of his soft bed. But his work was not done. He selected a chisel from his tool bench, and tapped it against the wood. Just a little more, he would do tonight. He thought ahead to Niall's journey. Niall would resist, argue, and, possibly do things his own way, despite the Laird's commands. Young men would be rash. He touched his chest, where the crucifix from the Monks of Monadhliath lay, praying that this young man, this time, would not be.

He sighed, thinking of the many hours of sleep he had not gotten and would not get. "Niall, I've my fears, but I'll do my best for ye if it kills me," he whispered, and once again hefted his wood-working tools. The things in front of him were close to done, but time was short. Maybe, in a night or two, he could sleep.

Chapter Two

Inverness, Scotland, Present

Shawn woke to steel drums pounding his brain, and a dozen timpani thundering in his ears. All of them out of tune, too. Sun poured through the window, and skimmed past the half-open curtains of the four poster bed, blinding him. He squinted at the clock; groaned; looked at Caroline, stretched cat-like on piles of rumpled pounds. He'd have to count those before Jimmy came. It wouldn't do to come up short in front of the man and his mates. He groaned again, rolled over on Caroline, and woke her with a few playful kisses. She giggled; protested, "I feel so good, I must still be drunk!" She wrapped her arms around his neck, kissing him. For a few minutes, the pounding in his head dimmed.

She gave a long, contented sigh and wiggled up to a sitting position, drawing the bed sheets and her knees demurely to her chest. "They were saying a couple of days ago that you were talking Gaelic with a Scotsman," she said. "Is it true?"

"Och, o' coorse it's true," Shawn said, rolling his R's. "And I've got all sorts o' talents ye've only just started to see, wee lahssie! What else will I shoo ye?" He grabbed at her sheets. The motion made his head spin again. He laughed, his face flushed.

"Stop it!" She giggled, pounding his chest. "Come on, I'm serious. I want to get to know you better. I mean, here we are...." she fluttered her eyelashes at him and blushed a dainty blush.

"You got to know me pretty well last night." Shawn growled, burying his face in her breasts and pulling more giggles out of her. "What more could you want?"

"I mean it!" she insisted, pushing his head away. "I want to know you. That's not the same as sleeping together. You really speak Gaelic? You're not pulling my leg?"

"That's not what I'd do with your leg." Shawn lifted three fingers. "Scout's honor."

She giggled. "You a boy scout! Hardly! How do you know Gaelic?"

"It's not that interesting," he said, lying back on the bed. The pounding in his head kicked up a notch. "Not as interesting as other things we could be doing." He cocked an eyebrow at her. She waited. "Okay, if you really want to know, my grandmother grew up on Skye. She met my grandfather during the war, married him, and came over. My father grew up speaking both Gaelic and English, and he spoke it in our house. And he was also big into the re-enacting thing. A Scottish unit, of course. He used to take me with him. Most of them in the unit spoke it fluently."

She laughed. "You wore a kilt? Tell the truth: what's under them?"

He wiggled wicked eyebrows at her, and lifted the bed sheet. "I only know what's under mine. Come and see!"

She squealed at his wit, daring a peek and professing delight. "Is that why you wanted the orchestra to come to Scotland?"

"To show you that? Na, I could have done that at home."

She punched him. "Because of your family connection."

"Yeah, the family history thing's cool," Shawn said. "It was also convenient. I grew up playing the music we're doing. We did it in the re-enactment camps all the time."

"You played trombone in a re-enactment camp?"

He smiled. The feeling of putting on a show lifted momentarily. Remembering those camps gave him a brief happiness. "No. They didn't bring trombones into battle. I messed around with harps and fifes and things."

"Tell me about your father," she said. "You never talk about him."

Shawn turned away, rubbing his throbbing temples. "He died when I was in high school."

"I'm sorry." Her hands crept onto his shoulders; her breath brushed his neck. "Was he a lot like you?"

"His looks—those Scottish genes run strong. I'm his clone."

"Personality," she said. "Was he like you?"

Shawn snorted. "Nothing like me. He was a nice guy, and I can tell you, they do finish last." He sat up abruptly. He didn't want to have this conversation with Caroline. He wanted Amy. "Not much else to say. But mostly," he added with a roguish grin, changing the subject back, "I brought the orchestra here because I heard such good things about the women." He grabbed at her again, scattering more bills to the plush carpet. This time, she let him. His head pounded mercilessly. But it stopped her questions.

Glenmirril Castle, Scotland, 1314

The Laird straightened on his bench, stretching the kinks out of his back. If the dungeon had allowed any light in, he'd be seeing the sun reach over the mountains east of the loch. Dawn came early in June. As it was, he saw the same smoky shadows flickering on the same dusky stone and earth walls that he'd seen all night. He set the drill down, and contemplated how to move the items out without being seen. He twisted his neck this way and that, easing sore muscles. Finally, he rested his eyes on the completed projects. He smiled slowly, pleased. They would do. Yes, they would fool his enemies.

Now where to get the energy to face the day? He sighed. There were cattle to be seen to, and preparations for the castle men who would join Bruce. Meat to be smoked, mounts to be readied, weapons to be fitted. He pressed a hand to his throbbing temple. It was a job for a much younger man. Or at least one who had slept more than a scattered hour here and there, these past two weeks. He rubbed his eyes hard with the heels of his hands, and stood up.

There was no younger man. Niall himself must not know of these preparations, lest he trust the wrong person. So he, the laird, would do what he must. His fake coughs and sneezes, letting his men believe he was ill, would explain away his exhaustion and the bags under his eyes, so that no one would suspect what really caused them.

He pushed out through the heavy wooden door, looked up and down the dank stone corridors, and locked it behind him.

He'd done what he could. Now if only Niall would do—for once— exactly as he was told.

Inverness, Scotland, Present

Shawn lay on the bed, hands behind his head, scowling, while Caroline showered. He didn't like her asking questions about his father. He tried not to think about it. He sighed, glancing at the sun streaming through the window. It was higher than before; a little closer to the Scot's arrival. Time to count the money and get the trombone back before Schmitz found out. He sat up reluctantly. He paused a moment, squeezing his eyes against the headache, before pulling on a pair of boxer shorts covered in glow in the dark trombones.

Then he drew the bills to him, pulling them from under the covers, and from beside the bed, counting as he went.

One hundred and forty-eight pounds.

He found more under the bed. Two hundred thirty-six. He shook out the thick, blue comforter, and more bills dropped out. A few fives and tens, even a twenty. He smiled. He'd known his friends wouldn't let him down.

He crawled the length of the floor, searched under the bed again, and felt alongside the nightstand. A five fell from where it had caught between the bed and the canopy's draperies. He opened the nightstand drawer. There was a twenty. He vaguely remembered putting it there himself, and thanked fate for his own forgetfulness.

Three hundred and sixty-nine. He groaned, felt a renewed thundering of the timpani. He needed another thousand.

Caroline came out of the shower, wrapped in a large white towel. "Guess what I found!" she chirped, and showered him with fives and ones. "They were in my clothes when I picked them up this morning."

He counted quickly. Three hundred ninety-six pounds. He kissed her. She made a soft sound. "Maybe now they'll only beat up half of me," he joked, and kissed her again. "I can't thank you enough."

"Oh, you're doing very well," she said, and dropped her towel.

* * *

Shawn finished showering ten minutes after Caroline left, considering under the hot spray how to get another thousand pounds. He groaned at the answer that presented itself. But the orchestra needed him. He needed his trombone. He shook the water from his long, thick hair, and emerged from the shower into a bathroom of granite and stone fixtures, a hot tub shaped like a seashell, and thick white towels, twice as fluffy and soft as any other towels. He dried off, and drew on jeans and a polo shirt. Within five minutes, he'd convinced Jim, the portly second chair trombonist, to lend him his instrument. "Just for a minute," he said, and the man reluctantly agreed. Not that he had a choice, when Shawn demanded.

Shawn retreated to his suite. Amidst the luxury, he blew a few long tones. After a couple of harmonic minor scales, slow and relaxed, he blew a few garbled notes, waited several seconds, and blew another few, as awful as he could make them. He packed Jim's trombone away and headed into the hall.

Several orchestra members were there already, staring in shock at Shawn's room, as he'd known they would. Amy opened her door, wrapped in a fluffy white robe, with jeans showing underneath. Her dark hair hung to her waist, damp from the shower.

"Was that you?" asked Rob. "Where'd you get...?"

Shawn shook his head sharply. Rob stopped.

"Yeah," Shawn muttered under his breath. "That was me. I've got a problem. Come here." He pulled them both into the room Amy shared with Dana, a cool oasis of greens. He glanced back at the group in the hallway. Narrowly avoiding several shirts laid out for consideration, he plunked himself on Amy's bed, swathed in forest greens to match the room's decor, and dropped his forehead into his hands.

"What happened, Shawn?" Amy asked. "Is our trip canceled?" She gathered the clothes, yanking a pair of shorts from under him.

"No, I wouldn't cancel on you," Shawn said. "But I went to do a little playing, and the tinagle connector snapped." He covered his eyes, the epitome of despair, he hoped, and heaved a big sigh.

"The wha...!" A pointed glare from Shawn cut Rob off. He recovered quickly. "The tinagle connector? That's *really* bad."

"What's that?" asked Amy. She re-folded the clothes, and laid them back in her dresser drawer.

"It's part of the lever," said Shawn. "Inside the ball bearings that open up the F attachment. I can't play without it."

"Get it fixed when we get home," Amy said. "We're done here." She disappeared into the bathroom.

"No, we're not. Schmitz wants me to do another concert."

"So don't," she called back through the closed door. Seconds later, she reappeared, dressed in jeans and a royal blue t-shirt, pulling her hair from where it had caught inside, and looping it into a long, thick ponytail.

"Amy, you don't understand," Rob chimed in. "Everybody gets a big bonus if he agrees. Shawn's under a lot of pressure from everyone— *lots of pressure*—to do one more. Shawn, how much is it going to cost?"

"A thousand pounds." He dropped his forehead in his hands again. "I'm out of money and we don't get paid for three days. What am I going to do?"

Amy twisted her ring. Rob patted his pockets and pulled out his billfold, making a show of searching it. "Ten pounds," he said, handing a bill to Shawn. "Amy, you got anything?"

She marched across the pale green carpet to the window, staring out. "I do not have a thousand pounds," she said curtly.

"Oh, come on. Amy, you're always so practical. I bet you have plenty for emergencies. This is an emergency."

"Did it ever occur to you I might have my own emergencies?" she snapped.

"It's a drop in the bucket to save the whole orchestra. I bet your bonus will be more than that, and Shawn will pay you back," Rob said.

"No." She twisted the ring again.

"But Amy..."

She stared out the window, at the gardens behind the stone walls. "Go ask Caroline."

"Ouch!" Shawn sat upright. He was sure Amy hadn't seen them come in. "What are you saying?"

"Amy, you're not accusing Shawn...?" Rob said in surprise. "Not

Shawn!" She turned to face him squarely. He dropped his jaw in astonishment. "You *are!* He didn't spend the night with her!"

"How would you know?" asked Amy. "She left with Shawn, and Caroline's roommate said she was out all night." She slid the ring up and down her finger in agitation. It flashed the light of the morning sun in Shawn's eyes. He tried not to stare at it, but it drew him, a starving man to succulent roast beef.

"How would...well, uh...." Rob fumbled for words. "How would I know? Because Caroline spent the night with me! That's where she was all night." A red flush crept from under his collar, spread up his neck, and over his face, to the roots of his white-blond hair. He stared and blinked at the gilt-framed pastoral scene on the wall.

"You?"

"Is that so shocking?" Rob blinked rapidly. But he looked her in the eye. "I'm not that bad looking, you know."

Amy cleared her throat, studying him. He was almost as tall as Shawn. In every other way, he was Shawn's opposite, with a wiry build, short-cropped blond hair, and blue eyes. Many women in the orchestra found him attractive. "I'm not saying you are," she said.

"Then give the man credit," Rob said in indignation. "He's always been faithful to you. Couldn't stop talking about you last night."

"She was really with you?" Amy asked.

Rob nodded energetically. The flush on his face deepened.

Amy stared down at her hands. Her lips turned down, tightening. She chewed at her lower lip and twisted her ring. Finally, she lifted guilty eyes to Shawn. "I'm...I'm sorry for accusing you," she said softly.

"It's okay," he said.

"And now his tintager conn...."

"Tintager?" Amy turned to Rob.

Shawn cleared his throat, drawing Amy's attention back. "Rob, the word is tinagle. You never can get it right."

"Yeah, sorry," Rob muttered.

"Whatever it is," Amy said, "I don't have that kind of money."

"Look, Amy, I wasn't asking you for money. I was just upset, having my horn break like this, and turned to the woman I love. Not for money. I wasn't.... Well, never mind. I'll see if I can fix it myself. Just hope I don't make it worse." He sighed heavily, his face forlorn. He walked to the door and opened it. Musicians milled in the hall. They turned, voices raised with a dozen questions, when they saw him.

"I won't be able to do the extra gig," Shawn told them dejectedly.

Groans went up. "Come on, Shawn. Why not?"

"This hurts us all."

"I was counting on that bonus to pay off my car repair."

"My trombone. Something snapped." He glanced back at Amy, trusting them to understand the significance of the look. "I don't have the cash till payday to fix it."

"Shawn!" Amy hissed. She yanked him back in. He pulled the door closed, shutting the three of them in the forest glen of a room. "I really don't have the money!" she said. "Why are you trying to put this on my shoulders?"

"I'm not," he protested. "Honest. You're my girlfriend. Is it so unusual I would tell you when something this bad happens? I'm sorry you thought..."

"I just don't have the money." She twisted at the ring again. She sounded less sure now.

He held back a grin. "But you could get it."

"How?" She started at her own words, and added quickly, "No, I can't. No, Shawn, no, don't suck me into this! I don't *want* to lend you money!" She dug in a drawer, took out socks, and jammed them on her feet, quickly followed by her tennis shoes.

"The ring!" Rob said.

Amy gave one sharp jerk to her laces and lifted her head to him in shock. "I am *not* selling my grandmother's ring!"

"Not sell it," Rob placated. "Just pawn it. We're here another week. We do the gig, get our regular paychecks and a nice bonus, and Shawn gets it back for you. No risk. Nothing to lose."

"This is my grandmother's ring!" Amy said. "I can't believe you would even suggest it."

"It's perfectly safe," Rob insisted. "I pawn things all the time at the end of the month. They hold it for two or three days, a week, whatever you need. I've never lost anything. You save the orchestra, you get everyone a nice bonus, all risk free."

Amy closed her eyes, shaking her head no, and took a deep breath. Shawn held his, watching her. Rob leaned back on the pillows of her bed, hands behind his head. She expelled the air. "Risk free?"

"They're all counting on you, Amy. You heard them."

"It would really be risk free? Completely risk free? This is the ring my grandmother left me. I loved her."

"I promise. Shawn will get it back, won't you Shawn?"

"Amy, you'd really do this for me? I honestly never meant to ask you for a thing like this. I swear I didn't." He stood up and crossed the room to take her hands in his. "I owe you big. I'll have it back for you in three days. Trust me."

"I didn't say I was going...."

"It'll be perfectly safe. Thank you, thank you, and thank you again!" Shawn kissed her with each thank you, hands pressed on either side of her face. "And thank you from the whole orchestra." He kissed her again. "And thank you from my trombone." He kissed her again, till she laughed, pushing against him. "Do you know how beautiful your laugh is? Do you know how beautiful your eyes are? Do you know how beautiful your smile is?"

She tried to wipe the smile from her face and look stern. "I never said...."

"You've saved us all," Shawn continued.

"I didn't say...."

"I'm going to show you the very best time today."

"With what money?" Amy asked.

Shawn pulled a stack of credit cards from his back pocket, fanning them like playing cards. "The magic plastic." He laughed. His eyes danced, and he raced on, leaving her no room to argue or think. "All over Inverness, the best lunch money can buy, a picnic like you've never even dreamed of, under the stars at the top of the keep where we'll...."

Amy looked pointedly at Rob.

"...have a great picnic," Shawn finished. "Thank you, thank you, thank you for saving me!" He led her out of the room. To those assembled in the hall, more now that word was spreading, he announced, "Amy has saved our last concert! Let's hear it for Amy!" Those in the hallway clapped and whistled, and Shawn kissed her again, long and deep. She pushed him away, blushing furiously. "I'll be ready in half an hour," she said, and ducked back into her room.

* * *

Shawn passed the next hour and a half pleasantly with Amy, exploring the cobbled roads, and shops of Inverness. They found the pawn shop down a narrow street, barely more than an alley, with dumpsters and boarded windows. A skinny man with torn jeans and a drooping eye puffed on a cigarette, watching them. Shawn convinced her to wait outside, and exhaled with relief when her only reaction was, "You will get it back, won't you?"

"We're all getting a big bonus. I'll have it back in three days."

Inside, he waited impatiently while the old man studied the ring under lights and lenses, and finally filled out some forms and handed him a thick sheaf of bills. He thumbed through, counting quickly, stuffed them in his wallet, and hurried out into the sunshine of an otherwise perfect day. He steered them back along the River Ness, walking hand in hand on its pebbled shore, toward the castle. "I forgot my camera. I want pictures of the most beautiful girl in the orchestra."

They climbed the stairs guarded by stone lions, and entered the huge wooden doors. Amy followed him toward the red carpet racing up wide stairs. "Stay here," Shawn said. "Rest up for all the walking we're going to be doing. Hey, Dana!" He waved, grateful for her presence. "You were asking about Inverness. Amy, tell her about the bridges." He dashed up the stairs, two at a time, leaving her behind. His heart pounded. Last night's adventures were getting dangerously close. Dana wouldn't tell Amy about the game. But he hoped Jimmy would come in a back door.

* * *

Dana's eyebrows dipped in concern as Shawn dashed up the stairs. "You okay, Amy?" she asked. "You look kind of pale."

Amy sank into a chair. "Just tired." The carpet stretched across the foyer. Dana would never have gotten into this mess, she thought.

Dana dropped down beside her. "Didn't those antibiotics help last April? Did your doctor warn you they can interfere with your birth control pills?"

Amy looked up, meeting Dana's golden brown eyes, so much like Shawn's. "They can?"

Dana nodded, her cinnamon puff hair shaking like a duster feather. "Medications, miss a day, take them a few hours late, even."

Amy closed her eyes, even now remembering Shawn's rage. His *sturm und drang* would be useless this time. Still, she dreaded it.

"Shawn would..." Dana broke off.

Amy opened her eyes to see Jim, the portly trombonist, come in from the castle's library. "What's up with Shawn's trombone?" he asked.

* * *

Shawn stopped at Caroline's room. Glee flushed her face when she saw him. He brushed past her, to her roommate. The woman turned, smiling, from hanging up a blouse. The smile faded at sight of his dark face. "I'll say it once," he snapped. "Do not ever, *ever* again tell Amy that I went anywhere with Caroline."

"I didn't mean...." Her hands fell limply from the hanger.

"Flutes are a dime a dozen." He pierced her with a hard stare, long enough to make sure she understood, before turning to Caroline. She lowered her eyelids; a smile curved her lips. He stepped closer, letting his body brush the length of hers, and lifted her chin. Her smile stretched lazily. "Even first chair flutes," he said softly. His eyes bored into hers. He punctuated each of the next syllables, with an ominous decrescendo. "Do. Not. Hurt. Amy."

He dropped her chin, stepped away, and addressed them both with his public bonhomie. "Rob's a great guy. I hear you had fun with him last night, Caroline." He turned on his heel, not closing the door behind him. That problem was solved.

It was in his suite, with the blazing noon sun enriching every shade of blue, as Shawn re-counted the bills, that he found the new problem: a faint smudge in the ink on one of the twenty pound notes. His heart picked up an extra couple of beats. He'd seen such a smudge, once before, when he'd gambled with the wrong sort and been paid off in bad bills. He examined the note more carefully, holding it up to the sun.

This couldn't be happening, not here, not now, not with a bad-tempered Scot coming for his money, and Amy waiting downstairs. He felt no great desire to be beaten to a pulp today, and even less for Amy to discover he'd lied to her. He pulled another twenty from the pile and compared the two. His heart sank. Such small details, but there it was. He studied the other twenty pound notes from the pawn shop. Two more were bad. Damn! Why did these things happen to him!

He was so intent on his scrutiny of the bills, that the pounding on the door nearly jolted him out of his skin. It settled back, quivering, around his shoulders. He crossed the huge room in a few quick strides, throwing around plans. What if Jimmy noticed? Jumping out the window wouldn't do. He didn't have another sixty pounds to give the Scot. He needed his trombone. Telling the truth, with a promise to scrape up the rest by tomorrow would lead to a scene, prevent him getting his trombone, cause trouble with Conrad, and even worse trouble with Amy. There was only one answer.

He shoved the bad bills back into the middle of the pile, smudged sides down. He threw the door open. Sixty pounds wasn't so much. His eyes darted from the large wooden case dangling from Jimmy's hand to the two large men behind him. The man was still getting a great deal of money he hadn't had before. Shawn greeted him with enthusiasm, shaking his hand with a big grin and a "Good to see you! There's your money!" The forgery was well done. Jimmy would never notice.

"Aye!" The Scot grabbed for the money with his big, reddened fist. He dropped the case with a thud that made Shawn's stomach turn, and thumbed through the money, counting, while Shawn's heart hammered in his chest. He considered the distance to the window. The numbers added up. Jimmy saw nothing else, and broke into a grin. "Come play poker wi' me anytime!" he said, and shook hands again, in earnest friendship this time. The men behind him grinned and pumped Shawn's hand.

"Any time!" Shawn said, and it was over. The door shut. He closed his eyes and heaved a breath of relief.

* * *

Amy seemed to forget whatever had been bothering her. Shawn's credit card and a small deli provided the perfect picnic dinner, complete with a new picnic basket. He ducked into a shop and bought himself a bell-sleeved shirt, a long, woolen tunic, leather boots, and a red plaid tartan to throw over his shoulder. His long chestnut hair completed the look. It brought a smile to her face. "No kilt?" she asked.

"Those came later," Shawn said. "This is what we wore in the re-enactment camps."

"No leggings?" She stared at his knees, hairy and bare, between the tunic and boots.

He grinned. "I'm not wearing tights, no matter what you call them." Considering what the counterfeit notes could have turned the day into, her answering smile lit him up inside. He was grateful, suddenly, to be here. He vowed there would be no more redheads, no more Carolines.

He rented a car to drive to the nearby castle, twisting along narrow roads. Amy gasped at the scenery. Scotland's stark hills rose around them, rich with the purples and violets of heather and bluebells, and lively yellow splashes of gorse. She laughed at his tunic and boots, as they hiked the countryside above the castle.

They climbed to the top of a monroe and looked down at the cattle milling in the bowl below. A man squinted up at them, shielding his eyes against the sun, before raising a hand and calling a greeting. Shawn waved back, and they continued climbing, the rampant bluebells grazing their ankles. "He was dressed like you," Amy said.

Shawn shrugged. "A lot of people stick to the old ways, here in the Highlands. Friendly, though, aren't they."

Amy nodded. At the top of the next rise, looking down on the loch, she stooped to pick a bouquet of bluebells. Their delicate blossoms spilled riotously over her hands. "This is what the song's about?" she asked.

"What song?"

She rolled her eyes. He slapped his forehead. "Bluebells, of course. Is that what they are? I don't know." He dropped himself into the sea of blossoms, staring down the boulder strewn slopes they'd just hiked, running steeply down to the loch, and the loch itself stretching like an azure ribbon, north and south under an endless sea of blue sky. The lowing of cattle drifted up from somewhere far below.

"You don't know the words?"

"Sure." He lay back in the bluebells, hands behind his head. His dark chestnut hair splayed across the blossoms. "My dad sang it all the time. Noble deeds, streaming banners, that kind of thing." He gave a roguish wink. "I just play it because it impresses people."

She stretched out next to him, propped on an elbow, and dropped the spray of flowers on the chest of his tunic. "What have flowers got to do with noble deeds?"

Shawn laughed, brushing at them. "The guy's from the Highlands, wants to get home where the bluebells are."

"Why is that piece such a big deal?"

"It isn't, really, not once you can do it. Just scales, arpeggios, a few octave skips. Easy. It's a show-off piece, you know, just because you can. Back in the day, people thought trombones could just play oompah-oompah—too rough and crude to do anything fancy like a flute or violin. Then Arthur Pryor put that together and showed the world there was a whole lot more potential there."

"Like you?" Amy dangled a single stalk, letting the delicate bell trace the outline of his jaw.

He turned away; took the flower from her hand and studied it. Nearby, a flock of ewes and their lambs grazed, giving him an occasional wary glance and warning bleat. "No," he said. "This is it. This is me. You see it all."

She fell silent. After several minutes, he gathered the fallen bouquet, climbed to his feet, and took her hand. They clambered higher up the mountain, digging their toes into impressions in the earth to climb almost vertically. He grasped her hand, helping her along, though his own soft leather soles slipped in the soft earth now and again.

They reached another summit, looking out over the stunningly blue waters of the loch, and hills undulating forever in every direction. Towns and fields stretched away below. Vertigo swept Shawn. He laughed, feeling alive! He turned to Amy. The sun warmed her smooth, pale skin. The breeze tugged at her long, thick braid. Life was good!

"It isn't," she said.

"Isn't what?"

"It isn't all. There has to be more to you, or you wouldn't be with me."

Shawn dropped onto a rocky jutting of stone, his shoulder toward her, staring out at the water. A bee buzzed around the flowers in his hand, and disappeared into a patch of gorse. "Look, no heavy conversations," he said. "It's a nice day, okay? Let's not ruin it."

But she persisted, joining him on the rock, her shoulder brushing his. "If you were nothing more, you'd be back in your room with Caroline. That's a 'nice day' for the person you show to the world." She twisted the end of his red tartan around her hand, watching him.

Shawn breathed deeply, saying nothing. Sunlight skipped along the loch's waters, making him blink. A wind blew fresh and strong, this high. And the drunken romp on the pile of bills didn't seem as fun, here in the light of day with Amy. It felt tawdry. He stared at the ground, muttering, "I was never with Caroline."

"Yeah, I know, she was with Rob. I'm just trying to understand you," Amy said. "I'm sorry." Dropping the plaid, she worked her fingers into his, and they sat, with her head on his shoulder.

The silence stretched again, till Shawn broke it. "Let's go down to the castle. Today's the last day for that living history group. I'll find a way to get in after they close."

* * *

They toured the castle in silence, holding hands. The southern half lay in ruins. Stopped only once for an autograph, they soon moved on to the restored half, swarming with actors in medieval dress. The men wore wide-sleeved shirts and tunics much like Shawn's own, though the tartans over their shoulders were blue. They went about the daily activities of medieval Scotland, cooking, carding wool, and sharpening weapons, for the benefit of tourists.

One of the men paused in the midst of cleaning a horse's hoof, staring at Amy. She glanced away. When she looked back, the woman next to him was staring at her, too. They turned quickly under her gaze, whispering to one another.

"Shawn." Amy gripped his hand a little more tightly. "Some of these actors are looking at me strangely."

He glanced around the courtyard, at the buzz of medieval life humming around them. "You're imagining it," he said, and returned to scanning the walls for a way back in; listening with half an ear as the short, elderly tour guide, swishing her voluminous dress across the grassy courtyard, described the castle and its history, battles and lords, and the days of the Jacobites and Covenanters.

"But he was looking right at me," Amy whispered, conscious of the other tourists. "They both were, and whispering."

The guide led them into the eastern wing, up a narrow, uneven flight of stone stairs, talking all the way about Robert the Bruce, switching his loyalty from the Scots to England and back again.

"They were probably looking at me," Shawn said. "They must recognize me from the posters."

"You're arrogant," Amy muttered, and dropped the subject.

He grinned at her. "Thank you."

"In the 1300's, these were the chambers of Niall Campbell," the tour guide said, ushering the group into a suite of rooms high on the third floor. Tall arched windows on the outer wall spilled in sunshine. Shawn wandered, as she spoke, running his hands along rough stone walls, barely glancing at the four poster bed and the tapestry of a man on horseback.

"Look, Shawn." Amy indicated the tapestry. "That could be you." He glanced at it, and moved on. A short, narrow staircase, carved in the very rock itself, twisted back into a recess, with another window looking down to the loch. Shawn stuck his head out, and pulled it back in quickly. The wall dropped thirty or forty feet, a sharp vertical descent to a small patch of ground at its base. Choppy waters pounded the stones hemming in the little patch of earth. They would not be climbing this wall.

"The laird, Malcolm MacDonald, sent Niall to raise armies to fight Edward Plantagenet at the Battle of the Pools. There, Niall Campbell walks out of history, and we dinna hear of him again. It is believed a traitor in the castle killed him before he could reach his goal. Or he may have died at the battle."

Shawn emerged from the recess, back into the room, where the group hung on the guide's every word. He sidled up to Amy, taking her hand. "Lots of death and destruction for a miserable pile of stones," he said. "They needed to all have a beer and lighten the hell up!"

Amy gaped at him.

The guide turned fierce eyes on him. "It wasn't so simple," she said in clipped tones.

Shawn cleared his throat and grinned at the other tourists. "You heard that?" He didn't have the grace to look embarrassed.

The guide pursed her lips. "I certainly did! Perhaps had Robert the Bruce been thinking only of himself, he would have—" she cleared her throat importantly, "'had a beer and lightened up!'" She uttered the words with distaste. "Although it was not beer they drank, which you would know if you knew your history!"

"Americans!" muttered a German in the back, and snapped a picture of the tapestry.

Shawn took the opportunity to push his point. "What kind of man is always busting at the seams to get into another war?"

"A real man," Amy muttered. "If war means protecting his family."

Shawn stared at her in surprise.

"A real man, exactly," the tour guide snipped. "The lord had others to think about. Those whom he must protect from the English. If they were driven out of the castle, they lost the land, too, their farms, grazing for their cattle. They'd suffer hunger and starvation. Would you 'have a beer and lighten up,'" she spoke scathingly, "instead of protecting your child from death?" She stared up at him haughtily, waiting for an answer that didn't come.

Amy's hand slid from his. She crossed her arms tightly over her chest.

"Why did you have to say that?" Shawn asked the guide. "You've upset her!" He yanked his tartan more firmly onto his shoulder, glaring at her.

The woman sniffed and moved toward the tower. Shawn fell to the back of the group with Amy, throwing, first, a cocky grin in response to the German tourist's scowl.

"Come on, Amy," he said. "She's an old bag. Don't take her words to heart!"

"Maybe *you* should take her words to heart," Amy said.

He dropped the hand reaching for hers. They finished the tour in silence.

Afterward, the guide waved a friendly good-bye to the others at the gate where the portcullis had once been. She showed Shawn out with a sniff and a stiff, "Good day to you! Hope you learned something!"

Chapter Three

Glenmirril Castle, Scotland, 1314

At the top of the keep, Niall waited for Allene. A light evening breeze lifted his dark chestnut hair off his shoulders. He wore a freshly laundered linen shirt, open at the throat, his tunic, and leather boots. A blue tartan hung on his shoulder. He didn't look forward, particularly, to the meeting. She had chosen the tower for its high walls enclosing the ten foot square area. He had a good idea why she wanted to meet him in privacy, and he would stand his ground. There would be a fight, most likely, as Allene would also stand hers.

He sighed. Nothing he could do about it right now. For the moment, his aches were dulled by far more than the usual amount of ale. He may as well enjoy the quiet evening and solitude of the tower. He would be leaving soon; the trip would be dangerous. His fist tightened on the parapet. If only they knew who was carrying information to their enemies! He wanted to survive.

He relaxed his hand, determined to bring happy memories on the journey, for courage, motivation and strength. He stared out at the heather-covered hills, rising on three sides, where he and Lord Darnley had so often hunted, after his own father's death, and the glittering, blue loch, where they fished. He was grateful for Lord Darnley, Hugh, and the Laird, who had taken him in, and given him the best education to be had, in languages, warfare, music. He would marry MacDonald's daughter and be the next laird.

Laughter and singing drifted up from the great hall. He smiled. Earlier tonight, he and Iohn had sung, his harp and their voices a cheerful addition to the loud conversations and scurrying servants and dogs fighting in the rushes over bones. He and Iohn were a favorite among the people; he knew it with some pride. Iohn played the straight man to Niall's comic remarks, and they sang and played together—sometimes songs of streaming banners and noble deeds, sometimes songs of love and fair maidens and double entendres that raised delicate blushes and knowing smiles from the married women, and sometimes, just for fun, Niall adjusted the lyrics to make them laugh, to see how long it took a lord to notice he was now the subject of an old, familiar song.

He hummed to himself. At dinner, MacDonald had drifted off over his mead. Niall had gradually slowed *Blue Bells of Scotland* from the rousing battle tempo they'd been taking to a lullaby, encouraging the laird's nap. Guilt tickled his insides—he had an idea why the poor man was so tired—but mischief overtook him, and he changed the lyrics. "*Oh, where, and oh, where,*" he sang softly, "*has my highland lairdy gone?*"

A couple of ladies at the head table tittered, hands to mouths.

"*He's sleeping, he's sleeping, while his minstrel sings a song.*"

More heads turned toward the unfortunate man. Niall sang a little louder. "*He's drifted off to sleep, falling in his mead.*"

The laird's head lolled gently and came to rest atop his large pewter cup. A robust snore lifted from his slumbering form into the great hall.

"*And it's oh, how the ladies laugh at his mead-covered cheek.*"

Laughter swept across the hall. Allene, beside her father, met Niall's eyes. She tried hard to look stern. He wiggled his eyebrows at her. She covered her mouth and cast down her eyes. Iohn nudged him, and, with a wink, took over.

> "*Oh, where, and oh where,*
> *Has my highland lairdy gone?*
> *He's drifted, he's drifted off to the land of nod*
> *He's dreaming such sweet dreams*
> *Though his snores wake all the men,*
> *And it's oh, in my heart, I hope I can sleep again!*"

The crowd burst into full blown laughter. The Laird bolted upright, wild-eyed and shaking his head. Droplets of mead flew from his beard. The crowd laughed harder. He looked suspiciously at Niall.

"My lord!" Niall bowed deeply. "Why do you look at me so?" He took a long draught of his ale, easing his aches.

"Twas me singing," spoke Iohn. "My lord Niall is innocent."

"This time," grumbled the laird. "Did I think otherwise, 'twould be another arrow he'd have in his arse!" The crowd roared. Niall rubbed his posterior and grimaced, bringing on more laughter. He winked at Allene, who blushed and lowered her eyes swiftly.

"I sang your praises, my Lord," said Iohn. "You slept through it."

The laird narrowed his eyes. The crowd held its breath. "My praises!" bellowed MacDonald, danger in his eye. "Aye, 'twould be very different praises you'd ha' be singing had I been awake!" He wiped futilely at his beard and let out a big laugh. "Praises to my sweet-smelling beard, aye!"

The people roared in merriment and relief at his good humor, and the meal went on.

"What were you doing looking in on the cattle today?" Iohn asked Niall later, as they ate their dinner.

"I was nowhere near the cattle," Niall said. He speared a piece of meat from their trencher. "I had plenty to keep me busy and would scarce be making such a climb before I must."

"Odd," said Iohn. "I thought I saw you with a lass. She had long, black hair. She appeared to be wearing trews."

Niall shook his head. "A lass in trews! 'Tis me with the head wound, man!" He grinned. "But now, I do indeed have a lass to meet." He took a last gulp of ale, wiped his lip, and slipped away to meet Allene.

At the top of the keep, now, Niall studied the darkening loch. Mist thickened on its surface, swirling like a cauldron. Despite the mirth in the great hall, the ever-present threat of war lay over the castle. If they could stop England's aggression, at least his children, if not he and Allene, could live in peace. He glanced at the moon, just peering over the top of the eastern mountains, and sighed.

The gray stones darkened before Allene arrived. Her lady trailed discreetly behind, and waited patiently, eyes on the ground, by the stairs. Allene extended her hand. Niall bowed over her fingertips, kissing them. "My lady," he said. "You summoned me?" She rose just past his shoulder. Her hair blazed red-gold in the dying sun.

"You know I did." Allene handed him a basket overflowing with bluebells that had graced the hills outside the castle just this morning.

"My favorite." He bowed his head in thanks.

"Aer you still seeing double?" She pushed his hair back, grimacing at the bruises on his temple.

"You're well worth seeing two of, my lady."

"So ye've said. Your jest wears thin."

"'Twas no jest," Niall said solemnly, meeting her eyes.

Allene's cheeks turned a delicate pink. She lowered her eyes and spoke briskly. "Aer ye running a fever, Niall? You're sweating on this chill night."

He brushed it aside. "I'm fine."

She frowned and asked, "Ha' ye been drinking? The ale is strong on your breath."

"I hurt, Allene." The extra ale had damped the worst of it.

"Do ye be careful not to get drunk. Ye've an early meeting with my father on the morrow."

Niall smiled, amused at her scolding. "'Tis only to dull the pain so I might sleep well." He touched her hair, leaning his forehead against hers. "The journey will go better on a good night's rest, aye?"

"Niall, you needn't do this," she whispered.

"Meeting you, my lady? But of course I am your servant!"

"'Tis not funny, Niall!" She pulled back. "You needn't go for Hugh. You needn't join the fighting. They say Edward has gathered an army such as the world has never seen. My father would keep you here to defend the castle."

Niall's jaw hardened. "What kind of man runs from war?" He gave his own answer. "A coward! Would your father still find me fit to marry you, an I show myself a coward?"

"There'll no be much left to marry, an the MacDougall kills you the first night out," she said. "You know well someone is giving him information. If he doesn't kill you, the English will, on the road or at Stirling. 'Tis dangerous."

"God will go with me."

"As God went with my brother? Much good it did him." She stared hard at the corner of the tower, blinking back tears Niall knew she would never shed in front of anyone. She was her father's daughter, after all.

He set the basket down, took her hands in his, and spoke gently. "God will grant His protection or not, as He sees fit. I trust Him, Allene." He squeezed her hands. "We all grieve Alexander. An I do my job well, I'll save others from his fate. Think you I've forgotten my own brothers? Or my father at Falkirk?"

"I hate this never-ending war!" Allene said fiercely. "Let us run away into the hills and live a thousand miles from it all and raise our children there!"

Niall squeezed her hands. He'd entertained the same dream. But dreams were useless. "We'd no be safe. If Edward defeats Bruce at Stirling, he'll be in our Highlands next." He led her to the northern face of the tower and pointed out, where the slopes stood black against the last coral streaks of sunset. Velvet blue night touched their pinnacles. Silver pinpricks of stars danced above. Mist floated across their faces. "If we hide in the hills, he'll hunt us like animals. We must fight." Allene said nothing. Niall knew her better than that. More was coming. Into the silence, he spoke again. "I'll go for Hugh, and I'll fight beside Bruce, that our people will not suffer war this time."

She looked up, her eyes bright. "Then I'll go with you."

His heart gave a hard thump. So that was her plan! "Doona be foolish, Allene! You canna go!" He grasped her shoulders. "Do you no mind how Bruce's own sister lived in a cage, on public display, at Roxburgh? And the Countess of Buchan, likewise, on the turrets of Berwick. Think you, they'll treat you better?"

She yanked away from him. "I'll no get caught. I'll pass for a lad as I did last time. I can fight as well as you. Doona make me wait at home again!"

"No, Allene," he said, gently. "You'll stay, and pray for me day and night. You'll set the example for the other women, by tending the children and keeping their spirits up, and fighting here if need be."

Allene glared. "I'll no stay home waiting again, Niall Campbell! How would you, to know I was out there in danger while you sat home sewing?"

"Were sewing my duty," he said, his voice rising, "then I should sew. Someone must prepare for the men who will come home wounded."

"I'll not sit home sewing your shroud!" Allene insisted.

"If you prevent me doing my duty by following where you dinna belong, there'll be more shrouds needing sewing," he said, equally fiercely. His eyes grew dark in the setting sun. His face colored in temper. "Other women wait for their men. Did your father raise you to think you are above them?"

She clenched her jaw and stared at the stone floor. "My father raised me to do my part. I'm strong. I can fight."

"Which is why the women need you here," he said softly.

"You'll be safer if I go!"

"No." He saw her in a cage, displayed like an animal, like poor Lady Mary. Over his dead body. "You'll not endanger yourself."

"Our people are safer if two go." She hurried on. "If you are injured or caught, I can finish the journey and raise Hugh."

"I leave on the morrow. Alone. I had hoped for a pleasanter good-bye."

"Then say I can go."

He touched her shoulder. "Give me a proper good-bye, because I am going. Alone."

"You'll not get a proper good-bye, because I'm going with you."

Niall touched her cheek, despite her anger. He would not see her for many weeks; if things went poorly at Stirling, forever. He grabbed her, kissing her with a passion he'd rarely dared, his hand pressing in her thick auburn curls. She hugged him tightly, returning the kiss.

Equally suddenly, she shoved him back. "You'll no turn me from my purpose like this! You'll see: I'll be with you when you leave." She spun and marched to the stairway, brushing by her lady. The maid dipped a small curtsy to Niall, avoiding his eyes, and followed her mistress.

Niall thought of the revelry in the hall below: a last night of merriment before the morning's final conference on his journey, and the danger that would follow close on its heals. His blood churned. Damn her! She'd be fuming and plotting. He'd be loving her and angry all at once. The festivities below lost their pleasure. He glowered out at the loch. Mist bubbled like a witch's potion, creeping high up the castle walls. A wisp of it curled around his feet. He tucked his tartan tightly around himself, bunched his cloak into a pillow, and curled up against the tower wall. He thought about Allene and the future he'd envisioned with her. If only she didn't go and make his job difficult! He shifted, trying to get more comfortable, and hoped, at the very least, for a good night's sleep before his journey.

Glenmirril Castle, Scotland, Present

They waited, with the picnic basket, by the loch behind the castle. Shawn skipped stones across the water and made small talk, soaking in her long, black hair and small, white teeth, the lyric sound of her voice.

She pulled off her shoes to wet her toes. "Cold!" She shivered. "I wouldn't want to swim in it!"

When the last car left the parking lot, he pulled her to her feet. "I found a way in," he said.

For the first time, she smiled a real smile. "Shawn, we can't. We shouldn't be doing this."

"I like seeing you smile." He stopped, facing her. "You used to do it all the time. Come on! Let's go!" As enthusiastic as a young boy, he pulled her up a steep, bramble-covered embankment. With some agility and more luck, he boosted her on the top of the wall, and handed the basket up. She lowered it gingerly to the other side, leaning dangerously far down, then helped him climb up beside her. They dropped down, rolling in the grassy courtyard. Shawn trapped her under him and kissed her. She lay still. He ran his hands over her long hair, spreading across the grass, and touched her face.

"Why are you so different when we're alone?" he asked. "When we're with other people, you act like you can't stand me kissing you."

Amy rolled to her side, pushing him off. "When we're with other people," she said, "you kiss me like it's a show to put yourself in the spotlight. When we're alone, I feel like you really mean it."

He nodded, with a slight frown, and after a moment said, "Let's have our picnic. You're going to love it!" He grabbed the basket, grasped her hand and pulled her to her feet. "Last one there is an out of tune oboe!"

"That's redundant!" She laughed, racing him to the tower. Inside, with the sun just beginning to dip, it was dimmer than it had been.

"Up to the top," Shawn said. "The view's something else!" He led her up rough, stone stairs, past an arched window with a stone cross set in its aperture. They emerged into a ten by ten square, shielded by high walls, and the peculiarly bright light that comes just before the real sunset. Hills and loch stretched beyond the horizons. Mist floated in ribbons on the water's surface.

Amy shivered.

"What's wrong?" Shawn asked. "It's warm up here." But he took off the red tartan, and wrapped it around her shoulders. He stretched out his arms, feeling the glow of the sun and the warm evening air on them. The scent of the bluebells, tucked in the picnic basket, drifted across the tower.

"I don't know," she said. "It just feels...." She paused, looking around the tower. "The flowers have such a strong smell." She took them out, smelling them, and with a shake of her head, laid them in a corner.

"They're in a smaller space."

"But it's open here. On the stairs, it would have made sense. But —it just feels like—like tension up here."

"Tension?" He looked around the tower. "Come on, you've read too many ghost stories about these old Scottish castles. What is it, the ghost of the woman who picked too many bluebells?" He laughed. "Let's eat. Roast beef? Boiled potatoes?" He settled himself on the flagstone floor, pulling plates and food from the basket. Next came six bottles of beer and a fluted wine glass.

Amy groaned. "I told you I hate beer. Especially now."

Grinning, Shawn lifted out a slender, ruby bottle. He held it up, enjoying the pleasure that lit her face. "I listened this time."

She took the bottle. It sparkled like a jewel in the evening light. She gave a small gasp and delighted laugh. "It's the Merlot I love! I didn't know you knew!"

"I know more than you think." He uncorked the bottle with a pop and poured her a glass. "To us."

She raised the glass hesitantly to his beer bottle. Her smile slipped a little.

"No toast?" he asked. She hesitated. "Out with it," he said. "What's wrong?"

She lowered her glass, untasted. "You were right," she said. "We're having a nice day."

"But?"

"Shawn, you don't want to hear it."

He stared at her for several moments, not missing her hand resting on her stomach. He took a deep swallow of his beer. "Maybe not," he said. "Are you...?" He stopped. He didn't really want to know if she was pregnant again. He wanted this moment, this time in his life, to go on forever. "I was thinking," he said, instead, "about what you asked me earlier. Why I'm with you." She raised her head, watching him with less than the trusting eyes he'd hoped for. "I don't really know. I just know I feel different with you than with...." He stopped.

"With Caroline, with that backstage bimbo?" She finished for him. "How flattering."

"She was with Rob." He stared at the flagstones. She had no proof. Caroline wouldn't say anything. Everyone in the orchestra knew better than to upset him; and carrying tales to Amy upset him. Nobody told her. Ever.

"Uh-huh."

He wondered, uncomfortably, if she did know. He hated hearing her sound so cynical, but he'd never given her any reason to doubt him. He didn't want to hurt her. He kept all of it well hidden, after all, never carried numbers, canceled the history on his cell phone, never opened his e-mail in front of her. He took another slow swallow of beer, watching her.

She shook her head suddenly, as if making a decision. "I can't help it, Shawn. I know you don't want to hear it, but even with these wonderful days, something inside me is dead. Ever since the baby...."

He set the beer down, hard. "I don't want to talk about that."

"You're not the only one here! *I* want to!"

"It's over. You know it was the only thing to do!" He scoffed. "Can you imagine me as a father!"

"Yes, I can," she whispered. "I see so much in you." Her eyes softened. "I could see you as a father then, and I still can, if only you could see that good in yourself!"

"I see plenty of good in myself!" He shot to his feet, the beer bottle dangling from his hand. "So does everyone in this orchestra! I make them a ton of money!"

"Yes, you've done a lot for this orchestra. We were only half alive before you came. Think how much good you could do for your own child!" She scrambled to her feet.

He thumped his arms onto the northern wall, glaring out at the mists curling up the mountain's black face. "You agreed to it."

"*I did not!*" she exploded. "We fought for two weeks over it! I was afraid of being abandoned. You said my parents would disown me. I was afraid I'd lose my job." She lowered her voice. "Like other people have."

His shoulders stiffened. "We're not discussing it. We're alone in Scotland's most romantic castle, and you want to ruin it!"

"I'm hurting inside, Shawn!" Her hands fell on the shoulders of his tunic. Her breath brushed his neck. "I've tried it your way, stuffing it in, ignoring it, hoping it would go away, and I can't! It's eating me alive, that I did it, that we did it, that I have this awful secret, and there's no one else I can talk to! And we have to face it again...."

"Well, you can't talk to me, either!" He turned abruptly, shaking her hands away, and stabbed her with a stony gaze. "Life's about having fun. A baby—that's not fun for me. This carrying on, like it's something to cry over. That's not fun." He gulped the last of the beer, willing it all away. *Caroline! Pregnancies! Angry Scotsmen and counterfeit money!* Why did these things *happen* to him!

She stepped back, stricken. Her lower lip tensed. "I want to go home."

"Well, I don't. We came here to have dinner and make love in the sunset." He dropped back to the floor, patting the stones beside him.

Amy quivered with tension, glaring down at him. "You just told me to shut up and stuff my feelings back out of sight so they don't bother you. And now you think I want to make love to you?"

"Yeah. You always do."

She shook her head. "Not this time. I can't do it anymore, giving myself to a man with a stone where his heart should be. Give me the car keys." She thrust her hand out.

"You didn't get your international license. You can't drive."

"Watch me."

Shawn laughed, digging in the pocket of his baggy, medieval trews. "I know you, Amy. You won't jaywalk on a deserted street. I paid good money for this meal. I'll be out when I'm done." He flipped the keys at her, much harder than necessary.

She caught them in a neat overhand.   "I will expect my grandmother's ring back as promised," she said in clipped tones, "or I will raise a holy hell in every possible corner of your life, till you wish you'd never thought up that idiotic story about tinagle connectors." She threw the tartan down at him.

"I didn't make...."

"Stuff it, Shawn. I saw Jim while I was waiting in the lobby. He almost died laughing, said there's no such thing on a trombone. Thanks for humiliating me, on top of it. Maybe some day you'll come clean about what you needed—make that wanted—the money for."

"Hey, that's not fair!" He jumped to his feet. "I needed that money! There was this big Scot. He was coming with his friends to beat the living daylights out of me!"

"Did you sleep with his wife? You probably deserved to be beaten to a pulp." She shoved past him, glaring back from the arched doorway at the top of the stairwell. "I cannot believe I've stayed with you this long!" She spun on her heel. Her voice floated back up from the dark staircase. "I cannot believe I kept thinking there was something better in you!" He ran to the western wall to see her emerge from the tower into the courtyard. Mist swirled around her ankles. "Everybody told me there was nothing better there!" she shouted up at him.

"Bull!" he shouted back, leaning over the tower. "They love me!"

"You have no idea what they say behind your back," Amy yelled. "Selfish, self-centered, obnoxious, loud! They're just afraid of your temper. Arrogant!" She turned and stormed across the courtyard, tearing through tendrils of mist grabbing at her legs.

"I am not loud!" he bellowed. She disappeared into the gate tower without looking back. Shawn leaned against the wall. After a minute, he yanked out another beer, wrenched the cap off, and threw back a long gulp, his Adams apple bobbing. They were his friends. They loved him. Amy was just mad. Damn Jim for telling. Aw, hell, thought Shawn. He couldn't have known.

Now the abortion. That disturbed him on some level. But it wouldn't, if she'd let it go. He crossed the tower, sipping his beer, and gazed over the wall toward the loch. Its waters had turned deepest blue with the dying light. Mist had thickened and crept up the castle walls. In the distance, a cow lowed, and a car engine rumbled to life.

He spun. A car engine! He dashed back to the western wall, peering frantically across the mist-filled courtyard and the gatehouse walls on time to see the small white rental car roaring out of the parking lot above, spewing dust.

He swore violently. "Amy!" he shouted at the top of his lungs. The cow lowed back in response. She'd left him! She'd actually driven off, stranding him fifteen miles from the hotel, with night falling! He swore again, and kicked the wall. His leather boots offered no protection against stone bulwarks. He grabbed his foot, hopping up and down and swearing. "Hey, my wallet's in the car!" he shouted after her, but with less force. "My ID, my credit cards!" He shivered in the cooling air. He was stuck fifteen miles from his hotel in this ridiculous tunic and medieval shirt, and not even a few dollars to get a taxi.

Aw, damn it, he swore again. She'd come back. She'd get a mile down the road and have a panic attack at having driven illegally; she'd cry and beg him to drive her home, and he'd win her back like he always did, insist first that she allow him to show her the depths of his love, here at the top of the tower, under the stars.

Yeah, he thought. This night isn't over. He smiled smugly, wrapped the tartan around himself, and finished off his beer.

An hour later, he finished his third beer and looked out over the walls again. Mist boiled on the loch's surface and filled the courtyard, like a fog machine at an abandoned rave. The castle walls and buildings floated, ghostly, above the bubbling stew. Tendrils of mist shaped themselves, into a man, into a horse, and melted away again. He blinked.

Maybe he'd read too many ghost stories himself.

And he realized she wasn't coming back.

He swore one last time, without much energy. He thought about walking the fifteen miles to the castle, but wasn't sure he'd find the way in dark. And, though he'd never admit it to anyone, he wasn't sure he wanted to walk through that deserted courtyard, with its swirling ghosts. He drank the last three beers, pulled out a bottle of whiskey, and drank until he collapsed on the tower floor beside his half-eaten meal.

Near Loch Ness, Scotland, 1314

The clearing was warmer than the last time they'd met, but just as dark. Mist snaked through the wood, gripping Fearchar and Tearlach's legs with cool fingers. MacDougall had brought three of his men. "In case," he said grimly, "someone changes his mind." Four hands settled firmly on sword hilts, assuring that no minds would change.

"I've told ye all I know!" Fearchar glared around the circle. The trees pressed thick around them. As well as he knew the land, even he would not get far in such inky darkness. And Tearlach's courage would not stretch that far. "There was no need for this."

"We need more," spoke the large man from the last meeting.

"I can give ye no more, no matter how many men with swords ye bring! I know no more."

"But ye do," spoke the MacDougall. "You say they'll send him through the Great Glen, but spread a rumor he is going north around Inverness. What about the loch?"

"He canna cross the loch. We've no boat sturdy enough."

Tearlach spoke. "And Niall doesna care much for water."

MacDougall grunted. He and his men leaned close, whispering under the heavy pines. Fearchar and Tearlach waited, not daring to speak, till he emerged from the huddle. "MacDonald is wily. If he knows someone is carryin' tales, would it not be foolish to send him through the Glen when he's told the lords of the castle that is what he'll do?"

Fearchar snorted and spit. His waning courage waxed. "That's where you need to know our Niall. It matters not what MacDonald tells him."

"Niall is confident. Perhaps over-confident," Tearlach added.

"He knows the Glen better than anyone," Fearchar said. "'Tis the quickest way. As soon as he is out of the Laird's sight, he'll do as he pleases. He will go through the Glen, because he knows all its secrets."

"He is not the only one, I am told." A gust of wind whipped suddenly through the clearing, twisting his cloak around his legs. MacDougall's men ducked against the chill. Tearlach turned his head into his collar.

The wind died as suddenly as it had risen. Fearchar yanked his cloak, straightening it, and met MacDougall's eyes, black eyes glittering back at him in the moonlight. There was a long silence. Fearchar pulled his cloak more firmly about himself as the cold realization set in. "You are asking me to track him myself."

"I am demanding you fulfill your promise."

"I told you what I know. I dinna promise to kill him."

"A shame." The clouds shifted, and the mist thickened and rose. "There will be others eager for that land Edward will have after the battle. And we canna risk ye goin' back to the MacDonald now, warnin' him." The four men around MacDougall stepped closer. One of them pulled a dirk, idly cleaning his fingernails with it, watching Fearchar the while.

"How am I to explain leaving the castle?"

"There's a fair stramash up there, now, preparin' for Stirling. Ye say he's sendin' the first group of men on the morrow." He waited till Fearchar nodded. "Ye come wi' us now. Yer friend tells them ye've gone wi' the first group."

"MacDonald will no believe that."

MacDougall and his men looked at each other. MacDougall spoke again. "Tearlach is no so prominent. They'll no miss him. He comes with us to guarantee you'll show, the day Campbell leaves."

Fearchar studied the men and their swords. There was no way out.

MacDougall laughed softly, his hand on Tearlach's trembling arm. "Did ye think to get yer land fer nothin'?"

* * *

He hadn't drunk enough, Shawn thought, briefly conscious in the midst of his own dreams, as he occasionally was. When he drank enough, he didn't dream. But now, his father's reenactor friends twisted through his memory, probably brought on by seeing the actors on the castle grounds. They roamed his dreams, his father, his father's friends, with hearty beards, drinking around campfires in their tunics, hose, and gambesons, singing of love and war, arguing fiercely over the proper pronunciations of auld Scottish words that no longer mattered, before ending the feud with another swig of ale, and more laughter.

His father's camp always hummed with Gaelic lilts and life as people clamored, like children to a carnival, to his father's good nature, good humor, good fun. His father's kindness drew them. He was always ready to lend a few dollars or give a lift or share food. He took in strays— dogs, cats, and children from less fortunate homes.

Then came the battle, as it always did: the reason Shawn drank himself into unconsciousness whenever possible. He'd loved watching them re-enact battles, imbibing the nobility, virtues and heroism of times past. But this battle—this battle had never happened except in his dreams, and here it happened over and over. The young reenactor, the one his father had taken under his wing, rising up with a sword that was real when it shouldn't have been, and his father's death and his father's blood running red and real on the battlefield when it shouldn't have.

He twisted on the hard flagged floor of the tower, trying to look away, and vowing to himself, as he did each time he watched his father die again: he would not follow in his father's footsteps. He would not end up innocent and trusting, and tricked, and dead. Finally, he sank back into dreamless sleep, to the sound of a horse whinnying.

Chapter Four

Glenmirril Castle, Scotland

Niall woke with the hard stones chilly beneath him, bracing morning air crisp around him, and the sweet smell of the bluebells filling his senses. He jumped to his feet. The ache of the arrow wound brought him up short. He rubbed his posterior and grinned. It had been a foolish trick, but well worth the re-telling. They'd be talking about it for years.

Energy pumped through him. Not even the ache at his temple could dull his eagerness. Allene's determination notwithstanding, today was his last day in the keep for some time. Heat raced suddenly up his neck and face. He crossed to the eastern wall of the tower seeking a cooling breeze. Mist danced a languid reel on the loch below, and drifted in wisps up the pines across the water. It was here Saint Columba had driven off the monster. The curling mist made it easy to imagine such mysterious happenings.

With the flush on his face cooled, Niall lowered himself painfully to his knees, crossed himself, and thanked his Lord and Savior for the day, the beautiful loch, a safe place to sleep. It was more than Allene's brother, or his, had had for months before being tortured and murdered by the English; more than Hugh and his men had, hiding in the forest for so long. He prayed for them. His own protesting body, flushed with prickly heat, must not take precedence over their needs. Hadn't the Bruce kept going, even fighting battles, through a wasting illness? Niall would do no less.

He gripped the crucifix around his neck, and prayed: for Gil, still burning with fever; for wisdom and safety on this journey, and the safety of his people. He beseeched God to look with favor on his prayers, though he was hardly the man the Laird was. "And, Lord," he added, as dizziness pressed on his brain, "if it takes a miracle, please, heal me, too. Someone must reach Hugh."

He crossed himself, struggled to his feet, and leaned on the battlements looking over the northern hills, silver-green beneath the mists. He suspected MacDonald had something up his sleeve. And he suspected he wouldn't like it. Going north would take twice as long. He pushed his hand through his hair, letting it fall back to his shoulders. The Great Glen was the obvious way, and thus where his enemies would search. But he knew its secrets better than any man, thanks to Darnley and Hugh. He could outwit anyone there. It wasn't a difficult decision: he would go through the Glen.

He turned back to the loch, showing bright patches of blue through the mist now, and spoke to God once more. "Watch over Your servant, whatever the following days hold," he prayed.

Glenmirril Castle, Scotland, Present

Amy and Rob pulled into the dirt parking lot, heavy with swirling mist. Dawn shone on the castle, casting a rose-silver sheen over the gray stones. Rob stared up at the massive walls hovering above the mist. He shivered. "Can you imagine spending the night here? I can't believe you left him."

"I can't believe you helped him lie to me," Amy retorted. "That ring has been in my family for five generations. It was a last gift from someone I loved dearly."

Rob stared straight ahead. A tinge of color touched his cheeks. "Yeah, well. Haven't you noticed people have a tendency to do stupid things under Shawn's influence?"

"More than you'll ever know," Amy said. "Myself included."

She stared down at her clothes. She had become accustomed to dressing to please him. Today, she'd put on her favorite jeans, and a pink t-shirt he hated. "But my ring is still gone. And you still helped him. You want to start making amends by telling me what the money was for?"

The color on his cheeks erupted and spread, up to his blond hair and down his neck. He gripped the steering wheel, white-knuckled. "Not really."

"Women, drinking, gambling?"

Rob blinked hard at the castle.

"It's not like Shawn has any new tricks up his sleeve," she said. "It was one of the three."

They sat in silence for another minute before Amy muttered, "I can't believe I stayed with him this long. I'm such an idiot!" She threw open her door and climbed out.

Rob climbed out on his own side, and leaned over the car. The sun, just reaching over the castle walls, made him blink and shield his eyes. "Why *did* you stay with him?"

"I guess everyone wonders." Amy turned away from him. She shivered in the cool morning. "Why is Amy such an idiot? Because he was fun and exciting and colorful. All the things I'm not. I thought no one else would ever be interested in me." She slammed the car door, hard. "I *am* an idiot," she said, marching toward the castle. Damp fog twisted like a chilly cat around her jeans.

Behind her, Rob's car door slammed. "Yeah," he yelled after her. "You are an idiot."

Amy turned, glaring. The cool morning chilled her bare arms.

He leaned on the roof of the car. "You're an idiot to think no one else would be interested in you."

The anger drained from her face. Her heart skipped a beat. But she spoke cautiously. "There haven't exactly been any other offers."

"Of course not," Rob said. "Who's stupid enough to hit on Shawn Kleiner's girlfriend?"

Amy became still. She walked slowly back toward the car. "Is that how it is?" Her left hand moved to twist the ring, but found only a bare finger.

"Sure." Rob took his arms off the roof and rounded the car. He boosted himself onto the hood, and patted it, inviting her to join him. She hoisted herself up. "When you decide you've had enough of him, there are a few guys who would ask you out." She gazed at the castle walls, mulling his words. Rob spoke again, more softly. "And I don't believe you stayed with him only because he's fun and exciting. I don't think you're that shallow."

Amy turned to him, studying him a few moments before saying, "No. I stayed because I saw so much more in him."

"I don't know what you fought about last night," Rob said. "I'm not asking. But you got mad enough to leave him. Even he keeps telling you there's nothing more to him. Do you finally believe it?"

Amy hung her head. Her mouth stiffened. "Yeah, he finally convinced me."

"So is that it?"

"Is it over between us?" she asked. "Yeah, it's over."

"He's going to try to change your mind."

"This was pretty big." Amy paused. "But if he showed me...really proved to me...." She shivered in the cool morning.

"Not gonna happen." Rob shook his head. "He's exactly what he says he is." He put his hand on her back. "Let's go find him. I hope he's not too mad."

"But if he was," Amy persisted. "If he finally showed me he's the man I think he is, I'd go back to him in a heartbeat."

Glenmirril, Scotland

Early morning sun pierced Shawn's eyelids. He groaned, feeling the first poundings of the timpani. The aftereffects of too much beer and whiskey swirled in his stomach. His head sank into something soft; the sweet smell of bluebells nauseated him. He pressed the heels of his hands into his eyes, turning away from the sun. His world shifted, his head once again sinking. He groped beneath his head. His jacket? Somewhere in his beer-logged brain, he thought he hadn't brought one with him.

Never mind. He covered his eyes with both hands. Amy had left him. Amy, the ever-law-abiding, had driven without a license. He smiled. A little backbone? It would certainly make life more interesting.

A voice drifted up to him. He groaned. The tour guide. Wouldn't she have plenty to say, finding him here bright and early in the tower where he didn't belong. He pushed himself up, his eyes still clenched against the sun; the stone floor cool under his palms, and the sun golden-warm on his skin. He gave himself another minute, his head down against the swirling nausea. Then he opened his eyes, squinting tightly. There was the basket of bluebells that was so overpowering. He glowered, and climbed to his feet.

He leaned his head against the parapet, but the floral scent wrapped around him. Voices reached out again, from far away. His head spun. He risked opening his eyes. There were no cars in the lot. Funny. Whose voices had he heard? He crossed to the east side of the tower, reeling as the rising sun speared his eyes. He raised a hand against the glare, and squinted down at the pebbly beach below. Two women, in full skirts, ambled along the shore with a man in a gray tunic. The water glittered under the rich greens of the mountains behind it. He swore. What was with these damn reenactors? Didn't they have a life, that they were out this early in the morning playing dress up? They really needed to join the real world.

Ah, well. Time to get back to Inverness. In the light of day, he could do it. He turned to grab the picnic basket. Maybe he'd refill it and take Caroline up here. He stopped.

It wasn't there.

The basket in the corner curved up on the bottom, open on either end. Piles of bluebells lay lengthwise in it. He scratched his ear. He couldn't remember any basket, apart from the one holding the picnic. He turned slowly around the keep. That one wasn't there.

The sweater? A dull throbbing grew behind his temples. It was hard to think without his morning latte. But he remembered laying his head on something soft. There in the corner—a dark brown woven... *something*. He crossed the keep and picked it up, shaking it out. One of the reenactor's cloaks. He screwed his eyes shut, seeking a path through the confusion. So they'd found him here already and given him a cloak to sleep on. Strange. He'd have thought they'd wake him up with a little annoyance. Oh, well. He'd go down and thank them and ask for a lift back to the hotel.

But first, he sat down for just a minute, cradling his head in his hands. Just another minute to let the head-pounding and nausea quiet down. He wondered, for once, why he did this to himself, and whether it was worth it. It didn't even stop the dreams, anymore.

A commotion erupted on the stairs, a flurry of female voices, a swish of fabric against stone walls, and the light, hurrying steps of a woman. He groaned. The floor shifted under him again. Time to face the dragon-lady tour guide. *"Dh'fhàg mi an seo e a-raoir,"* said one voice. *I left him here last night* drifted lazily through Shawn's brain. "'Tis unlike him not to appear for the morning meal." Shawn rubbed his ear and shook his head. He was still hearing the Gaelic lilt from his dreams, although garbled and hard to understand.

Two young women emerged at the top of the stairs. Young women? He scoffed. Jailbait, more like it. But oh so attractive, even if they were two more of those ridiculous reenactors. One hung behind, clutching a small wooden bucket. Dark hair hung in plaits down the back of her plain brown dress. Plaits? Shawn thought. Where did I get that word? She kept her eyes on the floor. The one in front—now there was a force to be reckoned with. Fiery red hair shimmered around her face; blue eyes flashed. Freckles danced across her pale skin. A fine blue kirtle emphasized a small waist and fell to her toes.

"There you are!" she burst out.

To Shawn, it was an explosion. "Turn down the volume, will you?" he said. "My head is pounding."

"Drank ye too much ale?" she asked suspiciously. She turned to the girl behind her. "What gibberish is he speaking? It sounds like some drunken form of the Sassenach tongue."

Shawn stared. She *was* speaking Gaelic! Maybe it was the whiskey that made it sound so strange. He squeezed his eyes tight and opened them again, sure now that he was awake, and yet she *was* speaking Gaelic! These people, he thought for the second time this short morning, really needed to join the real world. He laughed out loud. The girl gave a suspicious stare. "'Tis hardly funny. My father and all the lords await. Did ye drink more?"

He switched to the Gaelic of his camp days and his grandmother. "What's it to you? Listen, I need a lift...."

"He speaks strangely, my lady." The quieter girl cocked her head at him. "And he seems not to recognize ye."

"D' ye not?" The redhead frowned.

"Should I?" he asked.

Her face softened. "'S *mise*, Allene." He struggled to make out
words. *It's me, Allene.* "Is it your head?" She reached for his hand. It
wasn't what he'd expected. But what the hell. Even half-drunk, he
recognized an opportunity. He pulled her down, tipping her off balance.
Their lips met. She softened for just a second, then yanked back.

"You!" She spun to the girl behind her, grabbed the bucket, and
doused him thoroughly with cold water. "Ye *are* drunk! I told ye not to!"

Shawn gasped and spluttered, shaking his hands and head, and
scrambled to his feet. Water dripped liberally from his eyes, hair, and
nose. The icy water chilled him down to his bones and brain. He gasped
sharply for breath, glaring. "What the hell was that for!" he demanded.
He had not forgotten how to swear in Gaelic.

Behind the fiery girl, the more docile one gasped. "D' ye no be
talking to my lady like that!" Her words belied her mild voice.

Shawn stared in fascination, sifting words from her garbled
dialect as he wiped water from his eyes. What an actress! She sounded
truly shocked, as if she'd never heard the word before. "That's good," he
said. He switched back to English, not wanting to play their silly game.
"Sorry about your dad and the lords, but...."

"Stop this gibberish," the girl with the fiery hair said.

Shawn sighed in irritation and repeated himself in Gaelic.

"What are you wearing?" interrupted the princess, as Shawn was
already thinking of her. "That is not our plaid! That is MacDougall's!"

Shawn glanced down at the tunic, and the plaid hanging
drunkenly off one shoulder. "Oh, this. Yeah, I just picked this up for
kicks. Wanted to feel a little authentic, you know. Oh, I get it. You
thought I was...." He groped for a Gaelic word and could think of none.
He substituted English. "You thought I was one of the reenactors."

"You're drunk," the girl snapped. "You make no sense. I've no
idea what a...a *re-en*...what that is. My father will not like to see you
wearing his enemy's plaid. You may in your drunken state find it good
jest, but I assure you, he will not!"

"This is enough." Shawn switched back to English. She stared at
him in such confusion that he wondered if maybe she was one of those
from the far west who spoke only Gaelic. He pushed himself to his feet,
picking up the cloak. "Is this yours?" he asked, giving her the courtesy of
her native tongue. "Thanks for the loan, even if you did follow it up with
a bucket of cold water. There must be someone here with a car."

"Would that I had another bucket of water!" the girl said in
agitation. "What were ye *thinking* to get drunk at such a time!"

Behind her, the lady in waiting spoke mildly. "My lady, however
upset ye are, he must be rid of that plaid before your father sees it."

Lady Allene pursed her lips. "Cover the plaid with that cloak. Go to your room immediately and change. And in the name of the Good Lord Jesus, I pray thee never get this drunk again. You are addled!"

"I told you, I'm not one of the reenactors. I have no idea what room you mean. My things are in Inverness."

"He's speaking nonsense, my lady," the maid said. "Are you sure 'tis only the drink? 'Twas a nasty blow he took to the head, bringing home the cattle."

"What blow?" Shawn asked. "What cattle?" He misunderstood their garbled speech, surely.

The redhead stepped forward, reaching for his head. Shawn jumped out of her reach, starting the nausea in his stomach again. "Uh-uh," he said. "Stay away from me."

"Follow me," said the girl, showing a little more concern. "He was sweating last night. Perhaps the arrow wound has become infected and addled his mind?"

"Arrow wound? What arrow wound? I'm not addled."

She ignored him. "He was still seeing double last night. Keep the cloak tightly closed, Niall. Who knows who is about in the hall."

Shawn shook his head, spilling drops of cold water down his nose, and wrapped the cloak around himself. Fine. Play along. At least he'd get some dry clothes. Or maybe the coffee his body craved. He followed the girls down the dim, twisting stairs, past the window with the stone cross inset, to the courtyard.

It bustled with life: women cooking, boys fetching, soldiers calling, and all of them hustling among the fingers of mist pulling at their clothes. They had their children there, dressed in what looked to be fairly authentic garb. They even had sheep in the courtyard! He wondered that they had moved all this in while he slept. And—something else—something not right with this picture. Even apart from the fact that it lurched like a ship on high seas now and again.

But despite the cold shower, the hangover clung to his brain tenaciously, and he couldn't put a finger on what was wrong.

He followed the women across the courtyard. Men offered him brief bows—nods of the head, really—and women dropped him quick curtseys. He nodded, grinned, winked at them in turn. I could get used to this, he thought. The insides of his head swayed pleasantly, with the hangover and the pleasure of flirtation.

Allene led him to the wing adjoining the tower, up more stairs, and down a stone hall with arched windows letting in light and morning sounds from the courtyard. He remembered coming here on the tour. She opened a large wooden door. He remembered this room. The historical society had furnished it as it might have appeared. It hit him! He stopped abruptly. "Yesterday was the last day for the living history."

"Go 'won wi' ye, my lord." The meeker girl pushed him in. There was the huge four poster bed, and the heavy draperies at the open window. He stared harder. Hadn't the hangings been red? Of course, he hadn't paid much attention. He'd been thinking about Amy and finding a way back in. Because there were the hangings, a deep blue. And the tapestry of the man on horseback—he looked for it. There were several, but none looked familiar. It must be a different room, after all.

Regardless, Allene implied it was his. They'd made a huge mistake. He wondered who his character was, the person they mistook him for, to deserve bows and curtsies and this huge room. "Nice," he said. "What am I supposed to do, again?" He put a hand to his pounding head.

"Get rid of that awful plaid!" snapped the lady in waiting. "Shall I fetch the physician, my lady?"

Allene crossed the room briskly and drew, from a huge wooden wardrobe, a clean linen shirt, tunic, leather boots, dirk, and a fresh plaid. "Haste!" she said. "My father is waiting and none too happily! Angry as I am at you right now, I'd not see you hang!"

"I'm sure you'd love to see how I'm hung," Shawn shot back. "And if you ever want to know what's really under my tunic..."

She slapped him.

Hard.

The blow sent new shock waves through his pounding head. He stumbled back into the room, a hand on his stinging cheek. "Hey! You're carrying it a little far, don't you think!"

"Change your clothes!" she snapped. "Iohn will be up directly. See you're ready." She closed the door with a dull booming thud.

Shawn dropped on the bed, cradling his thundering head in his hands. Why in the world were they mistaking him for this character? Maybe he looked like the man, or maybe they'd never met him. Maybe this was a new group of actors, different from yesterday's. Maybe there was some special production today. He tried to remember any mention of such an event, but couldn't. There had been posters at the gift shop, but he'd paid no attention. Too bad. It might have given him some clue who these people were, taking their little playacting so seriously.

He rubbed his cheek and looked at the clothes 'Lady Allene' had thrown out for him. He couldn't see, in his hung-over state, much difference between this plaid and his own she found so offensive. Red, blue, who cared? He wanted to march out of the castle and head for Inverness and break it off with Amy. This whole morning so far had him in a foul mood, and it was her fault. On the other hand—he looked at the clothes on the bed. At least they were dry.

He changed, and found himself more comfortable. He dropped

his own things in a heap on the floor. Opening the wardrobe, he found a hat with a plume, a bonnie plume, he might even say, and shook his head. Being around these people was messing with his mind. He put it on, wishing for a mirror.

A brisk knock landed on the door, and it flew open. A man with jet black hair and—Shawn squinted, to be sure—mismatched eyes, one blue and one green, filled the doorway, wearing the standard costume. So much for variety around here, Shawn thought. Except for the unusual eyes.

"My Lady Allene is distressed with your behavior," the man said, curtly. "Would that you stop teasing her. Your jests wear thin at this of all times. Would you have her send for a physician?"

"I doubt it. You people are so into this, he'd probably bleed me for the sake of realism."

The man frowned. "He'd no bleed you for drunkenness, though MacDonald might throw you in stocks, were your journey not so vital. Think you not, that you'd best let me accompany you? Allene is worried about sending you alone in this condition."

"No, I'm fine," Shawn said. He tried to work his liquor-logged brain around the mention of a journey. He'd just journey right on up to Inverness, without this man's help. He glanced at the bed, hoping he could sleep off this hangover, first.

"Well, then, I would that you show better behavior in front of the Laird, than the drunkenness you've shown my Lady. And bonnie though it is, the hat is perhaps not appropriate."

"I'm not drunk," Shawn muttered. He tossed the hat on the bed. "I'm hung over. I *wish* I were still drunk." He'd had a brief relationship with a girl who had been deep in the whole Ren-faire scene. He remembered her friends as a much looser bunch, winking and nudging at a good hangover, not threatening stocks. The 'ladies' among them had not been averse to a little bawdy humor, nor for that matter, to following it up in the nearest barn with even more fun. None of them would have slapped him. These Scots must be different.

He hastened beside the man back down the hall and stairs, and across the courtyard. He caught a quick but bold glance and a pretty blush from one of the girls at whom he'd earlier winked. Then he saw another one just like her. He grinned. "Oh, man, twice the fun!"

A jolt to the head threw him off balance.

"Twice the fun!" Shawn rubbed his head. "It's the Wrigley's commercial. What the hell do you have against Wrigley's? Are you some sort of gum hater? I'm still seeing double!" He laughed out loud, leering at the two girls.

"Your double vision is hardly cause for mirth right now." His escort glared at him. "Not even for a jest about the Morrison twins. You'll not long remain the Lord's future son-in-law with that behavior. He'll no have milady Allene mistreated."

"So what's he going to do? Demote me to pig farmer?" Shawn rubbed the back of his head irritably. The vigorous blow had set off the timpani, and another wave of nausea crashed around his stomach. "What the hell is up with all the smack-downs around here? Can't I just go back to bed and sleep this off?"

The man yanked him into an alcove, behind a huge outdoor oven. Shawn started. It hadn't been there yesterday. He was sure. It was only a result of the hangover, he told himself, but he thought there'd been only ruins. He was about to ask, but his questions were stilled by another buffet to the head.

"Hey!" he cried in real anger this time. "Do you know who I am? Don't you people know you can give someone brain damage doing that? Are you so stuck in your make believe you don't read the papers?"

The man gave him a curious, almost pitying, look. "Pig farmer! We've only sheep and cattle. Friends we've been these twenty years, I'll not watch you anger my Lord. I'll be behind you and the next inappropriate word, I will deal with the flat side of my sword."

"Can we stop the play-acting for a minute?" Shawn said. "I'm not part of this. My hotel is fifteen miles over that hill, and I'll be back in my own world, even if I have to walk the whole way."

"You speak like one bewitched," the man said. "Would that it were play-acting. Come along."

Shawn yanked from the man's grip. They continued across the courtyard. But Iohn's genuine perplexity, the oven that hadn't been there yesterday, sheep in the courtyard—they unnerved him.

"The sheep!" Shawn stopped abruptly. "How did sheep get here?"

Iohn took Shawn's elbow, steering him forward. "Keep moving, Niall. People will talk."

"But how did the sheep get here? They had to have been trucked in. But there's nothing in the parking lot." He threw in English where he lacked Gaelic words.

"*Trucked? Par King?* Try, Niall! For all our sakes, try to regain your senses! You brought those sheep yourself. Has the blow to the head affected you so?" He pushed Shawn into the great hall, where five men in tunics, cloaks and great red and gray beards lined a huge wooden table. Five stone, hard faces, Jimmy's ancestors, stared at Shawn.

Glenmirril Castle, Scotland

Hands on the cool stone parapets, and the rising sun bright in his eyes, Niall drank in one last glance of the mist-shrouded landscape. He knew this loch; he loved this loch. He'd grown up on its shores, surrounded by friends and family. Some had died of illness or in battles. He thanked God for those who lived. If he could complete this mission, they would be spared. He prayed God it would be so.

Voices reached him, from far away; just briefly before drifting off. He adjusted his tunic and tugged his shirt into place—his morning's version of freshening up—and turned back for his cloak.

It was gone.

He stared at the empty flagstones where it had been. Odd. Who would take his cloak? Who could have? Only Allene was angry with him, but it seemed a childish trick, unworthy of her. The Laird would provide a new one, but he didn't like to appear careless. He started for the stairs, but something else caught his eye: the bluebells. He took a wary step closer.

Allene's basket was also gone. The blossoms lay on the floor. Who would take a basket and leave the flowers? His eyebrows drew together at this oddity. He glanced for reassurance at the knife tucked in his leather boot. He turned slowly, studying the rest of the tower.

As he did so, he saw the third mystery: a large square basket. "What is this?" he murmured. He lowered himself to one knee, grimacing at the painful wound, and opened it. It contained a mess of half-eaten food. He sniffed a slice of roast beef and considered tasting it. But with enemies everywhere, it did one no good to go about eating unexplained food, mysteriously appearing where it didn't belong. He might have believed it was Allene's peace offering, but that it had obviously been well-sampled already. Maybe one of the laird's great hounds had been up here in the night. But it seemed unlikely.

He searched deeper, and found an elegant vessel of glass, enclosing a dark ruby liquid. He held it up to the rising sun. The color sparkled and deepened. *Fascinating.* He studied the unusual script on the bit of parchment stuck to it. *Merlot,* it said. He imprinted the strange lettering firmly in his memory and sniffed: some sort of wine or ale.

He put it back and picked up flat pieces of metal: a dull, weak knife, something with prongs, and a metal spoon too small to be of any use in cooking.

Returning them to the basket, his fingers skimmed something smooth. He pulled out a sheet of parchment, slick to the touch, glossy as a lady's satin gown, and bright with text and miniatures. His eyes widened, but he was too much the soldier to gasp. Never had he seen paintings so realistic. Or so small.

Words were written over the paintings. Peculiar. He spoke fluent

English, thanks to his foster years near the border. But the spelling was unlike any he'd ever seen. He studied it, settling the words in his mind. It was a story of some sort. He studied the paintings. Several were of a castle on a loch, much like his own, but for its crumbling walls. A bead of sweat broke from his forehead and trailed down his jaw.

He climbed to his feet, as abruptly as his wound would allow, disturbed. He would take these things to the Laird. He'd traveled widely in his youth. If anyone would know, he would.

He looked around the tower one last time. It was as it had always been, ten feet square, with stone battlements rising to his chest. So why did he feel he'd overlooked something, that something more was very wrong here?

* * *

Looking up at the castle's imposing northern walls, and the broken-down southern battlements, Rob said, "I'm sorry, you know, about the ring." His gaze shifted to the misty ground, his face red.

"Apology accepted," Amy said. "But you still need to get it back for me if he doesn't. Think he's still there, or did the dragon lady tour guide find him and carry him off to her lair?" She lifted her hair and let it fall again down her back.

"What an unpleasant surprise for her if she did."

"I thought you were his friend."

Rob shrugged. "Yeah, sure. He's my best friend."

"But you're feeling sorry for the dragon lady."

Rob laughed. He crossed his arms over his chest and looked into the distance. "It's different for guys," he said. "We drink, we party, we have fun. That's best friends for guys, not like you girls, always yakking about your feelings, and joined at the hip even to go to the bathroom. We just hang out, you know? I can feel sorry for the Dragon Lady."

Amy laughed. "Yeah, girls expect more than hanging out from a best friend. Should we try to get in?"

"We could—maybe—look around a little. He's probably still sleeping it off. This path lead down to the lake?"

She nodded, looking at him quizzically.

He flushed again. "It's just—I'm not much of a rule-breaker," he confessed. "I'm not sure I can bring myself to break into a locked castle. And I've never been the kind to steal my best friend's girl."

Amy's eyes widened. Elation swelled her heart. "I...yes, I think that's the path. We could just walk around, or sit there, until the castle opens. Maybe we'll see Nessie." She laughed uncertainly. He put his hand on her back, under her hair, and guided her down the pebbly path.

* * *

With sweat beading his forehead, Niall twisted down the rough hewn stairs curling down inside the tower. Sunlight skimmed through the archers' slots and the distinctive cross window, throwing a silver cast on the walls. In the courtyard, Niall looked around. Residence wings rose, three stories of gray stone, at right angles to the keep. Across the bailey, to the west, stood the chapel, and beyond it, the gatehouse. Mist drifted across the courtyard, rolling up around his ankles. A chill shuddered through him.

And now Niall understood the unsettled feeling. It wasn't just the missing cloak. Far from it. Nor the missing flower basket or unexplained hamper full of foreign things.

The courtyard was empty—worse than empty. Apart from that brief sound of voices, it was silent, utterly desolate. At the back of his mind, he'd noted the unnatural silence at a time when sheep should have been bleating and wives stirring and horses whickering. Missing was the smell of the fire in the great hall. Where could they all be? The MacDougalls couldn't have returned so quickly for vengeance. They couldn't have emptied everyone out so swiftly and silently that he slept through it.

Niall stooped to slide the dirk from his boot. Its smooth metal blade ran cold up his leg. A bead of sweat inched down his jaw. He scanned the desolate castle, right and left, and straightened, pushing the long, dark hair from his forehead. The walls: they were like his castle walls, but—he studied them—not quite.

A wave of dizziness crashed over him. He squeezed his eyes shut, braced his hands on his knees for a moment, and pushed himself back up, staring at the ruins where the stables, blacksmith, and armory should have been. The close was no longer beaten earth, grazed by sheep, but soft with dewy grass, like an English garden.

He touched his temple, under his hair. The lacerations were still rough, tender to the touch. The wound ached as if it were only days old. Had it caused him to sleep long enough for people and sheep to disappear, for grass to grow?

...and walls to crumble?

Intense unease laced his stomach.

He edged across the courtyard, his back against the wall, his eyes missing nothing. The oven was gone: the oven behind which he'd first kissed Allene and been chased out by her father. He smiled. It was the only time he'd ever been terrified in his life. Sheep had scattered in their ambling fashion, chickens lifted amid squawks and flurries of feathers, and women screamed and dropped their wares as he and the Laird plowed through. He'd whipped the young Niall and told him a man must court a lady properly. And from that day, Niall had found himself under the Laird's wing, learning all he knew, and, after that, all that the best tutors of Scotland could teach him. He wondered that the man had seen something in him.

But a brick oven couldn't disappear overnight.

He reached the door of the eastern wing and slipped in. The hall was empty, as lifeless as the abandoned, roofless church he and Iohn had once found in the forest. A bird trill sliced the silence. He inched up the stairs to the third floor. Sunlight and cool morning air streamed through tall windows. He looked up. A nest was wedged in the cross beams of the arched ceiling. A raven shrieked and wheeled away, beating black wings as it soared out the casement.

He came to his room. The door was gone. Checking the hall again, he stepped in, looking around. Tapestries hung on the walls. One showed a man, vaguely like himself, riding a pony and laughing back over his shoulder at his pursuers. The corner of Niall's mouth lifted in wry amusement, but the unnerving desertion of the castle and prickle of fever prevented real humor. He surveyed the rest of the room. His curtains, bed hangings, and cover were garnet red. The smile, small as it had been, disappeared. What sort of enemy took people and animals, tore down walls...and changed the bed linens?

All while a man slept.

Fear crept higher in his chest; deeper and more terrifying than being chased by MacDonald. Then, at least, he'd known what was happening. He leaned against the stone wall, gripping his dirk and waiting out another bout of dizziness. It passed, and he tried to think again.

Something had become of his people, including his beloved Allene. He considered, nonetheless, rationally, devoid of emotion. He could not save her till he could first do something for himself. His military tutors had pounded that lesson home.

He moved to the window overlooking the loch. The fog had thinned. Two people walked on the shore. They wore strange tunics, reaching only to their waists. One had short hair, the white-blonde of a Norseman. The other had long black hair all the way down the back. But what sort of woman did not wear a skirt? He checked that he was still alone, before studying them further. They moved peacefully, ambling toward the large rock where he and Iohn had played at soldiers and cattle-raids, as children. They showed no sign of fear or imminent danger.

A good sign, Niall supposed. Nonetheless, he kept his dirk to hand. He moved with a bit more assurance out of his room, through the silent halls. In the great hall, the windows soared high, letting in a view of loch and hills. Tapestries hung between them. One was a poor imitation of the Laird's favorite. The rest, he'd never seen.

Outside again, heat slicked his forehead and chest as he stared at the crumbling wall to the service close. Maybe it was delirium. He turned to the water gate that led to the loch. Its massive wooden doors, designed to keep an army at bay, had been replaced with a dainty picket blockade. He clambered over, onto the pebbly path, and headed down to the shore, dagger in hand, in search of the couple.

Chapter Five

Glenmirril Castle, Scotland, Present

The sun burst over the mountains, scattering mist and bringing the loch's waters to glorious life, sparkling like sapphires; picking out the flecks of silver and bronze veining the pebbles at their feet. Amy and Rob sat on a large stone at the water's edge. A slim, young alder sprang from the rocky soil, spreading June leaves just over their heads. Bits of greenery and tiny white blossoms burst out among the stones.

"My dad's dream come true," Rob said. His leg touched hers. "One of us kids playing professionally. He taught high school band for thirty years."

"My parents gave me all the lessons," Amy said, "but they think I could have done better things, like be a doctor or a lawyer."

They talked about Shawn.

"He decided we were having a Bash for Brass." Rob laughed; the sunlight flashed off his blond hair. "All the brass players. He wouldn't take no for an answer. He had this huge cookout for all of us, families and everything. He pulled me in, asked my advice, treated me like his best friend. Kind of let me know I *was* his new best friend, you know, and what Shawn says, goes."

Amy nodded, understanding. "Remember how he came into the first rehearsal walking on his hands? He was looking at me the whole time, seeing if I was watching. And he kept it up through that whole rehearsal. Kept turning his head. He hung around when I was talking to other people, for weeks, and I didn't get it, because he was so upfront with all those other women, asking them out, and well—you know what that means with Shawn. But he never talked to me, at first."

"You turned him down when he finally asked you out. Twice. He told me about it over beer once. What changed your mind?"

Amy stared over the water to the pine-covered hills. "I saw a different side to him," she said. "When my mother was so sick, he bought me a ticket home to see her. He slid it under my door, and tried to run away, but I caught him. I made him come in, and he was a different person. He talked, like a real person, not like the strutting bravado in the spotlight he always was at rehearsals. He told me his dad died unexpectedly and how important it was to say good-bye to my mother, if...." She paused, biting her lip. "If it came to that. That's when I started to fall in love with him." Rob grabbed a pebble and shot it hard, skipping it—two, three, four staccato, accented beats—across the water. Amy went on. "And when we do the arranging together, he's different. It's like he's ashamed of this good person inside him."

"He's not ashamed." Rob snorted. "Because that good person really isn't there." He glared at the water, slapping gently at the rocks, just inches from his tennis shoes. "He knows how to put on an act, that's all."

"I just can't believe it was an act that night," Amy said softly. They were silent for another minute before she said, "We were here yesterday. Right on this rock. Do you ever look at things that have been here for hundreds of years, and wonder, who else sat here? What things have happened right in this very spot?"

"Children fishing, boys playing soldiers," Rob said. "Couples falling in love."

Amy smiled. She didn't pull her hand away when he took it in his. "How mad do you think he'll be?"

"With Shawn, it's a big explosion, but then it's over. Or he might come out and make a joke of it. Try a prank on us, maybe."

"Yeah, I can see Shawn trying a prank," Amy said. They sat silently for another few minutes. She stared at the water. Rob's hand wrapped warmly around hers. It could be so much better than it was with Shawn. She'd never be afraid of angering—really angering—Rob. He would even welcome a child, she thought. So why, inside, did she feel only emptiness at the touch of his hand?

The slightest of sounds drew her head around, and she jumped up with a short, sharp scream, eyes wide, hand on her chest. "*Shawn!*" she yelped. "You scared me half to death! Put that knife away!"

Glenmirril Castle, Scotland

Shawn faced the five stone faces, two clean, three with bushy beards in shades of red, gray, and silver. Fake, he wondered? How did they manage three such similar actors? Another discomfort took up residence in his brain. He rubbed his temple, wanting coffee. A day shouldn't start without it. Iohn pushed him to the side. "Hold your tongue a moment, Niall." He stepped forward, bowing to the assemblage.

"Young Iohn," the man in the center rumbled. Shawn struggled to understand the man's accent, even as he studied the craggy face, weathered and as red as his beard. A scar ran from his temple to his jaw.

Heavy white and auburn eyebrows rose in fury above blue eyes, as piercing and brilliant as the water outside. "You found him."

"My lords." Iohn rose from his bow. "I beg your leave this once. I know not what has happened, but my lord Niall is not in his right mind. See how even now he rubs his head?" They all looked at Shawn. He dropped his hand. "He has never once missed an assemblage or shirked any duty. He has been babbling nonsense and behaving oddly. I fear he is taken ill, perhaps from the arrow wound? Or his head? He took quite a blow, the night of the cattle raid."

Shawn watched studiously. If these were indeed actors—noting how the word *if* had crept into his vocabulary—they were playing it to the hilt. Not a sign of a wink or nod, or noticing he wasn't playing his part. As if the script had indeed been written for an addled Lord Niall to step into the middle of their playacting.

Which it certainly could not have been.

No cars in the car lot. Sheep transporting themselves in without a truck. His head hurt. He didn't want to think this hard. A giant brick oven where there had been ruins, and people who freely buffeted others, mindless of lawsuits and brain injuries. He looked around the hall, at the tapestries, roaring fires in the giant hearths, rushes on the floor.

"Step forward, Niall," rumbled the clan chief.

Shawn stepped forward, weak-kneed and grateful he was no longer wearing the tartan of these people's enemy. Don't be ridiculous, he chided himself. But he wondered if he'd been kidnapped from the tower and carried to the most rugged, wild part of Scotland where old ways still held sway. Maybe they meant to hold him for ransom. He was an important man, after all. He shook his head. Then it made no sense for them to be calling him Niall. So they must be living history actors.

"Speak, Niall."

"I'm...I'm not Niall," Shawn said. A thud to the back of his head sent a new jolt through his unhappy body, and suggested this was not an acceptable answer.

"Niall, your jests are well known. Usually, however, they are in good form. This is not. You missed a very important meeting."

"If he is ill, my Lord...." suggested Iohn.

"He looks the picture of health. He is robust and has color in his cheek. Though his speech is odd."

"'Tis too much ale," said Iohn.

"Can I speak?" Shawn asked.

"Speak," commanded the Laird.

"No more punches?" He cast Iohn a dirty look, rubbing his head.

"Punches?" asked another of the stone faces.

"He appears to mean buffets," suggested another, smaller man, studying Shawn curiously.

"Ah," said the first. "Pu-unches." He tasted the word. "Punches."

"No buffets," the chief commanded Iohn.

Shawn pulled himself to his full height, though it increased the nausea in his stomach. *"I'm Shawn Kleiner."*

He waited for their awe.

The men looked back and forth, quizzically, at one another. "What is he saying? He's not so old."

Shawn cocked his head at this odd statement before remembering the Gaelic word *sean* meant old.

"Why does he talk of shawms?" asked another.

"I did say he was speaking strangely," Iohn said.

"I'm a musician," Shawn snapped. The pounding in his head kicked into another violent crescendo. Whoever they were, they ought to have at least heard of him. Unless he really was, somehow, deep in the wilds of Scotland.

"Yes, Niall, you've great skill on the harp."

"No!" Shawn shook his head, making drums pound inside. "I don't play harp. I mean, I play loads of instruments, I can play a little harp, but not well. I play trombone."

"Trumboon?" A voice creaked from one of the craggy faces. "What's this?"

Shawn struggled to think. If this was the wildest, oldest part of Scotland, what could he tell them? "It's long. It's got a bell." He gestured with his hands. "It's got a slide." He motioned with his right arm, in and out.

Most of the faces remained blank, but the Laird's awoke with understanding. "Niall, my lad! You were listening when I told you about sackbuts! But you've never touched the one the gypsies gave me."

Beside him, Iohn coughed loudly. "O' coorse he hasn't."

"O' coorse not," echoed one of the five, a young man. "'Tis but a fantasy woven in his delusions. Mayhap the blow to the head is more serious than we knew."

The chief studied Shawn. "Niall, tell us why you missed the council."

He spread his hands helplessly. "I'm trying to tell you...."

"No more of this nonsense!" roared one of the older men, half rising to his feet, and Shawn felt uncomfortably certain this was not acting. He stepped back.

"Look at him stepping back from us," said a man on the right. "Can this be the bold young Campbell who stole a kiss from the Laird's own daughter!"

"That will not be discussed!" thundered the Laird. "Young

Campbell knows what will happen ere he touches my daughter again before they are wed! You say you did not know of the meeting, Niall. Where do you say you were last night?"

"I was just visiting yesterday. We drove out here."

"'Visiting?' You live here."

"Drove what? Cattle? 'Twas two days ago."

"A car," Shawn said. They stared at him blankly. "I was having a picnic in the tower."

"Picnic?"

"I was eating dinner in the tower."

"What a peculiar thing to do!" said the man to the Laird's right, stroking his beard. "You ate in the great hall, at this very table with us."

"No, I didn't...." Shawn paused at the look on their faces. He made, perhaps the mistake, of glancing down. Under the table were five pairs of legs, three of them rough and old, covered in leather boots, two pairs young and sturdy. From the top of each boot jutted the hilt of a large knife. How would they react to a stranger in their midst? He had a feeling xenophobia didn't begin to describe the situation here. His gut twisted. Perhaps it was best to become who these people thought he was.

"I had dinner in the tower...later," he amended. "I had something to drink, and I fell asleep," he finished lamely. The Lady Allene—he would enlist her help. There was talk of a journey. He would simply walk away, as soon as he got out of the castle. The orchestra would be wondering where he had gone. Certainly Amy would have the decency to tell them, and they'd come looking.

And what would they find? Had he somehow been taken to a place similar to Glenmirril, or had they come into the castle while he slept? But that, of course, was ridiculous. They couldn't build the castle up around him and bring in sheep and change bedroom decor while he slept. He gave his head a shake, willing the room to stand still. *I had too much to drink,* he told himself. *Somebody put something in my drink. This makes no sense.*

The men at the table watched him closely. His decision made—he would be this Niall until he could get away—he bowed, as Iohn had done. "My Lords...." The words sounded foreign, but he was used to fooling people. This would work. "My Lords, I beg your forgiveness. I drank too much. I overslept. I forgot. It won't happen again."

A nodding of heads and a string of reprimands flowed and ebbed around the table.

"I truly beg your forgiveness," Shawn said. "I'm ready for the meeting and anything I need to do today. Although...." He had to account for not knowing the things they would expect *Niall* to know. "I think...I remember hitting my head in the..." What was it Niall had been doing? "In the sheep raid."

"Cattle, Niall, they were cattle," said the smallest lord, looking worriedly at the other men.

"Yes, I meant cattle, and my head has felt...foggy...since. I'm having a hard time remembering...uh, remembering some things. I beg forgiveness...." It seemed like a good expression; it had brought nods of approval last time. "If I seem not myself."

He committed himself to charming a few girls and finding out what he needed to know. And he wondered again if the orchestra had noticed he was missing. Schmitz needed an answer, and would come looking for him. Damn Amy for leaving him here and getting him into this mess. What in the world had got into her, anyway? He wondered, not for the first time, why he attracted such temperamental women.

* * *

"Bring this woman some clothes!" Niall averted his eyes from the woman, and addressed the man.

The white-haired man in front of him looked—stunned. He should jump, show fear perhaps, or defiance, but this dazed look on his face—was the man an idiot? Were they both idiots, let loose by uncaring kin to wander the shore half dressed? Barely dressed, Niall amended. He tried to keep his eyes off the woman, not wanting to shame her.

But the man looked at her, and she at him. Agitated gibberish flew from her mouth.

"English, Shawn," the man said dryly, turning back to Niall. "The atmosphere's great and all, but we still don't speak Gaelic."

"English?" Niall switched tongues. His back stiffened. His eyes narrowed. He scanned the loch, its misty water lapping just inches behind the man's feet, and the mountains, rising as they always had, beyond. He raised the dirk an inch.

"Very funny," said the man. But he gave the knife a dubious glance. "What did you say?"

"Bring this wooman some clooz." Niall spoke slowly in English, his eyes on the man's.

The woman gave, suddenly and inexplicably, a laugh, looking down at her small, tight garments. The shirt, a shade of pink Niall had never imagined in clothing, bared her entire arm. She wore trews! "You're joking! I mean, you really are joking, aren't you? I know you hate this shirt, and I'm sure you're mad at me for leaving you in the tower."

Niall turned his attention full on her, dumbfounded, meeting her eyes. She spoke so quickly, and such a bastardization of the English tongue that he caught only half her words. But she was clearly not the least ashamed of her state of undress! And leaving him in the tower? Was she mad? He turned back to the man, who looked at him curiously with another nervous glance at the dirk. "Shawn, maybe you should put the knife down," he said. "The joke's gone far enough."

"Where did you get that?" the woman asked. "Was it in the picnic basket?"

"The bahsket?" Niall asked. They seemed to think they knew him. Delirium, he told himself. He wasn't feeling well. They were a bad dream. "The bahsket in the tower? Thaht's yours?"

"It's yours. You bought it." She turned to the man with a frown. "I don't think he's joking. Do you think something happened to him?" Her hand fluttered to her chest. "I never should have left him. Shawn, what happened?"

"My naeme is Niall Campbell." He drew himself, against the throbbing in his head, to his full six feet.

"He's pulling your leg," said the man. "He's getting back at you for leaving him in the tower."

But the woman shook her head. "Maybe he hit his head? Could he have fallen?"

Niall's hand flew to the head wound, inadvertently brushing the hair back at his temple and revealing the lacerations. The woman jumped forward, saying, *Oh!* her mouth and eyes round in concern. Niall's knife flashed upward. She leaped back, fearful, scuffling stones under her feet. Wisps of fog swirled around her trews.

"He's hurt, Rob!" Her hand and voice hovered, as if she wanted to reach for him, touch the injury as Allene had done, but she kept her distance, her eyes flitting between his dirk and his face.

The man, this Rob, gaped at the bruise. To the woman, he said, "It looks like he hit it something awful." And to Niall, "Could you put away the knife?"

"I'm fine," Niall spoke clearly, pushing back at the disorientation pressing in on him. These half-dressed village fools were treating him like he was the one with addled brains! He wondered himself what illness had taken a hold of him. Regardless, these people would speak *to* him as the future Laird, not *about* him as a simpleton. He ignored the man's suggestion to put away his 'knife,' and said, "Name yourselves."

"It's me, Amy." The woman was obviously distressed now. "Rob, what should we do? He's hurt because of me. I'll never forgive myself."

"And you, Sir?"

"What's with the outfit?" the man asked, instead of answering.

Niall looked down at his own clothes: a perfectly serviceable pair of trews, a sturdy belted tunic, leather boots, and a plaid thrown over his shoulder. Surely they couldn't fault *his* clothing. He looked back at them in annoyance. "You will dae me the respect...." he began.

The woman ignored him. "He bought it yesterday." She looked more closely. "Shawn, you didn't steal that tartan from the displays here, did you? Wasn't yours red?"

"Sairely nawt!" Niall snapped. "The MacDougalls wair red. The MacDonalds wair blue. Whoot nonsense is this! Sir, your naeme."

"Funny, Shawn." The man slid his arm around the woman, and drew her back. He spoke with less certainty now.

She nudged him. "Just tell him, Rob. They say you should humor them."

The man eyed the knife.

"You think I'm dangerous?" Niall noted his look with amusement. "I'm verra safe as long as you air no threat to me or my clan. Apart from battle, I've only ever killed a MacDougall an' tha' for haerming my nephew."

The woman stepped back. The man's face blanched to the color of his hair. "Easy, Shawn. I'm no threat," he said. "I'm not a MacDougall. I don't even know any MacDougalls."

"Quit messing around, Shawn," the woman said weakly. "It's not funny." But she stared again at his temple.

The man leaned close to the woman. "Where's your phone?" he asked.

"In the car." She kept her eyes on Niall.

Niall pitied them. Such gibberish. *Foon! Khar!* "I'm nawt this Shawn," he said. "Sairch the cahstle yerselves if ye think such a pairson is here. But I dinna think sae." He waved his hands at them, as at a flock of chickens. They jumped, looking frightened. The man edged the woman behind him. Niall realized he was still holding the knife, and, deciding they were no threat, pushed it into his boot. "Check the tower!" he said, irritably. Every part of him ached, the dizziness was closing in again, and he wanted to know what was going on. "Go find this Shawn ye think is here!"

"How did you get in last night?" the man asked the woman. He cast a doubtful glance at the thick stone walls, rising behind Niall.

"Come along," Niall said. He led them back up the stony path, pushing through ribbons of fog, to the water gate. This time, he gave it a good kick, tearing apart the lock. It burst apart.

"Shawn!" the woman gasped. "You just broke it!"

"Twas obviously not built well," Niall replied.

"Never mind, Amy," the man whispered, ushering her between the broken slats. "We've got bigger problems."

They stared at each other, in the castle's inner close, now. Niall gestured toward the tower. "Go 'won!'"

They looked at each other uncertainly. "I need to get the basket," Amy said.

"Uh-uh." The man shook his head. "I'm not staying here alone with him." But he did stay, staring at Niall. The woman, Amy, strode toward the tower. She looked back once over her shoulder, then broke into a run across the grassy courtyard, her long hair swinging, and the last of the mist darting in and out between her flying feet.

The man looked after her for just a moment and turned back to Niall. He steeled his eyes and lowered his voice. "This isn't funny. Don't hurt her." Niall bristled. He did not harm women or children. "I know you can get me fired," Rob added. Niall wondered if he meant at the stake, or fired at, with arrows. "But I'm not going to let you hurt her."

Brave man, Niall thought, noting Rob's wiry build. But then, such men were sometimes stronger than they looked. Still, he'd not dignify such insult with an answer. He hardened his jaw.

Rob gave Niall one last hard stare, then yelled after the woman, "Amy, you're not going to find anyone up there!" He gave a darting glance at the knife jutting from Niall's boot, and hurried after her.

* * *

Amy and Rob hurried across the courtyard, shaken. "Amy, either he's pushing this joke to the limit, or he needs a doctor." At the tower entrance, they stole a quick look back at Shawn, lounging against a wall, watching them. "Think he's laughing at us?" Rob muttered.

They entered the dim interior, onto the twisting stone stairs. Amy stumbled once on the uneven surface, despite sunlight pouring through the archers' slots. Halfway up, under the window with the stone cross in its center, she bit her lip, and leaned against the wall, hugging herself. "What have I done, Rob? What have I done to him?"

"The question is, what are you *doing?*" Rob asked.

"Just getting the basket." She shivered.

"Are you sure?" He lifted her chin, making her meet his eyes. "You know he's not up there, right?"

"I know. I know he can't be, but...."

"If he was, he'd be mad." In the cool, dim stairwell, Rob slipped an arm around her, smiling. "Maybe I'd rather see him hung over and in a rage up here, than unbalanced and wielding a knife back there."

Amy laughed uneasily. "I don't want to think I did that to him. So if he's not up here, that has to be him, right?"

"Of course it's him. That's a pretty vicious blow to the head."

"To give him an accent, though? He's like a different person."

78

"Head injuries do strange things. Remember Phineas Gage?" Amy shook her head.

"A steel rod went through his head in an explosion, back in the 1800's. He survived, but he was a totally different person afterward." He put his hands on her shoulders, turning her toward him. "He'll be okay."

Amy leaned her head on his chest for a moment, then pulled quickly away. "Shawn!" she shouted. The sound bounced around the silvery stairwell. She darted up the uneven steps, suddenly believing she would see Shawn, hung over but healthy in his red tartan, the tartan of the MacDougalls. She burst into the sunshine pouring over the parapets.

The tower was empty.

* * *

Niall lounged by the gatehouse. *Never show weakness* his military tutors had taught him. Though sweat trickled icily inside his tunic, and he leaned against the wall for support, he put a cocky expression on his face and cleaned his nails with his dirk, striving for nonchalance. He gazed around the deserted bailey. He'd felt the fever growing. But he'd known dreams of delirium, and this felt too real. Maybe it was some doing of the MacDougalls.

The man and woman appeared at the bottom of the tower, staring at him, heads leaned close, whispering. He studied them, through eyes half closed, breathing deeply to steady the dizziness. They looked back up at him and crossed the courtyard. They seemed harmless; scared of him, in fact.

He tucked the knife into the top of his boot and straightened as they reached him. He strove to keep his voice strong and his eyes direct, despite the heaviness pressing on his brain. "Where aer the MacDonalds?"

The woman's face fell. She and the man, Rob, exchanged glances. She whispered with a tremor, "Come to the car."

He pushed himself off the wall, tensing every muscle against growing weakness. With his hand on her back, Rob guided Amy through the cool stone breezeway of the gatehouse.

Niall breathed hard, both from the physical exertion of following them, and from the shock of seeing a stone bridge where the drawbridge had been. It arched over a pleasant grassy glen where the loch's waters, only last night, had flowed into the moat. King Herla flashed across his mind. But that was ridiculous. A steady drumming throbbed in his head.

Rob spoke over his shoulder. "Conrad's really pissed this time."

Niall fought to concentrate through the growing haze. Sweat beaded his brow. "Conrad?" he asked faintly. He followed them across

79

an empty lee that should have held sheep, chickens, and a kiln; through a gate that wouldn't stop MacDougall's dullest bairn, let alone an army, to a field of beaten earth. On it crouched a beast on giant black paws, with a flat back, big enough to swallow several men. Sunlight glinted off its flanks. Its glassy eyes stared at him. It bared a wide row of teeth.

Rob and Amy walked right up to it.

Niall stopped abruptly, grabbing for his dirk. He studied the thing, watched Amy and Rob circle it fearlessly. Seeing no motion, no sense of danger, he approached it, ran his hand over the smooth, white surface. It was metal like his dagger, but white as a newly washed shift!

"Toto," intoned Rob, "I don't think we're in Kansas anymore."

Niall looked up. He no longer feared these people. "What is it?" he asked.

Amy grabbed the beast's flank, ripped it open, rummaging within. Niall closed his eyes, taking a deep breath, and opened them again. Sweat broke from his forehead, trickling down his jaw. The thing had no innards. Amy's voice floated out. "Shawn, you're really scaring me." She sniffed. He closed the gap between them. She stood up, a colorful parchment in her hand, turned, and jumped. He wanted to brush away the forming tears.

"Please, doona cry," he said, softly. "I've no wish to scare ye."

She gave a start; her hands fluttered. She dropped her gaze to the ground, met his eyes, and turned away again. Niall wondered that she seemed so unnerved by an apology. But then, it must all surely be a fevered dream. She raised her head again. A verra nice dream, he thought, looking into eyes as dark as the loch on a moonlit night.

From across the beast, leaning on its back, Rob cleared his throat. "The brochure, Amy."

"Yeah." She broke the look between them, wiping at her nose. She unfolded the parchment, muttering, "The MacDonalds."

Niall gave the beast one last look, dismissing it as harmless, despite its odd appearance. He slid his hand onto the parchment over hers, and took it, holding it over his knife. He frowned at the colorful miniature paintings, the plethora of script. It was like the thing he'd found in the basket. "What is it?" he asked.

"A...a brochure. It tells about the castle."

Niall ran his finger over the script, studying shapes, forming words. He'd never known a monk to copy such tiny letters. This couldn't be the MacDougall's doing. "Does it say where my clan has gone?" It seemed unlikely. They'd been there last night. Nobody could create this piece so quickly, telling the story.

His vision wavered suddenly. He put his hand on the beast to steady himself. A shudder wracked his body. Cold crawled through him, under the heat of the fever.

She reached up to touch his cheek. He jolted at her brazenness. She gasped. "Rob, he's clammy."

Dizziness swamped him, like a stormy wave on the loch. From inside the dark wave, he heard the woman shout. The dirk fell from his shaking hands, clattering to the ground, and they were on him, the man catching him as he fell, the woman crying, "He's burning up!" and her cool hands on his cheek, her lips on his forehead. She smelled sweet and clean. He tried to pull his head out of her warm bosom, but lacked the strength. His limbs flailed like a newborn babe. "What have I done to him!" she wailed. The wave swallowed him and sucked him down, shutting out light and sound.

Glenmirril Castle, Scotland

"Join us, Niall," said one of the older men. Shawn found himself growing accustomed to their accent. He inclined his head in respect—it seemed like a healthy habit here—and seated himself at the table. Iohn sat beside him.

"Let us review for Niall."

"Could you start with the basics?" Shawn asked. "What year is it?" He touched his head to keep them aware of his excuse for any peculiar behavior he was bound to exhibit. What year is it—the first question doctors always asked concussed patients.

Silence sprang up around the table. They all stared at him.

"Just the head injury...wound," Shawn said. "Just...just checking. Joking, really," he finished lamely. "Jesting."

"The year of our Lord, thirteen fourteen," said the smaller man.

"You're...." Shawn studied each of their faces. They gazed back solemnly. Clearly they weren't joking. Actors, he reminded himself. In the camps, they'd always told visitors it was the historical year they were re-enacting. The actors yesterday had said it was, what, 1413, 1430? Maybe they'd said 1314. They lived it and breathed it. Clearly these people were firmly entrenched in their own world. They would send him off on Niall's mission, and he would find a phone and call Rob and get back to his own world. And a latte. Hot, strong coffee and a bed to sleep it off were really all he asked of life right now. It wasn't so much.

"Edward is sending reinforcements to Stirling," intoned the Laird. His old, blue eyes met Shawn's. "If Stirling falls, the English invade Scotland, taking our land, killing our people. We need Hugh, but he and his men are in hiding. You remember naught?"

"Couldn't you just let him have the castle?" Shawn suggested. "I mean, it's a big country, there are castles to go around."

Two men drew their dirks from their boots and placed them firmly on the table, giving him stony stares. "What traitorous speech is this?" queried one.

"Would you have us all dead?" demanded another, leaning forward. "Have you forgotten your own brothers?"

"Have you forgotten what the English did at Stirling Bridge?" asked the small lord in shock. "Have you forgotten your own father at Falkirk!"

The Laird scrutinized Shawn's face, and held up his hand for peace. "Niall has ever been the most loyal, dutiful, and courageous among us. Were it not so, his life would have been forfeit that day behind the oven."

"For...." Shawn started to say, For *kissing* your daughter? Oh, man, you don't know how much more I have in mind! A glance at the daggers gave him a moment's wisdom. He held his tongue.

"The blow to the head has undoubtedly affected him. He does not understand what he is saying. Niall." He turned back to Shawn. "The English will not stop at Stirling. Do you not remember the slaughter of the Camerons at Falkirk? Your mother's own people, women and children run through. Wee bairns hanging by their necks. Surely you remember? Would you see your kin here suffer the same fate?"

Shawn shook his head, unnerved. He recalled the name Falkirk, though barely: there had been a very pretty and buxom girl in history, far more interesting than old, dry stories. These people were deep in their game; their acting so impeccable, they appeared to fully believe the danger.

"D' ye remember, Niall?"

Shawn nodded. He would leave on this journey, walk back to Inverness, and everything would be fine, as it always was in his life.

"Do you understand the importance of Stirling?"

Shawn nodded again.

"If Niall has become forgetful," one man asked, "if he doesna ken the year even, how will he reach Hugh? He is the only one who knows the way."

Inverness, Scotland

The sounds reached Niall first: hushed footsteps and voices, drifting like the whisper of the loch through his window at night. He listened with half an ear, the rhythm and cadences brushing over him like the steady *lap, lap lap* of water against the tower walls. Next came small clinks and whirrs and hums, and he felt a firm mattress beneath him. Soft clouds pillowed his head in darkness.

"Coming 'round," said a man, speaking a peculiar English. Niall's mind wandered to the puzzle of the broken down walls, but as quickly slipped back into darkness, a darkness filled with bizarre dreams of shiny metal wagons hurtling down wide roads at incredible speeds with no horses to pull them. *Delirium!* It had to be delirium! Inhuman voices had screeched and wailed, and lights spun and flashed like a thousand comets streaking through the night. A choir of urgent, white-robed angels tumbled him onto a cot with wheels and shot down a white tunnel, shouting in demonic voices.

The dreams faded to blackness. The whispers came again. "Lucky! ...just on time." Black faded to gray. Niall twitched, feeling for his knife.

"Is he waking up?" It was the woman, the woman from outside the castle.

He tensed. She was real.

Her voice trembled, as Allene's had, on learning of her brother's death. "I'll never forgive myself."

The gray paled, and became a bright light shining through his lids. He squeezed his eyes shut, remembering the broken walls, and fought his instinct to scramble to his feet fighting. He relaxed his face, relaxed his arm under what must be her fingers on his bare skin, and listened.

"He's moving." That was the man, Rob.

So they were both real, not delirium. Then were the broken down walls real? And the crouching beast? Those must be fever-driven hallucinations, even if the man and woman weren't. He lay still, breathing slowly. His head felt much better. He could think clearly. His body felt cool again. They'd healed him, he realized. He must be in their castle, with their physicians or monks.

"Thank goodness we left so early to get him," the woman said.

Footsteps sounded, and a man spoke. "He should be wakin' up any minute now, lass. Ye say he was fine when ye left him last night? I've never seen an infection move sae fast. He'd ha' been dead in a day a' most. And an arrow wound...."

"That's insane," said the woman. Amy, Niall remembered. It rolled through his mind pleasingly, and he almost drifted back to sleep, thinking about her long black hair. He gave himself a sharp reminder he was betrothed, and kept listening, hoping for answers, and accustoming himself to the cadence of their speech. Bit by bit, they became easier to understand. "How in the world could he have been shot by an arrow?"

"It appeared several days old." The heavy voice spoke with authority.

"That's impossible," Amy said. "He was fine last night. I know I shouldn't have left him, but I was back in less than eight hours."

"The police have some questions," the physician said.

Heavy footsteps sounded, a scraping on the floor, a settling of bodies, new voices, both male; more talk. Niall tried to weave some tapestry of explanation from the tangled threads of events and conversation. They thought he was someone called Shawn. The raven-haired woman in undergarments thought she'd left him in the tower last night. Guilt consumed her, though why, Niall couldn't quite pin down.

"He was gambling." The man, Rob, spoke tentatively. "But he paid the guy off." A flurry of anger erupted from Amy, shouting about a ring. The new voices begged for calm. A brief silence fell.

Then Amy spoke again. "He said he was Niall Campbell." Niall's ears strained at the sound of his own name. "He didn't seem to know us. He was talking about MacDonalds and MacDougalls."

"'Tis Glenmirril," said one of the new voices. "Ye said ye took the tour. Niall Campbell is mentioned on it, is he not, Angus?"

"There's a tapestry of him," said Amy, "and it's funny, it's just a tapestry, but he looked like Shawn, the long hair, something in the eyes."

"Niall Campbell is known to those who study Glenmirril's history," said a rougher voice. "He was betrothed to MacDonald's daughter. He went to raise troops for the Battle of the Pools."

Niall's mind sharpened like steel on whetstone. The Pools was what the English called the boggy area south of Stirling—the place Bruce would likely gather his army. And though the Sassenach tongue was his second language, they seemed to be speaking of him in past tense, as he would speak of Kenneth MacAlpin.

"They say he was injured stealing the MacDougall's cattle just before leaving on that mission."

Niall's hackles rose. *Those were our cattle!* But he held himself quietly, waiting for more information.

"History never mentions him again after leaving to raise the army," continued the rough voice. This one spoke the Sassenach tongue more in the manner to which Niall was accustomed. "They believe he died in the wilderness of his injuries."

"Now tha's no what I heard," said the other. "I heard a castle traitor hunted him down, sold him to the English, watched him hung, drawn, and quartered." They argued briefly over how he had died.

Niall breathed deeply, torn between amusement and disbelief. Only one answer accounted for broken walls and these people speaking about him as if he'd been long dead. But that was impossible. He did not believe a word of old Rabbie's tales, not King Herla, not Thomas the Rhymer, none of it.

Amy interrupted them. "Okay, but why is Shawn saying he's this guy? That was seven hundred years ago."

Niall grunted, only forcibly keeping himself from shooting upright. *Seven hundred years!* He reassured himself quickly. Only a fool believed everything he heard. Especially from the English. One did not skip centuries any more than one skipped heather-covered hills. A ruse, that was it!

"Is he okay?" asked Amy. A soft hand fell on his forehead. He forced himself to lie quietly. He needed a calm head. But her touch tingled through him.

The man who must be the physician spoke. "He's fine. Just coming to. Serious infection and fever like his can cause delusions. I'd say he heard the name, and it stuck."

"He wasn't paying that much attention," said Amy.

"But you pointed out the tapestry to him." That was Rob. "You showed him this guy looked like him. That would stick, for Shawn, and then he hits his head and gets a high fever, and it all gets mixed together."

"But the accent," said Amy.

"I've heard of that," Rob said. "I saw on the internet about these people who could only speak with foreign accents after a head injury."

It was without a doubt a Sassenach deception, Niall decided. The two newcomers began asking questions. Niall listened, feeling strength grow in his arms. Whatever they'd done for him, he hadn't felt so good since the moment he lifted his tunic to the MacDougalls, just before the hiss of that arrow.

While they talked about this Shawn, he listened, wondering why the English would heal him. Perhaps the ruse was on them, and they really believed him to be this Shawn? He lay still, deciding his next move, soaking in the patterns of their speech, rolling their accents around his mind, and feeling the motions of his tongue that would reproduce the sounds, just as he copied the Laird or old Rabbie.

Heavy footsteps trod away. The room became quiet.

Maybe this Shawn they spoke of *was* the enemy? They were English, after all. A lucky break for the ill-fated Edward to find someone who looked like Niall, the only man who could find Hugh? They knew there was a traitor in the castle. He pursued this possibility through the chambers of his mind, behind his closed eyelids. Could someone have put a draught in his mead and carried him to this place while he slept? Then someone in the kitchen was working with the traitor. He vowed, with steeled jaw, he would find the man and run him through.

A sniffle, a woman crying softly, broke into his thoughts. "He'll be okay," said Rob. "Uh, do you want something to eat?"

He'll be okay. The words rolled through Niall's mind, feeling the shape of each vowel. *Do you want something to eat?* More footsteps left the room. Lighter footsteps entered, accompanied by a chirpy feminine voice. Niall felt pressure on his arm, a tug, something cold sliding against his flesh, and his eyes flew open wide.

"Ah, there ye are!" A young woman dressed all in white smiled at him. A long silver needle dangled from her hand. "Ye're just after havin' your I.V. pulled. Ye're doin' grand. The doctor's wantin' to see you down the hall. I heard you play last Saturday, Mr. Kleiner. Wasn't that something!" She bandaged his arm, and danced out of the cell, her voice trilling ahead that 'Mr. Kleiner' had woken up.

Niall stared after her, shocked at her dress kilted all the way to her knees. He pulled his eyes back to the chamber. Bits of metal and things he couldn't name flashed and beeped. It was too much! He shut his eyes. Seven hundred years in the future? It couldn't be. But never had he heard of such things as these.

Amy grasped his hand. "Shawn?" she whispered. "It's me, Amy."

Niall opened his eyes slowly. The words played in his mind. *Shawn. It's me, Amy.*

"Amy." He repeated the word carefully.

Glenmirril Castle, Scotland

Shawn listened intently to the discussion, the nausea and headache having thankfully subsided a little. But being effectively captive in a room full of hardened men with wicked-looking daggers, pretending to be someone he wasn't, did nothing to quell the unease in his stomach. He listened for anything that would help him get back to Inverness, once they sent him out. Their fate most certainly did not rest on him. Wasn't his problem, even if they were talking about some actual battle. Which, of course, they couldn't be. This time tomorrow, when he'd figured out what was going on, he'd find it funny, how he'd misunderstood, how he'd actually thought they were telling him he'd traveled back in time.

The men talked endlessly, arguing over the best time to start, the best route for Niall to take, the dangers of nature and man.

"The Great Glen is steep and slippery in places," one lord said.

"Nothing our Niall can't handle."

"With his injury?" the first lord persisted. "He's no yet healed."

"But if there's a quicker or safer way...."

"Edward's spies are everywhere. 'Tis best to stay out of sight."

Several women—the beautiful Allene among them, Shawn noted with appreciative eyes—carried in platters of food and mugs of mead. He felt eyes on him, and turned to see an older lord glaring at him. He pulled his eyes off Allene quickly, not needing another knock on the head.

"Secrecy is paramount. They'd no expect him to go north around the Loch!" declared Conal, one of the young lords, as a woman set a trencher in front of him.

"It would take him directly past MacDougall's kin," said the small, wizened lord. "Well away from any of them is best. Speed is paramount. Can he no cross the loch?"

"In the leaky boat?" said the Laird gravely. "We're no equipped for him to cross the loch."

"And besides, 'tis the obvious way, what Edward's men might guess," retorted Lord Darnley. "Speed is no use if it is into their waiting arms he flies."

"Secrecy is no use if he wanders right up to the portcullis of MacDougall's kin. They'd argue only whether to hang him themselves or turn him over to the English for greater sport."

Another rush of nausea swooped over Shawn. The man appeared to believe this was a real possibility. "I've seen *Braveheart*," he volunteered. "I'll take the safer route."

"Braveheart?"

"William Wallace?" Shawn queried back.

The old lords shook their heads with laughter. "You were a bairn in your mither's arms in his day," the small one said. "Now there was a great man, who asked what would help his people, not—" he pierced Shawn with a hard stare, "what was *safe*." The others nodded, and the man continued. "'Tis a question of odds. But it remains that Niall was the one trusted with Hugh's hiding place. We canna be sure of the best way to go when we're not even sure exactly *where* he's going."

"Allene!" the Laird called, as a trencher was set in front of the last man. "Send the women out. I want no extra ears. You'll serve as needed."

She dropped a curtsy, her eyes low. "Yes, my Lord." She clapped, and the women filed out the great door swiftly, pulling it shut behind them.

The Laird's booming voice took over the discussion. "The problem remains," he said, "that Niall appears to have lost all memory overnight; including where Hugh is. We know little, beyond that he must go east. And that when Hugh does not want to be found, the devil himself willna find him."

Shawn looked at the food on his plate. Between a hangover and discomfort over his future, it looked none too appetizing. He searched for utensils, and found none. The other men dug in with fingers, or speared the meat with daggers. He lifted the large tankard in front of him, and sipped, testing this new drink.

"My Lord," Allene murmured, gliding up behind her father, and dropping a curtsy. She stole a bold glance at Shawn; he swore he saw a triumphant smile ghost her lips. Over what, he couldn't guess. The old Laird turned to his daughter, who whispered in his ear. He nodded gravely. She threw a bolder glance at Shawn, tossed her head, and stepped back against the wall, once again dropping her eyes demurely.

Inverness, Scotland, Present

Niall sought indications, inside these people's castle, of where he might be. Amy, Rob, and the chirpy woman in white—a *nurse*, Amy called her—led him through a maze of halls more confusing than MacDonald's dungeons. He studied everything, words and pictures, memorizing as quickly as he could. He watched every motion, and wondered how the English had spirited him away to another place, abounding with wonders surpassing even what the Polos had found in Cathay. But why the elaborate ruse of pretending he'd skipped times? So he wouldn't try to escape? He'd hardly run anywhere in this ridiculous linen shift. He twitched at it, trying to keep his nether parts covered.

A melody trilled, a shrill odd sound unlike any instrument he'd ever heard. Amy pulled a small black object from her clothing, and spoke into it. "Oh, Dana, thanks for calling." She stopped speaking. "Yeah, he's okay. Sort of." She stopped speaking again. Niall stared at her, perplexed. She was speaking to herself! She stared back at him, her eyebrows furrowed. "He seems to have lost his memory. Doesn't know who he is." She spoke a bit more, and snapped the thing shut. She stowed it back in her clothing and frowned at him again.

They passed a window showing a vast town, roofs stretching as far as the eye could see, but no moat or bridge. Strange. But then, these men, at least those whose legs he could see under their odd cut-off trews, carried no protection. Those in the long trews, he reasoned, couldn't get at a dirk anyway, reaching up under such impractical garments. Safety and defense, it appeared, were not issues in this peculiar Inverness, or wherever he was. If these were indeed the English, they were very sure they had naught to fear from the Scots.

"Shawn! Shawn Kleiner!" Rob and Amy stopped and turned. He realized the girl rushing up from behind was talking to him. "Will you sign this?" Breathlessly, she pushed a sheet of parchment at him. He stared at the short black spikes sticking up from her head. It took a moment to realize it was hair. He'd never known demons to make themselves visible, but surely this was what they'd look like.

She held up a small silver box, Amy threw up her hand, Rob jumped in front of him, and the thing flashed lightning.

"Security!" Rob yelled.

"He's sick," Amy snapped. "Can't you ever stop!"

Two men burst out, yanked the girl away and wrestled the box from her. Amy steered him forward, while Niall wondered what danger they'd just averted. The *nurse* chirped about a hundred things, till Niall tuned her out and went back to his deliberations. Much as he'd prefer capture by the English to traversing time, they did not have wonders such as this.

"Here ye are now," the nurse sang, and left them in a chamber crowded with chairs.

Amy and Rob sat. He did the same, though carefully. Scattered on low tables were dozens of glossy parchments similar to that in the basket, but larger and with many more pages and words. Pictures burst with color more vivid than illuminated manuscript. He ran his finger over the page, marveling at the smooth gloss.

"Since when do you care about Prince Edward?" Amy asked.

"Who?" He looked up.

Rob slid his arm around Amy, staring hard at him.

Amy nodded at the parchment. A man in a plaid tunic covered by a heavy woolen shirt stood on a rocky hill. The Prince Edward he knew was an infant. "Prince Edward of England?" she said. Concern filled her voice. He lifted his eyes from the parchment to hers. Certainly he had an ally in her. He'd need allies.

"Of course," he said, carefully imitating her vowels. "Read it, please."

She frowned, but slid the parchment from his hands. He leaned close, holding the edge, and studied the script. It resembled the writing he knew. But the spelling was atrocious, like a language foreign even to the English.

Amy's voice was soothing, reading about Edward, Prince of England, who smiled up from the glossy page. He studied the script, trying to find where she was, and listened to the words she spoke, soaking up her vowels, her inflections, and repeating them in his own mind, as he did when listening to a traveling minstrel play a new piece.

When she turned the page, his eyes scrambled to the top, trying to follow. But between her strange accent and the bizarre spellings, he saw mostly gibberish.

"Show me." He took her hand, placing her finger on the page. Rob cleared his throat. Amy glanced from him to Niall, before dropping her gaze back to the words and continuing. His mind soaked up sounds and shapes, as her finger slid under each word.

"Shawn Kleiner?"

She stopped reading and stared at him. He stared back.

"Shawn Kleiner?"

"Why did you stawp?" he asked.

"Don't you hear them calling you?"

"Och, 'twas no...." He realized his mistake quickly, but not before her eyebrows puckered in distress. He stood up, and found himself facing another *nurse* in another embarrassingly short white dress.

He stared at the walls with their strange glassy paintings, at anything rather than this woman in her undergarments throwing come-hither looks over her shoulder. He stared at the large desk they passed, with blinking, flashing, pulsing lights. But it was the small square of bleached parchment on the wall, with its stark few words that stopped him cold, his heart pounding erratically.

* * *

"Shawn! Shawn, come on." Amy tugged at his arm.

"Mr. Kleiner? Are you okay?"

Niall pulled his eyes to the *nurse* in front of him. He'd heard them use this word *okay* many times now. He thought he understood it. "Yes," he said.

The woman stared doubtfully for a moment. He wondered if he'd misunderstood the word *okay*. But she looked to the wall that had unnerved him. Finding no cause for alarm, she ushered him into a room smaller than the monastic cells at Monadhliath, and nearly as bare. "Only one, please." The nurse looked pointedly at Amy and Rob. Niall clutched Amy's arm and pulled her in, leaving Rob to fume.

Through the nurse's ministrations, Niall kept his eyes averted from her immodest clothing. This, he concluded from all he'd seen, was normal here—now, if the parchment on the wall was to be believed. Still, he couldn't bring himself to look at her. She wrapped a black band around his arm, squeezing tightly, and used devices to assign numbers to his height and weight, although why that should interest anyone, he couldn't guess.

His mind wandered while she pushed his tongue down with a wooden stick. He'd decided their words, while he pretended to sleep, must be a ruse. They *had* to be! But along with the crumbled walls he remembered, and the wonders around him, it was impossible to discount the parchment. It was far too thorough for a deception; and a useless and ridiculous one, at that. But King Herla's adventure was not possible.

With a bright smile, and a cheery, "The doctor will be right in," the nurse left. Niall grabbed Amy's arm, even as the door clicked.

"You lost ten pounds since we got here?" she said.

His own concern took first priority. "The parchment on the wall."

"Parchment?"

"Behind the desk. It had a date."

"*Parchment?* You mean the calendar?"

He nodded. "Tell me what it said."

"What's with the reading things to you?" she asked.

"The head wound," he said. "I see double. Is the date correct?"

"I'd think so." She narrowed her eyes. "Why?"

Her tone of voice made him examine his own. He'd seen wonders here. Maybe skipping centuries was normal, too. He forced himself to think, to roll their accent in his mind, to remind himself they thought he was Shawn, before asking, with deliberate calm, "Do our people know how to change times?"

"Our people? Change times, like how?"

"Like King Herla."

"*Who?*"

Did they not know the story? Everyone knew King Herla! "He goes into a dwarf's cave and comes out three hundred years later."

"You're asking if we can do that?" Her eyes opened wide. "Of course not."

"What would happen," Niall asked carefully, "if someone said they did?"

"They'd be locked up!"

Niall wondered what their dungeons might look like. Everything else seemed tame compared to his world. Regardless, he couldn't be locked up. He must reach Hugh.

"What happened to you out there?"

He carefully copied a word he'd heard them use. "Nothing." He leaned back against the wall, his face passive.

She stared at him, her jaw tight. "You say nothing happened, but you don't even know the date."

"I know the date," he said. "'Tis June 9." And well into the twenty-first century, he added silently to himself. Supposedly.

* * *

The physician studied the wound on his head, and the other. A nurse came in with linen pads and scrubbed it clean. The doctor asked questions. And, apart from an arrow wound and not knowing the American president—he knew the date—pronounced him the healthiest man he'd ever seen. Niall firmly rejected what they told him was pain killer, in a long, silver needle. He closed his eyes and clenched his teeth as they stitched him up. It hurt far less than the way the castle physician had torn the arrow out in the first place, and he wondered at their amazement that he made no sound.

"So unlike you," Amy said. "You usually kick up a fuss about having a splinter pulled."

"An arrow in the arse!" the doctor repeated for the third time. "How could this happen? The police must knoo." Niall noticed that he and the nurse spoke an English much more akin to what he, himself, knew. He wondered why Amy and Rob spoke differently. "We canna have people shootin' castle visitors with arrows!" the doctor said gruffly. "Who did this?"

Niall wondered if there were MacDougalls in the twenty-first century—if indeed that's where he was. Certainly not the MacDougall who'd shot him. In fact, their shock suggested that arrow wounds were not daily fair. That helped explain why they felt no need for protection.

The *police* returned, a short one, and a tall, broad man with short black curls and a ruddy face. He recognized the voices, though their outfits surprised him. At least they were fully dressed. Blue trews covered their legs all the way to the floor.

He said as little as possible, answering their questions with, "I dinna ken," which made Amy frown, and, "I remember nothing." He studied their every movement. They scribbled furiously with featherless quills—the Laird would be fascinated—on blanched bits of parchment strung together with something stiff. In the end, they left, scratching their heads, appearing more confused than Niall himself felt, promising they'd send a man to look around the castle.

He wavered between relief and disdain, that they gave up so easily, employing none of the Sassenach's usual unpleasant practices for getting answers. Even the MacDougalls would have been harder to fool. He would take it with relief, he decided, and thanked God. This wasn't, after all, an entirely bad place, disconcerting and distressing though it might be to be here.

Glenmirril Castle, Scotland

The Laird leaned back, and without a word, commanded silence in the hall. "He'll go south through the Great Glen. We'll spread rumors he's gone north."

"My lord! I dinna object to the Great Glen, but look at him!" The small man gestured at Shawn, who gave a hard stare back. "He doesna even remember how to drink his mead! He sips like a wee lass with a mug of warm milk!"

Shawn banged his mug down hard on the large, scarred table, half-rising to his feet. The Laird held up a hand. "Peace, Niall. 'Tis no consequence how you drink your mead. You'll be right in no time." The fire crackled in the huge grate behind the Laird, merry and loud in the momentary silence.

"He himself," the other man continued, "admits he has no memory of Hugh's whereabouts, or much else. We'll be slaughtered in our beds by the English ere he finishes gathering bluebells in the hills."

"I'll be fine," Shawn said. "It's coming back." He gulped his mead, stronger than the beer he was used to, and glowered at his critic, ignoring the churning of his stomach as the mead hit. He'd follow the loch north to Inverness. If they decided he was incapable, he'd be trapped here. He wondered why no one had come for him. Surely Amy had told them where he was. Temperamental though she was, she always got over it.

"He will go," repeated the Laird.

Shawn suspected the man's decision rested on whatever Allene had whispered. He turned to her. Her eyes remained demurely on the floor, but even with her head bowed, he could see her fighting back that same, victorious smile. He hadn't exactly won her over this morning, he thought, and wondered if she herself would be the one to sell him out to the English. He looked forward to a talk with her. His charm had never failed before, and it wouldn't now.

"Niall! If you will remove your eyes from my daughter." The Laird spoke more than sharply. "Betrothed you may be, but not yet wed!"

Shawn turned quickly away, but not before catching her lifting a hand to her mouth to suppress a laugh. Betrothed! His mind spun with kaleidoscope possibilities. "My apologies," Shawn said. "It is only that your daughter has such lovely eyes."

A wave of disapproving frowns washed around the table. Iohn thumped his head, setting off another round of timpani. Shawn rubbed it, glaring at him. The stone walls wavered for a second, and settled down. The arched window with the blue sky split into two and moved back together. He glanced at Allene, who also gave him a sharp frown. Clearly, these people did not approve of compliments. "My apologies," he mumbled. "I didn't mean anything." He turned to the parchment spread across the table, scratched with marks and lines in a rough estimate of Scotland, hoping they'd go back to their discussion.

Conal tapped the parchment. "Pay close attention. All our lives depend on it."

"The Niall we knew only last night would not need to be told." Darnley spoke with heavy disappointment. "Will we at least send one with him to make sure he does not wander off in his strange state?"

Anger boiled in Shawn. Never had his competence been questioned, much less to his face. No one, after all, liked to be on his bad side. He considered his options. A glance at their daggers narrowed those options significantly to courtesy and re-gaining the trust the real

Niall, whoever he was, had obviously had from them. "I'm not addled," he said. "Things are coming back."

"Will you send another with him?" Lord Darnley asked again.

"I have spoken," the Laird said. "He'll sup early, then rest. Lord Darnley, you will prepare his provisions. No one beyond these walls is to know anything. Niall, you leave an hour after midnight." His beefy finger pointed to their present location. You must be well clear of open areas before sunrise, lest anyone see you."

He traced a line from the castle to the rough depiction of a copse. "From here to here is nine miles. Dawn comes early, so you mustn't stop till you have cover of trees."

"Nine miles?" Shawn asked. He almost asked why nine miles should take from one a.m. till daybreak, but thought better of it. Apparently, he was walking, and that was obviously a given to these men.

"The forest will shelter you till you reach the Great Glen, which you'll follow until *Ku Chuimein*." His finger continued along the trail he'd drawn.

Shawn dared not ask what the Great Glen was, or how he would follow it. This, too, seemed a given to these men. Besides, he was going north, regardless of their plans for him.

The Laird raised his eyes to Shawn's. "Hugh must meet us at Stirling, or all Scotland falls, and our clan with it." He turned to his men. "I would talk to Niall alone. Lord Morrison, d' ye bring the robe to Niall's chambers, now. Ye'll find it in my wardrobe." The men, all but one, stood, unquestioning, gave respectful bows, and crossed the half-acre of the great hall, out the huge wooden doors.

"My Lord," Darnley said. "You must send one of us with him, at least! Tell me how to find Hugh, and I will get him there safely."

"I have spoken, Lord Darnley," the Laird said.

"My Lord, you must see...."

"I have spoken," rumbled MacDonald. His eyebrows drew together.

"'Twill not do...."

The Laird rose, thunder in his eyes, to his feet. Lord Darnley bowed, his mouth pursed tightly, and removed himself.

The Laird seemed to have forgotten Allene, standing in her drab gray-brown dress against the gray stones. Shawn, though he kept his eyes to himself, was powerfully aware of her. Her presence filled the hall. He wondered if he could find her room tonight. If they were engaged, certainly Niall had been there before. And certainly he could easily get back in her good graces.

The Laird spoke softly for a change. "A guide will go with you," he said. "The lad knows where to find Hugh."

Shawn nodded, not happy with this decision. But a lad would be easy to slip away from. "What lad?"

"Lower your voice," MacDonald warned. "Walls have ears, and there are those who have ambitions beyond their present position. Trust few, and you will live longer. Be clear on that, lad: trust no one, not even your closest friend. D' ye understand?"

Shawn nodded, stifling the urge to give a theatrical gulp. But these people had no sense of humor.

The old man waited; for what, Shawn couldn't guess. "Ye'll no argue?" he finally said.

"Why would I argue?" Shawn asked. All he wanted was to get out.

The Laird shrugged. "Ye've never yet failed to speak your mind. Surely you remember the *deaf and mute lad* who came with us last time." He stared at Shawn, boring deep into his eyes, and Shawn had the distinct feeling the words were supposed to mean something other than what they appeared to mean. He didn't even try to guess what.

"Aye," said Shawn, and almost choked to hear the word come out of his mouth. The Laird, however, seemed unsurprised.

"Two more things: follow the lad wherever he takes you. Aye?" Again, the eyes bored deep into his, and Shawn guessed he was not going the way laid out in such detail on the map. "An' you value your life and those of us in the keep, do not question me now. Clear?"

Shawn nodded. A shadow of fear niggled at him. This man was serious; dead serious. "And the other thing?"

"Lord Morrison will lay out clothes. Put them on immediately, and go to sleep. You'll be roused when the time is right."

Sleep sounded good. "Will there be coffee then?"

"Caw—caw. Fee? What is this?"

"Okay, so you're into historical accuracy. No coffee."

"You'll be given what you need. You'll cross the hill to the copse. Fast. My lad will lead you from there. When he gives the signal, change into the clothes you'll find among your provisions, and play the part."

"What part?"

"You'll understand when you open the sack. You've a gift, Niall. Now is the time to use it for more than a winter night's entertainment."

Shawn could think of only one gift he had which provided for winter nights' entertainment. This man couldn't possibly intend for him to seduce women across Scotland, so Niall must have another gift, with which to save Scottish civilization. He was curious what that might be.

But then, it didn't matter. He was going to Inverness.

95

Chapter Six

Inverness, Scotland, Present

It was another hour before they let him out. Niall scrawled a signature on the parchment they pushed in front of him, taking his best guess at how to spell Shawn. Judging by the other signatures on the page, script need not be legible. That suited him well.

Amy stuffed his tunic, trews, and boots into a bag, over his protests, and handed him wide blue hose of some stiff material, instead. *Jeans*, she called them, swiping at her eyes. When she left, he pulled his own clothes back out. He wouldn't parade publicly in such a short, immodest shirt.

Amy returned, sighing at his garb. "Never mind," Rob said. He slid his arm around her waist.

"Conrad planned to be here," Amy said over her shoulder. "But he had things to deal with."

Planned...things to deal with. The words shaped themselves in Niall's ear. "Conrad?" He kept his words to a minimum, till he could copy their language more carefully. The name sounded familiar.

Her feathery eyebrows drew together. She frowned. "You don't remember Conrad?"

"I remember nothing."

"Conrad leads the orchestra," Amy said.

So Conrad was a leader: a king, an earl, a duke? "Is he the laird?" Niall asked.

"What?" Amy sounded shocked. "There's no laird here. You don't remember the orchestra?"

"The doctor said the memory usually comes back quickly," Rob told her. "Let's get him home." He hoisted the bag of clothing and dropped a hand on Niall's shoulder, steering him toward the door. "A brief history of Shawn Kleiner. You play trombone." Niall wondered if that was a game of some sort. He tried not to stare at the cots on tall spindly legs with wheels at the end. So they hadn't been a dream. "You're a big star."

"Star?" He could make no sense of that.

"A big shot. Important. King of the hill."

Niall nodded, committing the expression *big star* to memory. He listened with one ear while sorting out the situation. Amy had left Shawn, the big star, in Glenmirril and come back to find Niall. So where was Shawn? In Glenmirril's tower, in Niall's time?

History said he, Niall, died on the journey, perhaps of his injuries. Well, he was healthy now, thanks to their medicines. If he'd really come forward in time, he'd just go back, King Herla's apparent failure aside. He had a job to do.

They strode out of the passageway, into a large front chamber. People turned to stare. Silence fell; then a girl squealed, "It's Shawn Kleiner!"

"Unbelievable," Amy muttered.

Rob warded off the stampeding girl, saying, "Leave him alone. He's hurt." The group that had massed for assault drew back; Amy and Rob ushered him to a large wall of glass. It slid open, without a hand touching it. Niall sucked in his breath, but said nothing. Just outside the incredible wall of moving glass, waited the one thing he'd hoped had been only a dream: the beast that had crouched outside the castle, one of the large metal wagons that shot like an arrow with no horse to pull it. Despite his intentions to learn and copy, to fit in, he took an inadvertent step back. His hand fell on the hilt of his dirk.

Rob stared at him. "Toto," he intoned.

Amy punched his arm. "Shut up, Rob."

* * *

Niall searched one last time for another explanation, on the drive to the *hotel*—an inn, judging by their conversation, what he could make of it through their broad, flat vowels. He'd steeled himself for the jolting against his injured parts. But the seat was soft, and the ride surprisingly smooth. He closed his eyes against the buildings speeding by, however. Behind closed lids, he soaked up their language, while searching for another possibility.

It wasn't delirium, it was far too elaborate for a ruse, and the notion of skipping across time like King Herla was too disturbing. Could he be in a fairy knowe? He'd never believed in those, either, but it seemed a touch more likely. Fairies were said to be tricksters. They'd have the means—if they existed—to create such things as he'd seen.

He let the morning drift through his mind, each detail of the broken walls of Glenmirril. But fairy knowes—so Rabbie said—held worlds more beautiful than man's, not tumbled-down copies. And even if Auld Rabbie's tales were true—which he doubted—elfin folk never came in pairs, nor bore such common names as Rob. And they captured men who wandered into their mysterious places; they did not venture into men's homes. Amy and Rob wore strange clothing, but not the beautiful things Rabbie described, and no thread of green. Fairies wore green.

Rabbie told of a people confident, devious, and sensuous. Amy had shown only forthright concern. She had not tried to seduce him with fairy kisses as the Elf queen did Thomas the Rhymer. Her eyes had flickered nervously to the knife, outside the castle, with no hint of the fairy folk's deviousness or cruelty.

Even now, she naively took his closed eyes for sleep and leaned forward from the back of the monster, talking softly about him, or rather, about Shawn. Shawn, then, whoever he was, had clearly disappeared.

"I shouldn't have left him," she said. Uncertainty trembled on every word, a sparrow in a storm. Her hand brushed his forehead, setting off pleasant tingles. He held still with some effort, trying once again to fit the facts to a ruse or kidnapping. Maybe Shawn had taken his place. His heart thudded. Surely Allene would not be fooled! Would this man, this *big star,* be near her?

He opened his eyes. Another of the man-carrying beasts hurtled straight toward them. He squeezed his eyes shut, tensed for death. When nothing happened, he lifted one tentative lid. The thing streaked past, almost skimming the sides of their own. He let out a thankful breath and closed his eye again. It helped not to look.

He explored the idea of kidnapping, while fighting the lurching of his stomach. He'd be held for ransom. And yet—where had he been taken? A place that looked exactly as his own castle might, in seven hundred years.

"Are you okay, Shawn?" Amy asked from the back seat. Only when her hand fell on his shoulder did Niall realize she was speaking to him. He opened his eyes, and wished, at the sight of hills flashing past, that he hadn't.

"I'm well," he said, curtly, and shut his eyes again. He listened to their voices, as they spoke with each other, and let his mind drift back to his prior thoughts, to *cars* and *phones* and leaders called *conductors.* He wasn't in England. Captors did not ask their victim to come along, nor looked so scared of, or for, him. And it served no purpose, pretending to think him someone else. They seemed genuinely perplexed and concerned. Especially Amy.

The car slowed as it entered the fringes of a town, which quickly became a city, with stone buildings rising like gullies on all sides. Parts of it seemed vaguely like the Inverness he knew, but full of cars and people in clothing even stranger than Rob's and Amy's. He braved the view of all those cars shooting every which way, to lean forward and study the city.

Giant versions of their own car, towering two stories high, rumbled by, ready to topple on them. Women bustled along in twos and threes, carrying heavy sacks. Men sat at tables sipping from delicate, white tankards with no handles. Paintings hung everywhere! Outdoors! He wondered if they needed to be replaced often, if they were brought in on rainy days, or if these people had paints and canvas that withstood the elements.

Seven hundred years. It would explain everything. When you've ruled out all else, his tutors had taught him, what you are left with must be the answer, no matter how unlikely.

The car stopped in front of a painting of himself. A man lolled in a field of bluebells wearing a tartan wrapped around his waist, a linen shirt with billowing sleeves, and an idiotic grin. Two busty women draped themselves over him with moon-eyed gazes. Niall sat upright, staring. The man looked just like him, yes, but how could these people ever mistake him, Niall, for such a dolt!

He studied the script at the top of the painting. *S-H-A-W-N.* The car lurched forward again.

Glenmirril Castle, Scotland, 1314

Iohn, waiting outside the hall, whisked him to his bedchamber after the meeting, gripping his elbow. He gave Shawn no time to charm women in the bailey, or talk to Allene. Iohn followed him into his room, with the massive four poster bed and the arched stone window showing glimpses of the loch, and pulled the door shut. "Niall, I've asked ye before not to make this trip."

"Have you," said Shawn noncommittally.

"You've a reason not to go, now. You're injured. No good can come of it. 'Twas a fool's errand to start. Now, in your condition, 'tis madness. Tell me how to find Hugh. I'll go in your stead."

This mission they were all fired up about was Shawn's only chance to get out of the castle and get to Inverness. "I'll be fine," he said.

"At least let me go with you. You've an arrow wound and are disoriented. There are those who would see you dead. I can fight at your side."

And have his escape back to the orchestra thwarted? "I'll be fine," Shawn said again. "Things are coming back to me. The arrow wound...." He had no idea where the arrow wound was supposed to be. He gestured vaguely. "Can't even feel it. I'm great."

Iohn stood awkwardly for a few moments. "Sleep well, then. You leave after the moon is high?"

The Laird's words, *trust no one,* leapt to mind. "Much after that,"

Shawn agreed. "Way past. You sure you can't scare up some coffee?"

"Sure 'tis your sense of jest, this caw-fee," Iohn said. "Is it really time for jesting? Ye're no acting like my friend who trusted me with everything."

"The head," Shawn reminded him. "Sorry. Nothing personal."

"Godspeed, then. Would you would let me help you." When Shawn didn't answer, Iohn took one last look around the room, and left, pulling the door softly behind him.

Shawn looked around the room, following the path of Iohn's gaze. The Laird's orders had been followed promptly. Clothes for his night's journey lay on the bed: a monk's habit. He chuckled at the irony, but put it on, along with thick, warm leggings and sandals, and lay down, grateful to sink back into bed. It was not yet noon, but it had been a long day. He closed his eyes, planning his return to Inverness. Wouldn't the orchestra get a kick out of seeing him show up in a monk's robe! Caroline would like that!

Inverness, Scotland, Present

Niall's stomach swirled with nausea as the car approached the castle that served as an inn, suitable for the likes of whoever Shawn had been. Niall studied each detail, memorizing. Stone walls rose high. Flags fluttered on the towers, reminding Niall that castles had not really crumbled and fallen. Here was one, strong for all the world to see. They must have taken him to a very old castle, or one torn down by enemy weapons. He must believe that. He must believe there was still an explanation which had not yet occurred to him.

They drove through a tunnel of trees dappling the road. Beyond the boulevard of trees, sweeping lawns surrounded the castle. Someone shouted from an upper window. As they pulled through the massive arched gate and onto a curving path, a crowd of colorful people erupted from the wide doors, and flooded down broad stone stairs: a dozen women or more in their undergarments; a knot of men in trews chopped off above the knee, and shirts in minstrel colors with hardly any sleeves. They surrounded the car, shouting. With adrenaline racing, pumping him with the calm, clear head needed for battle, Niall searched them for weapons. He saw none.

Rob threw open his door fearlessly. Niall spun his head, barely catching the motion of his hand. He flexed his own fingers, copying.

"Back off!" Rob yelled. "The man's had a rough night!" He marched around the car, waving his arms at them, as at a flock of sheep. He spoke with humor, and Niall realized these people were friends. His heart rate slowed; the adrenaline subsided. Feeling safer, he studied the faces again, noting each detail. They had backed a bit away from the car.

"Are you getting out, Shawn?" Amy asked, from the seat behind him.

"Aye," he said, resolutely, and fumbled with the door, imitating Rob's motion. It sprang open. He climbed out gingerly, resisting the urge to rub his aching posterior.

The group surged in. A waif-like girl, with short red hair jutting from her head like a ruffled grouse, eyed him with concern, before going to Amy. A busty woman, wearing even less than Amy, edged out the others and threw her arms around him. Her blonde hair tickled his nose and eyes. "Oh, Shawn!" she cried. "I was so worried! Poor Shawn! How awful for you!"

"Aye," he agreed, barely able to breathe, and carefully disentangled himself from her web of arms and hair. She seemed oblivious to having been dismissed, and hovered behind him chattering about her fear for him. He studied the other faces. He saw naked curiosity, excitement, admiration. One young woman, with hair as pale as Rob's, hung back, throwing shy glances his way.

Men pressed forward. *Tell us what happened!* Women hung on his arms. *Are you hurt, Shawn?* and everybody spoke at once. *Did you see Nessie?* His heart pounded uncomfortably. *Conrad scheduled the concert for Saturday morning. He couldn't wait for your decision.* He studied each face in turn, making assessments.

"What are you *wearing?*" someone demanded.

"A hot bath! I'll run you a hot bath, you poor baby!" the bosomy woman chattered behind him.

"Dress-up day at the castle?" asked a man.

A young man, with jet black hair, stood apart from the rest, back by the castle door. He alone paid Niall no attention. Niall followed his eyes and saw that he stared steadily, sadly, at the platinum-haired girl casting shy, hopeful glances toward Niall.

A man grabbed Niall's hand, and pumped it. *Good to have you back!* Niall fought the desire to grab his dirk. They pressed too close for him to reach it, inside his boot. "Amy!" he snapped. "Taeke me to my room!"

"Why's he talking like that?" came out of the crowd.

"That's Shawn, all right!" someone else said. A hand slapped him on the back. The crowd parted before him, and he followed Amy up the stone stairs.

Behind him, the blonde woman huffed.

"Rob!" Niall added. "Send for Conrad. Now!"

* * *

101

The conductor proved to be a short and very furious man, his face brick red, arms flailing, and white hair crackling upright with irritation of its own. "What do you mean by disappearing like that!" He stamped across the sitting room of Shawn's huge suite, narrowly avoiding a mahogany table and overstuffed divan. Niall tried not to stare at the blue-papered walls and frescoed ceiling. He started as Conrad turned back suddenly, pounding a fist in his palm. "You *knew* I was waiting for your answer!" A vein throbbed purple in his neck. "The whole orchestra was waiting for *you.*"

"I'm the one who left him there," Amy said.

"If you left him, he gave you darn good reason," Conrad snorted.

"This is all my fault," Amy whispered, turning as pink as Conrad was red.

"'Twas nothing to do with her." Niall pulled his attention from the box with a black glossy front. He wondered what it held.

At the same time, Conrad turned to her in almost equal outrage, yelling, "I will not have you taking blame for his stupid, irresponsible, thoughtless, selfish, pig-headed behavior!" The vein pulsed dangerously. "And where in the world did you get that outfit?" He looked up and down Niall's full-sleeved shirt, tunic, and trews. "Those boots!" he added with a harrumph. His eyebrows quivered.

Niall looked down at his boots. He rather thought the cordwainer had outdone himself on this pair. Conrad hammered out another lap up and down the chamber. Thank goodness it was so large, Niall thought, concerned for the poor man's health. "This takes the cake!" Conrad thundered. While Conrad ranted, Niall returned to his study of the room. Its size rivaled the Laird's. He tried to imagine MacDonald's chambers being used by someone like the person this Shawn seemed to be. "Of all the things you've done, this tops it!"

Niall stared in fascination as the angry torrent washed over him. Amy said there was no laird, but obviously he'd do better in this man's good graces.

"Nobody else is hurt," Amy said. She sat in the window seat, rubbing her right hand back and forth on one finger of her left hand. Her hair fell over her shoulder, brushing her leg. "No hotels are damaged."

"I guess that's an improvement," Conrad grumbled.

Niall gazed through the doorway into the bedroom, to a massive four-poster with dark blue hangings. Matching drapes framed the leaded glass windows in the sitting room. Turning from the bedroom, Niall wandered to one of the windows to look down, Conrad's angry words wafting over him unheard. A lawn stretched for acres below, smooth and green, with a few scattered trees. It begged for young children to run across it. At the far end was a stone wall, beyond which lay a garden awash in color. He'd heard the English had such things. Imagine. Walling in flowers. He thought he saw fruit trees, and vowed, forgetting Hugh for a moment, that he'd take a walk in this garden and have a piece of fruit.

"Arrows!" Conrad spit out behind him. "How do you do it, Shawn! How do you attract so much trouble?"

"This is different," Amy said, trying to calm Conrad. "He didn't do it this time."

"No, thank goodness! After lassoing the waitress in Edinburgh, I guess I should be grateful he isn't the one who *did* the shooting!"

"Lassoing?" Niall turned from his survey of the distant gardens.

"You don't remember?" Conrad pounded his fist in his hand. "You don't remember that?" The vein throbbed. He drew a deep breath and added, "Maybe that's just as well if it means you've turned over a new leaf."

"I know nothing of who I was," Niall lied, carefully flattening his vowels.

"He's not himself," Amy reminded him.

"Causing trouble is exactly like him! How could you do this?" Conrad shouted again.

"I beg your forgiveness, sir." Niall bowed his head low. "I wish to assure you, it will not happen again. I need to ask...."

"What's this?" roared Conrad, his white mustache quivering. He stared in shock at Niall, then turned a demanding look to Amy, who shrugged helplessly.

"I told you he's acting—different."

Niall darted a furtive look at the heavy, golden torch holders on the wall. The torches in them looked nothing like the torches he knew. They gave steady light, with no flame. Amazing! "It won't happen again," Niall repeated. Conrad stared, dumbfounded. Niall stared back, equally perplexed. Why did the man seem so baffled and angry to be given the assurance he clearly wanted?

"Well, I'll be...." Conrad let the sentence hang unfinished. He squinted, just barely, studying Niall from a slightly tilted head. "You're actually apologizing?"

"Indeed I am, my Lord," Niall said. Clearly, this Shawn had not a reputation for showing proper respect to authority, given their reactions to an apology.

Conrad's face turned slowly red again. Amy hurried over, taking Niall's arm. "I think 'sir' would have been better," she said. To Conrad, she added, "I don't think he's trying to be facetious."

"He's got a history that would suggest otherwise," grumbled Conrad. "Shawn, this is one stunt too many. Let me be blunt.

Regardless of the impact on the orchestra, you're half a step from being fired. The cost of your behavior has gotten too high. I couldn't wait on your answer. We scheduled a late morning concert for Saturday. Same music."

"Yes, my—yes, sir," Niall said. He didn't know what a concert might be, but it sounded as if he'd be burned at the stake if he failed. If it involved music, surely he could pull something off, if, of course, he was still caught here five days hence. Music, he could do. "But I must ask...."

"He really is behaving strangely, isn't he?" Conrad peered more closely.

"I'm fine, sir. I need...."

"There's a horrible bruise, and cuts," Amy said. "Shawn, show him." She pushed his hair back from his temple. Her intimate touch jolted him, tingling.

Conrad stared, fingering his mustache, and muttering. "Not that courtesy and co-operation aren't a welcome change, but this seems too good to be true."

"Sir." Niall stepped into the brief silence. "I must ask...."

"The doctor says you're fine," Conrad interrupted, leaping with vengeance back to his pacing. "The concert, then. Anything you want, ask when you've given me a good concert. Otherwise, you're fired. Rehearsal tomorrow at nine. Same music."

Niall shook his head sadly, wondering how he was going to reach Hugh. Had he realized he was going to get trapped in these people's lives, threatened with *firing*, he'd have demanded to be taken back to the castle to work it out on his own. He imagined co-operating now would give him the greatest freedom to get help and leave when he must. "I'm sorry. I doon't remember the music."

"Don't remember! We played it two nights ago!"

"Just tell him," Amy said. "It'll come back."

"*Annie Laurie*."

"*Blue Bells of Scotland*," Amy added.

"Och! I knoo *Blue Bells*!" Niall said excitedly.

They stared at him. He wondered, uneasily, what he'd said wrong. His goal, he reminded himself, was to gain this man's favor and help.

Conrad studied him silently, doubt dawning in his eyes. "Get out your trombone!" Suspicion lined his voice like soft cotton batting.

"My...." Niall searched his brain, shifted vowels around, trying to guess what this word meant. Rob had used it, too. "My what?" He wondered, at that moment, if he was capable of earning this man's favor. Might it not be better to run now and figure out a way to help himself? But it would take a full day to walk back to the castle, if they didn't catch him and lock him up or set him ablaze.

Amy was already pulling a long, narrow case, bulging at one end, from the corner of the room. She laid it on the bed next to him. He studied it, ran his hands over a fawn-colored covering, dark brown leather around the edges, and brass studs, till he realized they were, with equal intensity, studying him.

He glanced at them, and quickly back to the case, not sure what to do. Then, he saw the latches, and, with a little fumbling, popped them. He lifted the lid to reveal the finest golden instrument he'd ever seen, a curved pipe with a flaring bell. Letters were engraved on it. He traced them, sounding them out. Conrad tapped his foot. "Edward's?" Niall looked up, excited at understanding the letters. "Edward played this?" Past and present swirled around him like the loch's mists.

"Very funny, Shawn." Conrad folded his arms across his chest.

"Of course," Niall said. Edward was seven hundred years ago. What a stupid gaff. He pulled out the curved pipe with its flaring bell. It seemed to be a horn of some sort.

"The slide?" Amy said. She reached in the box and lifted out a long, narrow part, that wrapped back on itself. She took the bell from him and fit the pieces together, looking at him with real concern.

Niall stared in dismay.

It had been a Sunday. William begged the Laird to come attend the sheep. William always had a story; he'd keep the Laird away a good long time. Niall and Iohn slipped into MacDonald's chambers and dug out the shiny new sackbut the gypsies had traded for turnips. All the way from England, they said, and such a rich, deep tone. All the Laird's musicians had tried, but none could produce anything that might be called rich.

At thirteen, Niall was not allowed to try. That didn't stop him. He and Iohn admired it, moved the slide up and down, laughing with hands pressed over mouths at their clever machinations against the Laird. Even now, he'd be hearing a long-winded list of things William had noticed about the sheep, with detailed accounts of every event that had happened on the moors leading up to these discoveries, and a lengthy discourse on the care and breeding of livestock in general. Niall blew into the instrument. A wheezing gasp of dry air came out the end.

Iohn shuddered. "Let me try," he said. He grabbed the sackbut from Niall, sucked in a deep breath, and blew, before Niall could see how he'd done it. The sound filled the chambers. Not the glorious sound described by the gypsies, but powerful.

"How did you do that?" Niall demanded. He reached for the instrument, but Iohn skipped away, laughing. "I'm better," he gloated.

A heavy stone ground in the bottom of Niall's stomach. He was invariably just a little faster, a little stronger, a little bolder. And though Iohn could sing, he couldn't make sense of the harp strings, ever.

Niall grabbed for the instrument again. He blew and blew, and produced only squawks and grunts and wheezes, while Iohn laughed louder than necessary, clutching his sides in exaggeration.

Niall glared. "'Tis a foolish thing anyway!" He shoved it back at Iohn, who blew again and got that same powerful tone. It slipped up to a higher note without a movement from the slide. Iohn took it away from his mouth and stared in delight. Niall left the chambers and never tried the sackbut again.

"This better not be for real," Conrad muttered, his arms locked like steel across his chest.

Niall stared at Edward's sackbut. Adding up all he knew of Shawn, the images all over town, the cocky, grinning face so like his own and yet so different, the talk of a concert, he understood what they expected. His face fell. He could not please this man. He saw his chances of gaining his trust and cooperation, and getting back to Hugh, dwindle to nothing. Scotland was lost, and there was naught he could do. "I canna play a sackbut," he said sadly.

Chapter Seven

Inverness, Scotland, Present

After another brief drive along the River Ness, Conrad and Niall reached a small castle of bricks and glass. Inside, several women huddled behind a low wall, under another of the large paintings. In this one, Shawn, once again with a plaid wrapped around his waist, lounged in a small boat with another buxom woman behind him, gripping his shoulders, her mouth and eyes in round O's of surprise. SHAWN KLEINER read the words above him. His sackbut stuck out like a fishing pole, reeling in a long-necked creature rising from the water. *The best* was all Niall managed to read of the words below, before the women popped up from behind the wall, giggling and blushing.

"Oh, I looove your shirt, Mr. Kleiner!" one of them squealed. She was far too old to be squealing like a love-sick lass, Niall thought. He looked down at his wide-sleeved shirt, laced at the throat, no different than any other man wore. Amy had refused to let him wear the tunic. He'd refused to be stuffed into Shawn's bizarre clothing. She'd relented and allowed him the trews, shirt, and boots.

"They'll all be dressed like that by tomorrow," Conrad grumbled. "Why can't you just be normal for once?" He brushed the women off and bustled Niall up a wide open flight of stairs, into a cavernous chamber larger than any great hall; greater, he was sure, than even Edward Longshanks had had in his glory days.

Niall took in the odd sight of hundreds of plush seats, cushioned like thrones, all facing the same way. No straw on the floor. He rather liked that. A path alongside the seats ended at a dais, though it rose higher than any he'd ever seen, higher than a man's waist. On it, dozens more chairs, small hard ones, faced a low raised platform. A single beam of light fell from above, as if from Heaven, on one large pillar, standing before all the chairs.

"The harp is onstage," barked Conrad. "This better be all you say it is, Shawn. You're on the brink...." Conrad snapped his mouth shut.

Niall glanced at him. *Of being fired,* he finished. He could play harp. There'd be no reason for Conrad to set him ablaze or shoot him. He'd play and get this man's cooperation. Easy.

He searched the dais for a small clairsach like his own. Not seeing one, he turned back toward the free-standing pillar. Its ethereal gold shone in the light. Carvings adorned the top and bottom. He walked toward it, seeing now that it sat on a base, and now—the strings stretched out in an orderly row behind the magnificent column.

This was the harp? The words almost came out of his mouth, but he remembered what they thought of his reaction to the sackbut. The *tromboon,* he corrected himself. He must remember the proper name.

Raised a soldier, and having learned his lesson, he kept his face impassive. But inwardly, his jaw fell, his eyes grew wide. He reached the dais and stared, in awe, at the harp rising above him. Its magnificent soundboard swelled out, swirling with floral, gold-inlaid motifs. He touched the base, the gold cool to his fingers, feeling the raised designs. Magnificent! If only the Laird could see this! He'd not quit his workshop till he'd built one himself! He studied the harp's features, memorizing every detail for the Laird.

"The stairs, Shawn. On your right. We don't have time." Conrad's grumble registered through his awe.

"Aye, sir," Niall said, forgetting that Shawn apparently did neither *ayes* nor *sirs.* He glanced to his right, found the stairs running up to the black-coated platform, and went up quickly, and back to the harp. It rose as tall as a man. "This is a harp!" he whispered.

"I like your outfit." A soft voice spoke behind him. He jumped, and turned to see the girl from the crowd this morning, the one who had hovered in the background. Hair flowed down her back, pale honey, almost to her knees. "The red strings are C." Her large blue eyes looked up at him through dark lashes. "The black strings are F. Remember when I showed you...?" Her voice trailed off. Her eyes returned to the floor, darted up again briefly to him. This must be Celine. Conrad had said she would meet them.

"No," he said softly. "I don't remember." He studied her young, innocent face, the way her eyes met his, hoping, and had a strong intuition Shawn had also shown her things. It appeared she was still smitten with him, and from her hesitant manner, he suspected Shawn had given her enough hope to keep her so, but not enough to embolden her. Scoundrel, he thought in disgust.

He turned to the harp, disturbed. She indicated the stool behind it. He seated himself, pulling the huge instrument down onto his right shoulder. The weight was greater than his small instrument, solid and gratifying.

Part of his mind stayed on Celine, hovering—and hoping—on his left. He felt for her. His insides raged, both at the man who would treat her so, and the idea that this is what people now thought of him. He touched the strings, wondering at this new complication. But it wasn't his complication, he told himself. His job was to get back to Hugh.

He sighed, and plucked a few strings, enjoying the instrument's deep reverberations. It felt good to play. It was his favorite thing, but with the cattle problems, the MacDougalls, and the looming battle with the English, there'd been little time of late. He wondered that these people led lives so easy and comfortable they could do this any time they wished!

He tried a few more strings, and played a scale. It now became easy to run his fingers over a familiar melody. He played it once, and lifted his left hand to add chords. Peace washed over him. He lowered his head, feeling nothing but the music. The bulk of the instrument, and the unfamiliar, heavy strings caused him to miss a few notes, but for the most part, he found it delightfully easy, playing this much larger instrument.

The clapping of two hands, slow and methodical, burst from the dark, jolting him from his reverie. "You've caused a lot of trouble in this orchestra, Shawn." Conrad's voice boomed from the dark. "But I always give credit where credit is due. Truly impressive. How have you managed to keep this secret from us?"

"You told me you couldn't play," Celine murmured.

Niall glanced from Celine to Conrad. "Just something I— learned," he said helplessly. And to Celine, "It seems you're a guid teacher."

"We usually do *Blue Bells* in D," Conrad said.

"In D?" Niall looked helplessly at Celine. "What dooz that mean?"

"Here." She edged in close, her leg coming over his. He jumped, shocked and wondering what she thought she could do with the real Shawn here in front of Conrad. Anything seemed possible in a world where women wore undergarments, and less, in public. "The pedals," she said. "I need to change the pedals." He looked down. Seven gleaming brass pedals jutted from the base. She pushed two with her foot. "Now play."

He touched the strings again. This time, *Blue Bells* came out all wrong, even though he'd hit the right strings. "What happened?" he asked.

"You have to transpose."

"I don't know what this transpose is," he replied, copying the word carefully.

"What happened to you? They're saying you were shot by an arrow."

"Transpose?" Niall reminded her.

"Play every note a step higher than it was?" she said, perplexed.

"Ah." His eyes lit up. He understood the concept, although he'd never heard the word. He pushed his hair back from his temple, and she gasped at the bruise. "It's made me forget much," he said. He took a moment to think, then played *Blue Bells* again, moving everything up a step.

Conrad clapped. "You'll do," he said, delight in his voice. "Keep playing. I'm going to move around the hall and get a feel for the sound." Niall inclined his head in acknowledgment, remembering to ease off the ayes and sirs. Conrad's footsteps faded away in the dark.

Niall wondered, uneasily, what was expected of him. He and Celine stared at each other. "I'll need help," Niall said, breaking the silence. "I don't know the music. Play it or sing it to me, and I can do it."

She smiled shyly, and worked her way in between him and the harp. He was startled, given her demeanor, at the boldness of the move. This was what she'd been asking him to remember. Shawn had done this before with her, he was certain. He stood abruptly, thinking of Allene, and backed away.

She turned to him in shock. Her face fell. Her cheeks turned bright pink, and she hung her head. "I'm sorry," she whispered. "I know you told me.... But I thought, when you wanted me here today...."

"Conrad asked you here," he said, and realized, seeing the tears glisten in the corners of her eyes, that he sounded harsh. He touched her back, where she sat on the stool, awkwardly, and pulled his hand away. He was aware of Conrad still moving around the hall. "Show me the music. We'll talk when Conrad leaves," he said softly.

She nodded, and lifted graceful fingers to the strings. He took in every motion. Music flowed magically, gentle yet powerful enough to fill the chamber. The colored patterns of the strings, under her fingers, sparkled on his brain, leaving a trail for him to follow.

He sighed heavily, thinking of his need to reach Hugh, as he watched, and wondering if he'd made the right choice in coming here. Nonetheless, he was somewhat trapped, and would do what he could with the situation into which God had placed him. He leaned forward and studied her right hand, memorizing the patterns her fingers danced on the strings.

"Again, sloo-er," he said. She played again, obediently. In his mind, his fingers moved with hers. "Again." He closed his eyes and listened intently, letting his fingers, in his mind, follow the pattern. "I'll do it now," he said.

She stood, silently. He played it twice, three, four times, each time fixing mistakes, until it came out perfectly. Even as he stood to let her take the stool, his mind was once more reviewing the piece, settling it firmly into his memory.

"I don't know how you're doing that, Shawn," came Conrad's voice from the back of the hall, "but it sounds great. Celine, teach him the whole program. I'm going to talk to the board. We'll see you at rehearsal tomorrow."

A band of light appeared at the back of the hall, and Conrad's silhouetted figure disappeared out of the door. It swung shut, leaving the hall once again in darkness.

Onstage, in the glare of the spotlight, Celine waited for Niall's nod, and started the next piece. She played it several times, before he once again took his turn. "A singer will do this one with you," she said.

"Sing it, then." Niall rolled a chord. Deep reverberations resonated through his body. He fought back a thrill at the sound and touch of this magnificent instrument. After all, he was supposed to be getting back to Hugh, and this wasn't doing it. Her light, clear voice joined in.

> *Young Ian did a friend betray,*
> *A friend he did betray,*
> *He took him to the English King*
> *And he a price did pay*
> *Young Ian with his golden voice*
> *Did have the blackest heart*
> *Young Ian in his crimson cloak*
> *Betrayed his dearest friend.*

He rolled another rich chord to end the piece. "A sad tale," he said.

"In England, the same ballad treats him as a hero."

He leaned forward, and lifted his hands to the strings once more, remembering Lord Darnley, William, and Iohn singing with him on many a winter's evening by the great fire. He closed his eyes, smiling as Celine began to sing once more.

> *With eyes of loch and forest glen,*
> *With eyes of loch and glen,*
> *Young Ian spoke the falsest words,*
> *Pretending he was a friend*
> *But as the battle round him broke,*
> *He raised his voice in song,*

Young Ian with his crimson cloak,
Betrayed his dearest friend.

"I don't remember the rest," she said. "I'm sorry." He ran his fingers up the harp strings in a long arpeggio, and struck a low note, finishing off the song.

"Beautiful!" he said in amazement.

She taught him ballads, jigs, and dance pieces. She knew the story behind each, and Niall fascinated to hear this history of his country, things that would not happen until hundreds of years after his own birth. "Enough for one day," he finally said, rising from the stool. "Now we talk." He pulled up a chair, knee to knee with her.

They stared at each other awkwardly. He didn't know where to start. He couldn't tell the truth, of course. He'd be locked up. And even this quiet girl would most likely slap him for such a story. Allene certainly would! He wondered if Shawn had met Allene and earned a slap from her yet. He smiled.

He cleared his throat and met her eyes. "When I wook up in the castle, I dinna know who or where I was." It was almost true. Still, he hated himself for telling stories to this vulnerable girl, as Shawn had most definitely already done more than once. He only hoped she would see the sincerity of his intent in his eyes; hear it in his tone. "I canna say what happened." That was true enough. "But I tell you this: I don't remember you and I. I don't remember what I did, but I think I wasn't nice."

A single tear trailed down her cheek. "You said you loved me when you came to my house that night," she whispered. A sheet of long, honey hair fell over her shoulder, shielding her face. "You brought me a rose and said it was over with Amy. You said you didn't want to hurt her, and we had to be discreet until she accepted the inevitable."

He touched her shoulder awkwardly. Shawn had lied. Even he, stumbling into the situation, could see it had never been over with Amy.

"I'm sorry," he said. Her pain hurt him. She, he could see, would not tread on a rose petal for fear of harming it. "I was wrong. I lied. I...."

She looked up at him, her china blue eyes wet. "You lied?" She looked down at the floor again. She wiped the back of her hand against one eye, and after a few moments said, "I always knew you had. I just...I just didn't want to believe it. I don't lie. I don't understand lying."

"Remember I don't know who I was," Niall said, taking her hand. "Tell me: why did you wait for him—for me—when you knew?"

"I wanted it to be true." She stared at the floor. "I didn't think you'd lie to *me*."

"Why?" he asked. "Why did you want it to be true that he felt something for you?"

She studied his face.

"Look at me." Niall spread his hands. "I'm seeing—myself—as if I had been another pairson, and it seems he was not a verra nice pairson."

"Sometimes you weren't," Celine admitted.

"Then why?"

"Because you were kind and gentle to me."

"Aye," he snapped. "Casting you aside, leave you waiting when I finished with you was kind and gentle?" He wasn't sure if he was more angry with Shawn's abominable behavior, or with Celine for buying it.

"You're right." She bit her lip. "I was a fool."

"You weren't a fool," he said. "Shawn—I mean, the auld Shawn—was skilled at deceiving. Do not let him do it again. Do not think you're worth so little."

She nodded.

There was a moment's silence, in which Niall's head spun. He'd gone to sleep, only last night, in the fourteenth century. The many events of the day spun through his head, the fresh morning air off the Loch, the revelations in the hospital, the stomach turning car ride, and the bizarre hero's welcome at the castle. It was this scene that ran most strongly through his mind, and he suddenly understood something. "Have you never considered," he said slowly, feeling for the right words, "that there may be someone who would treat you so much better? Someone you'd have seen had you not set your feather for Shawn?"

"You speak like you're someone else," she said.

Yes, Niall thought. He must be careful of that. "I feel as if I am," he said. "I remember nothing. Was there never another?"

She nodded. "You knew I went out with Aaron a few times."

"Aaron? The young one with the black hair?"

Celine nodded. "You said he didn't love me like you did. You said he wouldn't want me anymore. You said if I'd just wait...."

"I'm truly sorry." Niall almost choked on the words, pretending to have been such a foul person. "I'm sorry for who I was, and what I've done. Do you not see the way Aaron looks at you? Do you feel nothing for him?"

"I thought I was in love with him. But then you—you were so important, and you treated me so well. For awhile. It's hard to compare."

"Poor Aaron," Niall said. "He doesn't glitter like Sh...like I do. But perhaps he is the real gold. Did he ever leave you waiting? Did he lie to you? Did he take you away from what was good in your life?"

"No." Her head hung.

"Shawn did. Remember that when you look at me." It occurred to him that the real Shawn might be back. "No matter what I say in the future," he added. He laughed inwardly at the joke. Everything he said was seven hundred years in his future! "No matter what I say," he repeated for emphasis, "remember who treated you well. It was Aaron."

"Yes, I'll remember," she said.

"Now kiss me," he demanded.

Her eyes widened, hopefully. "You mean it? But you just said...."

He slapped his knee angrily. "No, no, no! This is what I'm talking aboot! Do you not learn! This is where you slap me!"

She heaved a sigh. "I don't understand."

"You're an innocent," he said. "You don't understand lying and deception because you dinna do it yerself. Shawn—the auld Shawn—is a liar and a deceiver. I dinna know what happened in the castle, but the pairson I am now—I want never to hurt you again. Ye must understand I may be a liar and deceiver again, in a week, in a day. When I am, you must slap me if I try to take you from the good in your life."

She still looked uncertain.

"All right, you must learn one way or another," Niall said with determination. He offered his cheek to her. "Slap me."

She lifted a limp hand, and grazed his cheek.

"Sad!" he barked. "Think of all the lies!" He rose from his chair. "Think of the days you could have spent with someone who cared aboot ye! Think of the days in your room pining for him while he was having fun with Amy, not carin' a hoot aboot ye!" He'd guessed, from the young lasses he'd seen behaving the same way, and saw in her eyes he'd guessed right. "Did ye see me walking the gairdens hand in hand with Amy," he taunted, "while ye sat in your room?"

Her eyes blazed up at him.

"I wasna even thinkin' o' ye," he mocked.

Her slap stunned him. This time, it stung hard and sent him reeling into the chair behind him. His knees caught it, and he fell, pushing over two more chairs as he went down. He landed in a heap amidst the chairs, his cheek stinging, a chair biting into his back, and the stitches in his posterior burning. He laughed in delight. "Verra guid!" he said. "Now kick me for guid measure!" She did, and he groaned. "Did ye have to get the stitches?" He rubbed hard, hoping she hadn't broken anything open.

"You're right about everything, Shawn." Her china blue eyes spit fire at him. "I'm a fool. I'm even more a fool that you have to convince me yourself how awful you've been. I knew it and I didn't want to see it."

"You're a fool with someone who's verra much in love with ye," Niall said in delight. "Go to Aaron and never, ever look at me again as someone worthy of your time! I beg you!"

Laura Vosika

* * *

Conrad called the three senior members of the board of directors together. They gathered at the round mahogany table in the luxurious director's suite. "He can't play trombone," he announced.

Dan exploded from his chair, pounding his hand on the table. The water in the glass pitcher trembled. "It's the last straw!" he roared.

"He gets no break this time?" Bill asked. "They're saying he was shot by an arrow, hit in the head, beaten up. Amy did leave him."

Peter, the concertmaster, scoffed. "You're not going to find a single person in this orchestra who will hold that against her." He poured himself water and gulped it.

Bill held up his hands. "I'm not *blaming* her. I'm just saying it's not his fault this time."

"Most of them are cheering her on for finally sticking it to him," Peter fumed. "He's asked for it, the way he's yanked the poor girl around. I begged her not to get involved with him!"

"Fire him." Dan fished for his cell phone. "This young guy, this trumpet player, Zach, call him right now!"

Conrad held up a hand. "I'd agree except—get this! He offered to play harp instead."

"Shawn doesn't play harp," Peter said in disgust. "Arrows, head injuries, harp! The rumors are ridiculous!"

"You'd be surprised what Shawn can do," Bill said. "There's always been more to him than he lets on."

"But harp?" Dan insisted. He turned back to Conrad. "Do you have any reason to believe he can actually do it?"

"Celine met us at the concert hall." Conrad raked a hand through his hair, making it stand up like white dandelion fluff. "It was the damndest thing. Surreal. He spent a couple minutes feeling the strings, asked about the reds and blacks. It was like he'd never really seen such a thing before. He said how big it was. Then he started playing, like he'd been doing it his whole life!"

"Shawn knows what the red and black strings are." Bill looked perplexed.

"Right," said Dan in disgust. "He had quite an affair with Celine. He was always hanging over her, asking questions, pretending he didn't know, picking out pieces. And it was just another lie. He knew all along what he was doing."

"Maybe he forgot?" Peter said with disdain. "We all know it wasn't the harp he wanted to get his hands on."

"Be that as it may," Conrad said slowly, "I've never heard anything so beautiful in my life. God only knows how, but he can play! I

115

don't know what happened to him out there, but maybe this one really isn't his fault. And he seems to have come back a nicer person. Maybe we can make a go of this, really make a selling point of his versatility."

* * *

Niall spent his brief respite, after playing Celine's harp, in the hotel lobby, picking up the many *brochures* lying around; large, glossy ones like those at the hospital.

The woman with the ruffled-pheasant-feathers hair appeared, touching his sleeve. Close up, Niall saw the sprinkle of freckles across her nose and eyes the color of cinnamon. "Shawn, you should have called me," she said.

"Excuse me?" He lowered the *brochure,* and tried to keep his eyes off her hair.

"Didn't you have your cell phone with you?"

He closed the *brochure,* frowning. "My what?"

Her eyebrows furrowed. She looked close to tears. "It's me, Dana. You don't remember me at all?"

"My apologies, no." His mind spun, trying to think what he could ask to get more information about Shawn. But she blinked eyes that pooled like dew on the bluebells, blinked fast and hard, and hastened away, almost running from the hall.

He sighed and turned back to the *brochures.* It took some searching at first, difficult with the print and spelling so odd to his eyes, but he found what he was looking for. Though the months varied, they all, without fail, were dated well into the twenty-first century. The Sassenach could not possibly set up such an elaborate ruse, with wonders unheard of, with people pretending to know and care for him, with an amazing tale of time travel.

They *wouldn't* have, when they could have just kidnapped or killed him.

After seeing the date for the ninth time, he went to his room, where he fell on his knees, head bowed, not even knowing what to pray. He clenched his hands, till his knuckles turned white.

When Amy came for him at dinner time, God had still granted him no wisdom or hope. But he'd regained a sense of calm and duty, and saw sense in giving in this time when she insisted he wear the stiff leggings, the *jeans,* that constrained and clung oddly to his legs, after a lifetime in loose trews and tunics; odd, short hose that came only to his ankles; useless, tight black shoes that bound his feet in and would never do for running or hiking or fighting; a white shirt with small buttons and short sleeves that ended well above his elbows.

She led him to the great hall. She called it a *dining room*.

He stood at the door, when they reached it, needing time to adjust to this unexpected sight. The *dining room* had no straw on the floor, but the same soft carpeting as the other rooms. It had a fireplace at one end, but no fire was laid. He looked for the head table, where an important man such as Shawn seemed to be, would sit. But all were identical, round and covered in white cloths. Women in short, black skirts served the food; not boys. They did not scurry, but walked placidly. The Laird would bellow at such complacency! There was not a dog in sight.

Heads turned. "There's Shawn, waiting to see who notices his grand entrance!" a man shouted.

"Come on, quit making a show of it," Amy whispered. "Why do you always have to do this?

He moved forward, among the tables, stiffening his spine resolutely as the future leader he was. He understood immediately, from the greetings of a number of men and the coquettish smiles of many women, that Shawn was a great favorite. But neither did he miss those who turned the other way as he walked past. He said little, merely nodded gravely to those who hailed him. He saw the looks of confusion on their faces, and their hands fell lifelessly.

He saw and felt the whispers swirling behind his back. Obviously, this was not the way the real Shawn would have behaved. He didn't worry. The head injury would cover a multitude of inconsistencies.

Amy led him to a table, with Rob and the pheasant-haired woman —Dana, he reminded himself—and several others. A serving woman in a short, black skirt rushed to slide a soft cushion on his chair. He seated himself carefully, nodded courteously in response to their greetings. Dana barely glanced at him, but slipped a comforting arm around Amy's shoulder. "How are you doing?" she asked, and Amy murmured back.

The servant girl hovered. "Bring me ale," Niall said to her. The seven other faces at the table turned toward him.

He looked back at them, questioningly.

"You usually prefer lager," Amy said, softly.

"Ale," Niall answered. The serving woman nodded and left.

"I hear you play harp now," one of the men said.

"What's this about an arrow in the butt?" asked another.

"It can't really have been an arrow," Amy said. "He must have gashed himself on a rock or...or something.

"You finally got Amy mad enough to ditch you," hooted another man.

"Maybe it was Amy who shot you. What did you *do*?"

"Would you stop it," Dana snapped.

Beside him, Amy turned red and stared at her napkin. "I told him

I'm sorry," she said.

"She's not to blaeme," Niall said, feeling for her. Remembering his experience with Celine, he felt sure Amy was not at fault in anything, regarding Shawn.

The servant returned, bearing a tankard—a tankard of glass! Niall picked it up and stared at it in astonishment.

"Shawn! Put the mug down!" Amy hissed.

"Never seen a mug?" one of the men asked.

"He hurt his head," Amy explained.

"Sir?" said the woman.

He looked from the others' surprised faces, to the serving woman, and set the mug down. From a glass bottle similar to the one he'd seen in the basket, she poured what must be the ale, flowing gold, into the mug. He picked up the frothing mug, trying to recover his dignity. He gulped, wiped his mouth with the back of his hand to cover the sudden puckering of his lips, and forced back the urge to spit it out. It was strong and bitter, nothing like the ale he knew. They all watched. He swallowed, and smiled back, weakly. "Guid," he said. "Verra guid ale."

"Picked up an arrow *and* an accent overnight," one of the men remarked.

"An arrow, an accent, and an ale," said another.

"Aye," he agreed, for lack of anything better to say. But he vowed to listen and copy their speech more carefully. Thankfully, the woman returned, setting food in front of him: meat, peas, something like turnips, but bigger. He wondered if it would taste as he expected, or be as different as the ale was from what he knew. It smelled good. With a last, suspicious look at the so-called ale, he bowed his head. He crossed himself and folded his hands, his fingertips touching his nose. He thanked God, asked for guidance, crossed himself again, and raised his head.

The others stared, open-mouthed.

"Picked up an arrow, an accent, an ale, and religion," said Rob.

Dana glared at him. "You think this is funny?"

"Picked up an arrow, an accent, an ale, religion, and a couple of girls," said a third. Niall's ear processed his inflections for future use.

"Knock it off!" Amy set her fork down hard. Her lower lip tightened, as if holding back tears.

"Peace, Amy," Niall murmured, touching her arm. "Is the food *good*?" he asked the others, shaping his words carefully. He picked up one of the curious pronged forks they all favored, and copied their motions, cutting his meat with knife and fork and lifting it to his mouth. They nodded their assent, commented on the tastiness of the food, and slipped into conversation he couldn't entirely follow. He listened carefully throughout the meal, fully aware of their curious looks in his direction, as words became steadily more sensible, from the sounds coming out of their mouths.

"Are you okay, Shawn?" Amy asked him at length. "Do you want to go back to your room?"

The concern on her face reminded him what this odd word *okay* meant. He imitated their vowels carefully. "I'm *okay*. I'll stay," he said. He watched the man across the table lift a square of cloth to his mouth. He did the same. He had a great deal to learn from these people, if he was going to find a way out of this mess.

The women in short dresses came to clear the plates. One of them leaned close for his dishes, pressing her bosom against his cheek. "My apologies, madam." Niall pulled away. He heard Amy gasp, and noted the surprise on her face.

The girl in the short skirt giggled, and there was her bosom, right against his cheek again. He realized with shock that she was doing it on purpose. She slipped a bit of script-covered parchment in front of him. "Will you sign it?" she asked. "My friends couldn't believe I was going to see you tonight. Will you, please?"

Amy watched him.

"You want me to sign...my name?" he asked. She nodded so hard he feared her head would bob right off. He took the nib-less quill she offered. He thought back to the paintings of Shawn, picturing the letters that had spelled his name. He touched the quill to the parchment. Purple ink flowed from it. Purple ink! He realized everyone at the table was looking at him strangely. He lowered the quill and wrote *Shawn Kleiner* in his finest script. It dawned on him half way through that Shawn might not write in Niall's own fine hand, and that he himself had scrawled an illegible signature at the hospital.

He looked up at Amy. She stared at the elegant script in shock, and raised her eyes to his. Shockingly blue eyes. Shockingly upset eyes.

Glenmirril Castle, Scotland

A knock sounded on Shawn's door, seemingly minutes later. But the room was dark when he opened his eyes. He sat up, yawning, and scratching at his belly through the woolen monk's robe. The morning's hangover had passed, but not the craving for coffee. Outside the window, the moon hung low on the horizon in a pale charcoal sky. He stood up, stretching. The door eased open. To Shawn's surprise, the Laird himself came in, bearing a candle in one hand and a large bag slung on his back.

MacDonald must have seen the surprise in Shawn's eyes, even in the dim light, for he laid his hand on his shoulder. "I told you to trust few. I take my own advice. No one but you, me, and the lad must know the truth of your journey. You are my future son-in-law, and my heir. May God go with you, Niall. Ye've said your prayers?"

Shawn shook his head. Not since that last Mass, six days before his father's murder, had Shawn prayed. The old man pushed him down. He landed roughly on his knees, the Laird kneeling beside him with folded hands and bowed head. "God, our dear Father, grant Niall safety and wisdom on his journey. May God protect us all, especially my lad. In the name of the Father, Son, and Holy Ghost, amen." He crossed himself again, and they both rose. The Laird hefted the bag up to Shawn.

Shawn took it, wondering at its size and weight. Food? Thinking of the salmon and chocolate mousse they'd be serving at the hotel, his stomach growled. "It can't be past midnight," he said.

"Much earlier. Too many expected you to leave in the wee hours of morn. You must be well away before they start to watch for you."

"Wasn't it only the lords in the room who knew that?"

"Aye." The Laird did not elaborate. He pulled a rope from under the bed, and carried it to the window set back in the recess.

Shawn's stomach quelled again. "What's wrong with the door?" He went to the window himself, and looked out. Stiff wind yanked at his hair. He looked down, down, down into a bubbling witch's cauldron of mist. His stomach lurched far worse than any hangover. The rock wall dropped sheer, hundreds of feet. The rocky escarpment on which the castle stood dropped further still. Shawn's head reeled. He yanked it inside.

"You're kidding," he said.

"They may be watching the drawbridge. Hold the bag tightly, now." MacDonald tossed the rope out the window. It slithered down, slapping the wall. The Laird coiled the end tightly around his hands. "When you reach the bottom, run up the hill and down to the copse on the other side. Ye'll do it *my* way this time, eh, Niall?"

"Uh, yeah," Shawn said. He hoped the man didn't read his intentions to go his own way, directly north to Inverness.

"My way, Niall," the old man insisted. "Tweaking my plans may have worked with the MacDougalls, but not this time. Swear it!"

Shawn nodded vigorously, wanting nothing more than to be out of here. The Laird studied him hard, as if expecting more. "I'll do it," Shawn assured him.

"An' a last word of caution." The old man placed a short, thick dirk on the window ledge. Shawn eyed it. The old man eyed him. They eyed each other. "You treat the laddie proper. I'd no ha' sent him but for such desperate need."

"Yes, sir." He had no idea what the Laird feared, but the knife's sharp blade ran a cold finger down his spine.

"An' I hear a word agin you, we'll be having words." He tapped the handle of his dagger, glinting in the moonlight on the sill. "Am I clear?"

Shawn stared at the knife, blinking hard. He nodded. "Yes, sir! There'll be no complaints!"

"Good man, Niall." The Laird slid the dirk from the windowsill. With trepidation, Shawn took the oilskin bag, strapped it firmly across his back, and crawled up where the dagger had been. Wind tore at his legs, hanging out. He looked down, thankful he'd never been afraid of heights. This view, however, just might change that. "I hope you're strong," he muttered, and, clutching the rope, dropped over the ledge. He fell, slamming against the stone wall. The wind shoved at him. The rope slipped in his hands, tearing skin from his palms. He grabbed tighter, wincing at the burn.

"Hand over hand," the Laird whispered fiercely. "Careful with the bag. Ye cannna have it breaking. Hurry! My back is no what it was."

"I can do this," Shawn told himself. He managed to twist his feet in the rope—the leather sandals gripped it well—and, going against every survival instinct, forced himself to loosen his grip in one hand, then another, lowering himself down the rope. The moon, thankfully, had slipped behind clouds. Mist steamed on the loch far below; there was not a stirring of life anywhere.

He lowered himself another hand under hand, fighting the wind, and clung for several seconds, refusing to look down, before releasing his grip again.

"Hurry!" the Laird hissed from above.

Wild images of arrows in the back sprang to mind. It was a ridiculous thought. But it gave him impetus to lower himself another several feet. The rope slackened suddenly. He slipped another two feet, slamming against the wall. "I canna hold on," came the voice from above. "Faster!"

He glanced down. He was close, but not close enough. He hitched the bag up, and forced himself to lower his hands, wiggle his feet, inching toward the rocky outcropping. The rope gave a sudden lurch, and he was hurtling downward.

A foot!

Only a foot, and he struck ground. His legs buckled, throwing him to his knees. The bag hit the rocks hard. The rope slithered down beside him. He coiled it, and slung it over his body.

Clouds scudded for the edge of the moon. Soon it would be bright again. He looked up to the window; it was empty. He was alone in the world. There was the hill he must cross. He hefted the bag to his

shoulder, girded the monk's robe up around his bare legs.
And ran.

Inverness, Scotland, Present

Dinner lasted late, with thick, rich deserts Niall had never even imagined. He sampled several. Then there were drinks. A crowd gathered around his table, questioning him about his night in the tower, making wild guesses. "Shot in the leg, is the rumor," said a man with a thin goatee.

"Shot somewhere much more interesting is what I heard!" The men chuckled.

"Don't pay attention to ridiculous rumors," Amy snapped. "He'll be fine. He just cut himself on something, that's all."

"Allowed to be a little eccentric, anyway, when you bring so much business to the orchestra and the hotel," one of the men remarked.

The woman who'd given him the hero's greeting, with hair as white and soft as corn silk, and a garnet red dress clinging more tightly than any undergarment, dropped herself boldly on his lap, wrapping her arm around his head. Dana rolled her eyes and shook her feathered head. Amy glared. The bosomy woman smiled back, flashing teeth whiter than summer clouds, and cooed in Niall's ear. "Hope it hasn't hurt anything important. I was hoping for an encore tonight."

The words themselves made little sense to Niall, but a proposition in any language, he found, was not hard to understand. He stood, forcing the woman off his lap. "My lady, my apologies. You could not know, but I am betrothed."

A gasp went around the table. The woman looked as though she'd been slapped. They all stared at Amy questioningly. She turned red. "I... um...we talked...." she stammered, and finally said, "He's joking."

"Yes," agreed Niall, wanting to ease the embarrassment he'd obviously caused her. "I spoke in jest." At their curious stares, he remembered to copy their speech, and amended his words. "I am joking." He made no move, however, to sit down to accommodate the woman again. She turned on her heel and flounced away.

Niall resumed his seat. The uncomfortable silence continued, till one of the men cleared his throat and said, "Sounds like we might be here long enough to see the re-enactment." The focus off him, Niall sat back, listening. The word Stirling caught his attention, and he leaned forward. A re-enactment, he gathered, after some time, was men pretending to be warriors of times past, playing out famous battles. Not wanting to attract any more attention, he bit back his question: W*hy would anyone do such a foolish thing?* Were there not enough real battles and wars?

"...the Bruce," came the next words. "The Battle of the Pools."

The very battle for which Hugh was needed! Niall leaned forward. "This is what's being...re-enacted?" He tested the unfamiliar word, pleased at how quickly he was able to imitate their broad speech. His game of mimicking the Laird and Lord Darnley had a benefit he never would have guessed.

"Awful battle," another man said. "Edward destroyed the Scots. Not a single one of them left by the end. They even hunted down the townspeople hiding back on Coxet Hill and killed them all. Every last one."

The blood drained from Niall's face.

Loch Ness, Scotland

Shawn hadn't done much running since high school. Running from that angry husband last year didn't really count. The hill rose sharply, covered in heather and gorse, visible as darker patches against the dark hill. The loch stretched along his right as he half-ran, half-climbed the hill. At the top, a stitch pierced his side. He leaned over, hands on his knees, breathing hard, cursing Amy and wishing he were at the banquet with Caroline making promises with her eyes from across the room. She'd be wearing that red dress she knew he liked so much. He knew she would.

The ground leveled out. He had no idea where to go. Though Niall must know how to find the copse, he himself could only run straight over the hill as he'd been told, and hope for the best.

The heavy sack slapped him rhythmically on the back. The stitch in his side burned, but visions of English soldiers and feuding Scots clans lurked in the dark corners of his mind, waiting with arrows and daggers. The angry husband last year looked tame as a white rabbit next to the men populating his imagination. Gone was any thought of heading for Inverness. With fear growing, his only desire was to reach the cover of trees, and the lad who knew so much more than he did.

In daylight, he'd think about Inverness; he'd go straight for the nearest McDonald's and order the biggest shake they had to tide him over till he reached the hotel's buffet. They hadn't exactly fed him well at this place.

He pushed himself on, beaten by the bag on one side, burned by the stitch on the other, and his lungs ragged for breath between the two, and suddenly, the hill fell away, and there, at its foot, was a cluster of trees. He hoped it was the right cluster of trees. He hoped the castle traitors weren't waiting there. But he had no choice.

He stumbled downhill. In the copse's safety, he fell to his knees, gasping for breath, and gripping his side. The hill behind him suddenly exploded with moonlight escaping its cloudy prison. The back of his neck tingled, waiting for the imagined attack.

A short whistle sounded. His head spun frantically, seeking the arrow, before realizing it was a person whistling. His breath *whooshed* out in relief. "You're starting to believe their hallucinations," he muttered to himself. "Nobody's shooting arrows around here."

He peered into the darkness from which the whistle had come. It sounded again, short and sharp. He climbed to his feet, searching for its source, and immediately blundered into a tree. He flung his pack to the ground in anger. How in the world could Amy have left him in this mess! He could be in a soft bed with Caroline right now! He rubbed his forehead, sure a knot would be rising, and wondered again why he attracted such temperamental women.

His eyes adjusted slowly to the dark. Now he could make out the shapes of trees. Enough to avoid them, anyway. The birches shone silver in the moonlight. A smaller dark shape grew out of, and separated from, a tree ahead of him. This must be *the laddie*. His upraised arm beckoned Shawn. A cowl hid his face.

The laddie was older than Shawn had expected. He rose just past Shawn's shoulder. He supposed that made more sense than the ten year old boy he'd been expecting. The figure reached for him and pulled him to the western edge of the grove, pointing at the castle rising atop its hill, and the moonlit group of men, small at this distance, moving stealthily toward a cropping of trees looking down on the drawbridge.

Shawn closed his eyes, wanting to be anywhere but here.

Chapter Eight

Inverness, Scotland, Present

Niall went directly to Shawn's chambers, after dinner. There was no crucifix. Choosing a spot over the bed, he imagined his own, carved by the monks of Monadhliath, hanging there. He fell to his knees praying. He'd always prayed, but he had a disquieting awareness now that it had, in a sense, been a formality. Not that he didn't believe in God, or truly seek His guidance. He did. But he'd always been so sure and confident. He'd seen his choices and understood his situations, always, and talked to God as—as what? he asked himself. As merely Someone to listen to him.

Now, for the first time, he came before God lacking wisdom and seeing his need to do the listening. For the first time, he felt rudderless.

He knelt by the bed, his forehead fallen on clasped hands, and sorted through his facts: a broken down version of his castle, his things missing and foreign objects in their place; people who neither dressed nor spoke like anyone he'd ever met or heard of; people with amazing devices from the mundane to the fantastic, from their writing instruments to *cars* that shot down the roads faster than an osprey could fly, and they took it all for granted. They carried no weapons—perhaps the most fantastic thing of all!

Amy, the calendar at the hospital, all the shiny *brochures* all told him it was roughly seven hundred years past the Year of Our Lord 1314.

He rose, and paced Shawn's chambers, from the bedroom to the sitting room, to the leaded-glass windows with their diamond panes, and back. He was a soldier. He was trained to face and assess facts. There were only so many explanations. Fairy hills, kidnapping, an English ruse —it was clearly none of these. When all other possibilities had been ruled out, what was left must be the answer, no matter how improbable.

He must finally accept that he'd been swept into the future.

It seemed impossible, and yet—there were stories of such things. He stared out the window at the darkened lawn. It was fantastic, incredible. Yet it appeared to be true. He drummed his fingers, letting it sink in. He'd come to the future. He'd moved through time with less effort than others crossed the bailey.

How? Shawn had also fallen asleep at the top of the tower. Niall pushed his fingers through his hair. Beyond that, he could only guess. Was there some magic in the castle? Some connection between himself and this Shawn who looked just like him? Most importantly, how was he to reverse the situation and get back? Amy, living in a world with all these amazing devices, appeared even more shocked than he at the possibility of moving through time.

The questions overwhelmed him. He returned to the bedroom, and knelt silently, head bowed before the crucifix he imagined on the wall, letting his mind go quiet and waiting for an answer, a sign, a miracle —anything! Nothing came; certainly no peace or reassurance about the outcome of the battle. He shook his head. It couldn't end that way. It just couldn't.

At last, he crossed himself and stood up, staring around the room. He flicked the lights on and off. He went to the bath chamber, running his hand in awe down the granite walls, smooth and shiny as glass. He turned the water on and off, on and off, marveling. He examined a white box, pushing buttons and turning dials, awed at the music and talk and crackling sounds that came out. He looked at it, picked it up, ran his hands under it, followed the black rope trailing from it to the wall.

He took his time examining the box with the glass front, but could find no way to open it. He found buttons and pushed them. Lights and sound and color sprang to life! He jumped back, grabbing for his dirk. But Amy had insisted he leave it in a drawer. With the immediate shock past, he saw there was no danger, and stared in fascination. He pushed the button, and the glass went black. He pushed the button, and the images sprang to life, moving paintings, people talking. He watched and listened for some time, repeating their words, with their accent, in his head, and finally, out loud, shaping his words carefully. He imagined the Laird's face when he heard of these things, and smiled.

The smile, however, faded, thinking of the Laird's fate. What would *he* do, if he found himself in this situation? *Use what you have,* he would say.

Niall sat down on the bed, dejected. Opening his sporran, he saw a handful of coins worth little enough, his slingshot, and bits of flint. He had his dirk and the crucifix on the leather thong around his neck, which he'd intended for Allene. He fingered it, thinking about Allene and what would happen to her. He couldn't bear it. This crucifix, itself, would not save the world.

He straightened suddenly, looking around the luxurious room. He *did* have something! Something potentially powerful.

If only he knew how to use it.

Laura Vosika

Loch Ness, Scotland

Shawn scrambled through the copse after the boy, stumbling and bumping into tree branches. The harp banged against his back with the sound of gunshots. Each twig and leaf underfoot exploded like a backfiring car. He couldn't imagine the men on the far side didn't hear them.

They burst around the back of the hill, onto the rocky beach, the same one he'd been on just yesterday with Amy. Then, it had been sunny and blue and calm. Now, thick clouds scuttled across the moon's glow, and black water shifted with eerie shadows beneath the swirling mist. A gust of wind lifted a wave, far off, and sent it smashing back to the loch's surface. He gave an involuntary shudder. He'd teased Amy about monsters lurking beneath the surface, and kelpies lying in wait to plunge unwary travelers to the watery depths. It wasn't funny now.

Thank goodness they were going by land!

He hitched up his monk's robes, and turned south, realizing, as he did, two equally unpleasant things: going south took them directly past the hill of the waiting enemies. The other, equally discomforting, was that they would not be going south. For the boy was, even now, gesturing madly for help as he tugged, from among the boulders and brush, an object with a rounded bottom, a wooden and leather wok, big enough for two: a leather currach to cross Loch Ness.

Inverness, Scotland, Present

Niall pulled Shawn's sackbut from its case. *Trombone,* he reminded himself. It was bulky compared to the Laird's sackbut. With some effort, he put it together, and blew, wondering what sort of man played such an instrument.

There was a pounding on the wall and a muffled, "Shawn... midnight...sleep!"

He considered his encounters with Celine, Amy, and Caroline, and couldn't imagine Shawn playing this at the side of the sick and dying.

He laid the instrument down on the bed and searched the case. He found a long, metal skewer. A weapon? Part of the instrument? He turned it over and around. He had no idea what it could be. He set it aside and picked two pieces of cloth out of the case. He shook them out. They looked rather dirty, and his best guesses could not give him any inkling of how they might help him save Scotland. He felt under the material that lined the case, and found a flat piece of parchment. He pulled it out and saw the image of a laughing man and a boy of twelve or thirteen years. He studied the faces. The man looked like Niall himself,

127

but with cropped hair. Was this Shawn?

Admitting defeat, he put the things back in the case, wrestling briefly with the trombone before fitting it in properly. He turned to the chest of drawers. It held clothes such as anyone in this era appeared to wear. Nothing to make him stand out or mark him as a man worthy of the attention showered on him. Nothing to explain why these women were such fools for him. What was it, then, Niall wondered, that gave Shawn the power he appeared to have over other people? He pondered the man's remark at dinner: Shawn brought them money.

Somehow, with his talent, Niall suspected, Shawn brought them all money, and that gave him his status. He dropped to the floor, his back against the bed, and wondered what Shawn was doing, trapped in the fourteenth century—if that's where he'd gone—with no money to buy influence. He thought about MacDonald. He held authority, not for bringing his people wealth, but for giving them security. He held his authority through the force of his character and the respect his people had for him.

But Shawn was not the laird. If there was such a person here, it would be Conrad, and even he seemed somewhat under Shawn's control.

Niall pushed himself up off the floor and moved to the huge bath chamber, with its granite tiled walls and smooth stone floor, its massive bathing tub with the raised back blossoming out in the shape of a shell. He poked around the things on the counter.

He picked up a bottle; turned it over, studying its elegant shape, its smooth feel, curious what it was made of. It wasn't glass. Printed letters spelled out J-H-I-R-M-A-C-K. He twisted the word in his mind, trying a few pronunciations out loud. It sounded French. He turned it around and found smaller words on the back. He squinted, reading slowly: *Wet hair. Apply shampoo.* Whatever *shampoo* might be.

After a brief moment of trial and error, he opened the top, and sniffed a pleasant scent. So Shawn smelled good. He replaced the top in disgust. This information would not help him save Scotland. He examined the huge, fluffy, white towels, and an equally fluffy, white robe hanging on the back of the door.

Going to Shawn's sleeved cloak, hanging near the door, he felt in the pockets and came out with a handful of items. Apart from the coins, he couldn't name them. There were several flat, hard cards. Niall flexed them back and forth. Black and white keys, like a virginal, adorned the front of one. A forest scene was painted on another. A third had a pattern of red and white stripes and small, white stars on blue. He fanned them out: more than half a dozen. A game of some sort? Each bore a raised inscription: SHAWN KLEINER and a long string of numbers. He ran his fingers over the letters, pleased that he'd recognized

Shawn's name.

A leather case contained a bound sheaf of parchment. Each bore the words *East Bank, Shawn Kleiner, pay to* and *memo.* He flipped through, identifying what must be Shawn's writing and numbers, all of them large, and, finally, Shawn's bold signature.

Tucked behind the bound sheaf were a small square of parchment with the words *garnet ring* and the number *1000*, and two more of the miniature paintings: the man from the other picture, and one showing what could only be Shawn and Amy, in more of those embarrassingly scanty clothes, smiling in the sun. It unnerved Niall to see his own image staring back at him, dressed in clothes he'd never worn, in a place he'd never been, his arm wrapped around a girl he'd never touched.

He understood, looking at the image, why they believed him to be that man. The likeness was uncanny. And yet—was that a cockiness in his expression that was much more MacDougall than Campbell? He looked to be a man of boisterous humor, and not entirely kind.

Niall wondered about Amy's part in his life. They'd spoken of betrothal. So he must have been courting her.

Niall sat back, flummoxed, against the headboard of the elegant bed. He'd done as the laird would do. He had more than the coins and dirk at his disposal. He had the inherited life of Shawn Kleiner: all his possessions, power and influence.

And he had no idea what to do with it.

Loch Ness, Scotland

"You're kidding," Shawn said flatly. He looked from the choppy waters to the flimsy boat. "You have *got* to be kidding." The boy cut him off with a violent shake of the head, pointing up the southern hill in stern warning.

A currach on this stormy sea! "Look at that wind," he hissed. As if on cue, a gust slammed into a tree, shaking its dark limbs viciously. "You'll kill us!" But the laird had said the boy was deaf and mute.

The boy gestured again, still tugging at the little boat. Shawn looked up the hill. The Laird had said trust no one except this boy. Foolish old man! This boy was bent on self-destruction!

Still, every high-pitched whistle of the wind sounded like an arrow zinging through the air. He found himself all but heaving the suicide-craft into the water himself, glancing back over his shoulder for arrows and miscreants.

The boy lifted his robes and splashed in, throwing a leg over the currach's low edge. Shawn followed, the chill waters soaking his sandals and sinking sharp teeth into his bones. He waded in further, gasping wide-eyed at the cold piercing his legs, and shoving the currach before him. He pushed away thoughts of Nessie's tail snaking unseen below the water to entwine his feet. When he could stand the cold no more, he clambered in, rocking the boat.

Wind whipped across the loch, shoving the small craft six feet from shore. The force tumbled Shawn into the rounded bottom of the boat, all knees and elbows, his face in the boy's lap. The leather shifted under his knees. Only that thin layer of hide stood between him and hundreds of feet of dark, drowning water. The bag slid over his head. A hand shoved him; he hauled himself up onto the bench, and settled the bag back behind him. Wind roared in his ears. Arrows, right now, didn't seem so bad. Maybe he could get the boy to go back to shore.

But the boy thrust a pair of shovel-like oars at him. "To dig my own grave?" Shawn muttered. Inky water slapped the currach's side. He closed his eyes, swallowing hard, and pulled his oars, matching the boy's tempo. Monsters and kelpies loomed in his mind. He thrashed at them manically with the crude oars. A wave crashed over the edge, dousing his knees with ice. He hoped the oilskin bag would protect his change of clothes.

The boy tugged his hood tightly around his face, battling the wind, and returned to his oars. Shawn threw his back into his own rowing, surprised at the boy's pace. As the boat jolted over choppy waters, the wind carried a man's voice to them. The moon silhouetted him at the edge of the trees, on the enemies' hill. They rowed faster, stroke upon stroke. The man pelted down the hill, swinging in his left hand a deadly crossbow.

"Faster, faster!" Shawn snapped at the boy. Their oars dipped at a frantic pace, but the wind pushed the wrong way now.

The man leapt onto the large boulder at the water's edge, swinging the bow up in a fluid movement.

"Faster!" Shawn screamed over the wind. A tremor shot through the silhouetted figure on the shore; he arched back, his arrow loosed. He pitched forward. Shawn gaped. He didn't see the boy whirl and grab his hair; rather, he found himself on his knees, huddled with the boy, their heads on the bench. He heard the whine of the arrow. A thud jolted his body.

Inverness, Scotland, Present

After kneeling in prayer, Niall climbed into bed. He couldn't help but enjoy a thorough scrubbing in a very hot bath, the soft robe, and the bed swathed in rich coverings. But guilt gnawed, an incessant rat, at the edges of the pleasure. He'd managed to do absolutely nothing about

Scotland's fate. He made a decision then and there: he needed help. The question was whom to ask.

Conrad clearly carried authority here. He would be the natural choice, if one could get past his perpetual bristling. Worse, Niall didn't know what help he needed. But a man in authority was always a good choice. He would ask Conrad.

He rolled over, sinking into the deep pillows. But once again, MacDonald's advice came to him: *Consider all your options.* He had, Niall remembered, all of Shawn's resources at his disposal, and Amy *had* warned him he'd be locked up if he claimed to have skipped across centuries. A man in authority could also be a danger. He sighed, wondering who else he might consider.

Rob? He lacked Conrad's authority, but appeared to be Shawn's friend.

Amy? The same could be said for her. She seemed to feel responsible for the situation, but as she wasn't, it was hardly sporting to hold that over her.

Celine. No. He had no wish to give her any wrong ideas. Besides, he'd convinced her all too well to slap him if he did anything she thought was out of line. He rubbed his cheek; he'd leave her alone. He doubted she could do much, anyway.

Dana? No, something about her made him nervous. A woman's hair ought not to look like a ruffled grouse. He wondered if an illness had forced her to cut it. But it was more than that, something he couldn't name.

Caroline. He shook his head in distaste. She'd be more than willing to give him anything he asked. He didn't care to get close enough to do so, or to be beholden to her in any way. There was a woman who would call in what she thought was owed her. He'd try elsewhere, anywhere, before Caroline.

He lay back in the pillows, disturbed to find he liked this luxury. Tomorrow, he'd talk to Conrad. He was a reasonable man, after all, under the blustering. He'd taken the shock of his trombonist playing harp in stride—relatively. Surely he would see the truth of Niall's story, and not lock him up. Yes, tomorrow morning, he would talk to Conrad.

If only he knew what to ask for!

He settled into the smooth blankets and soft pillow, confident that God would guide him as necessary on the morrow.

Loch Ness, Scotland

Shawn stayed, face down on the bench, hands over his head, waiting for the pain, feeling the water push below the currach's thin leather. He'd felt the jolt. It had to be buried in his back. He remembered hearing that in the worst injuries, the body shut down, prevented the sensation of pain. He was going to die! Just when things were getting good with Caroline. Damn Amy!

He felt the boy rise, and lifted his eyes. The hooded figure beckoned. How appropriate.

But the boy tugged at something. The bag, strapped on his back, gave a jerk, and the boy held the arrow out to him. He took it, eyes wide. The boy took up his oars and started rowing again. Shawn stared back to shore where the man had been. His dark shape now sprawled across the rock. An arrow stood straight up from his back, quivering.

Shawn lifted his eyes to the castle parapet. A man stood high atop the tower, dark against the silver moon glowing through gray clouds, his huge beard glinting silver and copper in the moonlight. He lifted a hand in farewell, still gripping a longbow that stretched to the sky.

* * *

The Laird emerged from the dungeons into a short, earthen tunnel. Only after pushing his helmet firmly in place did he dare feel his way to the other end of the passage, and push through the brush covering the secret entrance.

He crawled out as quietly as he could, covered in chain, into the open, by the rocky base of the castle's southern end. Clouds once again covered the moon. He peered across the water, but mist and darkness had swallowed the currach.

He sighed. He'd seen men behave strangely after blows to the head. It would pass, and maybe it was a blessing in disguise. The Niall he knew would have marched straight into the Great Glen, regardless of orders, confident—perhaps over-confident—in his ability to elude his enemies. Niall forgot that his enemy, this time, was someone who knew him well, and could predict exactly what he'd do.

He crossed himself, thanking God for Niall's unusual burst of compliance, and praying for their safety. But his praying days could be up within minutes, if the archer had not been alone. He studied the rock. Moonlight glinted off the arrow's shaft. If the assassin had come with others, venturing out sooner was dangerous. His accomplices would be watching. If he'd come alone, waiting too long brought the danger of the body being discovered.

He scanned the hills south and west. Nothing stirred. But the trees would hide plenty. He saw no motion along the castle walls. The dark, silent world belonged, it appeared, to himself and the dead man draped across the rock.

He edged along the wall, clutching his sword. At the edge, he hunched, and ran. Reaching the rock, he planted a foot on it, yanked the arrow from the body, and heaved the man onto his shoulder. The wind screamed, washing an icy wave over his boot, and shoving the clouds off the face of the moon. He stood exposed in the moonlight atop the rock, carrying a dead man and gripping the arrow that had killed him. Plenty of battles had taught him to keep a calm head. He used the burst of light to see who else it might have exposed.

He saw them, on the ridge, staring and gesturing north. With a prayer they had not seen their accomplice or Niall and Allene, with a desperate heavenward plea they would not see him, he crouched and ran. The body thumped, dead weight against his back. The warm, sticky smell of blood filled his nostrils. His legs ached from the unaccustomed weight. His ears strained for footsteps or the twang of a bowstring as he raced for the brush covering. Breathing hard, he threw the body down, and slid in feet first, yanking it after him. "Now fer some answers," he whispered. "Who aer ye?"

He rolled the man onto his back, and cautiously lifted a branch. He searched, first, for any sign of pursuit. Breathing a prayer of gratitude at seeing and hearing none, he pushed the branch further aside, letting moonlight spill on the face of a man who had hoped to go home to a warm bed with his wife; a face the Laird had known as a boy, playing on the shores of the loch with Niall and Allene; the face of a man grown to be a father, watching his own small son play on the shore; the face of a man who would betray his own people.

The Laird wiped roughly at damp eyes, and grabbed the shovel he'd brought. He dug a grave in the hidden tunnel, the warmest bed the man would have from now on. He stripped him of his valuable weapons, made the sign of the cross over him, and laid Lord Darnley's son, William, to rest, grieving.

* * *

No more men appeared on the shore. Shawn could only guess if this meant no one else had discovered their route, or if they were, even now, launching boats that would remain hidden until the moment they burst from the mist around them.

They stroked in accented, vivace tempo. The loch that had been a painter's dream yesterday now brewed angrily. Waves slashed over him. Wind sliced through his woolen robe. He imagined Nessie sliding beneath the waves, queen of her dark and deadly castle.

Stroke, pull, stroke, in presto time, searching through the swirling, gray mist for signs of pursuit. The howling wind might be men calling, arrows flying, Nessie bellowing, kelpies laughing. A chill shot down Shawn's spine and raced back up his arms.

He shivered, glanced at the boy with his hood pulled up tight. They were alone, in a howling morass of mist, wind and waves. "Me and the Grim Reaper," Shawn muttered. He wanted to shake the looming fear with a rowdy drinking song, but dared not. "There is no Nessie," he whispered, instead. It wasn't a spirit-raising beer song, but it was better than nothing.

He closed his eyes—stroke, pull, stroke, till his shoulders complained—and hoped they weren't going in circles. Better not to think about the hundreds of feet of water below. Something eased under his foot, beneath the very thin layer of leather. Something large.

"Go, go!" he hissed. He pulled his oars harder; the boy matched his speed.

The thing slid away under them. He peered into the mist, jumping at every swirling shape. There was no Nessie, he told himself, but still he wondered if prehistoric monsters ate people, or played with them mercilessly before drowning them.

A moan crawled down the long, narrow loch, echoing through the hills rising on either side of the water; a moan like a monster rising from the deep. He wondered how big the thing would look close up. His heart beat harder. Something slid under his foot again, and tugged, a heavy weight on his right oar. He yanked, fighting panic in his throat. He almost leapt to his feet to get away from whatever was underneath, but the boy turned and put a hand on his arm, his face shrouded.

"'Tis naught to fear," came a feminine whisper through the wind. "Lest you tip the boot yerself." The sweet voice carried all the comfort of his mother singing to him and rubbing his back, when he was very young.

An angel?

He didn't believe in angels, but the voice calmed him.

He settled in his seat, fighting his oar. It flew up out of the water. Seaweed, dark and ugly and dripping, clung to it. He heaved in a ragged breath of relief, and shook it off. The thing underneath—just a fish, he told himself. Rob had raved about the phenomenal fishing in Scotland.

He and the boy fell back into a fast rhythm, shivering under waves that broke over the currach's sides. Shawn's shoulders and back ached now, his eyes were dry and red with the whipping wind, his whole body chilled, and his ears strained, listening for danger.

An eternity passed in silence, except for the splash of their oars and the cries of the wind as it pushed the mist across the loch's surface. The moon came and went as clouds scuttled across its surface and fled again at the wind's brutal hands. The small currach nearly tipped twice, under the force of the waves. And Shawn fought back, the whole time, visions of pursuing men and underwater monsters. It had been just seaweed, he reminded himself. His perverse imagination insisted on replying that because there was seaweed didn't mean there *wasn't* a monster. "There's no Nessie," he reassured himself again.

The boat thumped against something solid and unyielding. His heart careened off the walls of his chest; the oars nearly slipped from his sweating, clammy hands. *There is a Nessie, and she's just stopped our boat.*

* * *

With cold water seeping through his robe, Shawn turned slowly. His heart thudded like war drums, waiting for Nessie's attack. The boy scrambled from the boat even as the looming shape registered in Shawn's mind: a boulder jutting from the wall of a large cove on the far shore. He closed his eyes, rolling them heavenward behind closed lids, and let his breath out. He clambered after the boy, helped drag the boat up the pebbly shore, under thick brush, then raced to keep up with his wordless flight up a wooded hill, the bag slamming against his back.

"Hey," he whispered harshly. He glanced over his shoulder at the receding shoreline, fearful of pursuers, and nearly got a tree branch in his eye when he turned back. He slapped it away. Depending more on sound than sight in the blackness, he chased the silent, dark wraith weaving through the forest ahead of him. Trees pressed close on either side. They shut out the worst of the wind.

And suddenly, the shore was lost from sight. Sweat broke out across his forehead. Without the loch, he had no way to find Inverness. In the morning, he reassured himself. He swallowed hard. In the morning, everything would look better. He'd see sign posts and cars. He'd get coffee; he'd get to the hotel for its four-acre buffet, and have one of everything, maybe two. His mouth watered; his stomach rumbled. They'd gather around. He'd tell his adventures, and raise holy hell with the police for letting psychos with arrows loose in the country, and it would be another story they told for years.

The boy stopped so abruptly that Shawn slammed into him. The bag banged against his back. The boy yanked at it, motioning for speed. A shaft of moonlight pierced the trees far above, giving just enough light to see the small clearing in which they'd stopped.

Shivering in the saturated robe, Shawn swung the bag down, tugging with half-frozen fingers at the leather drawstring. The knot fell loose and the bag opened, spilling out a pile of clothes, a cloak, leather boots, and plumed hat. He tore off the monk's robe. Thoughts of the men watching the castle gave him haste, as much as the chilly night air on his damp, bare skin. He fumbled into a billow-sleeved shirt and long, heavy tunic, grateful for their warmth.

"What do I do with these?" Shawn indicated the robe and sandals. The boy gestured at the oilskin bag. Pushing the robe inside, Shawn's fingers touched a wooden frame. He felt further, and found strings. He looked down at his tunic. The weak moonlight showed him only that it was pale on the left and dark on the right. It was enough.

"I'm a minstrel!" he said. "I'm supposed to play the harp?"

* * *

They alternated jogging with quick walking, up steep hills, stepping high over the heather, a charcoal-drawn landscape in endless shades of black and gray. With no sign of pursuit, Shawn's panic eased, and boredom set in. He turned his thoughts to the lovely Allene, back at Glenmirril. By the time the boy led him over a hard-won ridge, he and his fantasy Allene had explored every corner of the castle with their pent-up passion, and moved on to a grassy bank by a rocky stream.

He emerged from his daydreams to see the boy far ahead, a small blur in the night, far down the slope. Fearful of being lost in this wilderness, Shawn scrambled after him, down into a deep glen. Black hills rose sharply on either hand. The ache never left his side now; the harp never stopped banging his back. Each breath drew cool night air, burning, into his heaving lungs. The ache moved to his legs. The boy walked steadily, silently, showing no sign of discomfort.

With his fantasy repertoire exhausted, Shawn's mind turned to the harp. He didn't expect to be around for whatever occasion the Laird expected him to play. But it was something to do. He tried to remember anything from his affair with Celine. Mostly, he recalled her Godiva hair like silk against his skin, and her light floral scent that had teased him in his dreams for weeks.

A rocky stream emptied into the glen, a soft pewter chain burbling along beside them and flashing back specks of moonlight. He tried to judge their direction by the moon's position, and failed. But the walking became easier, and Shawn decided to kill both problems: his boredom with the never-ending walk, and his inability to *really* play harp.

He started with *Blue Bells*. It was an old folk song, just the sort of thing these people would expect to hear. He imagined each note, transferred one by one, from his trombone music onto the harp strings in his mind. He played it back, seeing the strings, working out the fingerings. Celine had said never use little fingers. He chuckled. She'd blushed a pink Chablis at his bawdy comeback to that. But fine, he wouldn't use his pinkies. He played it again and again in his mind, a largo accompaniment to the stream's vivace bubbling. By the time the glen widened and the stream poured itself into a new loch, he was playing at a decent tempo, and even starting on the dancing, skipping triplet section.

The moon rose higher. They left the loch behind, veering into a wood. Birches rose like ghostly sentinels among the sparse scattering of firs. Anything for a latte, he thought. Or a beer. He wondered what food the provisions included. Probably not the McDonald's double cheeseburger with everything on it, fries on the side, and large chocolate shake he craved. The boy marched, unflagging, through the trees.

Shawn straggled behind, clutching now and again at his side. He stopped briefly, hands on knees. The boy gestured angrily. He shut his eyes, resting a minute beside a cluster of pines, despite the boy's annoyance, before heaving himself back to his midnight jog.

If he collapsed from a heart attack, he wondered, would the orchestra ever find him, lying among the wood's thick carpet of ferns. He entertained self pity for awhile, imagining the headlines. *Young Talent Lost Forever*. Amy would be broken-hearted. *Great Life Tragically Cut Short*. The moon crested at the height of the skies. *Musical Prodigy Dies in Highlands. World Grieves*. He pictured Caroline at his funeral in a black veil and that tight black dress of hers. Very nice! He smiled, enjoying his fantasy funeral. They left the wood for another bare slope and continued walking and jogging, climbing the rough hill, walking and jogging, in their endless cycle.

Bored now with the world-rocking news flashes, he began *Castle of Dromore*, once again transferring trombone positions to harp strings, steadily increasing the tempo. He chose chords, imagining his fingers on the strings. He was only mildly curious when the Laird expected him to play harp in the wilderness. Regardless, however, tomorrow, he was going to Inverness.

They stopped briefly at a river. Leaving the harp on the bank, he fell to his knees, scraping his knuckles on the rocks at the bottom as he scooped up great handfuls of cold water. Far too soon, the boy tugged his sleeve. With a groan, he clambered up and began once again to follow him.

As the moon sank to the west, they eased down another hill and he started on *Gilliekrankie*. As he finished working out an accompaniment, more trees appeared ahead. He sighed. Still no sign of a resting place. His legs threatened to mutiny. His back was no doubt permanently bruised from the harp. And the stitch in his side was a constant piercing now. He didn't have the energy to vent his anger at a boy who couldn't hear anyway. Another hundred yards, and they approached a town, nestled in a hollow high in the mountains. Hadn't the men decided towns weren't safe?

They trudged down this place's version of a main street: a dirt road with a few tiny thatched-roof cottages. Across a field, a cow lowed. A rooster crowed in the distance. Rich velvet blue now streaked the sky's eastern rim, above the mountains, where it had been black. The far end of town reached them quickly, and they passed through, to a dirt track rising once more into dusky hills. Shawn hovered between relief and disappointment. His legs screamed for rest.

With the western sky now midnight blue and the eastern horizon gray, the town shrank behind them, receding into its glen. Bright pink tinged the east by the time they paused atop the next pass. Far below, in a park-like clearing, surrounded by lawns and orchards, sprawled a rambling stone structure with a tower.

It wasn't a castle; it had no moat. Sheep dotted the glen. A bell tolled in solemn, deep tones. The boy led him, scrambling, down the last slope, through the orchards with small green apples, right up to the stone structure. He pounded on the door, a wooden affair studded with leather and brass like that of Shawn's own castle-hotel.

In Shawn's exhaustion, thoughts raced through his head: the boy was the traitor, leading him to his death. This could be the home of the infamous MacDougalls! But, having little choice, he followed.

The boy pounded the door again. After a long wait, in which Shawn peered over his shoulder, it creaked opened. From behind it, a monk in a brown robe appeared. The boy lifted the edges of his hood, showing his face to the monk, who bowed low and stood back.

Shawn and the boy passed through the towering doors, into a cold stone hallway. The boy kept going, as though familiar with the place and disappeared through a door on the left.

The monk took Shawn's sleeve and encouraged him forward. As they passed the room, Shawn saw the boy kneeling at an altar.

"Come, eat," the monk said, and Shawn followed him gratefully, forgetting everything else.

Chapter Nine

Inverness, Scotland, Present

The day's first sun filtered through lace curtains and skimmed past rich blue hangings. Blinking in the light, Niall pushed himself up out of the massive four poster, more comfortable than any king had ever enjoyed, throwing back covers softer than any queen had ever luxuriated under.

He missed his furs.

He missed, in the insular silence of the cavernous suite, the sounds and smells of the castle waking. He wanted to go to the great hall, so different from last night's *dining room*, and break his fast with the laugh of the scullery maids and sweet-smelling rushes under his feet and shaggy hunting hounds begging with large, doleful eyes for scraps, and Allene at table with her father, throwing him stolen glances. He sighed, and stretched himself out of bed. He settled the large, fluffy robe into place, yanking the belt tight.

With a wondering look around the room's wealth of frescoes, paintings, and fine woodwork, Niall knelt by the bed, under his imagined crucifix, and crossed himself. He guessed the Laird had decided to send him across the loch, down to the monastery. He shook his head. The Great Glen was much the more sensible route, knowing, as Niall did, every towering tree, every leafy trail, every cascading stream and waterfall, and, most importantly, every possible hiding place. Once he reached it, the English would never find him. He and Iohn had learned it far too well from Darnley.

Niall sighed, wondering how God could have allowed things to go so terribly wrong. Even if Shawn had been left in his place in the castle, he could never find his way through the Glen. Who would go for Hugh? Something niggled at the back of his brain, something he should remember.

He pushed it aside and pulled his wandering thoughts back to his prayers. *In the name of our Lord Jesus Christ crucified, I arise. May He bless, govern, and preserve me, and bring me to everlasting life.* He made acts of adoration and thanksgiving. He said a *Pater*, an *Ave*, and the *Credo*. The words took on newer and deeper meaning in this inexplicable turn of events, which he couldn't handle on his own.

A knock sounded on the door of the suite. He looked up in irritation—nobody interrupted his morning prayers!—before realizing his new reality: these people wouldn't know that. Still, the Laird had taught him to put God first. If one did not walk out on a king, how much less so on God. He bent his head again, fingertips meeting between his eyebrows. "My Lord, God in Heaven," he said, "I pray thee watch over me and grant me wisdom. I've always understood everything, and now I don't."

The knock sounded again. Niall looked up. Who would be knocking at Shawn's door? Conrad, maybe? Perhaps God had sent the very man who could help him.

He jumped to his feet. The door burst in, propelled by a heady scent and closely followed by the bosom-laden woman, Caroline. Corn silk hair floated around cheeks like blush rose petals. Her royal blue shirt brought out the startling hue of her eyes, and the delicate pink of her lips. Kicking the door closed behind her, she launched herself at Niall, hugging him with vigor.

"I'm sorry about last night," she cooed. Her breath on his ear jolted him. Her finger ran down his chest, where the robe gaped. Images burst in his brain, delightful and alarming. He pushed her and the images away in shock, and yanked the robe together.

"As am I," he said, striving for diplomacy. "I meant you no embarrassment." The floral scent floated off her, filling his senses. He gestured toward the door. "I'm in the midst...."

"You said you didn't want Amy hurt. I understand." She thrust herself forward, bosom first. "But Amy's not here, and *you're* hurt." Her hand shot up to his temple, pushing the hair aside and touching the deep purple bruise. Another tingle shot through him. He pushed her hand away. "Let me take your mind off it." Her eyes slid coyly in the direction of the bedroom, her lips curved in a bewitching smile.

Niall took a deep, steadying breath. Could a woman really be so blatantly offering things any man dreamed of? She was. And she was beautiful.

Beautiful like the Barns of Ayr. The English had promised a council of peace there, and instead threw a rope around each Scotsman's neck, as he entered, till three hundred of Scotland's finest twisted, like ribbons dangling in a tree, from the rafters. He rubbed his throat. He couldn't look Allene in the eye again if he betrayed her trust. "I'm sorry," he said, turning her toward the door. "I don't remember you." He twisted the gold door knob.

"I could help you remember." Her voice caressed him like a

summer breeze. *The Barns of Ayr*, he warned himself, swallowing.

"No, thank you," he said. He pushed her out the door, closing it firmly behind her.

* * *

Back on his knees, beside Shawn's bed, Niall forced his mind from the encounter with Caroline, to his prayers. "I lean on Thee, Lord God, for the wisdom I lack. I pray Thee provide for my people, now I've failed them. Guide me in all I do today, help me to do Your will, and get back to Hugh."

He sighed. Only God could possibly know what he needed, or how to get back where he belonged. Rising, he crossed to the window in the sitting room, pulling back the lace. Outside, morning sun skimmed across the manicured lawn, stretching away to a grove of trees, and a brick wall with a wrought iron gate surrounding the gardens. He reviewed the possibilities once more, but there was no escaping the awful truth. He was seven hundred years outside his own time. He dropped onto the periwinkle cushion in the window seat; his forehead fallen on clenched hands, incapable of even forming a prayer. *Thy will be done,* he whispered. *Though I confess I do not like Thy will over much right now.* He crossed himself, and lapsed into silence, listening for God's voice.

After a half hour, he rose, more unsure than he'd ever been in his life, of what the day would bring. He went back to the wardrobe in the bedroom. He'd barely finished dressing, struggling with the tiny buttons, when a knock sounded on his door. He fastened the last button and called, "Enter," hoping it would not be Caroline again.

Amy came in, her heavy, black hair falling free to her waist today. She wore a more modest shirt, and a swirling skirt, below her knees, although still showing far more, even, than her ankles. "How are you feeling?" She looked his clothes up and down. He wondered what he'd done wrong.

He bowed to her, relieved she had stopped blushing at proper courtesy. Obviously, Shawn had not been genteel. He rather thought Shawn a fool, as well, failing to appreciate what he had in Amy. "I am well," he told her. "Your doctors have wonderful medicines." The festering of the MacDougall's arrow was healing much more quickly than such a wound normally would.

She nodded, pausing as if framing words, and then said, "You might want to put on something more casual."

"Casual?" He did not understand the word

"You don't need to wear a dress shirt to breakfast or rehearsals. Especially with jeans." Her mouth twitched. He suspected she was laughing at him. "Here, try this." She led him across the sitting room to his bedroom, opened a drawer in the chest, pulled out a black woven shirt, and tossed it to him. The gesture reminded him of something Allene would do. "Why don't you change?"

He did so as quickly as he could, trying to hide his discomfort with working the small, unfamiliar buttons. He glanced up guiltily, and saw, though she said nothing, that he hadn't fooled her. He turned his back to peel off the dress shirt.

"Got shy all of a sudden?" Amy asked.

He didn't answer. The shirt fell away, and she gasped. He spun back quickly, startled.

"What happened to your back?" Her hand covered her mouth.

"My back?" The scars from the whipping were a distant memory to him.

"You didn't have scars on your back."

"No, I didn't," he agreed. "It was...." His choices flashed through his mind like lightning. How important was it for these people to believe he was Shawn? He had Shawn's life and power at his disposal to cope in this world and get back to his own. Would he be locked away as a fraud, or mad, if he now claimed not to be Shawn? "It was running through the trees. They scratched my back...they...I was in the woods."

"What were you doing in the woods?"

He spoke as the future laird he was. "Whatever happened in the castle, I dinna ken."

"You dinna ken? You mean you don't know?"

"Aye." He chastised himself for forgetting the proper words. "Yes. I was in the woods seeking help." He stared her in the eye firmly before yanking the new shirt over his head. "Now, I need to see Conrad."

"But those scars are...." Amy started.

"It's fine. Do you ken...do you *know*...where Conrad is?"

"But how could trees...?"

"I'm fine," Niall snapped. "I do not wish to discuss it. Do you know where Conrad is?"

Amy rolled her eyes. "Same old Shawn. You'll have a hard time finding him this morning. He might be with Peter doing arrangements for those new pieces you offered to do. Maybe down at breakfast, but not for long. Anyway...it's good to see you feeling better. I guess. People are really worried about you. Rehearsal starts right after breakfast."

Niall studied her. She was bonnie, with her long black hair, fine creamy skin, and large eyes of midnight blue fringed with heavy, dark lashes. Clearly, she and Shawn had been close. And yet, not betrothed. This Caroline, now, with her obvious expectation of a hasty roll in the hay: he wondered that a woman apparently of good breeding by her

142

looks, dress, and speech, should exhibit such common, scaffy behavior. The castle's blind beggar could see what relationship *she* had had with Shawn.

But Amy seemed to actually care for him, whoever he might have been. Goodness knows why. It was obvious Shawn had been involved with others. And it could be seen from Amy's own behavior that she was unused to proper treatment from Shawn. A real lout, he must be. A churlish oaf who unwittingly charmed a few, earned money for the rest, and thus mistakenly thought himself a man of stature. Yet here was Amy by his side, asking nothing of him.

"You ready?" she asked. "I guess you don't need your trombone if you're playing harp."

"I guess not." He pulled the door shut behind him, barely thinking of the coming rehearsal, and hopeful of finding Conrad soon.

* * *

Conrad was, in fact, everywhere and nowhere, impossible to pin down.

Niall found himself pulled along to breakfast by Rob and a shorter man, who came down the gilded hall as he and Amy left the room. "Forget Conrad. He's busy!" said Rob. He turned to Amy, taking her elbow. "What were you doing in his room, Amy?"

"He needed help," she said.

"Not from you."

"Nothing you need from Conrad right now, is there?" asked the shorter man. "You'll see him at rehearsal."

"He's got a lot of adjusting to do to the program for you." Rob's voice was as chilly as the loch in spring.

Niall's effort to turn and follow a glimpse of Conrad down a hall was thwarted, as Conrad disappeared around a corner, and Rob yanked him on. "Plenty of time later! Let's eat!"

Niall found himself swept down the wide red-carpeted stairs and back to the huge *dining room*, dragged into the growing line at a table flowing in white cloths and laden with food. Someone pushed a plate into his hand. He was so surprised at the expectation that he serve himself, that he didn't see Conrad at first. When he did, he started toward him. Rob yanked him back. "Utensils, Shawn!" he barked. Niall stared blankly at him.

"Unless your new persona includes eating with fingers," said the other man, dumping a pile of metal objects on his plate. Niall jumped at the clatter. Several others laughed. He swung his head to where Conrad had been. Conrad was gone.

"Come on, Shawn, you're holding up the line! We know you move faster than that!" someone yelled from behind. A group of men laughed. Across the buffet, Caroline grinned at them. Niall looked fruitlessly around the room again, before giving up and moving forward. He heaped his plate with the table's abundance, not recognizing half of it, and moved with the flow toward a white-clothed table full of men, all jostling and laughing and asking questions at once as he seated himself.

"They say you got yourself shot with an arrow!" one said.

"A little chilly in that castle overnight?"

"A little chilly between him and Amy, more to the point." They laughed and nudged each other.

"When did you learn to play the harp? That's not what you were really doing with Celine last month."

"And when," interrupted Rob loudly, "did you start eating garnishes?" He poked his fork at something green and leafy on Niall's plate.

Conrad appeared suddenly at Niall's elbow. "*Blue Bells* as the finale. The solo in the middle...."

"Conrad, I must...."

"Megan will sing with you on *Sheebeg Sheemore* and the other one, the one about the traitor."

"I need to...."

"Got all that? We'll talk at rehearsal." And Conrad plowed away through the tables. Niall jumped up to follow him, his eyes chasing him frantically through the crowded room. His chance to reach Hugh was slipping away. He took a step, and came up short, Caroline blocking his way with a red-nailed hand on his chest.

"You never mentioned the harp," she purred. Niall stepped to the left. Caroline stepped with him. Niall stepped to the right. "When you were showing me all the other things you can do," she said, and stepped with him.

The men hooted.

Niall looked across the room. Conrad had disappeared again. Amy, at the buffet, was watching. He sank back in his chair, Caroline's hand still on his chest. "Not now," he snapped.

She pulled her hand away. "Later," she whispered, and blew him a kiss. "When you're feeling more yourself."

* * *

Tension crackled over the table through the meal. Dana threw morose looks at him and whispered occasionally to Amy, who whispered back and cast him furtive worried glances. Rob spoke stiffly to Niall only when necessary, and continually tried to catch Amy's eye. Niall did not understand Rob's antagonism. He had seemed, at first, to be Shawn's friend.

Niall crossed himself and bowed his head over folded hands, giving thanks. He heard a whisper or two. Finishing, he looked up to see people staring. Caroline, at the next table, frowned, feathery eyebrows dipping close over cornflower eyes.

"When did you start praying?" Dana asked.

"Nice touch," Rob muttered. "Saint Shawn. He's playing you, Amy. I told you he would. Don't believe him till you get that ring back."

Niall turned to Amy for some understanding of the hostility. Amy stared back with something less than kindness, and said nothing. The silence grew awkward, as the four of them glanced at each other uncomfortably over their meals.

Rob followed Amy to the buffet when she rose for seconds, and Niall noted the way he leaned in close, his hand on her back, whispering intently, and throwing hard stares back at Niall. She shook her head vehemently, and moved away from him, her lips clamped, her eyes dark.

* * *

After breakfast, Niall followed her out of the dining hall, torn between relief at the meal being over and annoyance over the time the rehearsal would consume. The musicians trailed out to a gigantic silver beast, and climbed, laughing and talking, into the maw on the side of its head. "Go on, Shawn," said the man behind him, when he stopped. "Never seen a bus before?"

"Leave him alone. It's the head injury," said Dana.

The others seemed unconcerned about diving inside the beast. So Niall followed, forcing down the quivering of his stomach. The inside of the giant was lined with cushioned benches. Niall took the first one he came to, and sat, planning his day. He'd talk with Conrad. Amy seemed distressed at the thought of skipping centuries. But maybe, being a leader, Conrad knew things she didn't. Maybe, when he explained, Conrad would have a quick and easy answer, maybe even a tool or weapon to help him save the Scots at Stirling.

Amy and Rob squeezed through the narrow aisle. She met his eyes only briefly, and followed Rob.

As the bus rumbled to life, Niall closed his eyes against the ill feeling in his stomach. It was just a giant *car*, he realized. Nothing to worry about. He opened his eyes to see his own face grinning at him, from one of the paintings that festooned half the buildings of Inverness. *Shawn Kleiner* he read; *the best of Scotland!* Shawn gamboled in a meadow of heather, wearing his tartan. He held the sackbut to his mouth. His eyebrows lifted high; his eyes opened wide in delight and angled toward a buxom auburn beauty dressed in a similar tartan and playing bagpipes. She appeared to have something quite different from music on her mind, Niall thought. He lifted his eyes to heaven and closed them again. He didn't want to see any more of this ridiculous bampot of a man.

* * *

In the great hall, Amy pulled an instrument from a black case. It must be this century's version of a lute, Niall thought, noting the strings running up the long neck. But she tucked it under her chin, rather than holding it before her, and drew sound from it with a bow, rather than by plucking. She seated herself just back of Celine's great harp.

Conrad proved equally difficult to pin down at the rehearsal. He was, Niall thought, the king of his castle, in command, and everywhere at once, issuing orders, making adjustments and giving snap decisions like Wallace in his glory at the Battle of Stirling Bridge. Niall was rebuffed with, "In a minute, Shawn," and, "Not now," and, "Go warm up."

"I need but a moment. It's important."

"Just play what you did yesterday," Conrad told him, "and you'll be an even bigger sensation than before." He thundered toward the sackbuts—trombones, Niall corrected himself—not looking back.

Niall heaved a breath. He gazed around the gathering crowd, all with instruments, curious how so many planned to play together. He'd never seen more than a handful play at one time. He seated himself at the harp, at the front of the orchestra. He wondered anew at its magnificence and size, hardly noticing Conrad storming the podium at the front and rapping his stick on his stand. Niall touched the strings, ran his fingers through a rich, rolling chord—the power of which, his own small clairsach could never match—and began *Blue Bells of Scotland*.

"No, no, no, no!" Conrad shouted. Niall's head shot up. "What are you doing? I haven't given the downbeat!"

"My apologies." Niall inclined his head respectfully. Snickers rose from the middle of the orchestra. Niall turned, seeking the perpetrator. People busied themselves with their instruments, fiddling with keys and bows. Nobody met his eyes. He leaned his chair back on two legs, his head close to Amy's, and whispered, "What is a *downbeat*?" The elderly man in front of her gave a loud snort.

"When his arm comes down," Amy whispered back. "Although you hardly deserve more help from me."

He dropped his chair back on four legs, placed his hands, and watched Conrad, noticing now how the other musicians did the same, their instruments poised, still as statues. So that was how it was done! He watched Conrad. For a second, two seconds, three, his arms hung motionless. His eyes scanned the musicians. Then, suddenly, one hand swept to the side and up, and...SLASH!...*down!* Niall struck his chord, exactly as he'd done for Conrad yesterday, exactly as he'd done hundreds of times for the Laird.

"*You're late!*" Conrad roared.

"*Right* as he comes down," Amy whispered in his ear.

Across stage, from among the upright lutes, he heard a whisper. "...channeling his inner hack today!" When he looked, the players busied themselves inspecting their instruments and music.

Conrad raised his arms, and they tried again.

"And again, if you'd like to join us this time, Shawn," Conrad said.

The first small snicker grew to several. Niall remained silent, focused on doing what he must, to get back to Hugh. He considered, around the sixth try, getting up and walking out.

"Early, too early," Conrad barked.

He could follow the River Ness and the loch back to the castle, Niall thought. At the seventh try, he considered that it was a day's walk, and he had no idea how to make the switch happen again.

"Late again!"

On the eighth try, his fingers on automatic pilot, his eyes aching from watching Conrad, he feared he'd be locked up, or *fired*, if he walked out, with no explanation rational to these people. That would end all hope of reaching Hugh.

"He's got Van Gogh's ear for music!"

The ugly comment came from the brass section, hitting Niall as surely and squarely as spittle. The tone was clear, even if the words weren't.

He wished he'd demanded to be taken back to the castle. *This can't be what You want from me*, he berated God. He gritted his teeth and tried again.

At last, Conrad dropped his baton, his hand plastered against his forehead as he shook his head. "You start," he said to Niall. "Give me two chords. I'll bring them in on the third."

After two false starts, it worked. The music began to fall into place, and the snickers died down.

Niall breathed a sigh of relief at the end of two very long hours. Even riding home with the MacDougall's arrow in his posterior had not been so excruciating. And yet—the music had been beautiful. He smiled. He understood that on one level, he'd failed; Conrad had accommodated him. He didn't care. The beauty of the music breathed hope into him.

He shook the few hands proffered after the rehearsal, searching out Conrad over their heads; he nodded and smiled at the many exclamations of amazement—and noted those who gave him sour looks.

The young man with the black hair, the one who had watched Celine, approached him as the others dispersed. He held out his hand. "Do you remember me? Aaron."

Niall shook the proffered hand.

"You know I never liked you," Aaron said.

"I imagine not," Niall replied. He'd never even met Shawn, and didn't much care for him, either.

"I don't know what happened to you out there, but I always let bygones be bygones. Thank you."

Niall bowed his head, just a bit, over their clasped hands. Their hands dropped, and with a grave nod, Aaron took himself off after Celine.

Niall scanned the rehearsal hall. Conrad was gone. Niall sighed, and left the stage. He sought out Amy, and found her in the back room, a cavernous and dim place almost worthy of the name dungeon. She and Dana spoke together while Dana polished an instrument like a giant golden snail. Amy held in her hand the lute-like instrument he'd heard singing so sweetly behind him for the past two hours. She stared at him with barely veiled suspicion. Dana glanced at him and walked away.

"What a beautiful instrument." He reached out a hand. "May I?"

She looked at him doubtfully, but passed it over. He took a moment to see in his mind's eye how she'd held it, before tucking it under his chin. The corner of Amy's mouth quirked up, but she fought it down. "The other way," she said. "On the left side."

"Ah." As Niall shifted the instrument to his left shoulder, Rob entered the gloomy backstage, polishing his trumpet with a yellow cloth. Niall drew the bow across the strings. The thing screeched; he shuddered and lifted the bow. "Amazing," he said. "You get such a lovely sound out of it."

"Praying *and* giving kudos." Rob perched on the table. "My, you have turned over a new leaf." He laid his instrument in its case. The words were not entirely sensible to Niall. What leaves? He'd turned over nothing. But the strutting of an angry cock was strikingly similar in any time and place.

Niall glanced at him, looked back to Amy, still smiling faintly at the compliment, and thought about his difficulty tracking down Conrad. He made his decision instantly, pulled her aside, and leaned close. With or without Rob's noxious presence, he must ask her. "I need your help."

A curtain dropped over her eyes. She stiffened and pulled away.

"I told you so," Rob said. Niall gave Rob a hard stare, and edged Amy another inch from him.

"'Tis...not...it is not what you think," Niall said, softly. His insides shimmered with waves of irritation at Rob, like mist curling up from the loch just before a storm.

"Try again." Amy yanked her arm from his grip. "I helped you enough out there. No more help until I get my ring back." She stared at him steadily.

He closed his eyes. Another obstacle to getting back to Hugh. "What ring?" he asked, slowly. It had been mentioned at breakfast, too. He could feel Rob's eyes boring holes in his back.

"What ring," scoffed Rob.

Niall clenched his teeth, holding his temper.

Amy glanced around the now-empty room, before hissing, "My grandmother's ring! The one you all but stole from me!"

"He gambled away his trombone," Rob reminded her. "He needed the money to buy it back."

Niall pressed his hand to his eyes. Gambling, he understood. What a fool Shawn was! Amy set her lute in its case and snapped it shut forcefully. She turned on Rob. "You have a lot of nerve playing the cowboy in the white hat now, Rob. *You* helped him convince me. And you haven't exactly raced to get it yourself, have you?"

Rob flushed pink, and then red, right up to the roots of his Viking white hair. His lip twitched upward, like a mad wolf Niall had once seen. But his jaw jutted forward. He tore his eyes from Niall and looked back to Amy. "He's playing you, Amy."

She turned back to Niall, just pulling his hand from his face. "You should be embarrassed. I'm sorry you got hurt, but I don't care how bad your memory is all of a sudden, *I* haven't forgotten my grandmother's ring, and I'm not helping you with anything else till you get it back! It was helping you in the first place that cost me my ring! And for a lie on top of it! Gambling away your trombone! How stupid can you get!"

Niall sucked in his breath. Heat climbed up his face. Damn Shawn, the chanty wrassler! Useless and dishonest to the core, by all he'd learned of the man. He'd be darned if he'd help the baw juggler! And the man was most likely there in Glenmirril with his Allene, no doubt sitting by idly while death stalked her and all those he loved. The thought gave him pause.

Rob hoisted himself off the table and strode toward them. "Let's go, Amy." He threw his arm over her shoulder. "I'll get your ring."

"I'll get the ring," Niall snapped. His eyes bored into Rob's. They both tensed. Amy shrugged Rob's arm off her shoulder.

Rob stepped toward Niall. "I *said*, I'll get the ring."

"*I'll* get it." Niall stepped forward himself. He didn't know why he was demanding to fight the baw juggler's battles, but he couldn't seem to let go.

"I want to see Shawn keep a promise," Amy said.

A muscle twitched in Rob's jaw.

"Let's go, Shawn." Amy turned on her heel and marched out, leaving the two men to stare each other down.

"Setting her up to hurt her again?" Rob sneered.

Niall studied him closely, and saw, not anger, but pain, in his eyes. "I wouldna hurt her," Niall said. "I hope you wouldna, either."

Inverness, Scotland, Present

Out on the sidewalk, her lute having been locked in the green room, Amy walked quickly, not looking at Niall. Her skirt swirled around her ankles. "When I get the ring," he finally said, "you'll help me?"

"Within reason," Amy said. "Don't make the mistake of thinking that I trust you now, just because I feel guilty and you made a promise. I'll believe it when the ring is on my finger. You have your cash card?"

He patted the unfamiliar pockets of Shawn's jeans and jacket and pulled out Shawn's leather wallet. He flipped it open, revealing the cards he'd found last night. He stared at them helplessly.

"What? You don't remember which one is your cash card?" Amy took the billfold, rifled through the cards to a plain blue one, and handed it to him. "Do you remember the pin number or is that conveniently forgotten, too?" She stomped up to a wall—a brick wall sporting another of those paintings of Shawn. This time, he lolled in a bed of bluebells in his tartan wrap. The sackbut lay across his chest. His head rested in a young woman's lap, and she smiled down at him adoringly.

Amy followed his gaze to the painting. She rolled her eyes. "The money," she said. Niall saw now that set into the wall was a metal plate, and a glassy screen, like the moving-picture box in his room, set into that. Below the screen were numbered squares.

"I get money from here?" he asked. It seemed to be her intent, yet it was impossible! He was aware he was giving himself away with every word, but unable to stop.

"Our paychecks were deposited at midnight."

He shook his head; her words were gibberish. *Paychecks? Deposited?* But it seemed to be a yes of some sort. He lifted the shiny, blue card and stared from it to her. "What do I do?"

"Here, in the slot," she said. "I didn't know amnesia made people forget even the basics." He tried, and she said, "No, the other way." He turned the black strip upwards. "No," she said again. "Not that other way, the *other*, other way. Like this." She took the card and turned it. "See the picture?" She pointed at the machine. The machine sucked the card in, and Niall sucked back a gasp. "Okay, so you don't know the pin number," she said. "You were always pretty predictable. Probably something like a birth date. Let's try yours." She punched the numbered squares. The machine beeped back angrily. "Okay, not that. What else? Mine? No, you probably don't even know it. Your mother's birthday? What is it?"

"I don't know," Niall confessed.

"The model number on your trombone? Caroline's bra size?" She sighed. "Okay, your dad's birthday. You don't remember that, either? Let's try the obvious ones, then. A sequence." She stabbed at the buttons again. The machine beeped again. "You're not playing me?" She turned to him. Her eyes glistened with frustration. "You're not just pretending you don't remember? It was my grandmother's ring."

"Och, Amy," he said, forgetting to imitate their speech, "I wouldna do that to ye. How else can I get the ring?" It hurt to have someone think so poorly of him. He wondered that Shawn could go through life that way.

"I only get two tries before it takes the card." She hit another button angrily, and the card slid from the machine. "Do you have your checkbook?" she snapped, swiping at her eye. "Pawn shops don't usually take checks, but maybe you can convince them. You're good at that," she added dryly. She snatched the card, pocketing it herself, and set off briskly down the road. "Let me know when you need money. You can tell me the number then, and I'll get it for you."

He hurried after her, into a seedy narrow street, feeling in the pocket of Shawn's jacket for the sheaf of bound papers. "This?" he asked. "Is this the checkbook?" He had no idea how it might be used for money, and offered a silent *Ave* that he might figure it out when the time came. A wind shot down the close, billowing trash around his ankles.

She nodded. "That's it. Here's the pawn shop."

They stopped at one of many shops in the long brick building. Niall studied it, finding no sign of the Inverness he had known. It had big windows of glass, through which could be seen every sort of object known to man. A bell tinkled as they stepped through the door. It felt like stepping back into his own time. The thought made him disconcertingly aware that he'd come to accept as normal, the inconceivable thought that he *wasn't* in his own time.

It was a small, crowded shop, dark and stuffy and smelling of its own ancient goods, which filled every inch of space: counter tops, shelves, and walls. Red velvet hung at doorways and peered out from what infinitesimal bits of counter top showed between the jostling crowd of pawned goods.

A paunchy, old man pushed out between thick, red curtains. Amy looked at Niall expectantly. "We're here for the ring that he, that I left," he said. "How much to get it back?"

"Dae ye haeve yer ticket?" the man asked.

Ticket...ticket.... Niall remembered the stub he'd seen last night, and pulled it out of his—*Shawn's*—billfold. He had a moment's panic, digging through the bits of paper, before he recognized it.

The man fingered it. "A thousand pow-unds. I remember ye."

"You got a *thousand pounds* for my ring!" Amy exploded. "That's not what you told me!"

"I'm sorry," Niall muttered. *Chanty wrassler!* he cursed Shawn again. "I'll make it up to you." He placed Shawn's checkbook on the counter. As he did, he realized Shawn would say, and not mean, the exact same words. It upset him.

"Nae checks," said the man.

"You remember me," returned Niall, disgusted at pretending to be Shawn. "You know who I am." He pulled himself to his full six feet. He was a future laird, and Shawn—despite his personal misdemeanors—appeared to be a man to be reckoned with in his own right. He called on them both for a solution.

"Nae checks." The man set his jaw stubbornly.

"I'll pay you more than you require," Niall said. "But I need the lady's ring."

The man placed his hands firmly on the counter, pushing his bulbous nose close to Niall's. His mustache bristled. "Payin' extra dooz me nae guid if the check doesna clear!"

"But you know who he is," Amy insisted. "Shawn, show him your ID. This is Shawn Kleiner, the headliner with the American orchestra. His picture is all over Inverness."

"You know where to find us," Niall added. "We're at the castle down the road apiece."

"We'll be in Inverness for another week," Amy added. "Call the director and confirm it with him.

"I dinna ahk-cept checks," the man repeated.

Niall saw, not the counters or goods or a man who had possibly been cheated in the past, but another obstacle between himself and Hugh and the safety of those he loved. He looked around, remembering Amy's explanation of pawn shops. He had arrived in this time with nothing of value to trade. Still, he searched the shop, hoping for inspiration. Peering closely in the display case, the details of the jumble of items came to him: an old dagger; a heavy, gold necklace; delicate chains hung with jewels; countless gold and silver coins, some quite worn; a flower bed of rings, sparkling in more colors than the castle gardens.

"Aer ye interested in antiques?" the man asked, following his gaze.

"Aye." Niall pointed to the dagger. "It looks to ha' been a fine piece. Tell me about it."

"Shawn, who cares about some old knife?" Amy whispered. "I want my ring back."

He waved her off, ignoring the irritation that roiled off her like steam.

"'Tis over three hoondred years old." The man pulled the dirk up to the counter top. "It belonged to Clan Morrison in their heyday. See the jewels in the handle?" He regaled them with tales of the Morrisons for ten minutes.

"Aye." Niall nodded, touching the jeweled hilt. "How much?"

"For its age and condition, two hoondred fifty pounds, an' a bargain a' tha.'"

Niall hefted the dirk, testing its weight and balance. It was a good one. It would serve well in a fight. His own dirk, not so elaborate, but much older—and the man seemed to value age—and in better condition by far, nestled snugly in the sporran he had insisted on carrying on his belt, over Amy's protests. If he could get back to his own time, however, he would need his dagger. His eyes roamed over the other things in the case. The jewelry? He fingered the crucifix around his neck, the one intended for Allene. He wouldn't part with it.

Amy heaved an impatient sigh.

"Care to see the coins?" the man asked.

"Aye," Niall said, his mind working.

The knife disappeared back inside the glass case, and the tray of coins slid silently up to the counter top. "1857," the man said proudly, lifting a battered piece. Niall admired it, listening intently to its history. The man slipped it back in its place and pulled out another and another, giving dates and histories. Niall fingered the coins with respect, and studied them through the magnifying glass the man offered.

"This is a waste of time!" Amy hissed, when the man disappeared into the back of the shop to gather his private collection to show Niall. "Just get my ring."

Maybe she was right, thought Niall, but the inner tugging to listen to the man was great. He clasped the crucifix around his neck, asking for help in getting back to Hugh. "Showing interest in another is never a waste of time," he said. The Laird had always said so. "Let's see what comes of it."

"I'm going back to the hotel," Amy huffed. "You can forget any more help if you don't get my ring back for me."

He watched sadly, as she pushed through the door into the sunlight outside, her black hair swinging, and left.

The man returned, friendlier and more enthusiastic than he'd initially been, with a large, flat case which he laid on the counter. "The whole history o' Scaw'lan', right here in these coins!" he raved. "The post-union coins." He pointed. "The Edwards, the Williams, the Charleses...." His finger traced back, fascinating Niall not only with his detailed knowledge of the coins, but of history, which was, to Niall, the future, of Scotland itself.

The man recited tales of the monarchs and other images on the coins, working his way backwards in time. He had an almost full set of coins for each king. "But here," he said, passing through the interregnum period after John Balliol's failed kingship—Niall's own immediate past, and he found it fascinating to hear it through this man's eyes, seven hundred years later. "We come to John Balliol. Don' 'spose ye learned aboot him in the States?"

Niall grinned. He remembered King John's visit to Glenmirril vividly, and the messenger arriving breathless at the castle months later, telling of King John's tabard being ripped bare by Longshanks, when Balliol refused to send troops for Longshank's war against the French.

"The coins seem to ha' been struck quickly in the first half of his reign. See how rough the die is? I've pennies from the first and second halves of his reign. But the ha' pennies...." He indicated two empty slots, awaiting their treasures. "I've sairched the internet, with nae luck."

A word caught Niall's attentive ear. "Inverness?"

"Inter-*net*. Shairly ye've heard o' the internet?" The man grinned at his joke.

"I haven't," Niall said.

"Aw, go' won," the man protested. "Ye're havin' an old man on. A world traveler like yerself?"

Niall spread his hands in apology. "I've been so busy practicing for concerts," he said. "I miss things. Tell me about it."

"Why, you can find anything a' tall on the internet! Anything you want to know, just put in the words, and out it comes on the screen. Ye shair ye're not havin' me on?"

"I wouldn't do that," Niall said. "Where can I find this internet?"

"On yer computer, o' coorse. Ye *do* knoo what a computer is?" He narrowed his eyes.

Niall nodded, warding off the man's suspicion. But he repeated the word—*computer, computer*—over and over, to remember. Now he'd have to find out what this *computer* was. "So you can find anything except the penny you want on the internet?" he asked, bringing the subject back.

The man shook his head vigorously. "Och, 'twill turn up. Someone has one, and someone will want to sell it."

"How much would such a coin be worth to ye?"

"Hoondreds o' pounds!"

"What if I could get them for ye?" Niall asked. "The two for your collection and more, too. How much?"

"What? Both o' them? The first and second 'alves of 'is reign?" Niall nodded.

The man's eyes lit up. "Dae ye really think you could? I would ha' to see its condition."

"Like new." Niall couldn't resist a grin. "Like it came off the mint a few years ago at most. Much better than what ye have here."

"In the condition you see here," the man said, "four hoondred each. More an' its as guid as ye say."

"Aye, it's as good as I say," Niall assured him. "I've the ha' pennies you're lookin' for. I'll trade them for the ring and the extra in cash."

"If it's as guid as ye say, aye," the man agreed. "Bring it to me."

Niall dug in his sporran. The man's eyes widened. "Ye don' mean to say ye carry it wi' ye!"

"An' why wouldn't I carry my money with me?" Niall asked, in equal surprise.

"Ye canna be serious." The man eyed him briefly before his attention flew to the pile of coins Niall dropped, clattering, on the counter. He stared, then gaped, reaching for his magnifying glass and running his finger tenderly over them. He raised his eyes to Niall's. "This canna be real! The impressions are like new. They must be frauds!"

"Ach, noo!" Niall said, angrily. He reached instinctively for his dirk, slamming it on the counter. "I'm no liar nor cheater!" The old man pulled back, eyes wide, grabbing belatedly for his own coins. Niall remembered these people carried no weapons. The man, he realized, with shock, thought he was going to rob him!

"My apologies," he said quietly. He pulled back the musicians' accent, hoping the man hadn't noticed his slip. "It is the custom where I am from. I forgot myself. I'll not hurt you nor take your coins." He pulled the crucifix from under his shirt and held it out. "It's Him I'd be answering to. I do not lie nor cheat."

The man stared, enthralled, at the crucifix. "'Tis medieval, too, is it not?"

"Aye," said Niall. "'Twas made by the monks of Monadhliath in 1297 to be passed down through the Campbell family. 'Tis not for sale."

"Aer ye cairtain?" asked the man. He turned the light on it, and fingered it reverently.

"Certain," said Niall.

"Beautifully done," the man said. Niall slipped it off over his head, and handed it over. The man studied it with the magnifying glass, the figure of Christ and the narrow white piece inset in its back, ran his fingers over it, and turned it over and back again.

"1297, you say?"

Niall nodded.

"In forty years in the business," he whispered, "I ha' ne'er seen such a beautiful piece, and kept so well! Five hoondred pounds."

Niall met his eye firmly. "'Tis not for sale."

"A thousand."

"'Tis not for sale."

"A shame." The man's eyes caressed the piece. "If ye ever change yer mind, the offer stands."

Niall reached for his dirk, still on the counter, but the man, reassured now, laid his own hand on it. "From the Highlands, late twelve hoondreds, early thirteen hoondreds," he said in awe. "Or an incredible counterfeit. This handle is made of antler, is it not? How d' ye come by these things?"

"My father gave them to me," Niall said.

"An' ye carry them wi' ye."

"What's the point in havin' them an' I don't use them?"

"May I look?" At Niall's nod, he picked it up. He felt its blade, touched its handle, and studied it through the magnifying glass. "It looks as real as any I've ever seen," he said.

"'Tis," Niall assured him. "'Twas made in the Year of Our Lord 1301 and given to my Lord James Campbell by the Laird of Glenmirril. On his death, it passed to his son, Niall. 'Twas used in the cattle raids against the thieving MacDougalls and killed the son of Lord MacDougall's younger brother in 1314."

Having copied the man's style of weaving detailed stories around his pieces, Niall thought it sounded better in the telling, than the actual events. The man's death rattle, the pull of his body against the dirk, came to him at odd moments, though he'd had no choice in defending himself.

Clearly, however, the man appreciated the telling, and it seemed to lend weight to what was, after all, a rather ordinary dirk, much like those carried by the other lords.

"Amazing!" the man said. "An' how did it come to your father?"

"The ha' pennies," Niall reminded him, pushing them closer. "Look them over and satisfy yourself. I promised the lady her ring."

The man gathered the coins and took his time, turning them over and studying them from every angle under his magnifying glass and a strong lamp. At last, he snapped off the lamp and looked up with a broad smile. "I'll gi' ye the ring and two hoondred fifty pounds."

"The ring and five hundred." Niall pulled the coins back. The man's jaw dropped. Then a gleam came into his eye. "The ring and three hoondred."

"It's like new," said Niall, with the grin of a wolf, and a locking of eyes. "Ye'll never find another like it. The ring and five hundred."

"Three twenty-five."

"There's a coin shop down the street. They'll no doubt recognize their value. A shame not to complete that fine collection."

"They won't pay it. 'Tis not worth that."

"Not to them. But to you?" Niall let his gaze slide to the empty spots in the collection.

"Three fifty."

Niall collected his coins and turned to walk out the door.

"Five hoondred!" The man bustled back around the counter, blocking the door.

Niall said nothing.

"Five hoondred and the ring, an' a necklace to match."

Niall smiled, the smile of a lamb this time, and turned back. He dropped his coins on the counter with a pleasant clinking. The man disappeared between the curtains, and returned with a bundle of cash and the ring. He placed it in Niall's hand, glinting blood red in the dim light.

From a tray of necklaces, Niall took his time choosing a delicate chain with a matching garnet teardrop. It would be perfect against Amy's skin.

As he reached for it, a crucifix caught his eye, tucked away in a dusty corner of the glass case. Wooden, with a detailed figure of Christ, it reminded him of his own. "That, too." He pulled the cash back out of the bundle he'd just been given, to pay for it.

The man reached into the case, and quickly had it wrapped up. Niall slipped it into the jacket's deep pocket.

At that moment, Amy burst back into the shop.

"Still here?" She yanked a bundle of cash from her purse. "I'll get the ring myself, but don't ever ask me for anything again. Don't even expect help at rehearsals. It's over between us."

He turned to her, unable to conceal his pleasure at the surprise awaiting her.

"Don't smile at me!" Her eyes spit fire. "Move!" She pushed at his chest.

He didn't budge, but raised his hand, opening it before her eyes.

The anger flew from her face. She drew in a breath, then laughed, took the ring and pushed it hastily on her finger. She looked up at him. "You did it? You actually did something you said you would?" The ring glinted on her finger. She flew to hug him.

"The Shawn you knew was a chanty wrassler," he whispered into her ear. "That's not who I am now." He slid the necklace off the counter and held it up. "To make up for taking your ring. Accept my deepest apologies."

This time, she gasped out loud; threw a hand over her mouth, and touched the necklace gingerly. "You didn't.... This isn't you."

"No, I'm someone else altogether. Don't ever let go of your ring again." He pushed her shoulder gently, turning her around, and clasped the necklace around her neck, under her heavy hair. "And if in a few days, I seem back to my old self, remember me as I am now, today. But you still must not let him treat you like that."

"I won't," she whispered.

"You must stand by your decision that it's over, if he treats you badly," he insisted.

She nodded, overcome. "But how did you...?"

"The finest coins ye've ever seen," the old man gushed. "Here's your money, Mr. Kleiner." Amy's eyes widened as he counted out bills.

"What coins?" she asked.

"Come and see," said the pawn shop owner.

Niall closed his eyes, cursing the old man's enthusiasm. But she was at the counter, listening to his dissertation on the coins and their significance.

"Come along, Amy," he said, pulling her shoulder.

"No," she said. "No, this is interesting. Where in the world did you get these?"

"From my father."

"You never showed them to me."

"It didn't seem important."

"You had them the whole time? Then why...?"

"Dinner," Niall said, firmly. "It's been a delight doing business." He bowed to the old man, who was lovingly settling his new half pennies in place, and ushered Amy outside, blinking in the sunlight of the dirty alley.

He was immediately accosted by a girl with a billow of hair the color of summer peonies—he could hardly tear his eyes from it—giggling and bumping Amy out of the way without even noticing her. She stood on tiptoes and kissed Niall on the lips. A light flashed in his eyes.

"Will you sign an autograph?" she simpered. "Can my friend take my picture with you." She wrapped her arm around him, leaning her pink hair against his cheek and another light flashed. The friend, dressed entirely in black, with short white hair sticking straight up, was just lowering a tiny silver box. They both thrust papers and pens at him, leaning into each other and giggling some more. Niall looked at Amy questioningly.

"It happens all the time," she whispered. "Sign your name and they'll go away." He did so, and they skited off, tossing coquettish grins over their shoulders. *He's so cute,* one of them gushed in a whisper meant to be overheard. And the other, *His hair feels soooo nice.* Niall touched his hair, wondering what was particularly nice about it. Must be that French *shampoo* Shawn used. He'd tried it this morning. Amy rolled her eyes and shook her head. "You're so vain."

He didn't know what overcame him—some sprite of mischief. He ran his hand down a long tendril of her hair, grinning. "Yours feels much nicer," he said. "What's better than French shampoo?"

She looked shocked, then flushed with pleasure and laughed. "French shampoo? What do you mean? I can't remember the last time you said you like my hair."

"I'm saying it now." He thought of Allene and pulled his hand away. "Dinner," he reminded her. He led her out to the cobble-stoned streets, already planning his next move in the chess match that must get him back to Hugh.

Chapter Ten

East of Loch Ness, Scotland

When Shawn awoke, evening sun filled his room, and every muscle ached. Every inch of his body screamed for a double tall mocha. A new headache, of caffeine withdrawal, took up where yesterday's hangover had left off. The past two days' events jumbled in his mind, images of Amy and Allene melding in the tower, the scent of bluebells and heather, the taste of beer and mead and a cool, clear Highland stream; the silky feel of Caroline's skin beneath his hand and the sting of Allene's hand on his cheek, the remoteness of the castle and the neon bustle of Inverness.

Inverness! He bolted straight up in bed, tearing at sore muscles. He groaned, rubbed his protesting legs, stretched his back, and, finally, stood up. He studied the cell. It was bare, stone, and cold. A simple crucifix hung on one wall, next to a plain wooden wardrobe. The bed leaned against the other wall. He kicked one spindly leg, knocking the threadbare brown blanket—more of a burlap sack, really—onto the floor. It was hardly the four poster with silk sheets back at the hotel. Exactly what he'd expect in any monastic cell, though.

A chant drifted through the wooden door, disturbing and peaceful. His father had sometimes taken him to vespers at a monastery near his childhood home. The haunting drone of men's voices had always lifted him to a higher place, brushing the face of God. He closed his eyes, and felt himself surrounded by the white light emanating from the chanting. He saw his father's face, his father's kindness, his father laughing, and felt, just for a second, something of the man he might have been, had his father lived—or if he'd seen any benefit in the way his father had lived. He shook his head, and opened his eyes. His father's naiveté had gotten him killed, and taught Shawn to take charge of his own life and happiness.

It was time to get to Inverness! He groaned, thinking how long he'd been gone. Conrad would be having a cow—a giraffe, an elephant, several epileptic seizures. Not that he'd do any more than have fits, but Dan and Peter had a few sticks up the wrong places. They might do more than fume and bluster. He'd better find a phone and let them know what had happened.

He'd slept in the long-tailed, billowing-sleeved shirt he'd donned in the forest last night. He scooped the tunic off the floor, a heavy woven slash of holiday blue down one side, and carnival red on the other, and yanked it over his head. He laced the leather boots, and looked down at the get-up. "Ren Faire, here I come!" He chuckled. It would be a great story, showing up at the castle like this. Caroline would love it. He put on the floppy hat with its trailing green peacock feather. He strutted across the bare cell, strumming an imaginary lute, singing, "*Sumer is Icumen in, lhude sing cuccu!*" His theory professor would be thrilled he'd finally found a use for the stupid piece.

With sunlight and some rest, his fears of the previous night could be seen for the foolishness they were. The Loch Ness monster! "Did I really believe that?" he interrupted his medieval song to ask no one in particular. As to the arrow, there must be a rational explanation. It must have been a blunt arrow. He was being Punk'd. Yeah, someone might set him up on a program like that. Or he'd fallen in with some remote clan still clinging to the old ways. He'd file a complaint about the shooting business, but all in all, it had been an adventure, another story the orchestra would re-tell for years. But it was over. He'd tell the monks who he was. They'd help him.

He scanned the room for a sink. None showed itself. They must all be in a communal bathroom, he decided. He'd get a quick shower—he almost held his nose at the sweat and dirt he'd collected on their jaunt. Maybe they had some shampoo and soap. He rubbed a hand through his grimy hair. His public couldn't see him like this. Then he'd be on his way. Too bad about the boy. In Inverness or Edinburgh, there'd be ways to help him, give him a better life than his silent exile from the rest of humanity.

He let himself into the dim stone hallway. Far away, a shaft of sunlight shot through a high arched window and landed on the stone floor in a solid square. The chanting grew louder. The *Kyrie* rose a step, and another. Shawn heard, in his head, the 80's pop version his father had loved.

He moved his head from side to side, did a rhythmic jaunt with his shoulders, and sang into an imaginary microphone, "*Kyrie eleison,*" thinking of last night's endless hills and roads. He strummed an air guitar, throwing his head back and closing his eyes, and belted out, "*Kyrie eleison!*" feeling last night's dark all around him. He struck a mighty chord on the non-existent guitar, his face a mask of concentration, ready to slide onto his knees, arch back, and launch into a virtuoso air guitar solo.

A monk appeared, treading with cat's paws on the stone floor.

Shawn dropped the guitar back into non-existence, grinning at the monk. "It was going to be a great solo. Move over, Jimi Hendrix!"

"'Twas a novel *Kyrie*," said the monk. "I will pass it on to the singing master."

"Novel, indeed," Shawn said. "Toto in a monastery."

The monk looked at him quizzically.

"The group, not the dog," Shawn clarified. "Can't have dogs in a monastery." Still, the monk showed no comprehension. "It wasn't Toto?" Shawn struck his forehead. "Big Country? Mr. Mister? Loved them."

"Yes, well," said the monk, "the words are wise. Do we all need mercy on the roads we travel. The times are dark indeed. Dinner is in the hall," he added reverently.

"Great!" Shawn's stomach begged for some good strong food. A steak, maybe, with a salad and baked potatoes with sour cream and chives. Definitely, some coffee. "Then I need a phone, and a shower."

"Shower?" The monk stared blankly.

"You don't do showers? A bath, then?"

"Ah!" His face glowed with understanding. "Yes, we've a bath."

"Great! Do you have some soap to spare?"

Far away, the *Kyrie* rose another step, shimmering and echoing in the high stone hall, and dropped again. The monk's hands disappeared inside his sleeves.

"We bathe on Saturday. 'Tis several days off yet."

Shawn drew a deep breath, and, hungry and filthy, didn't fight his inclination toward sarcasm. "Surely you jest!"

"No jest, my Lord Niall. It has ever been so."

"You know...?" Or at least, he knew Niall.

"I've known you since you were a bairn."

Shawn nodded, processing the information. He wondered how the monks would feel about an imposter in Niall's place. Maybe he didn't need to tell them everything. "Okay, then. Which way to Inverness?"

"The dining hall is this way," the monk answered.

Shawn followed him down the hall. "How 'bout a phone?" The monk looked quizzically back over his shoulder, but said nothing. The chanting drifted after them, a tendril of sound floating on incensed air. "I really need a phone," Shawn said. "They're going to fire my a...a..." He felt his father's stamp on his personality, and couldn't say that word in a house of God. "...my posterior if I...."

"Yes, I heard you were injured," the monk replied.

Shawn wondered if he imagined the ghost of a smile in the words. He didn't really see what was amusing about being fired. "Dan and

Peter," he tried again. "They have no sense of humor. They want to hurt me, and...."

"My Lord Niall." The monk stopped, waiting for Shawn. "We are doing all in our power to prevent them hurting you. But 'twould help if you would make haste." He strode forward again, serene and brisk, a combination, Shawn thought, only a monk could manage. They seemed determined to send him on this journey. He'd have to tell them.

"The thing is," Shawn said, "I cannot tell a lie." He grinned, pleased with himself for quoting George Washington. "Actually, I'm pretty good at telling lies, but not to a holy father...."

"I am but a friar," said the monk. "Not the Holy Father. Here is the dining hall."

Shawn looked in dismay at the faces gazing at him from the long, narrow table. He didn't want to announce in front of the whole monastery that he wasn't who they thought he was. This must be what it felt like to be the victim of a conspiracy. He sighed. At least there would be a good meal. After that, he'd try again for a phone. At least he could tell Dan and Peter he'd tried.

A large table ran the length of the dining hall. The dozen brown-robed monks ate silently. Shawn's escort led him to an empty spot. He took his place, a red and blue peacock among sparrows. Someone set before him what must be the first course: a bowl of steaming stew, and a salad. "Got some salad dressing?" he asked. "French?"

A dozen faces turned to him in shock.

Ah. Silence at mealtimes. "Sorry," he muttered, and bent over the meal. The stew stared back at him, looking suspiciously like the evil twin of yesterday's meal at the castle. He watched as the monks reached into their bowls with their hands. Copying them, he fished out something like a scrap of potato with fingers less than clean after last night's doings. He continued eating, nonetheless, his hunger being greater than his aversion to sticking dirty fingers in his food. Still, the stew seemed less repulsive than it had at the castle; maybe because he was hungrier.

As each monk finished, he pushed his bowl away, folded his hands in his lap, and bowed his head. Shortly after the last monk finished, a bell tolled, slow and mournful. As one, they stood, and began filing out the far door. Shawn waited, not knowing what to do. There appeared to be no more stew, though he could have done with a second, and very probably a third, helping. He grabbed the sleeve of the last monk in line. "Where's the rest of the meal?" he whispered.

The man tugged his sleeve back, and hurried after his brothers.

"This is it?" Shawn said. "Where's the steak? The potatoes?" Several tonsured men frowned back at him. But no one stopped.

"Don't you even have coffee?" Shawn asked, more loudly.

"You must be on your way," Another monk spoke, *sotto voce*, behind him. He turned to see last night's guide—he surprised himself with his growing ability to tell them apart in their look-alike robes.

"You can't expect me to go on an empty stomach," Shawn said. The man tucked his hands into his sleeves, and turned around.

Shawn leapt from the bench and followed him out into the hall. "I can even survive without a milkshake, but how about a full meal at least!"

The monk led him silently to his room to collect his harp. Still grumbling about food, he started wrapping his monk's garb. "Leave it in the press," said the monk. Shawn hesitated, then hung it inside on a peg, with a dozen identical garments.

"I guess I'm ready," he said. Twenty yards down the hall, he tried again. "I need to know which way to Inverness. Or a McDonald's."

"Certainly."

"Thank God!" Shawn said. "Hallelujah!"

The monk smiled, a small, tight smile. "There's a MacDonald in the hall."

"You're kidding! They're even in monasteries now? How did I miss that?"

The monk didn't answer, but spoke to someone else. "He is here." There, near the door, stood the boy, his back to Shawn, his cowl up, and his foot tapping impatiently. The monk glided silently away, and the boy turned, flinging back his hood.

Shawn's jaw dropped.

Inverness, Scotland, Present

With cash in his pocket, and impatience in his spirit, Niall walked with Amy back through the old stone buildings of Inverness. They passed another of the infernal portraits of the frolicking Shawn. He sat on a ruined castle wall amidst green fields, holding the sackbut. Two buxom young women in tartan skirts and billowy-sleeved shirts leaned in on either side, painted in the very act of kissing him on either cheek. A third clutched enraptured hands to her breast. This time, Niall made out all the words: *Shawn Kleiner Celebrates the Best of Scotland!* Niall shook his head in disbelief. People thought this was him!

"You loved them when you did the photo shoot," Amy said. They reached the River Ness and crossed one of its seven bridges.

"I was a different man," Niall replied.

They strolled the sidewalk along the river till they reached the restaurant: The Two-Eyed Traitor. "A strange name," he said, studying the sign. Two faces, identical but for different colored eyes, peered opposite directions. "Having two eyes would hardly seem a noteworthy trait."

Amy glanced up at the sign. "I thought it must be a Scottish variation on two-faced. Either way, there's a story behind it." She laughed. "There's *always* a story. Way back when, some guy sold out his clan to the English in battle."

"People don't change," Niall said. "What battle was that?"

Amy shrugged. "There have been so many. I think his coat of arms is displayed here, or his tartan, or something."

Niall ushered her in. From the entry, he surveyed the pleasant flickering of a fire; soft lights, crisp white linens, finer than even Longshanks must have had. The wide expanse of carpet was soft under his boxy shoes, and as clean as if no foot had ever trod upon it. Music tinkled from the large, black instrument in the corner, vaguely like an overgrown virginal. Glasses clinked an ostinato and voices droned, with occasional laughter breaking out, like a dove bursting to carefree flight above the fray.

It would be easy to stay here, enjoying luxury and leisure beyond a king's wildest dreams. It would be easy to stop worrying about Hugh.

The scene darkened before his eyes. Edward's wildest dream was to slaughter the Scots. And though all appeared well for these people, seven hundred years later, it would not be well for Allene and the Laird and all he knew and loved. He must get back. He wondered—the man had said you could find anything on this *internet*—could he find if Hugh *had* been there? It was a ridiculous thought. Shawn couldn't accomplish that. If Niall could just get back and make his way through the Great Glen, all would be well.

A whisper ran through the dining room. Niall realized people were staring at him.

"Mr. Kleiner." A man in a black suit with a crisp, white shirt bustled forward, bowing low. "We are honored, sir." He glanced at Amy barely long enough for a head count. "Table for two?" He led them through a gauntlet of greetings, proffered hands, and enthusiastic comments about his last concert, to a secluded corner. A candle flickered on the table. "Your menu." The man in the black suit presented Niall with a large, shiny brochure. Niall stared, not knowing what to do with it. Amy open hers. He copied her. But his thoughts slid back to Hugh.

"You're a million miles away," Amy said.

"Hm?" He peered at her over the top of his menu.

"Your menu is upside down. Out there, it was like you were seeing something else."

Niall stared thoughtfully at the letters on the menu, turned it right side up, and studied them again. Reading was easier than it had been. The spelling looked less like gibberish. But he wondered why Amy wished to read before eating.

Their eyes darted uncomfortably at each other over the candlelight. A servant appeared with two crystal glasses of water sparkling on ice, each with a lemon floating in it. Amy started reading again. Niall did likewise, making out *venison* and *trout*. The servant reappeared, hovering quietly with a sheaf of parchment and poised quill.

"What are you having?" Amy asked.

"Having?" he repeated.

"It's a restaurant. What do you want?"

"I can...choose?" He had expected tables laden with repast, or a stream of servants bringing food as they did at the castle.

"Of course you can." She smiled. "You're paying."

"A loaf of bread, then."

"A loaf, sir?" the servant asked.

"A whole loaf?" Amy repeated.

"Soup, eel."

"Eel? Did you say *eel?*" the servant asked. The black-suited man hurried over. He must be the steward, Niall decided.

"Where did you find that?" Amy searched her menu.

The servant looked to the steward, who nodded furiously.

"Pigeon pie, woodcock, salmon," Niall added, thinking of all his favorite things at the Laird's table. The waiter scribbled swiftly. Amy would certainly be pleased with him for providing this fine feast!

"Can't you make it easy and order off the menu?" Amy whispered, a little fiercely.

"Of course," Niall said obligingly. "Venison and trout would be good! And as we're celebrating, a boar's head!"

"A *boar's head?*" Amy asked in disbelief.

"A...boar's head, sir?" The servant swallowed.

"Anything you like, Mr. Kleiner," the steward said loudly. He nudged the servant, who scribbled, frowning.

"Aye," Niall agreed cheerfully. "And plenty of ale!" At another table, a man handed his menu back to a servant. Niall did likewise.

"I'll have the chicken salad," Amy said.

"You'll not share my meal?" Niall asked in surprise.

She rolled her eyes, and handed her menu to the servant, who hurried away to consult with the steward.

"I've done something wrong," Niall said.

"Just—being yourself," Amy replied. "I keep wondering if this change is for real. You're so different, it's like it's not really you."

Niall said nothing. He didn't want to find out what happened to imposters here. In his own time, he'd be hanged. He wondered, uncomfortably, if Shawn was foolish enough to put himself at such risk, if he were, in fact, in Niall's time. He felt a twinge of pity for the man, who was most certainly not living the comfortable life to which he was accustomed.

"And then you're right back to your arrogant self, making people jump through hoops, just because you can. Look at them!" She nodded toward the steward, gesturing frantically at his staff. "They're actually going to dig up a boar's head for you!"

"Dig it up?" Did they keep boar's heads underground in this strange time? It didn't sound appealing. Maybe that was why she was displeased.

"I guess it's better than what you did in Edinburgh." She sighed. "I can't believe I stayed with you this long. You realize it's going to take them forever to find a boar's head. What was it you wanted help with?"

"The Battle of the Pools." He instantly dismissed the question of where he'd gone wrong. It was of little matter.

"The battle they were talking about last night?"

He nodded. "The man in the pawn shop said I can find anything on the *inter...net*." The word came out slowly, having been rolled around in rehearsal in his mind for the last hour.

"That's news to you?" She shook her head. "Sorry. I get the whole amnesia thing, but I've never actually known anyone with it. It's hard to understand you finding the internet big news."

"Yes," he agreed, for lack of anything better to say. "Can you help me find this *internet* and anything about the Battle of the Pools? And maybe a man named Hugh?"

"That's what you wanted?" she asked. "A man named Hugh. That's kind of vague." She sipped her water. "Of course I can help you with that, but...." One hand gestured futilely, as if reaching for some sensible answer. She settled for a weak, *"Why?"*

He smiled. "Let's enjoy dinner. But you'll help me afterward? You promised."

"Of course." She nodded. "That's easy. I thought you'd ask for more. I just wish I could understand what happened to you."

"You wouldn't believe me if I told you," he said softly, smiling over the flickering candle.

"So you *do* know what happened. You keep saying you don't. And there are so many things you don't remember. Or say you don't. What am I supposed to believe?"

"Can you believe I need help, and trust me?"

She stared at the tablecloth and blinked hard. "You've told me so many times to trust you. Why would I be stupid enough to do it again?" She raised her eyes, waiting for his answer.

Niall stared pointedly at the ring on her finger. It flashed in the candle's tiny flame. She picked up his gaze, blushed, twisted the ring, and cleared her throat. "I said I'll help. I will. Anything else, I still need more reason to trust you."

There was an awkward silence. Niall wondered how one held a conversation with a woman. The things he would have talked about with Allene would hardly do. He fell back on his supposed *amnesia.* "Tell me —remind me—about yerself."

"Remind you?" she said. "You probably didn't know half of it to begin with. I was never the important one here."

"Of course you're important," Niall said, in surprise. "You're talented, lovely, and kind. I took your ring, and still you helped me through that rehearsal!"

She blushed furiously. "It was nothing."

"You saved my life!" he insisted. "I thought Conrad was going to run me through with his baton!"

She laughed. He liked seeing her happy, instead of distrusting and angry. He added, just to see her laugh again, "I thought the brass were going to throw me from the tower, the things they were saying. But tell me about yourself."

She laughed again, clearly embarrassed, looking at the ceiling, at her hands, and finally at Niall. "I was born in New York."

"I know of York."

"Thank goodness you remember something. We play there a couple of times a year." She twirled her glass by its elegant stem. The lemon twisted in slow circles. "You know I play violin."

He kept his thought—*that's what it's called!*—to himself.

"What else is there?" she asked.

To sum up a life by place of birth and instrument! "Amy, you think too little of yourself!"

"So did you," she said. "I guess you convinced me."

"I was wrong," he said, hating Shawn. "How did you learn to play violin?"

He drew her out till she spoke freely about *schools* for music— entire buildings full of tutors—and a very important one called *Juilliard,* which she'd attended. "I just lucked out and played well on the audition." She'd named her cats Quarter and Half Note. "Kind of stupid," she apologized. "But at least it's not Ebony and Ivory." He wanted to tell her about his hobbin, an unusually affectionate pony, that whickered for him when he came into the stables, but he couldn't.

"I would love to live in the country and have a horse someday," she said, sipping her water.

"Is that not easy enough?" he asked.

She laughed. "You've forgotten how much things like that cost." He couldn't tell her his own dreams for the future, though he wanted to.

"I love Bach. The composer," she clarified at his blank look.

He found it hard to understand an entire life spent writing new music. In his world, music was handed down, one generation to another, around the fire in the great hall, on winter nights. But then, what he'd seen of music in rehearsal today was far more complex than anything he'd ever known. He couldn't tell her any of that, couldn't tell her how fascinating he found it, or his idea of trying to create such a thing with the Laird's musicians. So he asked more questions.

She painted. "The forest scene in my apartment, I did that."

She had grown patient babysitting five young cousins. "I found the twins one morning, stark naked feeding apple pie to the dog."

He laughed. They sounded like boys of his time. He resisted the urge to tell her about the Morrison twins' antics, saying instead, "You must love your cousins very much."

She nodded, her eyes going soft. "They like you, too. You're so kind when it's just us."

And her eyes, he slowly realized, were a deep sapphire blue in the candlelight, striking against her black hair. And he was leaning across the table, enjoying himself far too much. He looked away, breaking the moment that had stolen around them. He couldn't and shouldn't notice her eyes.

Thankfully, the servants appeared, a stream of them, bearing eel, and salmon, bread and ale and pigeon pie. The other patrons gaped at the magnificent boar's head, apple in mouth, carried high above the servant's head, on a huge silver platter, through the middle of the restaurant. They piled platters on Niall's table and an extra one nearby. Niall breathed in the sweet smells with a huge smile, eyes closed. He opened them to see Amy looking at him, shaking her head.

"How in the world are you going to eat all that?" she asked. The servant set her salad in front of her.

Niall smiled and dug in with his *fork*. "How will you get through the night on only that?" he asked in return. "It's for both of us. Help me eat. The eel is very good!" He pushed the plate toward her, laughing at her look of horror. "You don't like eel?" he asked. "It was such a treat when I was a lad, and someone caught one in the loch."

"What...do you mean?" Doubt and fear crossed her face. "A *lad?* You grew up in Minneapolis."

"A dream I had in the castle," he lied quickly.

"There are lots of lakes there. I guess with the head injury...."

He stabbed a bit of salmon on his fork and offered it to her. She tasted it, approvingly. "Now tell me about myself," he said.

"You can't tell?" She gave an unladylike-like snort. "Look how they just scrambled to get all this! Girls scream for you at our concerts. I keep expecting you to tear off your sweat-soaked shirt and throw it to them." She paused. "I guess that's hard with all those buttons." She poured a thick, white sauce on her salad. "You're a musical genius. You get things out of music no one else can. You make things happen. People do what you tell them. Sometimes that's good." She reached for another bite of his salmon. "And sometimes it's bad."

She sipped her water. "You're smart, but you got lousy grades, at least with the teachers you couldn't charm. You didn't care; you knew where you were going and figured you didn't need it. And you were right. You usually are. It's legend how Conrad hired you on the spot before you even auditioned. You're funny. You keep people laughing so hard they can barely breathe."

Niall smiled. Maybe Shawn had a redeeming quality or two.

"You're generous. You throw great parties, and make everyone feel like you threw it just for them." She told him, as he savored his eel, about his childhood, the re-enactment camps with his father, his mother. "You wanted to buy her a mansion. She said she'd rattle around in it all alone. So you gave her this beautiful house in the country instead. She despairs of you. She says your father is rolling in his grave, the things you do."

"What happened to my father?" Niall asked, thinking of the man smiling in the picture he'd found.

"Well, except for saying he died when you were in high school, you never talk about him. Except one night when you got drunk. Really, especially, drunk."

"What happened?" Niall asked again.

Amy hesitated. "There was a boy who took up with the re-enacting unit. Your dad took him under his wing. He didn't really have a father. Only his mom's boyfriends, awful guys...."

"Mom's boyfriends?" Niall asked. "I don't understand."

"His mother." Amy eyed the pigeon pie. "She had boyfriends."

"Was she a widow?" Niall asked. "Do you mean men courting?"

Amy's eyebrows drew together in disbelief. She looked at him sideways. "That's far too nice a word. She wasn't widowed, she was never married at all." She reached suddenly, and scooped up a helping of pigeon pie. Her next words tumbled out, as if she hoped he wouldn't hear them all. "This is really pigeon?" She poked at it on her plate. "If I just don't think about that, I'm sure it'll taste very good. You really want to hear this? You would never talk about it before." She gulped a bite. "It's really good. How did you know pigeon pie would taste so good?"

Niall reached across the table, touching her hand. "I've no

170

memory of it," he said quietly. "I assure you, it will not upset me."

Amy stared at her plate and spoke softly. "You were a wreck the night you told me. You were really, horribly drunk. I'm afraid to remind you of it."

Niall squeezed her hand. "Tell me."

She left her hand in his as she spoke haltingly, softly. "He let the boy live with you sometimes, when things were bad at home. He helped him with job applications and school. One day, after he'd disappeared for a few months, he showed up at one of the camps, wanting a ride home. On the way, he asked for money. Your dad knew it was for drugs...."

"What's this *drugs?*" Niall asked.

"You don't remember drugs? Marijuana, crack, cocaine, that sort of thing." Niall couldn't grasp these words. "It messes up your mind," Amy tried to explain. She mimed holding something to her lips and breathing in, lifted her eyes to heaven. "Some people do it for fun, and then that's all they want to do, ever. They can't keep a job. They steal to buy the stuff. Anyway, your dad wouldn't give him money. He pulled into a parking lot to talk; said he'd take him home. But the boy just wanted drugs, just wanted money. He pulled out a—well, you get the idea, Shawn."

"No," Niall said. "Tell me the rest."

Amy squirmed, staring at the table, at her napkin. She pulled her hand out from under Niall's and twisted her ring. "You were a wreck, crying, sobbing."

"Amy, tell me," Niall said.

She stared at the table linens. Finally, she spoke softly. "He stabbed your dad. A dozen times, two dozen, I don't know. A lot."

Niall said nothing for several minutes. He thought of his own father, coming to a less than pleasant end, fighting beside William Wallace at Falkirk. But it had been war. Niall had been eight years old, and barely remembered the man. He wished, suddenly, that he had a picture of his father, as Shawn did. He wondered, given his and Shawn's similarity, if his father might have looked like the man in the picture with Shawn. He tried to imagine that man wearing a gambeson, fighting in a schiltron on a battlefield...dying with a spear through his chest. He closed his eyes against the ugly picture.

"Say something, Shawn."

Niall brought his thoughts back to the present. Shawn had known his father, loved him. His father had been betrayed and killed by someone to whom he'd shown only kindness. That was different from dying in battle. Very different. He looked at her, saw the worry and concern in her eyes. "I don't remember it," he said. "It's but a tragic story to me. Tell me more of who I was."

She bit her lip, and told him, softly and stumbling at first, how Shawn had worked with his young cousin, teaching him trombone; how he'd run from an irate husband, and broken her heart by lying to her again. He and Amy arranged music together for the orchestra and Shawn's albums, traveled, walked by lakes, and sampled new blends of coffee. "You've been funny and kind and thoughtful," Amy said. "You've also been selfish. Self-centered. Thoughtless. Hurtful."

He slathered butter on a large, hot slice of freshly baked bread, and handed it to her. "Can you believe I'm not those things now?"

Amy took the bread. Their hands grazed one another. The sensation jolted Niall. "You've shown yourself to be those things. Over and over. The last few hours have been nice, but you've always been able to be nice for a few hours, even weeks at a time. I have to keep believing you're those things, no matter what I see now. Or I'll get another shock."

"No." Niall laid down his fork. It surprised him how much it mattered that she not think these things of him. After all, he would, somehow, get back to Hugh. The real Shawn would—maybe—be back. And he, clearly, did not care. "The person you knew was those things. I'm someone new."

"Prove it," Amy said.

Niall considered the possibilities. When he found his way back to his own time, would the real Shawn return? If so, Niall's words now would appear to be lies. Just another brief show of kindness to string Amy along. Might he find his way back, and simply disappear without Shawn reappearing? If so, his words might, again, appear to be lies. If he couldn't get back...? He had to admit, he had no idea if, never mind how, such a thing could be accomplished. He looked around the restaurant, at his table piled high with the best things in life. What an easy and pleasurable life it would be, trapped here. Not that he could allow that. He had things to do, where he belonged. And he missed Allene.

"What would prove it to you?" he asked.

"An apology." Amy wadded her napkin, throwing it in her lap. "A sincere apology carved deep on your heart. It'll never happen." Her eyes met his, hard and angry.

He stared at her, saddened for the pain Shawn had caused her.

The waiter broke the moment, appearing with the bill in a black, leather folder. The crest on the front caught Niall's eye. "Explain this," he said to the waiter, pointing at it.

"It's the crest of the traitor after whom the tavern is named, sir. He slept here, hundreds of years ago, on his way to meet them at the Battle of the Pools."

Niall's heart froze in his chest.

It was Darnley's crest.

* * *

They returned to the hotel on far better terms than they'd left. Still curious about his request, Amy showed him the computer tucked in a corner in the castle's sitting room. It was an anomaly of slick black casing amidst aged books and shelves, heavy, ancient furniture and a suit of armor. He jumped at first; then, seeing that no one else took notice of it, circled it: a suit of armor with no one inside! He rapped on it and lifted the visor, just to be sure. It was entirely too reminiscent of Edward's men for his liking.

He pulled off Shawn's jacket and joined Amy as she seated herself in front of the *computer*. Niall kept his expression neutral, watching every movement, memorizing, as she worked her magic, wiggling and clicking a small box—he had no words for the thing—and tapping her fingers on some sort of board, covered with letters, and suddenly, there on the computer screen, were incredibly life-like paintings of Stirling Castle! It was as if someone had captured the actual image and put it on the screen. His gasp slipped out.

She turned. "It's an impressive castle, isn't it?"

He dropped, eyes wide, into the chair next to her. She thought the *castle* was impressive!

Clicks, colors, and pictures changed faster than he could follow. A dark blue bar swept up and down words that appeared on one side of the screen, seeming to move with the motion of her hand, although that could not be possible. It settled on one word: *internet*. With another soft click, the *computer* hummed, and the screen changed, covered now with words and images. He shut his eyes—this was impossible!—and opened them again. She raced her right hand over the small box, back to the letter board, as he christened it. Her fingers flashed, and the image changed again, to a long list of words. *Pools!* The word jumped out at him, in heavy letters, over and over again.

"Everything you want to know, right here," Amy said. "Where do you want to start?"

"I—I don't know," Niall said weakly. "What *is* it?"

"You don't remember the internet at all?"

Niall touched his temple to remind her. "As though I never saw it. Explain it." The lacerations were rough under his fingertips; she blanched and accepted the excuse.

"I click on it," she said, matching action to words, "and it pulls up a page with whatever information you want."

"A page like a book...." Niall murmured. He fell silent, daring show no more ignorance. This *internet* must have been as well-known and navigable to Shawn as the Great Glen was to Niall. He understood.

This box, this *computer,* gave him access to a monastery full of books on any subject he desired! "I don't know where to start," he confessed.

"Let's start at the top, then." Amy clicked the box. Niall caught the motion of her finger, committing it to memory. The image changed to a black background with white and blue letters.

"Read it," Niall whispered.

"Is this something to do with what happened in the castle?" Amy asked.

"Please." Niall spoke a little more forcefully. He studied the shapes and spellings as she read. The wine bottle, brochures and menu had all helped. He could follow the words on the screen almost easily now, thanks to his previous attempts.

It might be what saved Scotland, his ability to learn quickly— including how she was doing this. He studied her hands and the movements of the small arrow on the screen, replaying them in his mind, even as he watched her next motions.

She seemed more than willing to pull up page after page on the Pools, while he memorized her every action. There seemed to be hundreds, and each gave the same dismal story he'd heard at the dinner table: the English slaughtered the Scots.

He studied them all, narratives, diagrams, and paintings of this battle he was supposed to be fighting. A machine copied a multitude of pages for him—he blinked and swallowed to see the images on the computer transferred to paper he could touch—till a thick stack stood on the desk. It would take all the monks of Monadhliath a year to copy so much!

"New interest, Shawn?" asked a musician. Niall barely heard him. His finger traced the shapes of battle, the first day's movements, the second day's movements, the directions from which the English approached.

"What's with Shawn?" someone else asked, more quietly.

Niall marked notes on one of the maps the machine had spit out. It was marshy land on which they'd fought. He knew it, somewhat, from his fostering years in the lowlands. It would be hard on England's heavy horses. Still, the news was bad—all bad. The Scots had simply been overwhelmed. He touched the crucifix at his neck, refusing to believe he'd be here, if there wasn't some way to make use of it.

The steward came in, clearing his throat. Niall was not to be deterred. Unsavory though Shawn had been, he carried influence. Niall turned to the man after the third entrance and throat-clearing.

"We've other guests waitin' fer the computer," the steward said.

Niall stood, rose to his full height, put on his best impression of the Laird, and, copying Amy's vowels and pronunciations, said: "I want a *computer* and *internet* brought to my room immediately!"

"I canna do tha'!" the man protested.

Niall remembered the comment from last night's dinner. "I can bring business to your hotel!" he barked. *"Or I can take it away!"*

"Spoken like the old Shawn," Amy muttered. She covered her eyes with one hand, shaking her head.

Niall had bigger concerns than being compared to Shawn. He faced the steward squarely. "I expect to be back on the internet, in my own room, in thirty minutes." He dredged his brain, trying to recall the word she'd used—the machine that spit out manuscripts. "Don't forget the *printer,"* he added.

There stood, in twenty minutes, on a new desk in his chambers, one of the amazing computers.

"Unbelievable!" Amy stood in the doorway, watching the men scurry to connect the last cable and rush out.

Niall nodded approval, satisfied he had discovered how to use the assets Shawn had left him. As he hung up Shawn's jacket, he recalled the crucifix. He fished it from the pocket, unwrapping it on the way to his bedroom. He removed the painting over the bed, setting it on the floor against the wall.

"Shawn! That's an original McTaggart! You can't do that!"

Niall spun, startled at the alarm in her voice. She was looking at the painting.

Niall shrugged, with a dismissive glance at the seascape. "I want the crucifix there." He hung the cross in the painting's place.

"Same old Shawn," she said. "And yet, not." She studied the crucifix. "You were raised Catholic. Maybe when you hit your head, it sort of—jolted—something?" She sighed heavily and went back to the sitting room.

"I'll try now." Niall joined Amy in front of the computer. He seated himself, recalling how she'd done it, and tried. Nothing happened.

"The start button," Amy said. Niall searched the letter board. "On the screen." She pointed, and he remembered. After several more mistakes, processing and learning from each one, he found his way back to the *internet,* his own personal monastery full of books.

"I have to go to bed," Amy said. She crossed the room to a sink and another machine. "I can't believe I haven't seen you drink coffee since you got back." She ran water into a glass ewer and punched buttons. "It'll keep you awake if you're going to keep studying."

With only a cursory glance at yet another machine, this one burbling like a stream in the Highlands, Niall turned back to the *page* he'd pulled up, leaned forward, and read.

Edward gathered an army like the world had never seen, to

175

*crush the Scots once and for all. Every possible man must be called
upon to defend the struggling country.*

Hugh and his men were needed, and nobody but Niall knew how
to find them. Except....

The realization hit Niall hard, a fist in the gut. His head shot up.
At the machine, Amy jumped. "What's wrong?"

"Nothing," Niall said quickly. But something was very wrong.
Somebody else *did* know. Somebody who should *not* be traveling to find
Hugh!

Central Scotland

In the gray, stone foyer of the great monastery, the huge leather
and brass-studded doors looming over them, Shawn gathered his jaw
back up to the rest of his mouth.   Brilliant golden-auburn curls
surrounded Allene's furious face. All thought of Inverness fled his mind.
Even the poor excuse for dinner and the lack of a double tall mocha no
longer mattered. Had he really just been handed four days—alone!—with
this beautiful girl? He couldn't believe his luck!

She, however, did not see things in the same light. "Ready at last,
aer we?" she demanded.   "We've lost fifteen minutes we could scarce
afford."

"Fifteen minutes, huh? Oh, no, call out the National Guard." But
a grin spread across his face. He was helpless to stop it.

"I've badly misjudged ye, Niall Campbell! O' course you're angry
I found a way to come along, though 'tis your own fault I'm needed!" She
tossed her head. "Mooning MacDougall, indeed! But I hardly thought
ye'd bear such a grudge."

"I'm not angry! Who said I'm angry?" Indeed, pleasant thoughts
—vivid thoughts—raced through his mind faster than he could enjoy
them. "I didn't want you to come along?" That, at least, explained her
look of triumph in the great hall of the castle. She and Niall must have
argued. In fact, he guessed, piecing together more of the puzzle, they
must have argued in the tower. She'd known exactly where to find him.
Niall had been angry, stayed in the tower, and fallen asleep. And woken
up—where? He was too interested in Allene to pursue the thought.

"O' course you're angry! Why else did ye give me no greeting in
the grove! Surely you were not afraid of my father there! Why else did ye
no say a word to me all night?"

"I didn't know it was you!" he protested.

"O' course 'twas me! Is it not the way we traveled last time?"

"Of course!" Shawn struck his forehead with his palm. "I forgot.
Still not right in the head, you know. Well, then!" He rubbed his hands

together, the grin refusing to leave. "Let's go! No hard feelings? Let's start fresh, okay? I'm really glad it's you."

"We must be on our way," she snapped.

"Well, hold on! If you're supposed to be my mute servant boy, I *couldn't* talk to you, could I?"

"Not in public, certainly, but 'twould have been aw' right last night."

"Just trying not to blow our cover," he said. "Tell me when, and we'll talk. I can't wait!"

She gave him a dirty look and yanked up her cowl. The monks raised hands in benediction. They swung the huge doors open, and Allene stormed out into the pink-streaked evening, Shawn all but running to catch up. His fantasies of the coming days overshadowed the aches of last night's exertions.

Inverness, Scotland, Present

Jimmy burst into the Blue Bell, waving the money he'd won off the American musician. "Next round on me, lads!"

A cheer arose. Barmaids hopped, taking orders and carrying brimming pints to the men gathered around the dart board. "There's a big game in Glasgow tomorrow night," said one of Jimmy's mates. "Five thousand pounds to the winner. Pay off yer bills and get the missus off yer back fer a bit. Ye got the entrance fee there, if ye don't piss it away on drinks."

"Where in Glasgow?" Jimmy asked. He eyed the bundle of notes, before pushing it into his pocket. He chose a dart from the tray, testing its weight and balance.

"The James and Barley."

Jimmy laughed. "I'm loiked none too well there. Got meself piss drunk an' in a fight once too often." He eyed the dart board carefully, and launched the dart. It landed dead center. He smiled.

"It's been a couple years," said his mate. "They'll've forgotten. Me cousin works there now. I'll ask 'im to put in a word fer ye. Five thousand pounds, Jimmy, think on it."

"I doona ha' to think on it," said Jimmy. "If ye'll do that, I'll go." Jimmy shook the other man's hand. Several men clapped him on the back and shoulder, wishing him well. "I'll not let ye down," Jimmy said.

Central Scotland

The moon came out, drawing Allene's nervous attention, but showing Shawn the landscape. The hills continued, rocky now and covered in short, tough grass, rather than forest. At times, they climbed almost vertically up grassy slopes. At others, they crossed broad stretches of moorland, lifting their feet high over the heather or stumbling on uneven, marshy ground. Mostly, they marched in silence. Now and again, in a dark grove, Allene let fly. "And here was I thinking ye a better man!" she said.

"I can be as good as you want, baby," Shawn replied, the leer coming through in his voice. It earned him a shocked gasp and another glare. She flounced ahead, still lecturing.

He shrugged. "Your loss," and went back to passing the time playing the harp in his mind while the real harp bumped against his back. He was beginning to enjoy the effort. He grinned, did a bit of the triplet section of *Blue Bells* in his mind, and thought about those enjoyable nights with Celine. Maybe when he got back, he'd surprise her with his newfound skills and take it from there. He enjoyed the thought, his legs moving steadily under him, while another of Allene's tirades washed around him. He started on *Gilliekrankie*, relegating her mutterings and outbursts to the background. She'd come around. He knew she would. Eventually she stopped, tramping in silence, every now and again giving an angry toss of her head, and Shawn himself a dirty glare.

At last, they came to a stream. It appeared suddenly, glittering in the moonlight, at the bottom of a shallow gully. Not the coffee he craved, but better than nothing. Allene threw herself down on the bank. Shawn removed the harp from his back, leaving it beside her, and edged down to the water. His leather boots slipped on the wet grass. But he reached the stream without mishap and dropped to his knees in the rocks, scooping up icy water, and gulping deeply. When he'd sated his thirst, he splashed his head and face, and up under his harlequin tunic and billowing shirt. It was the closest he'd come to a bath in two days.

He looked over his shoulder. Allene had edged her cowl back from her face, watching him. Moonlight gilded the outline of her brown robe. She plumped her arms across her chest, and turned her head away. He'd ignored her long enough. Time to start making up. First, an apology.

"I'm sorry, you know." He sat back on his haunches.

Moonlight glowed on the pale edge of her cheek. She turned her head further away, lifting her nose in the air.

"Come and have some water," he said, gently. He knew timing like the best comedian: time to turn on the charm.

"In me own time," she sniffed.

"Aren't we in a hurry?" Always show concern for what she wants.

"We've a moment."

"Come on, Allene," Shawn crooned. "Forgive me. I've been an

ass. I'm not trying to be. Sometimes I just can't seem to help myself." Self-deprecation was a powerful weapon in his arsenal of charm. She said nothing, but the silhouette of her stiff shoulders lowered perceptibly. Shawn recognized progress. "The water's good," he said. "Come down here, before you drop of thirst."

"Perchance," she said.

"You know I got injured in the cattle raid." A little vulnerability, a plea for help, always appealed to women. "Just a delayed reaction from the injury. If I'd been in my right mind, I would've known it was you. I'm still not really in my right mind. I've forgotten things. I wish you'd help me fill me in the gaps."

Allene edged toward the water.

"Let me bring you some." Shawn doffed his hat, the feather trailing, and made a show of filling it. He carried it up the short slope, water glinting in the moonlight as it spilled over the edge and seeped through the material more quickly than he could scramble up the bank.

Her scowl thawed.

Shawn reached her and stared at the damp, empty hat in dismay. "I know I filled it," he said. "Let me try again." He slipped and slid back to the stream, re-filled it, and carried it up, making a show of trying to keep the water in with his hands.

A corner of her mouth twitched as he once again reached her with an empty hat. He tried a third time, and now she laughed out loud, and stood to come down to the stream herself, allowing him to assist her. He took her chilly fingers, rubbed them warm, and kissed them. "I hate it when you're angry with me," he whispered. He didn't know or care how often Niall angered her, or what he thought of it. But it was a good line, and delivered in an emotional whisper, it rarely failed. It didn't now.

She gazed up with sad, blue eyes reflecting the silver moon. "Do you know how scared I am when you're gone and I wait in the castle for news of your safety? And now you're angry with me for trying to help."

"I know, I know. I'm sorry you had to go through that. Really I am." He pushed the cowl down, freeing the wild red hair, and dared kiss her temple—and what a temple it was, he sighed in exultation! She threw herself into his arms.

"You won't make me stay behind ever again?"

"No, never," he promised. He had no idea what Niall could or couldn't promise, and cared even less. "I'll never leave you again!" He hugged her back tightly, stroked her hair, held her close. All the things that showed great emotion; all the things that always worked. He kissed her temple again, worked his way down, kissing her cheek gently till he reached her lips.

"Niall!" she cried, laughing. "You know what happened last

time."

"That's one thing I'll never forget," Shawn agreed, recalling the lords' conversation. "That day behind the oven."

"Nor my father chasing you and whipping you?"

Shawn cringed. Poor Niall. "Your father's not here. And we're betrothed." He pressed his lips on hers, kissing her over and over. She pulled away, laughing. He grasped her hand; kissed her fingers, kissed the back of her hand, kissed her wrist.

"Niall, we mustn't. My father trusted you."

"His mistake," Shawn growled, kissing her forearm. She tensed; he sensed he'd made the mistake. "Of course he can trust me," he amended quickly. "I'll take good care of you. You can trust me." He pulled her closer, and lowered his head, pressing his hand in her thick hair. She gave in this time. Such a kiss! His knees quivered. His free hand dropped to her hip, his fingers hitching her robe up. Excitement rose in him. This voluptuous, incredible young woman! All his, here on the banks of the silver stream, under the stars. Tonight he would truly celebrate the best of Scotland!

"Niall!" She gasped. "Stop!"

"Oh, no! No, this will be so good," he whispered in her ear. His insides leapt and tingled. His hand found the edge of the robe and crept under, touching soft, bare skin.

"Niall, stop!"

"I can't!" He yanked the robe higher, inching his hand onto her rounded hip.

She jerked backwards. Something stabbed deep in his palm.

He jumped back with a shout. "The hell was that?" He clutched his hand, frantically scanning the river bank for archers. His heart raced. But they were alone. He lifted his left hand cautiously off his right. His head reeled at the sight of a deep gash in the soft pad between thumb and wrist. Blood flowed like wine. Nausea rose in his stomach.

"Niall! Surely ye'll no faint at the sight of blood!" Her gentle nature was gone, replaced once again by the shrew he'd come to expect. Never had a woman addressed him with such disdain. "Ye canna be the same Niall who dropped his trews to the MacDougall!" She yanked her robe into place, snapping it back down around her ankles.

He lowered his eyes and saw the short, vicious dagger in her hand. Indignation burst in him. "You stabbed me!" His hand stung fiercely.

"An what did ye expect, ye lout? I told ye to stop."

"You stabbed me?"

"Ye know well my father's expectations!"

"You! Stabbed me!" A slow, steady throb began in his palm and

coursed up his arm, pounding in his temples.

"And ye know I can take care of myself! I'll not be brought to shame by any man ere my wedding night. That includes you, Niall Campbell." She climbed halfway up the bank and glared back at him. "One more try like that, and there'll be no wedding night for you. Think ye my father would stop at a mere flesh wound had he seen that?"

Shawn stumbled a step or two up the slope after her. "He wasn't serious...." he began. With time and distance, the old Laird's threats had become idle words. Shawn gripped his hand more tightly, shutting his eyes against the burning. The Laird, he feared, was not only serious, but very capable. Already, he felt ghost pains in places other than his hand.

"Shit!" he spat the word. Allene promptly slapped his face.

"Damn, what was that for!" he shouted.

"The language!" she said. "And there's for the other word!" She swung again. Shawn stepped back to avoid it, and tripped on a stone. He found himself tumbling down the bank, and landed with a splash in the stream, soaking his finery. Several words formed in his mind, but between her knife and her right hook, he dared say none.

He'd let go of his hand, and the blood flowed freely in the water. "Give me something to tie this up with!" he shouted. "I need stitches, you deranged woman!"

"Ah, go 'won and quit bein' such a wee bairn," said Allene. "Next time, keep your hands to yourself.

"How am I supposed to play harp with my hand sliced up by your Ginsu knife?"

"Naught has ever stopped ye before," Allene said. "And now ye've delayed us so. Get out of the water, ye great oaf." She picked up her pack, and stomped away. Shawn scrambled from the water, snatching up the soaked hat with its sadly wilted feather, and jammed it on his head. Water dripped in his eyes and ran down the back of his neck, dribbling inside his shirt. He wiped at his eyes irritably, then yanked his shirt tails from under the tunic, struggling to tear a piece off. The material was strongly woven and wouldn't give.

"Come on, Allene!" he yelled. "Help me out!" A large bead of water fell from the hat, hitting the end of his nose and dripping off.

"Keep your voice down! Would ye have Edward's men join us?"

He stumbled up the dark bank, tripping again on the same stone. He snatched up the harp, still trying to staunch the blood. "Cut a bandage off this shirt for me! Are you going to leave me here to bleed to death? Who will warn Hugh?"

"Ye'll no bleed to death from that small cut," Allene scoffed. "An you do, I can certainly get to Hugh myself. Have ye forgotten, I am the one who knows the way?"

"Haven't you got a streak of human decency?" he demanded.

She stopped, stamped her foot, and whipped out her knife. It glinted. Shawn jumped back. "Wee bairn!" she said in disgust. "I'm only doin' as ye asked. Give me your shirt." He edged closer, warily, gripping his hand. She cut a long swath from his shirt, and helped him wrap his hand. She tied it so tightly he thought he was going to faint. "What has happened to you?" she asked. "Is this the same Niall who with an arrow in his backside turned back for one more cow, laughing the whole time?"

"Sure doesn't look like it," Shawn said in disgust. Who was this Niall, anyway, he wondered. And why the hell did everyone think *he* was so great? He hadn't even gotten past first base with his own fiance!

He elevated the injured hand above his heart, hoping to slow the blood loss. Damn Amy for bringing this on him. He swung the harp onto his back, and followed Allene across the moonlit moor, glaring and hating the sight of her, stiff-backed, ahead of him. He hit the chords on an air guitar, hard, and belted out improvised lyrics. *"Come on, Allene! Why are you so mean?"*

She turned violently, hissing, "Do you wish us both killed? We know not who's about!"

"Come on, Allene!" he crooned, his eyes narrowed in anger.

Tears glistened in her eyes. Her lip quivered. She turned and strode away, ignoring him.

His anger simmered for a good hour, thumping along behind her in silence with his hand aching and the harp banging his back mercilessly with each step. Staying with the blithering shrew had certainly not turned out to be the dream vacation he'd thought he'd won, back there in the foyer of the monastery. He may as well head to Inverness. He stopped, looking around. Hills stretched as far as the eye could see.

"Aer ye comin'?" Allene demanded.

He had no idea which way led to Inverness.

"Not the way I'd like to," he muttered, and started after her again. They'd reach a town eventually, and he'd find a phone. Out of habit, he passed the time by going through his small repertoire in his mind, but his deepest thoughts dwelt on wishing evil on everyone in any way remotely connected with his troubles.

Chapter Eleven

Central Scotland

Early in the morning, with pinks and grays streaking the eastern sky, they reached a squat, stone inn with a thatched roof. Allene had said not another word to him for the rest of the night, hiking without pause. There had been no more water breaks. She led him around the back of the inn, and tapped on the door. A great, robust man opened it a crack. As before, she lifted the cowl off her face. The man's blue eyes darted side to side, he pulled the door wide, and whisked them in. "Henry of Forth," he addressed Shawn. "And your poor, mute serving boy. My weary inn looks ever forward to your music. I've a meal fer ye, and a place to rest yer heads. Come!" He clapped Shawn's shoulder and pumped his hand. Shawn winced. His hand throbbed painfully even without the greeting. The man leaned in and whispered, "Welcome, my lord! May God go wi' ye."

"Henry?" Shawn asked. He looked the man up and down, from his baggy pants past his flour-smeared apron to his ruddy, bearded face.

Allene, the mute serving boy once again, with her hood covering her hair, gave him a piercing glare and nodded, raising a silencing finger to her lips. "D' ye no remember Fergal," she whispered.

The huge man led them into the dining room, empty but for a serving girl, up early to cook and clean. "Maeve," the man said. "We've a visiting minstrel who may entertain us tonight if we feed him well. Dish up some bacon and neeps. Be quick, girl."

"And something to drink." Shawn glared at Allene. His heartbeat pulsed in his hand. "A beer would be good."

Allene shook her head.

"What do you mean, no?" Shawn demanded. "What, do you only have ale or mead," he bit the words out, heavy with sarcasm, "in this primitive place?"

The man shushed him in alarm.

"I'll pay for naught to drink for ye," Allene hissed.

"I've had a rough night," Shawn hissed back. "Primarily thanks to you and your silly knife. You da...." He re-thought his language and tried again. "I'm wearing tights, for Chr...for Pete's sake, and you butchered my hand. I haven't slept in a decent bed in two nights! You can buy me a drink. Buy me a couple."

Allene pursed her lips, barely visible under the hood, and shook her head one smart, angry shake.

Shawn stood up, threw the plumed hat on the floor at her feet, and stormed out. Allene and Fergal didn't stop him. He slammed the wooden door as hard as he could, and stood outside, looking around. A few houses lined the dusty road. A cock crowed. Pale morning light silhouetted endless black hills, rolling like rough seas in every direction. Storming out became less effective with nowhere to go.

He wandered to the stable at the back. It was a small, wooden structure. A bony horse nodded sleepily in one stall. A wagon sagged drunkenly in a dark corner. By the far wall, a girl in a heavy woolen dress pitched hay. She turned to him with a pretty blush and lowered her eyes. He leaned against a heavy post, his arms crossed over his colorful tunic, watching. She turned to him again with the same blush and lowering of eyes.

A lazy grin drifted across his face. "Want some help?" he asked. "A pretty girl like you shouldn't be doing all this heavy work yourself."

"No, sir!" she giggled. "I couldna accept help from our guests."

"Oh, now, don't think of me as a guest. There are only friends we haven't met. Do you have another pitchfork?"

"Only the one, sir."

"A shame," Shawn said. "Maybe I could—help you—somehow. Like this?" He closed in behind, reaching around her to grasp the pitchfork. She giggled, as they clumsily tossed forkfuls of clean hay into a stall. "I didn't know hay could be this much fun!" he whispered, brushing his cheek against hers.

"Aye, sir, and sometimes even more," she said.

"Mm, how could that be?" Shawn asked, playing the game. He nuzzled the back of her neck as they tossed another forkful of hay.

"'Twould no be my place to tell a gentleman such a thing!" The girl pretended shock.

"So I'll have to try a few things and figure it out myself?"

She giggled. He kissed her ear, thinking of Allene by the stream. His bandaged hand slid up her front, tugging at the leather thong binding her dress. He turned her around, dropping his lips to hers.

And suddenly, a heavy blow landed on his shoulder, flinging him to his back in the hay. The pitchfork pointed dead center in his chest. And pressed hard. The big innkeeper stood over him, face red. The girl cowered at the back of the stall, clutching her dress.

"I offer you safety, Niall Ca...."

"Sh!" hissed Allene behind him. "Nobody must hear!"

"I risk my neck for you, *Henry*," the man roared in a harsh whisper, "and this is how ye repay me?" He gave the pitchfork a sharp jab. Shawn gasped, throwing his hands up for mercy. "An' I dinna ken ye for a braw laddie aw these years, I'd run ye through right now," the man said. "Count God on your side my Lady warned me of your strange behavior! Whatever MacDougall's injury did to ye, let us hope it is cured soon, afore another does run ye through. 'Twould be a waste of what has been...*till now*...a good and noble life."

He raised the pitchfork. Shawn rolled from under it, jackknifing to his feet. "No such thing as a little fun in these parts," he muttered, rubbing his chest. He could feel welts rising. He glowered at the man and started for the door.

"An apology is in order!" Allene snapped.

Shawn sized the man up. Now that he was on his feet, it would be a fair match. Except for the pitchfork. "My humblest apologies, *sir,*" he said. He sketched an elaborate bow to the man, with a black look of contempt.

Allene gasped. The innkeeper growled and jabbed the pitchfork at him.

"Peace, Fergal." Allene laid a hand on his arm. "All of Scotland is at stake. He must get through, though he hardly deserves it. See to your daughter. You." She addressed Shawn. "Come and eat. It may be the last meal we see ere we reach Hugh."

She led him back to the inn's rough wooden table, piled high now with fare. None of it was the hot omelette or black coffee Shawn wanted. But it satisfied his hunger. They ate in silence, but for the cries of the girl out in the stable. At last, she fell silent.

Allene slammed her knife down, looking at him in disgust. "Have ye no shame?" she asked. "Bringing such a thing on the girl? Ye were so kind to her, like a brother, the night her mother was killed."

Shawn's head shot up. An image of his father, the image from his dreams, slapped him full in the face. Hatred shot from his eyes. "Don't talk to me about parents being killed."

"'Twas long ago." Allene frowned. "Ye're no the only who's lost a father."

"How do you know...?" Shawn stopped. Understanding flashed across his mind. Niall had also lost his father.

The innkeeper returned, throwing a stony glare at Shawn.

Shawn stared at the table, his jaw clenched. His hand throbbed. And now his chest ached with the sharp pain of punctured skin and newly forming bruises.

"Maeve," Fergal called to the serving girl. "Go to the Grants for a

185

basket of eggs!" When she'd left, the man checked the windows quickly, and then dropped on the bench beside Allene. "In my *lower* guest room," he whispered urgently, "lies a monk, your height and size." He indicated Shawn with a nod of his head. Shawn noticed he was no longer *my lord.* "He was found by travelers, just south of the Great Glen. He'd been set upon and beaten. 'Twould appear to ha' been Edward's men. 'Tis a miracle he lives."

Shawn's insides went cold. He understood all too well.

Fergal stood. "Under the table," he commanded.

Shawn grumbled, his chest and hand aching. "I thought I was supposed to be the visiting entertainment."

"Ye dinna take this seriously, Niall," Allene said. "What e'er the head wound has done, we fear ye'll tell the English soldiers who ye are, or do summat equally foolish."

"So I'm supposed to sleep in a cellar?"

"Would ye rather die?" Allene snapped. "Perchance ye *like* being drawn and quartered?" They glared at one another.

With a last glance at the window, Fergal shooed them under the heavy table that ran the length of the room. He brushed aside straw, revealing a hidden door, which he pried open. "Give the monk a bit o' this to help him rest quietly." He slipped a package into her hand. "Edward's men stop here often enough. They may be supping directly above your heads."

Shawn dropped into the cellar first. Darkness opened its mouth for him, a dank cloth pressing in on his senses, and closing over his eyes. Fergal helped Allene lower herself. Out of necessity, rather than kindness, Shawn caught her. He winced as her weight dropped on his injured hand. He was too disgusted with her stabbing trick to even try for a glimpse up her robe.

She landed with a soft thump at his side. Fergal lowered a heavy skin, bulging with water, then pushed the trap door into place above their heads, and darkness swallowed them.

Inverness, Scotland, Present

As Shawn dropped into the musty cellar, Niall rose from his magnificent four poster. Sunlight shafted through the leaded glass windows and over the rich velvet bedspread.

His thoughts were as dark as Shawn's. The late night studying did not bother him. But he saw with dismay that he'd slept later than usual. The sad medieval eyes of Christ, hanging above his bed, gazed down accusingly. Shaking himself from the deep pile of blankets, he cast guilty eyes to the crucifix. Despairing accounts of the battle filled his mind.

But even that took second place to Allene: was she out there somewhere with that chanty wrassler, the baw juggler? He tried to guess what might have happened. He assumed Shawn had appeared in the tower in his place, though it was only a guess. Shawn would not have known about the council. Having left Niall in the tower, Allene would have looked there, and found the presumably drunk and confused Shawn. Would she have ushered him to the council meeting? Question after question attacked Niall's mind. Foremost among them: had Allene used this to her advantage? He knew her well. Of course she would! And what choice did the laird have?

And what of Shawn? He, Niall was sure, would use any situation to his advantage; for instance, being alone with a comely young lass.

He rolled from bed, fell on his knees, and crossed himself. "Lord, Jesus Christ, forgive me," he whispered, angry with himself. "I'm becoming lax. When will You deliver me from this place, back where I'm needed?" He began his morning offering, but his mind wandered to his own chambers in his own castle. Had it only been a week ago he'd woken, with Lord Darnley banging on his door in excitement, rushed with adrenaline for the raid into MacDougall territory to retrieve their cattle? He pulled his mind back to prayers, looking up at the crucifix.

...and remembered so many other days with Lord Darnley and William and Iohn, hunting and fishing. He missed them. A weight sank inside him, a knot of seaweed in his stomach. If the story was true, Lord Darnley was the traitor. He made the sign of the cross and said an *Ave* for Iohn. He would travel to Stirling with Darnley and the other men of Glenmirril. He wondered if William knew, or was part of it.

"Lord, protect Allene," he said out loud. He gritted his teeth, thinking of her out in the wilderness, alone with Shawn; then relaxed his jaw. He was supposed to be praying. "I offer this day to Thee." He said it more forcibly than necessary, in his attempt to keep his mind on his prayers. "Help me to know and follow Your will."

A long, sweet note floated through the wall. He opened his eyes, hoping, for an insane second, that it was the sound of angels appearing. But it was only a flutist, warming up somewhere down the hall. It drifted in, sweet and alluring. How incredible, he thought, to wake up in such a world, never fearing for one's safety or loved ones, always sure of the next meal. And surrounded by music and the leisure to enjoy it. These people were living in Heaven, and didn't even know it!

His mind was wandering again! He jumped to his feet, irritated with his inability to pray. He wanted—needed!—to be in the forest, making his way to Hugh. Why was God not doing that for him!

He paced Shawn's room like a caged wolf. The Laird would have wanted him to take a different route this time, but he knew better. He pushed his hand through his hair. No one knew the Glen like he did. It was by far the best way. That's where he'd be, just now emerging from its green depths, at its southern end by the new castle of Inverlochy.

He stopped pacing at the windows and stared out, between the leaded diamonds, to the garden across the wide lawn. It struck his fancy, far off behind its walls. He vowed to visit it someday, to remember every tree and leaf and flower and tell Allene all about it.

He turned back to his new crucifix and forced himself to kneel again. "Watch over Allene," he prayed. "She is my life. Please—guard her till You bring me back." The memory of their last kiss filled his mind. His stomach cramped at the thought that it might really be their last. Unless—an ugly thought occurred to him. Would Shawn try to kiss her?

Pray for Shawn!

The inner urging hit him so forcefully that he leapt to his feet, his face a mask of fury, and shouted, "No!"

At the same instant, a pounding landed on his door, forceful and loud. Was it that brazen woman, Caroline, again? What messes Shawn had left him! Niall strode through the sitting room.

He flung the door wide, his face like storm clouds over the moors. Amy jumped back, almost bumping into Dana behind her. Her hands flew immediately to twisting the ring. "I just came...it's breakfast time." She expected this behavior—from Shawn, Niall realized. Shame washed over him. He reached for her. She stepped back, shrugging his hand off her arm. "I wanted to tell you—I heard about a diorama of the Battle of the Pools. I thought you'd be interested."

"A di...a...a what?"

"A diorama. Like model trains."

"Muddle trains?" He imagined men training for war in the muddy carse.

"Only it's a battlefield," Dana clarified. "We thought, with your new interest...."

Niall wondered if he looked as confused as he felt.

"It's a model of the battle," Amy explained, "with all the horses and men in position. You can see everything exactly as it was, who was there, where they were positioned."

"Do you mean...." Niall paused, trying to imagine what she described. "I can *see* the battle? Like the re-enactment?" His heart sped up. Did these people have the means to watch the actual battle?

"No, not like that." She looked at him curiously. "This is just little figures." She held up a thumb and finger, an inch apart.

"Little...what did you call them? Like statues?"

"Yes! Little statues all set out in position, everything like it was."

She sensed his disappointment, and quickly added, "They put a lot of research into it, every detail, which clans and knights were there, how many, where they were positioned. You wanted to know what went wrong. This might be helpful."

"Yes." Niall's hand drifted to the crucifix under his shirt. The monks always said sometimes prayers weren't answered because it wasn't God's timing; perhaps other things had to happen first. He had this incredible knowledge available to him, to see from this future, what the English would do. "Yes," he said, more strongly. "I'll go." Once again, his heart sped up. Would he see a small statue of Allene? Of Shawn?

"It's just down the road. I'll see you at breakfast," Amy said, and left, her back still stiff. Dana glanced back once, her face in its perpetual shadow of concern under her ruffled cinnamon hair.

Niall stared after them. Amy was upset about his outburst. It was Shawn's fault. If it hadn't been for Shawn, she'd never have seen him behave like that. He was a better man than Shawn! He threw a dirty look back at the crucifix, visible through the bedroom door. *I've done everything else You've asked of me,* he told the Man hanging there, *but this is too much! I canna pray for that weasel!"*

Central Scotland

Standing blind in the dark cellar, sounds and smells pushed in on Shawn, darting close like the tentative brush of a hollow-eyed street urchin's reach, and swirling away again. A faint rotting odor hung in the air. A tiny scratching in the corner, and a skittering sound, might be rats. He shuddered, and wrapped his arms around himself. Disbelief assailed him. *I'm Shawn Kleiner. I belong in a castle.* Instead he'd just let someone lock him in a cellar full of rats. He spun in the dark, seeking an exit. "Let me out!" he shouted.

Allene's hand fell on his arm. "Aer ye mad!" Panic flooded her whisper. "They'll kill ye!" Her fingers, resting on his arm, trembled. "Do ye no mind what they did to my brother? To yours?"

He turned to her in the dark. Her fear snaked around him with cold tentacles, jolting him with realization. She wasn't a reenactor. This wasn't a game. Why it hadn't been on the news, he didn't know, but these people he'd fallen in with truly feared for their lives. Someone was really hunting them, seeking to kill them.

From above came the quick *swish, swish* of Fergal sweeping straw back over the trap door. Her hand fell away, and he stood alone, his insides trembling. Musty odors worked their way deeper into his nose. Darkness pressed in on all sides. He took a couple of deep, steadying breaths. "This is insane," he whispered. It couldn't be happening. His hand stung. The aches in his chest deepened.

"Shh!" came Allene's voice. "We mustn't alert the servant girl to our whereabouts. We doona ken if she'd betray us to the English. Be careful of the monk, now."

Shawn felt carefully behind himself, and found a bundle of burlap. He sank down on it, listening in the darkness for Allene's whereabouts. The cellar felt small and close. Her soft rustles filled it.

A groan rose in the dark, sending a chill down Shawn's spine. "Here now," came Allene's burr—so gentle when she wished, thought Shawn. A shame she didn't wish, with him. "Have a wee bit o' this." There came the soft, repetitive sounds of a man gulping. Shawn imagined his own head resting in Allene's lap, and rather envied the monk. He could use a little comfort himself. Fear prickled the hairs on his arms. There came another, softer moan, and then silence. "Rest, Niall," Allene whispered.

He didn't answer. The scratching started again in the far corner. He tucked his cloak tightly around himself, imagining a rat pushing its ugly nose up against his. But exhaustion gripped him. Tugging the hood around his face to keep the imagined rodents at bay, he curled his aching muscles up on the burlap sacks. They were hardly the hotel's four poster and silk sheets; but after the past two nights, they'd do.

He shoved a couple into position, and contented himself with images of Allene entwined in his arms and legs, maybe even saying something nice to him. Something kind and gentle. Something like Caroline might say. He twisted, trying to bunch a burlap bag into a pillow. It didn't help much. No, not like Caroline, he thought. She'd never really said anything *nice* to him. Not nice as in, really kind, like he mattered to her.

Allene's gentle voice brushed his ears, calming the injured man. A memory rustled, soft as a summer breeze, at the edges of his mind. He was drunk, horribly drunk. Amy wiped his forehead with a cool cloth. Amy held his head in her lap, even as Allene must be doing now for the monk, and stroked his cheek, and turned his head to the side, into a bowl, and wiped up when he vomited. Amy asked nothing of him, spoke soft, comforting words, her voice calming like Allene's. He didn't remember the rest, except that Amy had held some black cloud at bay.

He didn't want to think about it. The rat scratched in its corner. He forced his mind back to thoughts of Allene. But the images had lost their allure. He drifted off to sleep, Allene and Amy mixing in his dreams.

Inverness, Scotland, Present

Breakfast was an improvement over the day's poor start. At the buffet, Niall noted a gray-haired woman's limp and insisted she sit down. "I'll bring your plate," he said. She looked at him in surprise. Indeed, several in the line around them gaped. "Last week, you told me I was too slow and pushed your way ahead of me," she said. "Your friends all laughed."

Niall's mouth tightened. "I am truly sorry."

"Whatever happened in that castle has changed you," she said. It was not the shine on his pride it might have been, before Amy's disappointment in him, at the door of his suite. Still, it buoyed him. Other people could see he was not like that fool, Shawn.

He bowed slightly, not knowing what to say. He took her plate, silverware, and large mug of coffee to her table, and returned to the end of the line. It had grown considerably in those few minutes. The wait gave his natural optimism time to return. His apology to Amy had mollified her, although it had not entirely removed the sting from her eyes. But she would see, he vowed. She would see he wasn't like Shawn.

He thought of the comfortable bed in which he'd slept, the sunshine and flowers outside, with no fear of the English or MacDougalls to mar them, and the hearty meal bowing down the table before him. The duty demanded of him today was to practice the harp in preparation for tomorrow's rehearsal!

"What's that you're humming, Shawn?" asked the woman behind him.

He smiled, thinking how rarely he'd been shot with an arrow while playing harp. "Just an old song my mother sang to me," Niall answered. Weren't these people lucky! And after he practiced, he'd go see this model of the Pools and learn what he could.

***

Several hours later, after practicing on a harp whose touch was still unfamiliar, Niall walked along the river away from the city of stone buildings and spires, and found the place Amy had told him about. A group of young musicians played on the lawn; some with violins like Amy's and others with large lutes held between their knees.

Inside the museum, he found a cavernous room full of displays, with a glass case that seemed to stretch a furlong in either direction. It contained miniature rolling hills, swampy fields, and tiny figures of English and Scots. Tiny men thrust tiny spears. Horses keeled in pain in the mud. Little trees covered Gillies and Coxet Hills, where the town folk watched and waited. Stirling Castle, bristling with motionless snapping pennants, rose in the north, while Edward's enormous army streamed from the south, ablaze in reds, yellows, and blues, marking the houses of so many English nobles, and even some Scots. He recognized Comyns and MacDougalls among them, surging against Bruce's army. Bloody turncoats!

"Must you grit your teeth so, young man?" an elderly woman next to him said. Her mouth puckered with a hundred disapproving lines.

"My apologies." Niall forced himself to stop glaring at the little traitors. Music floated in from the front lawn. He circled the display, studying it from every angle, comparing it to the images imprinted on his brain from last night's study. Whoever built this display had all the men in the right positions. The horses were placed where the internet told him they had been. While it was fascinating—he could hardly take his eyes off it—to see it in three dimensions, it gave him no new information.

He studied Coxet Hill. If Allene had guided Shawn, and by some miracle reached Hugh, he would bring her along to Stirling and trust her to the care of the women on Coxet Hill. And where would Shawn be?

He stared at the tiny model, as if it could tell him something about such minor players. A man who gambled away his livelihood and stole his girlfriend's ring would most likely skite off. He'd probably find the nearest inn and be drinking himself into a stupor while other men fought and died. Niall had a strong desire to spit, thinking of Shawn.

Pray for your enemies.

The command was powerful enough to draw his head up. The old woman still stood there. A crucifix dangled from her neck. It swung over the battle scene as she leaned forward. His jaw hardened. *Pray for that chanty wrassler!* He wouldn't. The woman put her hand to the crucifix, and backed away from Niall. He shook his head in disgust and walked across the room, staring with unseeing eyes at a painting of the battle. English archers poured a volley of arrows into the Scottish schiltrons. The men pushed on toward certain death, obeying as good soldiers did.

Niall clenched his jaw and shut his eyes. He thought himself a good soldier. His stomach tightened in anger. Shawn was no better than a MacDougall, with his lying and cheating and stealing. He deserved no prayers. But Niall was a warrior. Disobedience did not sit easily with him. He jabbed at his forehead, *In nomine Patris,* his chest, *et Filii,* each shoulder, *et Spiritus Sanctus.*

Out on the lawn, a flute trilled and soared.

Ave Maria, gratia plena. He finished the *Ave.* Saying the words was the only obedience he could give. In his heart, he didn't mean a word of it.

Central Scotland

Restless dreams hunted Shawn through his sleep: pursuing soldiers, beating, stabbing, tangling him in the monk's garb and pushing him backwards into rivers roiling with blood. A golden-haired angel stood on the bank, playing a flute. Was it Caroline? He rose up from the river, calm and strong, and saw that, in the fluid unreality of dreams, it was not him, but his father, with flowing brown hair and beard, rising up, arms outspread. In welcome? In sacrifice? It was the boy, the straggler, stabbing at him. "I never regretted doing the right thing," the man in the river said. "No matter how I was repaid. I'm satisfied with who I showed myself to be."

"But he killed you!" Shawn shouted. He stood in the river, water icy around his ankles, dripping with water and blood. "He *killed* you!"

"You only saw the bad," his father replied. "Did you ever see the good in how I lived?"

In the dream, Shawn was suddenly, once again, thrashing in the creek. The soldiers stamped and shouted, "To the king! To the king!" Above it all, floated the incongruous melody, hovering on dove's wings, played by the reedy instrument in the angel's hands.

His legs ached with running, his hand throbbed, his chest stung from the pitchfork. Soldiers stamped and shouted.

He woke with a start. "To the king!" Deep voices shouted above him. He woke as he'd fallen asleep, a shroud of darkness lying against his eyelids. He licked dry lips. A gentle weight touched his mouth.

"Shh," came Allene's husky whisper. His hand throbbed. "Not a sound, either of you, an you wish to live." His chest ached. He rubbed it irritably. From above came stamping feet and a cacophony of rough voices. Someone bellowed for ale. More feet tramped into the inn. One voice started a ribald song; others joined.

Shawn squeezed his eyes shut, taking slow breaths, while the merry-making continued, like a looped tape, over his head. He tried to settle his mind by going over his pieces, but the dream kept intruding. A fine sifting of dirt sprinkled down through the floorboards, catching a speck in his eye. He rubbed it out, blinking hard.

"Are you aw' right?" Allene whispered.

"Aye," Shawn answered. "I'm thinking of my father." He didn't know why he said it.

"He died nobly, to save others," Allene said. The flute whispered overhead. The bawdy song continued, louder with the lubrication of more liquor. Shawn didn't respond. He was remembering a stranded driver his father had stopped to help, one January. His mother had warned him he'd get hurt one day, stopping for strangers. It had been a woman with infant twins, shivering and crying in Minnesota's frigid cold. The flute trilled overhead. He remembered another boy, Lazarus. The name had stuck with him. Lazarus had also stayed with them now and again, and under his father's guidance, grew from an abused and silent boy to a strong, confident young man heading for medical school on a scholarship.

He remembered a story in the paper two years after his father's murder. He'd crumpled it, torn it, stamped on the shreds, sworn. The boy who killed his father had publicly announced that he understood Mr. Kleiner had refused him the money for his own good. Someone cared for him, at any expense. The boy had joined, and soon led, a ministry in prison, which even skeptics admitted was changing lives. Shawn pushed the memory out of his mind.

The hearty off-key singing ended and a man bellowed again, "To the king!"

Shawn's stomach tightened. He was sure this was very bad news.

"King Edward!" thundered back a score of voices.

"To God and England!"

"To God and England!" echoed the score.

The blood drained from Shawn's face. He felt pathetic relief for Allene's calming fingers on his lips, and deep shame that, even in her anger, she should do this for him. Another stamping of feet sifted more dust onto his face. He brushed at it with his good hand. His right hand throbbed.

"You! Innkeep!" a soldier shouted. "Tell us what you know of Niall Campbell's whereabouts!"

"I've told you all I know," came Fergal's voice. "They say he would go by the Great Glen. The Grants have a lad who knows the Glen well. Shall I send for him?"

"We've a guide already who knows the Glen as well as Campbell."

In the dark, Allene squeezed his hand. "Who?" she whispered. "Who knew it as well as you? He'll keep following us."

"I don't know," Shawn said. "I can't remember anything."

His hand throbbed. Feet stamped, and *To the King!* echoed again down through the floorboards.

And suddenly he understood, listening to the shouts for King Edward, what his rational mind had been denying. There was no safety in Inverness, no castle, no orchestra to which to escape. There was a traitor from Glenmirril, on their trail with English soldiers who wanted to kill them. Somewhere near him in the dark lay a man they'd mistaken for him, and tried to kill. Fear rose, in the shape of nausea, in his throat.

These people were for real. The Laird had spoken the truth.

He was trapped in 1314.

Laura Vosika

Inverness, Scotland, Present

Niall sat on the bed that night, staring with disgust at one of the thick shoes that had smothered his feet all day. He'd tried to sneak out in his own soft hide boots, that let him breath and move and connect with the ground beneath his feet, but Amy had caught him. She'd pushed aside the hair at his temple, her fingers skimming the angry bruise, and looked at him with such concern that he'd relented and put on the *tennis shoes*. He wondered what *tennis* might be that required such awful things. He'd tied a sturdy knot in the laces such as he might use on a fishing line or his own boots. This had brought another, deeper, look of concern to Amy's face, and she'd knelt and re-tied them into ridiculous, floppy bows more suited to a lass's hair ribbons. He'd smiled his thanks and left before, in her kindness, she inflicted any more indignities on him.

He stared at the shoe and thought about his failure to do as Christ commanded. It disturbed him as much as his failure to find any helpful information about the Pools. It wasn't as if he *wanted* to pray for a baw juggler like Shawn. But he prided himself on following Christ. He lifted his eyes to the crucifix. Shame washed over him. *Just so.* Niall fancied he heard Christ's words in his heart. *You don't want to. If you loved me, you would want to pray for those I love, for my sake. Even when you don't understand.*

Niall turned the shoe over in his hands. He stared, unseeing, past the white rubber sole to the blue plush carpet. "No, I don't understand," he said. "I don't want to pray for him." He hung his head. "Help me want what You want."

Niall lifted his gaze to the crucifix. He stood abruptly and flung the shoe aside. It hit the wall with a solid thunk and slid to the floor. "I'm talking to a piece of wood!" he said, out loud. "I'm hearing voices."

He stormed into the sitting room, away from Christ. He poked buttons on the coffee maker, on the *TV*, on and off, on and off, poked the buttons that changed the pictures. Little men in fantastic colors, with wings on their backs, spoke Gaelic. He craned to look behind the box, seeking an explanation for this phenomenon. Were they moving images, or real people? He pushed a button.

"What kind of a rat is he!" a woman demanded. He waved his hand in front of her eyes. She didn't respond. He poked a button. One of the fast-moving metal wagons they called *cars* careened off a cliff, nose diving into deep water below. Niall cringed and poked the button. A man in black and white clothing spoke to an elegant woman wearing something slinkier and shinier even than Caroline's red dress. A young couple stood nearby.

"What kind of man do you want her traveling the country with?" the woman demanded. Niall snapped the TV off. It was quite disturbing. He took a deep breath. Maybe such wonders had been left out of the story of King Herla because no one would believe them.

He wandered into the cavernous bathroom with its granite tiles. He'd take a hot shower, he decided, tugging at his shirt. It would settle his mind. He turned on the water. From next door, Rob's trumpet started, low and smooth.

He climbed under the stinging spray with Shawn's fragrant shampoo. *What kind of man do you want her traveling the country with?* He wet his hair, irritated by the way these things on TV settled into one's brain. From next door, Rob's trumpet climbed up a lazy scale. Niall poured a dollop of shampoo in his hand and lathered. Well, Shawn was definitely no longer a kind of man with redolent hair. Niall chuckled, and immediately felt low for taking pleasure in Shawn's certain discomfort. He stood under the spray, rinsing the shampoo, listening to Rob move into arpeggios and faster and faster scales, and sighed. The hoped-for peace was not to be found in this shower.

The heart is restless till it rests in me.

The Laird had pounded that into his head. But where was there peace in a Christ who demanded that one pray for such a hateful man? *What kind of a man do you want her traveling the country with?* Niall snapped the water off, and dried himself in irritation. He pulled on his own baggy trews and linen shirt, and was pleased to see he'd gotten the coffee machine to work. He poured the steaming liquid into Shawn's mug with the golden trombone, and sipped, letting it warm his insides. What kind of a man *did* he want Allene traveling the country with?

He set the mug down hard. Torches flickered light across his mind. He wanted to strike his head for his obstinacy in not seeing it sooner. Praying for Shawn was the best way to protect Allene! A change of character on his part *was* her best protection. "I pray for him," he said. He stared at the tennis shoe, lying where it had fallen, and felt nothing but disgust for the man. He crossed himself and said, "God, go with him." He added an *Ave,* more heartfelt than the one muttered earlier today. The scales continued in the next room, soaring higher and higher; much higher than a trumpet should go. Niall jumped up. It was a flute. He crossed the sitting room in a few sturdy strides and flung the door open. Caroline and the other flutist sat in the hall, talking. They looked up at him.

"Who's playing the flute?" Niall demanded.

"That's Rob playing the trumpet," said the other flutist.

Caroline looked at him, her eyes traveling up and down his trews and shirt, as if he were the village idiot. "Cute outfit," she sneered.

Central Scotland, 1314

Shawn lay quietly on his lumpy burlap bags in the dark cellar. The monk wheezed near him. Allene slept, wrapped in his arm, her head on his chest, her breathing deep and even. Above him, the party had died down, though the reedy instrument played on, soft and low. His thoughts circled, a hungry wolf wary of meat in a trap, around the idea that he was in 1314. He couldn't bring himself to touch the thought and find it was real, even though he could see, hear, smell the truth all around him.

The rat scratched in the corner.

He squirmed on the burlap sacks, trying to get comfortable. It was useless. A thought he'd long ago skimmed over returned full force: if he was here in Niall's place, was Niall there, in his? If so, had he wandered off, or had someone from the orchestra found him and taken him back to the castle? He groaned. What was that goody-two-shoes doing with Caroline? Probably trying to teach her the Rosary.

He shook his head. He was in the wrong century, with people who wanted to kill him. Caroline would have to fend for herself. With his free hand, he tried to wedge the burlap sacks into a better position, angry nonetheless. The man was no doubt ruining his reputation. And traveling through time only happened in movies. There had to be another explanation.

But even in the farthest reaches of Scotland, they would not think Edward was king.

A door creaked in the inn above him, distracting him from his morose thoughts. Footsteps crossed the room. A scraping of wood on wood suggested a bench being pulled out. Or—he strained his ears—two benches. He thought about the concert. He knew Conrad well enough. He would have scheduled the concert. How would Niall explain his inability to play trombone? They'd have to cancel the extra performance, and the musicians would be irritated with him for costing them money. Something else occurred to him. He nudged Allene.

She mumbled in her sleep and stirred. "Wha...?"

"Shh," he whispered. "Does Ni...do I by any chance play trombone?"

"What?" She still sounded half asleep. The voices above them drifted down as mere murmurs.

"Sackbut? Can I play sackbut?"

Allene yawned. "The one thing ye couldna do. Do ye no remember Iohn riling ye that ye couldna make a sound?" She nestled more deeply into the crook of his arm. A moment later, a soft snore rose. Shawn turned back to the questions tearing through his head like a

Midwestern tornado. The when was obvious: they'd both fallen asleep in the tower and woken up in each other's places. How? He couldn't guess. More importantly, how was he to get back?

A thump above jolted him from his thoughts. "You've let us down so far," a voice barked. The accent was English.

"He's no yet reached Hugh, o' that ye can be sure," spoke another. "And what o' the rewards I was promised? I've no seen *them*."

An ugly tingle crawled down Shawn's spine. This was the voice of the man who would betray Niall...Shawn. It sounded familiar. But he'd spent so little time in the castle, he could not place it. One of the lords around the table?

The voices continued, and he realized his musings had distracted him from listening. He needed to figure out how to get back to where he belonged. His mind struggled through his nightly marches. Should he go back to the castle? Did the switch need to happen there? He tried to recall the hills and moors surrounding Fergal's inn. He had no idea which way the castle lay. He was a strong swimmer. He could cross the loch—if he could find it. And if he did, what then? Just knock at the portcullis, announce he wasn't Niall, had no idea where Niall was, and needed to take a nap in the tower, please? He'd be shot, hung, drawn, and quartered, before he ever made it back.

"...a cloak," said the English accent.

Allene shifted in his arm and muttered in her sleep. He put his fingers against her lip. But he'd missed more of their conversation. He tried to lift himself from under Allene's weight, with little success. He could hear nothing from above. But there'd been no sound of departure. Then there came a soft scuffle, and the familiar sifting of dirt on his face. His eyebrows drew tight in irritation. He wanted to be in his four poster with a double tall mocha and—his heart pounded as the realization hit him. He didn't want Caroline. He wanted to be in his four poster with a double tall mocha in one hand and Amy wrapped in his arm. Allene stirred, made a sound in her sleep. He smoothed her hair, whispering, "Shh."

"'Twill do," said the Scottish voice above. There were mumblings he missed, and then, "...quality." The thing he imagined to be a rat scampered closer. Nearby, the monk breathed heavily; a soft thump suggested he'd swatted the rat away. There were footsteps, and finally, the men's words became clearer, as if they'd moved more directly over the spot where Shawn lay.

"From Edward's own tailor. But MacDougall is angry with our failure thus far. He has become consumed with finding Campbell. He'll be at Stirling, if we don't catch him up before. MacDougall wants him, even then."

"For what?" demanded the Scottish voice. "'Twould be too late to do any good."

"Vengeance. He's making fools of us." A long silence stretched above him, before the English voice spoke again. "You'll get the land only if you turn Campbell over."

The Scottish burr rose to an angry pitch. "'Tis not what I agreed to. Ye wanted only to stop him reaching Hugh."

"Have you an attack of conscience now?" The English voice laughed. The sound shot a chill down Shawn's arms. Allene rustled. He tried to be still so she might sleep. "What you agreed to would have led to his death. Surely you didn't think otherwise?"

After a pause, the Scottish voice asked, "What will ye do to him?"

The man laughed again. "What concern is that of yours? If you want the land, point him out to us at Stirling."

Shawn wrapped his arm more tightly around Allene, squeezing out images of *Braveheart* and wishing he could put a face to the voice. He was sure he did not want to be pointed out to anyone at the battle, or any time before he could figure out how to get himself out of this mess and back to the orchestra.

Chapter Twelve

Inverness, Scotland, Present

Niall woke with his mind churning. All his research only raised more questions. He managed to settle his mind to a perfunctory *Pater* and *Ave* and prayer for Shawn—*God, may Your angels watch over him and guide him*—before Jesus could rummle him again with demands, but his real concern was Allene. He wrestled with the question of what must happen at the Pools to save his people, while he pulled on Shawn's clothes, even the hated *tennis shoes*.

Dressed for the day—he kicked his leg irritably in the stiff jeans—Niall poured coffee from the machine, marveling at whatever miracle allowed it to be hot and ready, with no human intervention. Well, he corrected himself, Amy had thoughtfully pushed some buttons last night, making it beep, and told him it would be ready. He sipped the strong, black brew, loving the way it brought his senses to life, and wondering how he'd readjust to not having it, if—when—he got back.

He took the steaming mug to the large table with his computer and printer. Papers lay scattered across it. He pushed them around, trying to combine their information with anything he might have gleaned from the model. He'd hoped that last night's studying would percolate in his brain while he slept, and the answer would be clear this morning, appearing miraculously and with no effort like the coffee. But the Scots were as hopelessly outnumbered this morning as they had been last night, and had been seven hundred years ago, and would be in the future, if he somehow got back to fight the battle himself.

He looked back through the bedroom door, at Christ on His cross. "I shouldna ha' expected answers in a dream, should I now?" He spoke his native Gaelic. "Even You dinna get aught for naught."

He raked a hand through his hair, and began organizing the papers into piles. He put maps to one side—hand-drawn maps, maps looking down from above as a bird might see things, maps with symbols and arrows and labels showing the movement of the armies. In another pile, he placed photographs. In a third, he put written accounts of the two days. He sipped his coffee and stared at them, thinking.

Laura Vosika

"None of it helps," he muttered. He pulled the maps toward himself, and spread them out, once again, comparing the movements of Bruce's army, on the hand-drawn maps, to what he could see of the terrain on the bird's view photos. *Did Bruce use what he had?* he asked.

He pulled over the sheaf of narrations, and thumbed through till he found an exceptionally detailed one. He studied it, irritated at having to wade through a foreign language in foreign script. What tragedy if Bruce lost because he, Niall, hadn't paid more attention to his English tutors. But he waded through, and, choosing a sharpened pencil from those Amy had brought, jotted a notation on one of the maps. He studied the account again, and made another notation, consolidating details to one source. He sat back in the leather chair, studying the amended map. It helped to see, on the map, what the account told him.

He traced, with his finger, the positions of the opposing forces. Bruce had arrived early and taken the western and northern high ground, a mile or so south of Stirling Castle, forcing Edward's mighty army to pass in small units through a narrow gap. Brilliant. Niall tried to remember the area from the time he'd been there. But he'd been more interested in getting a glimpse of Allene, riding tall on her horse beside her father. He shrugged. He'd been fifteen. How could he have known he'd need an intimate knowledge of the terrain some day? He'd have to make the best of what he had, and with any small blessings, it would bring back some helpful memory.

He turned back to the map, sipping his coffee. Bruce had lined his men up facing the carse bog. He imagined Edward's heavy, proud horses, covered in their nobles' colors, struggling to carry a thousand pounds of armor-covered knights and their array of weapons across that soggy marshland, and admired Bruce's strategy.

He read further, and jotted another note on the map, with little, pointed symbols: *caltrops.* He nodded approvingly. Bruce had thought of everything. His men had strewn the marsh with the sharp, multi-spiked instruments, a deadly game of jacks sprinkled across the field to pierce the horse's hooves, and tumble them, rider and all, to the ground, cutting down the rumored hundred thousand before combat even began.

Bruce had prepared and strategized brilliantly.

And yet...he lost.

Why? Niall asked again. They'd been hopelessly outnumbered at Stirling Bridge, and triumphed despite it.

They'd chosen their ground well. Bruce had turned the once defensive, immobile schiltrons—the walls of spears that the English found difficult to penetrate—into moving, offensive weapons. Clifford, an English knight leading seven hundred cavalry, had thrown himself and his men at a schiltron and been killed almost instantly. Even mounted

201

cavalry couldn't stand against them, so what had gone wrong?

Niall continued moving his fingers along the lines of writing, going now and again to pin a point on one of the maps, shuffling the papers to find better representations, and occasionally pulling out one of the photographs to check another detail. He drank the last of the coffee and shook his head. There had to be some information he hadn't come across yet, some question he hadn't thought to ask.

He turned to the computer. He pushed buttons, finally managing to bring up the bright *desktop* as Amy called it, of a Scottish castle. He smiled, trying to imagine the Laird's scarred writing desk covered with images of a castle. *Amazing!* He moved the *mouse.* He picked it up and studied it, now that she wasn't here to witness his wonder at what Shawn would no doubt find normal. Nothing happened. He studied the letter board. He hit a few, with no results.

He glanced back into the bedroom, to the crucifix. *Is this getting me anywhere?* He couldn't see that it was, but felt drawn, nonetheless, to search again. He wondered how much longer Amy would help him before asking awkward questions, and no longer believing the wound story. Still, he couldn't remember how she'd made this thing work.

He sighed, and opened his door. Music flowed from several rooms, the musicians warming up before breakfast and rehearsal. He smiled, enjoying the scales and bits of melodies. Such a peaceful life. No fears of death or war. He wondered that all these people didn't seem happy, in their luxurious and idyllic lives: Rob, angry about something, Niall knew not what, every time their eyes met; Conrad so worried about whether a concert would be played perfectly; Caroline upset that he rejected her brazen behavior. What did she really expect!

He walked down the hall to Amy's room and tapped on the door, giving a courtly bow when she opened it.

"Shawn, you don't have to do that," she whispered. "People are staring." Niall looked down the hall, and, indeed, Caroline was regarding him sullenly.

"I'm sorry to cause you discomfort," Niall said, remembering to drop the *my Lady*, which courtesy also raised eyebrows.

"Come in." Amy stood back, ushering him into a sea of calming greens. Unlike Shawn's chambers, hers had only the one room, holding a bed and chest of drawers, with a much smaller bathroom off to the side. He glanced at the parchment in her hand.

She blushed, and lifted it to him. "It's the letter you left under my door in Edinburgh. Sometimes I re-read them." She looked apologetic.

Niall took the letter in his hand, feeling he was stepping into a very private part of another man's life. Her hands gripped one another, less than an inch from his. He scanned Shawn's writing, not as bold and brash as it had been in the checkbook.

Amy, mo ghràdh, Amy, mo ghaol.

He looked up. "I spoke Gaelic?"

She nodded. "Fluently. Your dad and grandmother both spoke it. Have you forgotten it all?"

"No." Niall looked back to the letter. *I loved the underground tour. Thanks for going with me. I hope you had fun, too. Great ghost stories, great excuse to hold you in the dark. I'll remember it forever. Always yours.*

A flattened S was etched under the words, centered below them. He touched his finger to it.

"You don't remember?" Amy edged closer, peering up at him curiously. He shook his head. "A visual pun," she said. "It's an S for Shawn, or it's a trombone. You leave me notes and letters all the time, always signed with this." She glanced at the desk in her room, littered with several more pieces of parchment. He guessed they were more of the same. Her hand fell on his. His nerves danced, sending life up and down his arms. "It's one of the things that made me think you were so much more." Her voice trailed off. Her eyes bored a question into his, asking for the truth. *Who are you? Are you the man I believed in?*

He dropped his eyes, swallowed and pulled his hand from the thrills she was sending up his arm. "Will you help me again with the internet?" he asked.

"Sure," she said, and opened the door. He offered his arm. She smiled shyly, and took it.

* * *

Niall said a silent prayer with bowed head that God would lead him to the answer. *Yes, and for Shawn, too,* he added. He studied every motion as Amy pulled up page after page. It was all he could do, still, to contain his wonder at the moving figures! Amy's long, black hair fell occasionally, brushing his arm. "Shawn, what exactly are you looking for?" she finally asked, sitting back.

"Some weakness," Niall answered, suddenly knowing what he needed to find out. "Edward is a fool."

"Is?" Amy asked. "Isn't Edward a 'was?' He crushed the Scots once and for all, and solidified England's hold on Scotland for hundreds of years. Till well after the American Revolution."

"When was that?"

She harrumphed. "You don't remember the American Revolution? Oh, sorry, the amnesia, the injury."

"But *why* did the Scots lose?" Niall asked. He paced the floor.

"Well, because they were outnumbered three or four or even five to one, depending which site you read. It's not like you can go back and change that." She went to the coffee maker.

Not even all Hugh's men would help that ratio much, Niall had to acknowledge. "Maybe not." He dropped onto a chair. "But every army has its weakness. I *know* Edward!"

She spun, shocked, from the coffee maker. "You what?"

He corrected himself. "I mean, I know what I've read." He rose from his chair, his agitation pushing him back to pacing. "He's a fool and a weakling. He has taken...I mean, he took little interest in Scotland or his armies. He is the last man to be leading an army, but he will, because he is king." He pounded his fist in his hand, and dropped back into his chair.

"Shawn, this happened seven hundred years ago." She poured the coffee into Shawn's mug. "It's not he *will*, but he *did*. You're talking as if you can change it. Why this sudden interest? I mean—it's kind of scaring me, really." She set the steaming coffee in front of him, in Shawn's black mug with the gold trombone. "You haven't had your usual latte since you got back." She seated herself in a chair beside him, her thigh touching his.

"My...." He paused, sounding out the word in his head. "Latte?"

"Your double tall mocha." A sweet floral scent hovered about her.

"Yes, well." Niall chose his words carefully, having no clue what lattes or tall mochas might be. He knew he couldn't tell it from a short mocha. "I haven't thought about that." He wrapped his hands around the mug, feeling something of the man who had owned it. He'd miss *coffee*. He found himself wanting to drink it all day. He wondered how Shawn was surviving without it.

"Something happened in that castle," she said. "I wish you'd tell me. Why the change?"

"What change?" It was a foolish thing to say, but he didn't know how else to respond. And the touch of her leg and her scent were distracting him terribly.

"You're so serious now, and kinder."

He set the mug down. "But you stayed with him, I mean, with the man I was. Why?"

She shrugged. "Who would be stupid enough to leave the great Shawn Kleiner? Fear. Afraid no one else would ever notice me."

"Och!" He shook his head sadly. "You're bright and talented and beautiful. Any man would notice you."

She lowered her eyes. "You've never said that before. You always acted like it was you or no one."

"I was a fool." Niall stared at her, at her pale, smooth cheek and intelligent eyes, and knew Shawn must be a fool. He closed his eyes, in pain, sure this fool was even now with his Allene.

"I stayed because I saw something better in you. When we were alone, it was like the mask slipped and I saw someone I *wanted* to be with. Someone good and kind buried in there."

Niall nodded, trying to piece together the dichotomous images of a man he'd never met.

Amy murmured into the silence. "You haven't been pushing me."

"Shawn *pushed* you?" The words slipped out before he could stop himself. Men didn't shove women; only brutes did. "I'm sorry," he said, pushing aside his hair briefly so she could see the vicious bruise and jagged cut. "I still feel Shawn is someone else. It will come back. But...why did I *push* you?"

"It's an expression," Amy said. "You don't remember that? It means pressuring someone to do things they don't want to."

"I did that? What was it I—pushed—you to do?"

"What was it?" She looked at him incredulously. "You know what!" Her cheeks turned pink, and he understood.

His eyes opened wide! "We...?" He stopped. No injury would make Shawn forget that. She wouldn't believe it, and he'd find himself locked up or *fired*. "Yes, we did!" he assured himself and her with gusto. And to think stealing a kiss from Allene had been considered bold! "Did you...um, did you *want* me to *push* you?" So many temptations in this world, and so many strange euphemisms! He glanced uneasily at the cross, wondering how to stave off such expectations if she wanted that.

"No," she said. "It's nice just being with you for a change. I'm starting to feel like I could tell you...."

A knock sounded at the door. She sighed and stood to open it, her long black hair flowing down her back. He watched her, digesting the news. And yet, given the way these women dressed and behaved, he thought he shouldn't be surprised. He was disturbed to find he liked the idea. He pushed the thought from his head, with another guilty glance at the crucifix. There was Allene and all of Scotland to think about.

"Rob!" Amy said, at the door.

"Twenty minutes in his room and he hasn't gotten you in bed," Rob replied. "The changes just keep coming!"

Amy gasped. "What an awful thing to say!"

"It's been an awful way for him to treat you. Breakfast is on, and people are asking where you two are. Most are assuming, of course. Caroline's in a real snit." He scowled at Niall. Amy shoved out the door past him, glaring. He waited till she was gone before saying, "How long are you going to string her along with the Saint Shawn act? She deserves better."

"Yes, she does," Niall agreed. They stared at each other for several moments before Rob slammed out of the room.

Niall turned back, thoughtfully, to the pile of paper and pens, and his copious notes, diagrams, and maps of the Stirling area. Pushing Amy and his new-found knowledge of their relationship, and Rob and his anger, forcibly from his mind, he studied them again, turning them around, looking at them from every angle.

Hesitantly, he touched the mouse, moving the *cursor* as he'd watched Amy do. He clicked on the map and it responded. It took him a minute of study and deciphering the odd script, to realize he was now looking at a larger area. *Zoomed out,* Amy had called it. He studied this broader view of the area, waiting for the bolt of sudden insight he'd been sure Christ would send him. He took a long drink of coffee, staring at the maps over the golden rim. No bolt of inspiration came. Worse yet, his mind would not stay on the battle.

Niall sighed. He leaned back, tipping his chair on two legs, and pushed his hand through his hair. His thoughts kept returning to Shawn and all the bits and pieces of information he'd learned about him. He stood, finally, resigned to his inability to study the battle, and went back to the bedroom.

There, he pulled out the trombone case, opened it, and felt under the lining for the picture. He slid it out and stared at it, the man and the boy. As he did, the flute once again started its melody in the background. He looked up. Caroline or her friend must have skipped breakfast. A violin joined, playing long, slow notes, and still he stared. God knew more about Shawn than Niall could guess.

"I pray for him," he said softly. "God, may Your will be done in his life. May your angels guard him." The flute trilled and launched into a scale rising swiftly on eagle's wings. Niall's soul danced with it, anticipating something good. The sound lifted out of reach, leaving the room emptier than it had been.

A knock sounded on his door, and a man yelled, "Buses leaving for rehearsal, Shawn! Get downstairs!"

Niall gave the photograph one last, lingering look, trying to imagine the boy and his father as they'd been the day it was painted. Pity swelled in him, knowing what each had come to. He slid the picture into the back pocket of his jeans, and left for rehearsal.

Central Scotland, 1314

Shawn's heart beat hard and swift in his bruised chest. He lay trapped, injured and helpless, under the feet of men—brutes—who wanted to kill him, still trying to find a better explanation than what it appeared. There was none.

Another song started up. He couldn't guess how much time had passed. He'd woken several times, sometimes to silence, sometimes to talk and laughter, always with aches in every part of his body and the growing stench of the cellar in his nose. He looked twice at his wrist in reflex, but he hadn't worn his watch that day with Amy.

Above him, the men bellowed bawdy lyrics about a girl in the hay; the kind of thing, Shawn thought, he himself had been singing just days ago while downing ale. Beer, he corrected himself in irritation. Panic swelled at the thought of never again throwing a party for his friends. He fought it back: no escape had suggested itself yet. But it would.

The reed instrument kept piping the mismatched melody that bore no relation to the men's song. He couldn't believe they didn't clout the man playing it. People seemed willing to hit and stab each other for little enough in this time. If just a little kiss got you stabbed, then playing so badly out of tune deserved at least drawing and quartering.

He thought of the innkeeper's daughter, laughing in the stable. His hand stung; his chest hurt. He wondered where she was, and what her father had done to her. He wondered if she ached like he did, and felt another sting: of remorse. He twisted on the burlap sacks, seeking comfort he couldn't find.

Above, a woman squealed, men laughed, and feet pounded across the floor over his head. These men wanted to kill him! His hand throbbed. Distaste coated his mouth. He sipped from the water skin, grateful for it.

Allene's hand slipped into his. Sweat covered her palm. It surprised him. Cool, unflappable Allene, so at home in this bizarre world? Fear gripped her, too. He squeezed her hand. Nearby, the other man rasped; Shawn guessed he had woken, and was most likely sweating profusely under the heavy tread and raunchy humor of the men who not merely wanted, but had already tried, to kill him.

His hand throbbed.

He closed his eyes, waiting, listening. The rat scratched in the corner. His legs itched.

Allene's hand lay clammy and soft in his. She lay her head on his chest, over his pounding heart. "Remember the day we ran in the hills among the heather?" she breathed.

Shawn tried to picture goody-two-shoes Niall and the angry Allene running carefree. "No," he said. "The blow to the head, you know." But talking would ease her fear. "Tell me."

"It was my fifteenth summer. I was out with the women, collecting peat. You rode over the hill, coming home from your foster family. I slipped away to meet you. I knew by then my father had promised you my hand, and I knew the girls envied me. But I was scared."

"You kissed me behind the oven." *Pretty wild guy, that Niall,* Shawn thought.

"'Tis not the same as spending my whole life with you. I dinna ken how you'd treat me, as a husband. I sat on a rock while you took off your shirt to clean in the stream. And I saw the scars on your back."

Shawn waited, curious. "And?" he finally asked.

"I caught my breath, and you turned and laughed, saying 'twas naught. Then you saw how upset I was, and took my hand. I asked how could you bear to look at me when I'd brought that on you. You said you'd brought it on yourself, and 'twas by catching my father's attention you won my hand." Her breath flowed over his cheek. Her voice fell lower. "You said had you not kissed me, you'd ha' spent your life watching me from afar and wishing an' you'd gladly suffer it a hundred times more to marry me. No one ever loved me like that. You made me a garland of bluebells and sent me back to the women, saying you'd never again anger my father and risk our future. I still have that garland, all dried now."

Above them, the singing died down. The talk dwindled soon after, leaving a nerve-wracking silence, in which their every breath thundered out to the soldiers to come and find them. The tramping of heavy boots at irregular intervals suggested men leaving for their rooms for the night. Or was it daytime? Maybe they were leaving to search for him. The flute's soft melody died down last of all and drifted away. In the silence, one man's words sounded through the floorboards.

"You sure you haven't seen a monk come this way?"

Shawn jumped at the words. Did the soldier mean him, Shawn, or the real monk? Not that it mattered. He knew who they wanted, and could only imagine what the other man must feel, beaten and wounded and more helpless even than Shawn. The memory of the innkeeper's angry face swam before him, hovering over him in the stable. Allene curled in closer, seeking safety. He tightened his arm around her, and held his breath, waiting for the innkeeper's answer.

"No, my lord," said Fergal. "The road has been quiet."

"We're looking for an enemy of King Edward. He's disguised as a monk, raising armies against the king."

"No one has been here disguised as a monk, my lord," came the landlord's steady voice.

"You don't want to harbor enemies of the king." A long silence followed. The itch started again on Shawn's leg. Then the same voice said, "Niall Campbell. Has he been here?"

Shawn's insides cramped. His throat hurt from the tension in it.

His life lay in the hands of the man he'd thumbed his nose at, mere hours ago.

"The Campbells live some two days' journey west, my lord, on the other side o' the loch."

A sharp report jolted the floor above their heads; a great fist, perhaps, slamming down on the table? A man leaping to his feet in anger? Shawn tensed. He relaxed each muscle methodically. He slowed his breathing. "Well I know it!" the English voice bellowed. "Three days hence, he gave us the slip. We've not found him in the Great Glen."

"The Great Glen is deep," said the landlord, unperturbed. "There are great unexplored reaches. 'Twould be easy for him to hide there and not be found."

"He's not the only one who knows it well," the soldier said. "There is another who has taken us to all his hiding places."

In the cellar, Allene clung to Shawn's arm and whispered, "Thank God ye were wounded! I know ye, Niall. You'd ha' disregarded my father and taken the Great Glen."

"No..." Shawn said. His head swam from fear and hunger. His mouth became dry. Maybe Niall would have done that. He might be dead in the Great Glen, right now, had the switch not happened.

"Who knows your secrets, Niall? Darnley? William? Conal? Iohn? Try to remember. He'll keep following us. An' he doesna find us, he'll be at Stirling Castle, posing as a friend."

Shawn's jaw tightened. He had no way of knowing.

"We've begun to wonder," the soldier said slowly, and Shawn, relying on his sense of hearing as never before, heard slyness in the ugly voice, "if we were fed false rumors. My man swears it was monk's garb in which Niall was to travel." Allene squeezed his hand sharply. Shawn gasped in pain. He wracked his mind to think who knew about the monk's robe. All the lords. They'd discussed it in the meeting. "Maybe he changed clothes on the way? But we would have found the robe, under thick brush or thrown in a river, maybe even buried."

Shawn let out a breath. "The Purloined Letter," he whispered.

"'Twould be a job, finding one robe in the wilderness," replied Fergal.

"'Twould," agreed the soldier, "but that two score of the king's best men are searching. There are only so many ways to enter the Great Glen from Glenmirril. We've searched every one, far in, and far off the path. We were right behind him. There is no stone unturned."

"He's a genius," Shawn whispered. The soldiers might look right at the robe, hanging with a dozen others, and be none the wiser.

"So he must still be wearing it," the soldier concluded. "A monk should be easy to spot. We did find one."

Shawn breathed in relief. He, a minstrel in a fine-feathered hat, would pass unnoticed.

The voice above laughed. "Poor devil was half dead before our friend told us we had the wrong man." The monk, somewhere in the dark, rasped, and Shawn's relief dimmed. They would indeed find another monk. And that monk would die that Shawn might live to rouse Hugh and save Scotland. In a flash, he saw all the old Laird had done to see Niall safely through. He closed his eyes, sinking deep into himself, and suddenly he understood why Allene prayed.

He did so, himself, in agitation. *God, get me out of this! I didn't ask to be needed by these people! It isn't my responsibility! And I can't help them.*

Inverness, Scotland, Present

The bus whisked Niall, with the orchestra, through a drizzly Scottish morning to the great hall. Amy sat beside him this time. He closed his eyes, trying to quell the discomfort of his stomach. Her hand, in his where she'd put it, gave him some comfort. How these people laughed and sang inside this hurtling beast, he couldn't guess. The thought of the rehearsal did nothing to ease his stomach. The only upside was that it distracted him from the images of Amy and Shawn that had come with his new knowledge of their relationship. What disturbed him most was that Shawn didn't deserve her.

He hurried with the musicians through the rain, into the warm concert hall. Onstage, beside the harp, he squinted over the lights glaring up from the edge of the floor. A black cavern yawned beyond, its ceiling soaring up out of sight. He settled himself at the harp, a jangle of nerves.

Today, however, went much better than the first rehearsal. Thankful for the Laird's rigorous instruction, he played through his pieces, with only half of the previous rehearsal's mistakes—and only half the snickers. His confidence surged; he enjoyed the fine instrument leaning on his shoulder, and the magnificent music swelling from the orchestra behind him. He'd always done his best thinking while his fingers moved through well-known pieces, and his mind roamed freely across the battle as he played.

After the second piece, a young woman came onstage. Red hair swirled around her face. She reminded him of Allene. Pain seared his heart. He shouldn't be here! He should walk off this ridiculous *stage* right now, because this concert didn't matter! He glanced at Conrad, and feared he'd have him locked up, or, worse, *fired.*

And he wouldn't know what to do if he left, anyway.

"We'll do it with Megan today," Conrad said, and, with a swoop of his baton, he began the song Niall had worked on with Celine. He played an introduction and the first verse, rich chords rolling from his fingers.

Megan joined, in a throaty voice. *"Ian MacGregor a friend betrayed, a friend he did betray."*

"No, no, no, *no!"*

Niall jumped as Conrad's voice smashed through his reverie. The music behind him crashed to a halt. He heard a snicker, and sighed.

"He's an angel of music!" came a man's voice. "The angel of death!" Laughter came from the brass section. Niall turned. Rob polished his trumpet, not bothering to hide a self-satisfied smirk.

"Listen to the words!" Conrad shouted, waving his baton. "You're playing this thing like a battle march. It happens in the middle of a battle, but it's a ballad. A *ballad!* A man is betraying his friend!"

"Shawn knows about that," came the same voice. Niall clenched his jaw, but refused to acknowledge the comment in any way.

Conrad shook his head in despair, raised his baton, and said, "Try it again."

Niall placed his fingers, waiting for Conrad's downbeat. He played the intro, the first measure, and continued this time through the whole song, listening to the words, and feeling the betrayal. He knew it all too well, in recent weeks as he and MacDonald had discussed who might be carrying information from the castle—and especially now, knowing it was Darnley. He bowed his head, hurting, remembering so many days in the hills and by the loch with the man who had become a second father to him.

A crimson cloak he was paid
To sell his dearest friend
Lord Campbell charged that very day

He fumbled a string, looking up at his own name, but found his place and continued.

From out the wooded hill
But oh, Ian, his friend betrayed
In swirling crimson cloak.

There were lots of Campbells in Scotland, he told himself. His fingers ran through the melody and chords, while he scolded himself he did not know the piece well enough to let his mind wander. He glanced up as Megan started the next verse.

Lord Campbell thought that very day

To fight by Ian's side
As their fathers had before them done
To save auld Scotland
But Ian raised his voice in song
A greeting once they'd shared

Besides, he told himself, forgetting his own admonishment to keep his mind on the music, he knew no Ian. And he'd seen Darnley's coat of arms at the Two-Eyed Traitor. Ian might belong to any of Scotland's many wars. He hit another wrong note. The singer cast a look of concern, but kept singing. He smiled back in reassurance.

With the very song they'd shared,
He called the Sassenach laird
Never suspecting till the end,
Lord Campbell met his friend
And now he lies beneath the sword,
A-dying at Ian's feet
And oh, Ian his friend betrayed
In swirling crimson cloak.

Niall played through the chorus one last time, the violins tremoring on chords, and flutes singing a descant over his melody. He rolled up an arpeggio, and dropped to the lowest string to finish with a long gliss. His right hand hovered near his head, letting the sound resonate. Behind him, the orchestra poised like deer spotted in the forest. When the last reverberations died away, he looked up.

Megan smiled. "To think you don't even play harp." She shook her head. "You scared me once or twice, but that was wonderful!"

Conrad stepped down from his block. He pumped the young woman's hand, and slapped Niall's shoulder. "Great job, Shawn! I don't know how you do it! Always more surprises from you!" The musicians laughed knowingly. "I'm very happy with this one!" He turned to the orchestra. "That's the kind of emotion I want!" he said. "These two," he gestured to Megan and Niall, "had me feeling someone was going to stab me in the back any minute!"

Several musicians nodded appreciatively, and they moved to the next piece. Niall played alone, or with vocalists, pieces that he'd played many a winter night in the castle. They danced and skipped easily from his fingers, patterns he'd known for years, while the orchestra played Conrad's hastily-arranged accompaniment behind him. The familiarity of the pieces freed his thoughts to turn back to the upcoming battle. Make that, he corrected himself, the battle that had happened seven hundred years past. His mind drifted over the writings, pictures, and maps he'd studied in every spare minute, while his fingers moved through the music. His head bowed in concentration, but on the Pools. What had been the Scots' real downfall, apart from the little matter of being severely outnumbered? He'd studied warfare with the best tutors. Numbers alone need not dictate victory or loss. Conrad's baton swooped to a finish.

"Nice job," Conrad said. "Maybe a little quicker next time, but I'd swear you've been doing this all your life."

Niall smiled. "On to the next?" he asked. He watched for Conrad's signal, and began the song that always made Allene blush, sitting by her father, in front of the great roaring fire of an evening while he played, and gave a roguish wink when MacDonald wasn't looking. The memory warmed him. Judging by the gentle violin accompaniment Conrad had conjured, Niall thought he had no idea of the bawdy double meaning of the original lyrics.

His thoughts drifted back to the battle. Where had it really turned against the Scots? He reviewed the information again, pausing only when Conrad stopped the orchestra to work with the trombones. "You, timpani." He pointed to Aaron. "Imitate the trombones here. Back and forth. Heavy." Niall stared at the great, copper kettle drums in the back. He'd seen something similar once, when Longshank's army had marched across his foster family's land. An enormous horse with feathered feet had borne a rider and heavy drums. Lord Hayes said they were used to signal the army. It didn't help. He couldn't bring back a timpani. He couldn't produce a heavy horse, and they would be no good on that carse, anyway. Keith's cavalry would be light. Ponies, really. And he didn't know *what* to signal Bruce's army, to turn the tide of battle.

"Shawn. Shawn, are you with us?"

A snicker rose on the heels of Conrad's sharp words. "The tuner's on, but it's a little flat." He recognized Caroline's voice.

"My apologies," Niall said, and lifted his hands. He returned to the song Allene loved, but his mind stayed caught, a bird thrashing in briers, on Keith's cavalry. His hand drifted, during a rest while the flutes took over the melody, to the crucifix around his neck. *Pray for Shawn.* The words leapt, unbidden to his mind. He dropped the crucifix. "May your angels protect him," he thought, without enthusiasm.

What do horses have to do with it? he asked himself. *All they'll have is light cavalry against Edward's war horses. What am I missing?* He brought his hands back to the harp and joined the brass on the refrain. He smiled, remembering exactly where he'd winked at Allene. He frowned, thinking about the horses. He missed a note, and glanced up. But Conrad was focused on a violinist behind him. "A love song!

This is a *love* song," he shouted over their playing. "Hearts, lace, cupid!" He imitated an archer, pulling his baton back like the arrow. A few musicians laughed. Niall stared, unclear what archers had to do with love, or why anyone found this funny. His fingers moved; the harp rested solidly on his shoulder. He lifted his eyes into the black abyss beyond the stage, seeing drums and horses and arrows and....

The answer hit him. He fumbled a note, and a second note, and rushed the next few to catch up. Conrad threw him a questioning look. He kept playing, but his heart raced. He knew the answer! *He knew!*

"Slow down, Shawn," Conrad said. "A love song, not a race." Someone snorted in the trumpet section. Niall's fingers slowed, though his heart and mind sped. He had his first answer: how to turn the battle of the Pools.

* * *

Niall played through the rehearsal, impatient to get back to Amy and the computer for his second question: how to get the information back to Bruce and Keith.

After another hour, Niall's back and fingers ached. He grudgingly admitted some admiration for Shawn if he could play a sackbut for so many hours on end. He sighed with relief when Conrad put down his baton, shaking his fingers and stretching his back. "Until tomorrow," Conrad said, and the musicians began packing up.

Niall lowered the harp and turned to Amy, seated behind him. "Beautiful playing," he said. "You're very talented."

"About time you noticed!" The concertmaster harrumphed.

"The song." Niall turned to Peter. "You're knowledgeable."

Peter narrowed his eyes. "What do you want, Shawn?"

"What battle was it? Who were Ian MacGregor and Campbell?"

The concertmaster regarded him suspiciously for another moment. He polished his violin, and finally said, "Could've been anything. These folk songs get corrupted over the years, names change, they get mixed up with new verses added after another battle. Hundreds of years later, it's only guesses what they originally referred to, or whether anything in them was ever real."

"So maybe no one was betrayed?" Except he knew there was a traitor in the castle. So if this Ian in the song was not a clue, then it must be Darnley as the story said.

"Not your usual interest, Shawn." He wiped his violin, with slow strokes. "I'm glad to see the change," he added. "A lot of us are. You just might be the man Amy's thought you were all along."

Niall gave a slight bow—it was a habit he found difficult to break, though it drew odd stares—and turned to go.

"Pray for Shawn!"

He heard the voice audibly this time! He spun around. Peter polished his violin. Niall slid the picture from his back pocket and studied it. Compassion rushed over him, for the boy in the picture. He'd lost his father. He'd grown to be a man whom few really liked, not even those he called friends; a man whose peers did not respect him; a man who had now, most likely, been thrown into a wild, cruel world with none of his money or power to help him. Niall crossed himself and prayed with heartfelt compassion for the boy in the picture and the man he'd become. A flute fluttered and trilled, sailed away to a high note, and drifted off. He searched the orchestra. Caroline and the other flutist chatted while tucking their flutes into black cases.

Central Scotland, 1314

Time dragged like a funeral in the cellar. The flute started again, low and soft, barely audible. For the first time in years, Shawn was alone and sober with his own thoughts: no television, no parties, no women, no concerts to prepare. Nothing to distract his attention and keep it darting to anything but what mattered. The question of how to get back to his own time raged in him. His wounds ached. The innkeeper's daughter worried the edges of his mind. He thought of his father, suffering as his blood drained away. He tried to push the girl out of his mind. It was her father's choice, after all. The flute trembled and fluttered. But with each new ache of each bruise, he thought of her, nonetheless, and wondered if she hurt as badly as he did. With each sting of his body, grew the sting of his conscience.

With a deepening thirst as they rationed the water ever more carefully, the growing rumbles of his stomach, and the eventual necessity of relieving himself, Shawn guessed they had been in the cellar far longer than the day's sleep he'd expected. They huddled together through a second rabble-rousing party, holding hands. Morning or night, the dark womb around them never changed. The room stank of whatever the burlap bags held, of rotting vegetables, and of their own waste. They dared some quiet talk during the loudest of the party.

"Allene." Shawn cleared his throat uneasily, about to say words he'd never said in his life. She shushed him, but he pulled her finger from his mouth. "No," he whispered. "I have to. I'm...uh, I'm....I'm sorry." In the dark, he sensed her head turning toward him, her eyes opening wide. Although conscious of the monk nearby, it had to be said. "I've been a jerk. I never meant to, it's just...in my life, this is normal."

"Normal?" Her breath came out in a soft swoosh. "Taking

advantage of a woman is normal? Seducing a man's daughter behind his back while he's trying to save your life? Normal?" Loud voices bellowed a drinking song over their heads, with more enthusiasm than talent. Something soft sniffled at the back of his hand. He flung it, startled. It slammed against the far wall. Allene let out a muffled yelp. They fell silent for a moment.

Shawn squeezed his eyes tight, nauseated. A rat had touched him! He forced his mind back to their conversation. It sounded pretty bad, in her words. He tried to explain. "It's not really seen that way. Women—I mean, women in my world—they like that sort of thing."

"In your life? In your world? Niall, you're not yet yourself. This *is* your world. Have I not known you since we were both bairns? I've never known such women, except loose women." A loose woman, Amy? Hardly. She'd never slept with anyone but him. She made the Victorians look licentious. "Or desperate women," Allene added, "who appease a man to feed their children or have a place to lay their head." The idea unsettled him. Amy wasn't desperate. She earned her own way. She didn't need a man to feed or house her.

Feet stomped a raucous rhythm above them. Hands clapped. Dirt sifted down, a fine sprinkling into their hair and faces. He rubbed at his irritated eye.

"Niall." Allene's breath brushed softly against his cheek. "I'm scared. You're no the brave and giving man I knew but last week."

Shawn hung his head. He wanted to tell her he wasn't Niall. She couldn't possibly understand. "I'll try," he said. "I'll try harder to be that man." He couldn't say, himself, why it suddenly mattered. But he wanted her respect.

Above, the bacchanalian song ended, liquor-logged voices called to one another, and shuffling footsteps moved drunken men around the room. Several minutes later, someone spoke. Something scraped, a bench at a table, Shawn guessed. A voice rose in irritation. Shawn and Allene held hands, straining to hear.

"My men have gone farther into the Great Glen with your lad," said the voice from last night. He slurred his words. "We've not heard from them yet. Are you sure you've seen no monk, nor Campbell? Would we could check your cellar and find whether there may be a monk or a Campbell hiding among the turnips!"

Shawn's insides ran cold. Mostly. *I did the right thing. I apologized.* He felt his father's presence, strong, warm, and smiling, and the fear eased a little. He slipped an arm around Allene.

"Now, my lord," came Fergal's placid voice, "surely none would be foolish enough to hide the king's enemies right under the king's men! An' surely you don't think I'd trust a Campbell with my turnips!"

The king's soldiers guffawed. "Safer your turnips than the MacDougall's cattle!" shouted one.

"Those were *our* cattle!" Allene whispered indignantly.

"A fine jest," said Fergal. "Though the MacDougalls would no see the humor. A round on the house." The men cheered. "'Twill be another day ere the Grants and your men finish searching the Glen. 'Tis a deep wilderness, when a man does not want to be found. And Campbell is perhaps far away by now. Would it no be wiser to move on? Rumors have Hugh in the forest near Glasgow."

"Bah!" bellowed the first soldier. "I would feign search your cellar, drunk though you intend to get my men!"

"Surely not, my lord," said Fergal, mildly. "I mean only to keep them happy. To King Edward!"

The men cheered, but the commander shouted above it. "To the cellar!"

In the cellar, Shawn sweated. "We have to hide," he whispered.

"Trust him," Allene whispered back.

"It's the rest of them I don't trust," Shawn hissed. "He's just one man."

"The cellar is well hidden."

Shawn, nonetheless, began digging among the sacks and piles lining the cellar's walls. The monk rustled nearby, presumably doing the same. Feet stamped above, and he heard the brushing sound he'd last heard as Fergal swept straw over the trap door. He forced his muscles to relax; tried to slow his breathing; tried to settle his mind. Allene squirmed in beside him, yanking the rancid sacks over them both. He wrapped his arm around her. "You okay?" he risked asking the monk, under cover of the shouting above.

"We are in God's hands," the man replied, and they fell silent, waiting.

Shawn wished he could believe that. He lay back, Allene's head on his chest, and returned to mentally rehearsing his music on the harp—anything to keep his mind off the soldiers. It could only lead to blind panic. He had six pieces now, and wondered, should he be called on to actually perform, if that would be enough.

The harp! With a start, he realized he'd left it against the wall near the trap door.

He sighed. Maybe with a monk here, they *would* be safe in God's hands. But his heart pounded, a snare drum in the hands of a drunken percussionist. He'd feel better if God made Himself visible, preferably with a flaming sword in hand. Even a minor angel or two would do.

Above them, a soldier shouted. "Found it!" The men cheered. Allene curled more tightly into him. Her breath came in short, sharp jolts. Hinges creaked. Shawn squeezed his eyes shut. The putrid sacks pressed on his nose. "I'll go down," volunteered one. "Hand me my sword!"

Shawn swallowed hard, tightening his arm around Allene. Her faith in him was misplaced. He couldn't protect her.

The soldier shouted again. "I'll stab these turnips and see how many bleed like a Campbell." Great laughter greeted this apparently clever quip. Shawn, shrinking smaller under piles of turnips, onions, and burlap sacks, missed the humor. He wondered where the real Niall was. Flying home with the orchestra? Shawn didn't want to die here in his place.

A thud of feet landed on the cellar floor, along with a muffled voice. "I'm in!"

Inverness, Scotland, Present

Niall couldn't face the queasy bus ride back to the hotel. Besides, he wanted time alone to think through his next problem. If he could persuade Amy to go with him, he could risk asking again what her century knew of changing times. He'd word it more carefully this time, so as not to upset her.

"I'll walk," he insisted. The others, congregating around the huge bus in the warm afternoon sun, seemed to find this outrageous. "All the way to the castle?" Dana asked in disbelief. She shook her head and climbed on the bus.

"It's at least a mile," Amy said, her forehead wrinkling.

"It seemed but a few furlongs," Niall replied.

"Furlongs? How long have you been thinking in furlongs?" demanded one of the men.

"Not fer long!" another cracked. They laughed and punched one another's arms.

"Yes, I'm sorry, not furlongs," Niall agreed. "Miles." The men turned their backs, jostling to get their instruments into the storage areas under the bus, talking about the rehearsal and their plans for their free afternoon.

"Do you remember the way?" Amy glanced at his temple.

"I was hoping...." Niall began.

"He'll be fine." Rob rounded the bus, his face dark. "I've got a seat on the bus for us, Amy."

Niall's hackles rose, with a sudden, irrational determination to have Amy choose him. He looked with wide eyes at the glass and stone buildings, old and new, rising along the River Ness. He knew exactly where to find the castle hotel. But he wanted to talk to Amy. And Rob's possessiveness ground his nerves. "That way, is it not?" Niall said, pointing north.

"'Is it not,'" Rob sneered. "He knows it's south. He's playing you, Amy."

"Which way is south?" Niall turned west. His back to Amy, he arched an eyebrow at Rob, challenging him.

Rob's lip twitched. His eyes hardened. "I'll take you." Most of the musicians were on the bus now. He slid his trumpet into the great silver beast. "Amy, get on the bus."

Niall waved away Rob's offer. "Weren't you going fishing with the...uh," he almost said *lads*, but caught himself and substituted, "others?" He needed to talk to Amy!

"Yeah, we're going fishing."

"I'm slow." Niall rubbed his posterior, reminding Rob he'd been wounded there, too. Their eyes locked like rams' horns, showing none of the concern their words conveyed. "I don't want to hold you up."

"You haven't been moving slow." Behind Rob, someone pounded on the bus window. Rob glanced back, his shoulders tense.

"It was a long rehearsal," Niall lied. "I'm stiff."

"Then ride the bus."

"I need to work it out." Niall stared Rob down. "I'll be slow."

Rob's eyes narrowed. "They'll wait."

"Best not," Niall said. "The biggest fish bite before sundown."

A muscle twitched in Rob's jaw. "What do you know about fishing?"

Niall coughed. He knew plenty. Shawn, perhaps, did not. "I've heard they do," he said. "In the Highlands. You'd best take the bus." A breeze blew, rippling Rob's short, blond hair, while each man considered his next move.

Someone on the bus pounded a window, louder this time. "Let's go, Rob! The fish are waiting to jump in our boats!"

"I'll take him," Amy said, pushing her violin in with the other instruments under the bus.

Rob glared up at the window. It reflected the tree-lined boulevard. He slammed the big door of the bus's storage compartments much harder than necessary. "He's playing you for a fool, Amy." He shot Niall a last glare before swinging onto the bus. Niall couldn't resist a smirk back, though he chided himself such behavior was unworthy of a future laird.

He took Amy's arm, elated to have won, and hard-pressed to contain his excitement at retrieving the opportunity to question her. They crossed the street and set off down the sidewalk, along the river. Behind them, the bus roared to life, belching smoke, with all those people in its belly. Niall shuddered. He quickened his step, beside the silvery Ness.

"It was a good rehearsal," she said, hurrying to keep up.

"Yes," he agreed. His excitement pushed him forward, rashly, to his real concern. "Switching times," he said excitedly. Inspiration hit him. "Are there stories? In my time..." She looked at him sharply. He searched the corners of his mind for a correction. "In my time in, uh...in my time growing up, I recall stories of fairy hills and such. Stories of men who went into hills to visit dwarf kings and came out three hundred years later. Have we no such stories?"

"This again?" Amy stopped. "Who are you, and what have you done with the real Shawn?" He paled, resisting the urge to put his hand to the noose he felt twisting around his throat. She cocked her head. "I'm kidding." The Ness whispered beside them. "But what in the world happened out there? I want the truth."

"Nothing." The wraith noose slid away. Niall breathed more freely. "Something I saw on the internet. Are there stories?"

She started walking again, frowning. He knew he hadn't convinced her. "There are all kinds of stories. H.G. Wells and *The Time Machine*."

"What kind of wells?" Niall's heart leapt in excitement: stories of disappearing in time still abounded! He imagined a deep well on a fairy hill.

"H.G. Wells, the author?" Amy said. "In his story, the guy made a machine that took him through time. In other stories, people walk through stones on, well, fairy hills, like you said, or in magical places. There are just sort of—gates—into other times, and it happens by accident, where they say the crust between times is thin. There was a whole series about standing stones where that happened."

There were standing stones less than a day's ride from Glenmirril. Men whispered of witches and mysterious goings-on there. He and Iohn had talked of it. Maybe he needed to get to them, now in this time, to get back to his own. But it had happened without them the first time.

"There was one where the guy surrounded himself with things from the early nineteen hundreds and went to a hotel from that era, and just sort of believed himself back to that time. And as long as he believed he was there, he was. Then he sees a penny from his own time, and gets sucked back."

Niall thought regretfully of his coins, sitting now in the pawn shop. But clearly, seeing them hadn't taken him back where he wanted to be. Nor had believing he was in his own time, that first morning, altered the truth of where—when—he really was.

"But none of it is true," Amy said. "No one's ever claimed to have really traveled through time, and if they did, they'd be locked up."

"Maybe that's why they don't claim it," Niall murmured. He fell silent. He couldn't be locked up.

His hand slid from her arm, and he trudged along under the summer trees lining the walk. The river whispered its rhythm against the narrow pebbled shore. Her hand crept into his, and he jumped, guiltily. Memories of Allene flooded him, of climbing the hills together. How she would yell to see him walking hand in hand with another lass. But he could hardly pull his hand away, without raising Amy's suspicions more. A warm flush crept up his arm. He liked the feel of her hand, and hated himself for liking it. All night, since her revelation yesterday, he'd fought off images of her and Shawn *pushing*. The images returned, with himself in Shawn's place. The flush inched up his neck. That's what Rob wanted...he wanted to *push* her!

Niall almost groaned at the realization, and wondered why he hadn't seen it immediately. Rob was smitten with Amy. Niall wrapped his hand more tightly around hers. Rob was not right for her. He tried not to worry about holding her hand.

"Something's wrong," she said. "It scares me when you talk like this. I'm worried about you."

"Don't worry. I am well." The worry stayed on her face. He tried again. "I'm *okay*." He thought about Shawn, possibly in the wilds of Scotland, hunted by a killer. How Amy would worry if she knew the truth. He didn't want to see her hurt. He squeezed her hand, put a smile on his face for her sake, and, deep inside himself, fell to his knees before the throne of God, pleading for Shawn.

Anything, he begged God. *For Amy's sake, for Allene's sake.* In his mind's eye, he saw the innocent boy in the picture and the father who had loved him. *Yes, even for Shawn's sake. You love him. Whatever You want, God, I'll do, if You'll just be with Shawn.*

Central Scotland, 1314

Muffled? Sweat prickled Shawn's hairline and slicked his palms; his senses strained. The voice sounded as if it came from another part of the cellar. He couldn't have buried himself so deeply under the burlap sacks. Thumps and pounding came from behind his back. He rose from the fetid sacks, shedding them, as understanding dawned.

"Pray, sir," Fergal's voice floated down through the floorboards, unperturbed, "spare some turnips for your men's stew tonight."

"We'll spare nothing till we find Campbell!"

Shawn sat, a statue, straining to hear every detail of the ongoing sword fight against the turnips, the cheers of the soldiers and the increasingly disappointed reports of the parsnip slayer.

Allene pushed at the bags, rising from their stinking bed to her knees, clutching his arm. He laid his hand over hers. At last, things quieted down. They heard the thunk of the trap door dropping back in place.

"My lord," the innkeeper said, "would you had believed me. I know not how I will prepare your men's dinner with what is left in my root cellar."

The captain's answer floated down as garbled rumblings. Running and swift steps ensued. For a time, chaos reigned above.

Shawn, Allene, and the monk climbed to their feet, shaking the filth off themselves. "We are hidden behind the real cellar," Allene said, having reached the same conclusion as Shawn.

"Praise be to God," whispered the monk.

Shawn let out a long, slow breath. He closed his eyes. *Thank you, God!* It was his first prayer of gratitude in many years. Allene wrapped herself in his arms, her head lying on his shoulder as they slid back to sit on the sacks. He leaned his own head on top of hers. Her body trembled; he touched her cheek and felt a damp trail of tears. "It's going to be okay," he whispered. "I'll get you there. You'll be okay." He vowed he would. He leaned back against the earthen wall, kissing the top of her head.

He tried to remember a time when Amy had turned to him, trusting him to protect her. He had to admit he'd given her no reason to do so. The one time she'd needed him—the time she came to him and told him she was pregnant—he'd let her down.

He felt sick, a tightening of his stomach, remembering how he'd cajoled and bullied, driving her to the clinic insisting it was for the best, while she pleaded. Why hadn't he seen her tears at the time? He'd only seen a woman who couldn't work through her emotions to her own best interests. *His* best interests. He'd seen a woman threatening him, standing between him and the life he wanted.

He pressed his cheek against the top of Allene's head, holding her close. It felt good to be needed and trusted. So Niall hadn't gotten to first base. But he had something Shawn didn't. He had a woman with utter faith and confidence in him.

Shawn wanted more of what Niall had.

Chapter Thirteen

Glasgow, Scotland, Present

Jimmy reached the James and Barley, a place of dark greens, rich mahoganies, and low lighting, ten minutes before the deadline. He dreamed of his big win, of paying off bills and having a bit extra. He'd take the missus to dinner, and buy that ring she'd wanted for so long. His mate's cousin shook his hand. "I 'ad some talkin' to get the manager to let you in again. I promised there'd be no trouble, like."

"'Coorse not,'" Jimmy promised, heartily. "I'll no tooch a drop. I want to win some money and pay off me bills, is all. I thankee for getting me in. I'll no let ye down." They shook hands, and Jimmy took his place in line to register.

Nine minutes later, the manager had him pinned against the dark-paneled wall, his face red, his ham fist gripping Jimmy's shirt front. The mate's cousin and a policeman stood by, glaring. "What were you thinkin', tryin' to pass dodgy notes?" demanded the manager.

"I wasna...." He scanned the crowd in the dim interior, desperate for a friendly face, anyone who would vouch for him. Rough and tumble men lined the heavy wooden bar, glaring at him. More heads turned to stare.

"Did ye no think we'd be lookin' fer suchlike?"

"I tell you, I dinna...."

"I gave me word for ye!" shouted his mate's cousin, jabbing his finger in Jimmy's chest.

"I dinna...."

"Where'd ye get 'em from?" the constable demanded.

The pub manager interrupted before Jimmy could speak. "Ye've ne'er been aught but trooble!" he said in disgust. "Take him out o' here," he told the policeman. "And dinna waste yer time lookin' further fer who's passin' funny money. Yer man here's been a troublemaker from day one."

The Scot spent the next two days in a small local cell, protesting his innocence, and growing steadily angrier at the American who had cheated him.

Central Scotland, 1314

Several hours later, the trap door opened and Fergal's strong arms pulled them out, blinking and squinting against the fire blazing in the grate. Outside, evening colors streaked the sky red, pink, and orange. "'Twas safe no sooner, my lady," the innkeeper apologized.

"Fergal," Shawn said. Dryness scratched his throat. He forced his head up, made himself meet the man's eyes. The girl cowered against the wall. Her fingers flashed, pulling Allene's hair into a tight plait. She avoided Shawn's eyes. Heat flushed his face.

Fergal glared at him, and thrust a bundle of clothing into the monk's hands. "Haste! Change and go with them!"

The monk needed no encouragement. Stiff from his injuries, he pulled the fawn-colored hose on under his robe, tugged the robe off over his head, and donned a linen shirt and brown tunic in its place—but not before Shawn saw his slender body covered in purple bruises, abrasions, and gashes from the beating the English soldiers had given him: the vicious beating that would have been Niall's, had he disregarded the Laird's orders. He winced.

Fergal snatched the monk's robe and threw it into the fire, and soon all evidence of their stay had become ashes. "The soldiers should be far away," Fergal said. "They've gone back to the Glen, though they left two men in the village. Walk boldly down the lane, look neither left nor right, and be on your way." He thrust a package of food into their hands.

"Fergal." Shawn cleared his throat and added, "Sir." He closed his eyes, not wanting to say those awful words again. Something about them hurt.

"Haste!" Fergal snapped. He glowered at Shawn. His body hummed with angry tension. Allene touched his forearm.

"I'm sorry," Shawn whispered. The words stung, like having a splinter pulled. Or something larger. He found it difficult to pull his gaze up from the floor, but when he did so, Fergal's face had softened.

"You were e'er a good man, Niall. 'Twas the blow to the head. No more will be said on it. God go wi' ye."

"Tell your daughter...." He looked to the girl again, melting against the shadowed wall. She met his eyes and turned quickly away, face red.

"I will," Fergal said. He edged between Shawn and his daughter, and pushed him toward the door. "Go."

A weight lifted from Shawn's chest.

* * *

Out in the road, Shawn felt exposed and vulnerable. His colorful tunic was no longer so bright. The billowing white sleeves were crumpled and gray. But he straightened his spine, told himself he was a minstrel, and put a carefree grin on his face, no different from any performance. No different from putting on his stage persona, or the man who made Amy feel good. Performance, after all, was about making the audience believe what you wanted them to believe. He did it for a living, for far more sophisticated audiences. He could do it here—even if his heart sank in fear.

The night air felt good after the stench of the cellar, crisp and clean. It was Heaven on earth, this fresh air, and he'd never seen it! They sauntered down the dirt road, looking neither left nor right. The few stone cottages stretched further and further; the road seemed endless, with two soldiers remaining behind, and no guesses where they might be. As they reached the last house, Shawn's smile grew. He could do this.

Then he saw the cage hanging from a large and sturdy oak. A dead man—if what was left in the cage could be called a man—blackened with decay, his body picked over by birds, slumped inside. The stench drifted on the evening breeze, sending a wave of nausea roiling through Shawn's stomach.

"You! Minstrel!" shouted a rough voice.

Shawn turned slowly. The nausea grew worse. His heart gave two hard thuds.

Now he knew where the soldiers were.

They sat on a rough-hewn bench, their backs against the stone wall of the last thatched-roof cottage. They wore crisp white tunics. Rounded metal helmets lay at their feet. A wineskin relaxed between them, a third companion. A jagged scar ran down the younger man's face, pulling his lip up into a curl, and his eye down in a permanent glare. He was no living history actor.

Shawn inclined his head, feeling weak all the way down to the toes of his leather boots. "Good even." He tried to imitate the speech he'd heard here. He winced at the poor results.

"What are you called?" the scarred soldier demanded.

Shawn's heart thumped, trying to remember the name they'd given him. He eyed the pike leaning against the wall. The scarred man's thumb stroked the hilt of a sword slung at his side, giving the impression he'd like nothing better than to use it. Shawn's mouth went dry.

"Have you no tongue!" barked the older man.

"Allan a Dale," Shawn rasped. He grimaced. He ransacked his memory, flinging aside one hazily-recalled fact after another. King Edward. Which Edward? Was Allan a Dale before or after the Edwards? Had he even existed? Or would these men know he'd just stolen the name of a character from a book? The dead man, not fifty feet away, jangled his nerves.

The men didn't react to his choice of names. "And who are your companions?" The scarred soldier's good eye roved over Allene's hooded figure and the monk's brown tunic. His hand tightened on his sword.

"Little John," said Shawn, indicating the monk. He jerked his head toward Allene, her face once again hidden in her cowl. "And my mute servant boy, um...Francis Drake. He was dropped on his head as a wee bairn and has not...has no said a...um...a wee word since."

"Where are you from? Your speech is not of these parts."

A plus, Shawn realized, his odd speech. He couldn't possibly sound like the Niall they sought. "From over the sea." He didn't remember what the continent was called, to these people, at this time.

"Spain? France?" The soldier rose from his seat, circling Shawn. Allene lowered her head; Shawn feared they'd push her cowl back. Her fiery long braid would betray them. His eye strayed to the sword; he swallowed hard.

"France." He spoke boldly, stepping forward to draw attention off her. The image of the dead man burned in his mind.

"Allan a Dale sounds very English," said the older soldier. He leaned against the wall, studying Shawn.

"'Tis," said Shawn. "My mother was English." He gave himself a mental kick. His mother would not have passed on her English surname.

The man on the bench swilled from the wineskin. "Who were her people?"

"The Dales," said Shawn. Would this man never stop asking questions! He realized, belatedly, that the Dales would be his father's people, not his mother's. He wished his heart would slow down. A dead body did nothing for his thinking processes. But the men's wineskin, not so full as it had been, did nothing for theirs.

"And this man? What happened to him?" The older man indicated the monk's bruised face.

Shawn lowered his voice, man to man. "His wife caught him with the barmaid." He grinned, nudged the monk knowingly, who laughed and winked at the soldiers. They chuckled understandingly.

The scarred man leaned close, his breath fouling the air. He stroked the hilt of his sword. "Why are you leaving the village at night? Would you not stay at the inn?" He fingered the edge of Allene's cowl. Allene shrank into her robes, bowing her head low.

"The night is warm," said Shawn loudly. His heart pumped fast with the familiar fear of being found out. He'd experienced it often enough with Amy. And suddenly, with his feet on familiar territory, the lies and charm flowed, weaving their spell around his audience. "The innkeeper has no dinner. It seems his turnips were no match for the King's men. We'd lief be on our way in search of food."

The soldier's hand fell from Allene's cowl. Shawn remembered, too late, the food tucked under his belt. But he'd become a person he knew well, and he swelled his chest with confidence he almost felt. If they saw the pouch, he'd deny, deny, deny. He'd feign surprise. It always worked.

"Play for us, minstrel. 'Tis a long night."

Shawn drew in a breath. Confidence aside, he didn't relish this test; especially not with an enemy of the king dead and decaying in his sight. Not with medieval weapons waiting to disembowel him, should he fail.

Slowly, he swung the harp off his shoulder, and seated himself on a rock, taking a moment to review his exercises on the road and in the cellar. He touched the strings, drooping his fingers as Celine had taught him, willing them to stop shaking. The pike hovered in his peripheral vision. These strings had no colors. He plucked a few chords, listening for majors and minors, till he found a tonic. These men, hopefully, knew little enough about music that a few missed notes would not alarm them.

The scarred soldier resumed his seat, but he scrutinized Shawn's every move. His hand stroked his sword. *You're a performer,* Shawn reminded himself, tearing his gaze from the sword, and tugged that persona firmly about himself.

He plucked the strings, starting with his old standby, *Blue Bells.* The melody flowed, as he'd practiced it over and over in his mind, carrying him to a place with no fear. A missed note here, a step too high there, but nothing that would alarm anyone. In these days, his music history classes had taught him, music changed with the memory and style of each minstrel.

"Do you not sing?" demanded the second soldier. "What kind of minstrel are you?"

Shawn grinned slyly. "I usually sing for the ladies, my lord."

The younger man half-rose, knuckles white on his sword.

Shawn held up his hand, as he'd seen others do. He hoped they didn't see it trembling. "Peace, my lord. I'll sing. 'Twas but a jest, and a poor one at that. My apologies."

The man sank back on the bench, sipping from the wineskin.

Shawn began again, giving himself an entrance, and sang.

Oh, where, and oh where
Has my highland laddie gone?
Oh, where, and oh where
Has my highland laddie gone?

He's gone with streaming banners
Where noble deeds are done,
And it's oh, in my heart, I wish him safely home.

He ran through another verse on the harp alone, playing the melody with the chords underneath. He hit a few notes that made him cringe, but the men seemed not to mind. The scarred man's shoulders relaxed. The soldiers took turns gulping from the wineskin, leaning against the cottage. Shawn started the second verse. Beside him, a clear tenor joined, the monk at his side harmonizing.

Oh where and oh where
Does my highland laddie dwell
Oh, where, and oh where
Does my highland laddie dwell?
He dwells in merry Scotland
Where the bluebells sweetly smell,
And all in my heart I love my laddie well.

He played through the melody once more. The scarred soldier's hand slipped from his sword. The lip relaxed and looked less fearsome. Shawn moved into the triplet section. Allene stiffened beside him, at this twist, and he moved back to the melody. The man beside him sang alone. "And it's oh in my heart that I wish he may not die." Shawn finished with a gentle arpeggio, running the length of the harp, and just for fun, gave a gliss up the strings.

The soldiers' faces were solemn. Silence hung between them, while Shawn's heart pounded. Sweat slicked his palms, and the pike loomed large in his vision.

Finally, the scarred man spoke. "It 'minds me of my own lass waitin' at home. Would that she is thinkin' o' me so. I thank thee. A good journey to ye."

Shawn inclined his head. These men were real. These men who wanted to kill him had died hundreds of years before his birth, but here they sat, man to man, before him. They feared dying as he did. He stared at them, museum exhibits come to life.

Allene tugged his arm.

"I thank thee," Shawn said gravely, and with a lingering glance at the gruesome corpse in the cage, the three of them set off into the countryside.

* * *

With the never-ending hills and valleys rolling before him in the late evening light, the weight of his situation settled on Shawn. He'd somehow ended up here, with Niall's problems dumped in his lap. It wasn't his deal. He had a life to live. Niall would just have to get himself back here and take care of his own business.

"'Twas not your usual playing," Allene commented.

"Very different," Shawn agreed, pleased nonetheless. Glancing back and seeing that the village had disappeared and they were far out of the soldiers' earshot, Shawn risked asking the question burning on his mind: "What's with the cage?"

"Did you no hear the soldiers while we were in the cellar?" Allene asked. "He was hung there to starve to death, as a warning to others."

"A warning about what?"

"Standing against King Edward."

"Isn't that..." he swallowed hard over a tight, hot knot in his throat, "what *we're* doing?"

Inverness, Scotland, Present

Niall downed a quick lunch with Amy in the castle's dining hall after rehearsal, grateful for Rob and Dana's absence. Celine and Aaron waved from their table. He smiled back.

"She seems much happier," Amy commented. "What happened when you were playing her harp?"

Niall waved a deprecating hand. "She realized Aaron's a fine man, that's all." Amy stared hard at him. He grinned, pushing in a mouthful of the brown *pudding* he was coming to like very much. "You don't believe me? There they are."

A smile spread across Amy's face. "You did something," she said. "I know you."

"Not so well as you think." Niall couldn't resist grinning at his own joke. And he liked seeing her smile. The ghost of the tingle he'd felt, when she took his hand, crawled up his arm. He had to fight his face out of a ridiculous grin. Romance was not on his list. Finding a way back was. He'd had no control over coming here, and feared he'd have equally little over getting back. But looking at Amy, he thought he might suffer worse fates. He could be content with her. More than content.

He touched the crucifix, thinking of Allene, and what awaited her at the hands of the English.

He stood abruptly, wiping his mouth with the back of his hand. "I'll be in my room," he said. "You'll summon me for dinner?"

"Summon you? Sure, your highness. Or maybe I'll just call you."

At her assent, though her attitude baffled him, he excused himself from the table, and hurried to his room, giving waves and nods to those who greeted him. As he entered his chambers, the tubby chug-chug of the tuba began down the hall. He closed the door, dulling the sound, and settled himself at the *computer*. It took only minutes this time, only a few mistakes, to remember how to reach the internet and *Google*. Google, he said to himself. Google, google. Iohn would get a good laugh out of that. He imagined himself back in the castle, with the Laird and Allene and Iohn. Only to them would he tell this adventure. No one else would believe him. Not even William. He did, he thought somewhat ruefully, have a reputation as a bit of a prankster. It would not stand him in good stead, did he tell this story.

But, he had to get there, first. He studied the small box under the word *Google*, wondering what to enter. *Time travel.* That's what Amy called it. He closed his eyes, searching his near-perfect memory for the words. Seeing them, he leaned over the letter board, and hunted.

T-I-M-E. He tapped them in, one by one, *time travel*, and waited. Nothing happened.

Through the walls came voices and the sound of that overgrown shawm they called a bassoon, playing an old folk song.

He stood, pushed a hand through his hair, marched to the window and back, trying to remember how she'd made it work. The blank screen mocked him, silent and unhelpful. He stalked to the coffee maker, picked up his big black mug with the gold trombone—Shawn's mug, he corrected himself—filled it and drank. It was cold. He threw it down the sink, hit the button to start the machine, and went back to stare at the Google page again.

Then he remembered: the square underneath, that said *Google search*. He moved the arrow over the box and clicked. The image—the page, he reminded himself, determined to use correct terminology and remain inconspicuous—changed instantly. He smiled, appreciating the legacy Shawn had left him, which had acquired this fine *high speed internet* in his own chambers where no one would question his search on time travel.

He studied the listings, trying to recall how Amy had reached them. He needed her help. But he'd already pushed his credibility with her. Besides—he leaned back in his chair—new temptations swirled around her, rousing his imagination and senses, now that he knew the possibilities. No, safer all around to do this on his own.

He stared at the mouse, picturing Amy's motions in her many hours of helping him. He moved the mouse. The arrow onscreen moved with it, and settled on the first word. He clicked the button.

The screen turned purple and yellow, like heather and gorse in the hills around Glenmirril. He blinked hard and faced the bright colors again, running his finger under the words, and reading slowly. *Sagan on Time Travel*. He wondered what a *Sagan* might be.

He clicked, bringing up a new page, and continued plodding through unfamiliar spellings of what was still a second language to him. He couldn't guess what the letters P-H-Y-S-I-C-I-S-T meant, or what worms' holes had to do with time. Maybe it was similar to walking into the dwarf king's cliff? That, too, had been inside the earth. He grimaced at the thought of a worm whose hole was large enough for a man to walk into. There had to be a better way.

He pushed on. This, surely, was no worse than MacDougall's arrow. He grimaced, twisted on the cushioned chair for more comfort, and scrolled down. His brain hurt, trying to make sense of so many strange words. Then again, he decided, maybe he would rather be astride his horse, laughing back at the enraged MacDougalls. At least that had been fun for a moment.

A knock sounded on the door. Both relieved and irritated at the interruption, Niall raised his head and called, "Enter!"

The door swung open, admitting a stern-faced Conrad and two blue-clad men. "The police have a few questions," Conrad said. He pursed his lips. Niall eyed the men, hoping neither he nor Shawn had done anything that would get him locked up or fired, and joined them at the sitting room's table.

They set their hats with the black and white checked bands on the table. The older man came straight to the point. "We canna find any sign of the man who shot ye."

Relief coursed through Niall. He stuck to his story as they fired questions at him—he remembered nothing—till they stopped pressing. But when he rose to bid them farewell, they remained seated. Their expressions hardened.

"There's more," Conrad said. His white eyebrows bristled. "A man was caught with counterfeits down in Glasgow." Niall thought he must look as blank as he felt, for Conrad leaned forward, biting out each word, "Fake money." He paused. "Says he got it from you." They all stared at him.

Niall's eyes widened, understanding. He shook his head. "I'd do no such thing!"

Conrad stood, and marched back and forth across the room.

"You gave him a thousand in cash," said the younger man, with short black curls and ruddy cheeks. "Where did ye get it?"

Niall closed his eyes. "I remember nothing," he said. But he had a niggling feeling. Then, suddenly, he knew where Shawn had gotten money. Opening his eyes, he crossed the room swiftly to Shawn's jacket and dug out the parchment that had identified the ring.

The police took it, murmuring to one another, and nodding. Excitement grew on their faces. "Don't leave town till we've talked to you again," the younger man warned, and they took their leave.

Relief flooded Niall, till he turned and saw Conrad staring at the computer. A word of which the Laird did not approve slipped through Niall's teeth. He stepped forward, casting for an explanation.

"Amazing!" Conrad burst out. He turned to Niall, beaming. "You never fail to surprise me. Who would think you'd have such an interest?"

"I...." Considering Amy's distress at his interest in time travel, he didn't understand Conrad's pleasure.

"Fascinating subject!" Conrad said. He jabbed a finger at the screen. "Sagan, now!"

"What's saggin'?"

Conrad laughed. "Funny, Shawn. Not what. Who. Fascinating man. What do you think of his grandfather paradox?"

"I know his grandfather?" Niall asked. "The wound," he explained. "I've forgotten so much."

Conrad frowned. Niall suspected he'd made another mistake. "Not Sagan's grandfather. The grandfather paradox. What if you go back in time and kill your grandfather before he sired your father?"

Niall stared, shocked at the imbecility of such a question. "Nonsense! Why would anyone do such a thing?" he snapped. He had no desire to kill anyone! These people led lives of such ease they had to think up problems! "What if you wished to save people?"

"Well," Conrad drew the word out. "Save them from what? Does that mean somebody who wanted to kill them dies instead? Now *their* descendents are wiped out, and the person you saved has descendents he wouldn't have had. Everything changes."

Niall strode to the window, looking through heavy diamond panes to the riot of color in the garden below. If he succeeded, would this entire world appear instantly different? He shook his head. It did no good to think of such things. He'd do what he could for Allene and Scotland, let come what may. He had not their luxury for such games.

"Stephen Hawking," Conrad continued. He tapped at the letter board, making little clicking sounds like the scurry of rats' feet down in the dungeons. "Smartest man in the world. Says time travel is impossible—as proven by the lack of time travelers."

Niall turned from the window, grinning broadly. "I'd like to meet this man," he said. He doubted Mr. Hawking would believe him, could he introduce himself.

Suddenly, Conrad snapped his fingers. "You know who you should talk to! Aaron!" He jumped from the chair and dashed out of the suite, white hair flying, yelling for Aaron, before Niall could protest.

He sighed, and went to the coffee maker to fill his mug.

The door flew open. Conrad ushered in a startled-looking Aaron and flashed out again, seeking other targets for his energy.

Aaron pushed a lock of black hair off his forehead. It promptly fell back. He scanned the opulence around him. "An unlikely scenario, me being invited into your room," he said. "Is this a new interest or what? Something to do with what happened in the castle?"

It seemed a fair explanation. Niall nodded. "I saw and heard... things. People."

"If the Shawn I knew a week ago said that, I'd think I was being set up." Niall waited. "But you're different since then." Aaron frowned, then said, "I'll show you something." He crossed to the computer, tapped, and stood back, indicating that Niall should read.

"The head wound has made me see double," Niall said. "Read it, please."

"This was a friend of my grandfather's," Aaron said, seating himself at the computer. "I knew him—straight up, honest guy. He's been interviewed. It was in a book."

Niall held tight reins on his impatience. "What happened?"

"This guy and two friends were out in a field near Kersey, in England."

"I know of Kersey!" Niall said. The Laird had visited the place, years ago when England and Scotland had still been friendly.

Aaron looked at him askance, and turned back to the computer. "They heard church bells, climbed a fence, and the church was gone. And Kersey suddenly looked like it would have in medieval times."

"Mid...what?"

"You know, thirteen, fourteen hundreds."

"They are evil times." Niall sighed, thinking of Edward's army.

"What?" Aaron looked at him, perplexed. "Isn't that 'were?'"

"Were, yes," Niall agreed. "They just walked into another time?" Hope shot through him. "How did they get back to their own time?"

Aaron shrugged. "They just did. They walked through the village. It was deserted, meat hanging in the butcher shop turning green, cobwebs everywhere. They started running, turned a corner, and when they looked back, there was the modern Kersey again."

He clicked the mouse, bringing up another page. "In a lot of these stories, there's this eerie silence, but in some, they interact with the people from the past, even buy things that come back to their own time with them." Niall fingered his crucifix. It and the coins had leapt forward with him. "But here's a really wild one. This woman," he tapped the screen, "says she was at the coliseum and suddenly found herself surrounded by Roman gladiators. One of them stabbed...." Aaron stopped, staring at Niall with naked curiosity.

"Like someone shot me?" Niall raised one eyebrow, unsmiling.

Aaron swallowed. "They found her unconscious in a tunnel, with gashes in her leg. They were the exact distance of the prongs on a trident from 250 A.D. just like she described." He studied Niall, waiting.

"Suppose," Niall said, "that it was not she who was stabbed."

"But they found her. They saw the marks."

Niall leaned forward. "Suppose someone from 250 A.D. who looked just like her was stabbed and found in the tunnel."

Aaron stared at the monitor and bit his lower lip. "Then where's the original woman?"

"You know more than I. What do you think?"

"If that were true, and I stress if, then there are two women from two times, who look alike. Somehow they switched places."

"How would you switch them back?" When Aaron didn't answer immediately, Niall added, "Would it be the place that caused the switch, or a connection between the two of them?"

"I don't know." Aaron studied Niall, his eyebrows drawn together, frowning. "Put them both back in the same place, maybe, and hope." He leaned forward, regarding Niall. "You saw people. What year would you guess they were from?"

"The year of our Lord, 1314. They are preparing to fight England for Stirling Castle. All Scotland is at stake."

"You could tell all that from looking at them?" Aaron asked doubtfully.

"I could tell you much more," Niall said softly. He leaned forward, piercing Aaron with his gaze.

"If you were the Shawn I knew...."

"Am I?"

"No." Aaron studied Niall. A pulse beat rapidly in his throat. A muscle twitched in his jaw. "But you were exactly where she left him. Nobody would believe you if you said you weren't. Because to believe anything else...." He frowned, his eyebrows drawn together, his head tilted. Just then, a jingling melody came from his belt.

His mouth pursed as he fumbled for his *cell phone*. Niall stared in fascination as he flipped it open, speaking to the unseen person. He closed it, and lifted his hands in a gesture of resignation. "I was supposed to meet Celine." He paused and when Niall didn't answer, said, "Let me know if you have any more questions." He turned at the door. When Niall said nothing, he added, "Anything at all."

"I will," Niall said.

After a momentary silence, Aaron let himself out, looking back in curiosity one last time.

Central Scotland, 1314

They traveled through the night, slower than they would have liked, due to the monk's injuries, eating the hard biscuits, or bannocks as Allene called them, dried meat, and turnips Fergal had provided. Not exactly McDonald's, Shawn thought, but a sight better than nothing. And all of it better by far than being hungry in a dark cellar, smelling the stench of their own waste, or facing scarred men with swords. Allene stuck close to his side.

The monk, peering through bruise-ringed eyes, told his story as they walked. Brother David, newly ordained and assigned to lead an abbey's choir, had been hiking south through the Glen, singing, when Edward's men had set upon him. Ignoring his insistence that he wasn't Niall Campbell, they'd beaten him and left him for dead. He'd woken to find Allene pouring a draught down his throat.

"A traveler found ye and carried ye to Fergal," Allene said. She slipped her hand through Shawn's arm. Warmth climbed up his insides. He thought of Amy, back in Inverness, and his awareness in the cellar of letting her down. Moonlight danced off Allene's wild red hair, freed from the cowl, and springing in curls around her face. She'd ask questions if her betrothed pulled away. Amy would understand. Scotland depended on him.

"Aye, he saved my life. And they'll be wonderin' what's become o' me, at the abbey," Brother David lamented.

"You're safer with us for now," Allene said. "We'll send word when we can."

They lapsed into silence, but for Brother David's labored breathing. Moors and hills rolled away on all sides, looking to Shawn as they had the day he'd hiked them with Amy. He wanted to believe he'd imagined the soldiers, the body in the cage. But the stench lingered in the pit of his stomach. Fear echoed through his veins, afraid they'd be seen silhouetted against the moon on the empty moor or as they crested yet another hill.

"They'll be sleepin' off the ale," Brother David reassured him, as Shawn turned yet again to search behind.

Shawn nodded and continued in silence. He curled his toes up against the damp bog. It's real, he told himself. As the distance increased between himself and the soldiers, a flame of excitement licked upward. How his father would have loved this opportunity, to find out how much they'd gotten right in their camps! What archaeologist wouldn't give his last pick and shovel for this chance! He tried to study Allene's garb without staring. He wondered, when he got back, could he look her up on the internet and find out how she'd fared. Seeing his gaze, she patted her hair and checked her robe.

"It's nothing," he said. He looked across the endless mountain moors, with moonlight bright above and a canopy of stars shining brilliantly down, and the marsh sucking at his every step. They were safe now, he assured himself. But he remembered enough history to know it was a brutal time, full of mutilating weapons and killing diseases. He rubbed his chest: and humorless men with pitchforks. He had a life to live, back in the twenty-first century, and people who would be wondering where he'd gone. Pique replaced the burst of excitement. He belonged in his suite, surrounded by opulence, double tall lattes, and beautiful women. There had to be a way back.

"Allene."

She turned to him, questioning.

He tried to think how he might ask such a question. For all he knew, they'd hang him or drown him as a witch for even asking. But then again, he decided, they needed him. He'd blame it on the head injury. "You ever hear any stories, um, legends, about time travel?"

Allene's eyebrows furrowed.

"Going to a different time, do you mean?" asked Brother David.

At Shawn's eager nod, Allene exclaimed, "Do you no remember old Rabbie's story?" She proceeded to tell what had apparently been a favorite of Niall's: how King Herla went into a cliff to spend three days at a dwarf's marriage festivities, and emerged three hundred years later.

"Lousy way to repay a wedding gift," Shawn said. They trudged on in silence. The story gave him no hint as to how he might get out of this mess. The harp bumped against his back, a monotonous rhythm. The marshy land cushioned his steps as he beat the corners of his brain for an idea. But, except for getting back to the castle, his mind was a bare attic, giving him not even a cobweb with which to weave a plan.

"Do people routinely disappear hundreds of years into the future?" he asked after another long interval.

Allene laughed.

Normally, he appreciated his ability to amuse women, but he found her response unhelpful. "How did King Herla get back to his own time?" he pressed.

"You're like a bairn wi' your questions," Allene said. "He never got back. Mind the burn, now."

Shawn jumped back just on time, from another of the many small streams crisscrossing the land. Though they could scarce afford the delay, they knelt in the rocks at the water's edge so Allene could cleanse and re-bind Brother David's wounds. Shawn washed his own hand and re-bandaged it. He looked up, catching Allene's eye. Moonlight shone in her hair and glowed off her pale skin. She turned away.

As the morning dawned, they approached a forest. "We're getting close," Allene said. "But we must still take care. Wolves and boar roam this wood, and we're no yet safe from Edward's men. We'll sleep but a few hours, and say, if we're asked, that we're going to Edinburgh for the music festival. Allan a Dale." She smiled at him, and his heart melted.

Chapter Fourteen

Inverness, Scotland, Present

Niall arrived at the last rehearsal awash in elation, hope, and despair. He greeted a number of musicians, and took his place behind the harp. He watched for the downbeat, and began playing, setting his brain free, as his fingers danced through familiar pieces, to work through all he'd learned.

Time travel happened only in theory and stories. His fingers skimmed over a light ballad, and his brain skimmed past time machines and wormholes. It had happened the first time, after all, without either. His left hand glided up the strings in flowing arpeggios; behind him, the clarinets took up the melody.

"A little slow," Conrad said. "Keep your mind on the music."

Niall nodded, expecting more rude comments. None came. He listened for the beat, watched Conrad's arms, and settled into the tempo, warning himself against over-confidence. He thought once more about organizing something like an orchestra, with Iohn and William. But they didn't have the instruments to create such a thing.

"Nice job." Conrad drew the piece to a close. "That's in good shape for tomorrow! Pull out *Gilliekrankie.*" Music shuffled on stands behind Niall. "Ready?" Conrad asked him.

"Ready." Niall watched Conrad's baton, an expert now, and began another song about another battle. What a sad history, he thought. Sadder, still, if all he knew and loved were destroyed when he could possibly save them. Without machines or wormholes, there was only the element of chance, with which this whole thing had begun. One story after another showed exactly what he'd experienced—some sort of connection via place. All the stories seemed to contain elements of strong emotion.

The trombones and kettle drums thundered out the melody with a powerful beat. He was sure his harp couldn't be heard over them, but he kept playing and pondering. So what, he wondered, was the secret of picking the right location. Maybe he should have gone straight back to Glenmirril. But what-ifs did no good. Herla and his men, and the people in Aaron's stories, had simply walked into other times. Perhaps he could, too.

His fingers slowed, gliding into the ballad section of *Gilliekrankie*. But what if Shawn had not been in the tower that night? Would he still have made the switch, Niall wondered.

Conrad waved his arms suddenly, cutting off the orchestra. "Flutes, flutes, flutes!" he cried in exasperation. "Late again! You're with Shawn." Was Allene with Shawn? Niall closed his eyes, knowing Shawn's habits with women. "Shawn, bring out the melody there, so the flutes can hear you."

Niall waited for the snickers. He turned, and sure enough, one of the trombonists was speaking. "How do you know there's a flute player at your door?" he shouted. Several musicians turned in expectation.

"Knock it off," Caroline snapped.

He ignored her. "They can't find the key and don't know when to come in!" The orchestra laughed. Caroline glared. The man picked up the spray bottle for his slide and sprayed it in the air. A fine mist descended over Caroline. She shook her fluff of corn silk hair and brushed irritably at the water spots on her shirt.

"Children, children," said Conrad. "If we could all come in at the *andante*. Shawn?"

Niall let out his breath. He was no longer the butt of comments. Without that, it would be pleasant here, playing music all day, having his food set before him, Amy loving him and...willing. He smiled, and started on the *andante*. The flutes sang with him.

And his mind wandered again. If Glenmirril was key, even if he made the switch there, he'd never reach Hugh on time. And if the connection was between himself and Shawn, how did he know where Shawn was right now?

Gilliekrankie drew to an end. He ran his finger up a final gliss, as Conrad cut off the orchestra with a graceful circular motion of his hands. The instruments hung, suspended in midair, letting the last notes reverberate. Conrad lowered his arms; the instruments drifted down.

And Niall made a decision: his best chance was being where Shawn was. But where would that be? At Glenmirril? In the Great Glen? Dead? He sifted through possibilities while Conrad talked, bullied, and cajoled the musicians with pointers on the next song.

Through the rest of the program, through his solos, through the piece about Ian's swirling crimson cloak, Niall's thoughts simmered, deciding where he might reasonably expect to find Shawn. He could be anywhere! What would he have done, waking up in a strange place as Niall had? Niall made his best guesses, his fingers dancing a lively jig on the strings. And, as the music flowed around him, a plan formed. No matter what he did, he was taking a chance.

Conrad stopped the orchestra to lecture the percussion. Niall waited patiently. His plan might not work. He knew that. But the only other choice was to do nothing. If it didn't work, he'd try something else. He listed, in his mind, what he would need. He'd need Amy's help, for starters. He couldn't do it on his own. He would need to figure out....

"Shawn?" Amy murmured behind him.

Her voice brushed over him, a soft caress. Hadn't Shawn been lucky. Niall wished for a few more days of her gentle voice. If time was fluid, after all, he could enjoy this life for awhile and go back when he wanted. Maybe he'd ask her....

"Shawn?" she said again.

"Hmm?" He shook his head, knocking away the images. Allene needed him. He would never turn his back on her where the least hope flickered. Scotland and Bruce needed him! What was he thinking!

"Your solo. They're waiting."

Niall looked around. Conrad and all the musicians stared. Embarrassment washed over him. He coughed, lifted his hands, took a moment to put himself in the mood, and began. It was a piece he'd learned from MacDonald and played while Iohn sang, a lament for the men who had died at Falkirk.

He closed his eyes, and found himself on a winter's night in Glenmirril's great hall. Tapestries warmed the stone walls. Stars twinkled through high arched windows. The survivors of Falkirk listened quietly. Never did the song finish without some eyes being wiped. Niall began humming as he played, feeling the great fire roaring in the grate, driving back the winds that howled outside, and his mother and the other widows setting down their goblets, leaning close and clutching one another's hands.

Almost without realizing it, he began to sing, softly at first, in his native Gaelic. His voice grew stronger, as he saw the battle his song described, as he felt the sorrow, death, and loss. He lived because of his father's sacrifice at Falkirk. He swallowed, letting the harp sing alone when the lump in his throat stilled his voice. He could almost smell the peat fire and feel the rushes under his feet. The Laird would not approve of letting emotion overtake him.

Pushing aside thoughts of his father—protecting his family was what a man did after all—he breathed deeply, and sang the second verse, full of hope for Scotland, and tribute to her heroes. His voice drifted off. He repeated the verse alone on the harp strings.

He finished, and sat with closed eyes, thinking of those men, of his father, of their sacrifice for Scotland; thinking of his plan. The silence behind him was complete.

Then he heard a sniff.

He opened his eyes, disoriented to find himself on a stage in the future Inverness. Lights glared down on him. Heavy blue curtains soared high at the edge of the stage. An older woman in the cello section brushed her eye. "That was the most extraordinary thing I've ever heard," she said, meeting his eyes. Murmurs of agreement whispered around the orchestra.

"Amazing," Conrad agreed reverently. "Do it just like that at the concert tomorrow." He lifted his head to the orchestra. "A round of applause for that truly phenomenal performance!" Everyone stared at Niall, smiling and clapping. He stared back, still half in Glenmirril's great hall, feeling disembodied and out of time. He had to figure out where Shawn would be, and he had no idea how.

Peter, the concertmaster, stood. Others rose behind him, hands reaching out. Peter took Niall's hand, and shook it, the other hand gripping his shoulder. "I'm honored to play with you," he said.

Central Scotland, 1314

The next day passed without incident. The moor swelled once again to hills, which in turn gave way to more forest. Oaks and pines soared, springing from the slopes like gazelles. They followed trails overlooking deep gullies. Forest greens bordered aquamarine and diamond splashes of stream twisting along their route, snaking sometimes nearer and sometimes farther away. Rays of sunlight skimmed down through the trees, glinting off Allene's copper curls. Shawn's eyes lingered a moment before his thoughts drifted back to Amy.

They finished Fergal's provisions, and turned to berries and roots Allene and Brother David found. This seemed to be second nature to them, and she fretted that *Niall* had lost such knowledge. Their stomachs growled, but hunger in the open cathedrals far surpassed hunger in a dank cellar.

This war business, this was Niall's problem. Shawn wanted to get back to Amy. But he had no idea how. He barely even knew what was going on around him. Knowledge was power, and for once, he was the one who knew nothing.

"Will you humor me?" Shawn finally asked. His harp bumped against his back. They pulled themselves up the steepest parts of the trail by roots and tree limbs. The ache in his thighs faded, as his body strengthened. The ache in his chest dulled, and the sting in his hand came less often.

"Humor you?"

"Play along," Shawn explained. "Let's say it's not this head injury.

Let's say I'm from another time and place."

"Well surely you can't be, as I've known you all my life." Allene marched steadily under the dappling trees.

"What if you could go back to the time of..." His poor memory of history left him grasping for an example. "When they built Stonehenge."

"What is Stonehenge?"

"You've never heard of Stonehenge?"

"It's a stone circle built by the Druids hundreds of years before Christ," Brother David supplied. A grunt escaped him as he climbed a small incline.

"Why would I want to go to such a time?" Allene asked. "There can be naught worth seeing or knowing before Christ!"

Inspiration struck Shawn. "The time of Christ, then. What if you woke up in the time of Christ?"

Allene stopped, searching the wood for Shawn knew not what, glanced at the stream on their right, shaded her hand to scan the hills on their left, and moved toward the stream with confidence. "Alright," she said. "I wake up in the time of Christ. 'Twould be witchcraft, surely."

"What if that happened...to me?" Shawn asked.

"'Twould be witchcraft still," offered Brother David.

"Never mind what it would be!" Shawn smacked his forehead, earning him a worried look from his companions. "That's not the point! Wouldn't you feel lost? Not understanding what was going on?"

"But I know the Bible well. My father reads from it every night. I would recognize my Lord and Savior."

"Well, what if you didn't end up right next to Him? What if you landed in Herod's court, say, and you didn't understand the wars and battles going on, or who people were, or how to do things?"

Allene considered. "'Twould be confusing," she said.

"Pretend that's me."

"In Jesus' time?"

"No, in this time."

"But you know what's going on in this time." She stopped again, studying a rock formation and a massive fallen tree blocking the path.

Shawn boosted himself onto the log. He reached down for her hand. "Pretend I don't. Pretend I lived all my life hundreds of years from now."

"I thought we were pretending you went to the past." She gripped his wrist, hoisted herself up, and yanked her robe back over the flash of calf and knee. Her eyes met Shawn's, seeing that he'd seen. A small smile touched her lips.

He swallowed. It had taken flashes of more than Caroline's leg to make him feel this way. It was a different world. He looked away and cleared his throat. "But if you pretend that I spent my whole life, till last week, in the future, then for me this is—would be—the past." They both reached down to help Brother David up, and the three of them sat for a moment, contemplating the short jump down on the other side.

"I see," she said. He was sure she didn't. A bird trilled above. "Why are we pretending this?"

He was beginning to wonder, himself. "Let's just say I was," he repeated. "What would you tell me about your time?"

She turned suddenly to face him. "The story of King Herla! Is that what you're thinking?" At Shawn's nod, she looked pleased with herself. "But as if he went backwards," she mused. Shawn jumped down, landing silently in his leather boots. He helped Allene and Brother David, the monk landing with another grunt of pain, and they resumed their hike.

"I would say," said Brother David, gripping his side, "that we are blessed with many churches. We are Christians."

"That wasn't quite what I meant."

"But you asked...."

"How would you describe it, then?" asked Allene.

"Brutal," Shawn shot out. "Vicious and brutal."

"Certainly not!" Brother David sounded indignant. "We do not worship false gods like the pagans and druids. Nor do we offer human sacrifice or slaughter helpless babes, as did they."

"You kill people! You hit people. *You stab people!*" He stared pointedly at Allene, and wondered what had brought on those warm feelings toward her. Amy would never do that to him!

Allene gave an indignant toss of the head. "And this time you might come from? Did you dream about it in a delirium from your wound, Niall? Is it a time when men treat women like trollops to be pawed and groped, and force themselves upon them like enemy soldiers?" She pushed aside a branch and let it snap back in his face.

Shawn caught the branch, glared at her and fell silent, giving up hope of getting information. They followed a level track now, with ferns rising to waist height and spilling over the path. Birds sang from the treetops and undergrowth. A deer stood frozen in the underbrush, hoping not to be seen.

"Would I had a bow," Brother David sighed.

"'Twould be a fine meal," Allene agreed.

"See, this is what I mean," Shawn burst out. The deer's head sprang up, alert to the gunshot of his voice in the still wood. It turned in one graceful motion and leapt, its tail flashing white fear. Allene and Brother David sighed at the loss of their venison dinner. "In this time I'm...I imagine...what if people were shocked by that?"

243

"By what? Eating a fine meal?" Allene pulled her sad gaze from the retreating deer.

"No, getting back to nature, seeing a deer, and the first thing you both want to do is kill it! What's up with that?"

"We're hungry," Brother David said. "Would it be wise in this time you imagine to starve rather than eat what God provides?"

"Such a people would not long survive!" Allene stopped again, listened—this time Shawn heard the burble of the stream, louder than it had been—and chose a barely-visible path climbing steeply uphill.

"So imagine again." Shawn started over, not wanting to argue the point. "Tell me who the king is."

"Robert the Bruce, of course."

"Of England."

"Not of England, of Scotland." She squeezed through a heavy growth of ferns.

Shawn strove for patience, something he'd never had much of. "I *mean*, who is the king of England?"

"The king of England is Edward. Everyone knows that."

"Not someone who just got dropped in and doesn't know what's going on. Which Edward? The first, second? How many were there, anyway?"

"Only the two, of course, and he's the second. His father was Edward Longshanks. A far better king, they say. At least for the English. For us, he was brutal and cruel." She stopped to pull berries from a bush. Shawn and Brother David each accepted a handful.

"How long has Bruce been king?" Shawn tossed a berry high in the air, threw his head back, and caught it. He had years of bar peanuts to thank for the trick. Allene was not, however, as impressed as the women in bars usually were. He sighed.

"Nigh on several years now," said Brother David.

"And they're going to war?"

"Scotland and England have long been at war. 'Twould have been fine, had Alexander not insisted on going home to his bride that night."

"Who's Alexander?" Shawn asked.

Allene gave him a funny look. "You know far more than I. It is you with whom my father discusses these things."

"Pretend, remember? What would you tell a stranger about Alexander and his bride?"

"'Twas a dark and stormy night," Brother David began.

"You have got to be kidding," said Shawn. "Jesting," he clarified at the monk's blank stare.

"No jest, Allan a Dale. It was snowing, a ferocious storm. The ferryman told him 'twas no safe to cross, but he insisted. Men told him to put up for the night. He would go on. In the dark, his horse went over a cliff and he was killed."

"What was so special about Alexander, that his death sent England and Scotland to war?"

"'Twas not Alexander himself," said Allene, "but that he left no heir. There was only his granddaughter, the Maid of Norway, and she died on the journey to Scotland to take the throne."

"So how did Edward get involved?"

"Longshanks saw a chance to take Scotland," said Allene. She spotted a large, flat stone, incongruous in the midst of forest, quickened her step, and made an abrupt right when she reached it. Shawn slowed to help Brother David over the rougher patches.

Brother David took up the story. Of twelve contenders for the throne, John Balliol and Robert Bruce had the strongest claims. Fearing war, the abbots asked Longshanks to choose. He chose Balliol, expecting to set his puppet over Scotland. And so it was, until Balliol refused to send troops for England's war against France. Longshanks stormed north and subdued the Scots.

"So then he gave the crown to Bruce?" Shawn gripped Brother David's hand, helping him up the steep incline.

"No. Bruce and John Comyn fought over the crown. They met in Greyfriars Church. Bruce slew Comyn there before the altar. He was excommunicated for it."

"For killing someone?" Shawn couldn't hold back his sarcasm. "That seems to be the national pastime around here!"

"Dinna be foolish," Allene said. "He was excommunicated for killing a man on holy ground."

"My mistake," Shawn muttered. "So how did he become king?"

"He took himself hence to Scone and had himself crowned king by the Countess of Buchan."

"And that's that? How does Edward the Younger come into it and this war we're raising an army for?"

"Longshanks died. His son, Edward the Second, is not the king nor the general his father was. Under his reign, we have regained most of what Longshanks stole, but for Berwick and Stirling. The English still hold those. Nigh on a year ago, Edward Bruce...."

"Bruce is Edward's last name? Not Longshanks?"

"Edward Bruce is Robert Bruce's brother."

"So there are three Edwards running around: senior and junior over in England."

"Edward Longshanks...."

"That's the senior?"

"Longshanks, the father, is dead," David said.

"Ed, junior, is top dog now. And there's Edward the Bruce Brother here in Scotland?"

"Yes." David looked at him peculiarly. Shawn understood he should know these things. "He raised an army to take Stirling."

"Who raised an army?"

"Edward."

"Which Edward?"

"Bruce."

"Gotcha," Shawn said in English. He had no Gaelic equivalent.

"Bless you!" Allene handed him a handkerchief.

David continued the story. Edward Bruce laid siege to Stirling. The commander, Philip de Mowbray knew he couldn't hold out forever. He promised to surrender if reinforcements did not arrive by midsummer's day. Being perhaps overconfident, Edward Bruce allowed de Mowbray to request help from King Edward. David crossed a stream. "Edward is angry."

"We're back to Ed Junior?"

"The King of England, yes. He has raised the largest army ever seen, to crush the Scots once and for all."

"And the Bruce Brothers are going to stop him?"

"God willing." Brother David crossed himself. "But every clan is needed."

"And we're risking our lives to let one man know? What good is one man? What is he, like...*the Terminator* or something?" Shawn laughed.

"The termi...what?" Allene looked at him in puzzlement. "What nonsense is this?"

"The Terminator. It was....never mind." Shawn held aside a low-hanging branch while Allene slipped through. Her hood fell back. Her golden-red hair, having escaped its braid, tumbled down her back. He could almost believe it was a pleasant walk in the woods with a beautiful girl. If he could get Brother David to move on ahead, maybe she'd hold his hand again. Maybe he could manage a little kiss, behind a tree, if he didn't let his hands wander. Maybe.... He thought of Amy, and wondered if maybe he could go without a kiss this once. Amy would have liked this walk.

"I don't understand why you question us going for Hugh."

"Well, one man won't make much difference against the largest army ever seen on earth, will he?" High above, a bird trilled.

"Do you mean...?" Brother David stopped, stared in amazement, and laughed out loud. "My Lady, he seems to think Hugh will come alone! Just Hugh!"

Allene, too, laughed. They reached a stream and dropped on the bank to drink. "Of course he'll no come alone! He'll bring his men."

"What's that, like another twenty?" Shawn leaned into the water, splashing his face and hair.

Allene stared at him. The humor left her face. "Niall, I thought you were regaining your senses."

"I am," he reassured her, sitting up and shaking the water vigorously from his hair. "I mean," he touched his temple, where he understood Niall to have hit his head. "Mostly. But do you see, to someone who doesn't know the time, they'd ask that."

"Hundreds, then," Allene said. "Hugh's men number in the hundreds, including horsemen and bowmen. And his word carries great weight. Other clans will follow him."

"And each clan is hundreds of men?"

Allene nodded.

"Explain this, then." Shawn sat back on his heels. "Edward is coming to crush Scotland. Why would any clan *not* fight for Bruce?"

"The Comyns will fight against Bruce," Brother David said, "because he killed their kin. They'll not have him as king."

"Others, like the MacDougalls, and Robert de Umphraville, Earl of Angus, will stand with Edward because they have lands in England they wish to keep. The Buchans and Dunbars will stand with him because they wish to be on the winning side."

"If that many Scots will fight with England," said Shawn slowly, "how do you know what our man Hugh will do?"

"He will stand with my father," Allene said. "He is my father's brother."

The sting shot, sharply, through Shawn's hand and up his arm. He remembered all too clearly the Laird's threat, on the window sill. Maybe Allene wouldn't see the need to tell her uncle what had happened, back there by the stream. He wanted to ask, *Is he as bloodthirsty as your father?* but dared not. Maybe, if he behaved himself, she'd forget that little incident. Maybe, with the looks she'd been throwing his way, she already had.

"And once we deliver the message," Shawn said, "we'll go back to Glenmirril, right?"

Allene looked at him in surprise. "You, and perhaps Brother David, will fight with Hugh."

"I'm—" Shawn stopped dead in the forest. "I'm supposed to *fight?*"

Inverness, Scotland, Present

Niall shook numerous hands, working his way offstage after

247

rehearsal. Conrad pumped his hand, nearly taking his arm off, crowing, "Tomorrow will be your finest moment!" He rubbed his hands together, chuckling, and relishing the moment when people discovered the great trombonist Shawn Kleiner could also play harp like a master.

Niall moved through the crowd, stopping for those who pressed in, wanting to talk. In the wings, he met a violist whose daughter had taken ill during the orchestra's tour. "How's your lass?" he asked.

"Doing better," the man assured him. "Any chance you could sign a recording of tomorrow's performance? She'd love to hear you play harp."

"I will," Niall said. He planned to be gone immediately after the concert. He filed a mental note to leave something, anything, signed with Shawn's name and best wishes to the young girl. Such a thing, apparently meant a great deal in this time. It was a small enough favor.

Dana sidled up to him. "You're incredible, Shawn," she said softly. "I wish your memory would come back." She squeezed his arm and left, lugging a heavy round snail of a case.

When the last musician walked off, rapping drumsticks against the concrete wall, Niall found himself alone in the narrow hall, but for Amy, waiting at the stage door. A single bare bulb illuminated the white cinder block walls.

"That was amazing," she said. She drew close, half an inch between them, looking up at him in the dim light. A scent of flowers drifted off her. Her hands rested on his chest.

A jolt shot through him. He swallowed. She expected things of Shawn. Anything he wanted could be his. His hands covered hers.

"Your mother said you were so different before your father's death." Her eyes, full of hope, held his. "She's waiting for that man to come back."

She was beautiful and kind, and he wondered what it would be like, up in that big four poster bed. The thought inflamed him.

"Where did you learn to play like that?"

Niall studied her intently. He wanted to tell her. He wanted to share his life and himself. But he smiled sadly. "Just something someone taught me." A shadow crossed her eyes, and he realized she thought he meant Celine. He couldn't tell her the truth. He couldn't kiss her. He touched her cheek; only because he must play the role, he told himself. They studied each other, awkwardly, neither knowing what to say.

She smiled uncertainly, finally. "Well, I guess I'll see you at dinner." She pulled away and headed down the hall. She looked back, once, over her shoulder.

He watched her go. He'd disappointed her. He wondered if he'd disappointed himself. A kiss, just a kiss, with no laird to anger. He didn't think Conrad cared what he did with Amy. Would it really have hurt anything? A bar of light appeared at the end of the hall, as she opened the door. Her silhouette hesitated, then slipped out, and the door shut, leaving him alone under the bare bulb.

He boosted himself onto the forlorn table that had held musicians' cases during rehearsal, contemplating his decision. It seemed insane, suddenly, to seek one man in hundreds of miles, separated by seven hundred years. If Shawn and Allene were in the wilderness, they may not have even survived. He might find he'd gone back for nothing. To find those he loved already dead and gone. Maybe God, for reasons Niall couldn't fathom, had given him a second chance here.

But he wasn't one to second guess himself. He would move ahead with his plan. He would play this concert, as they called it, as he'd played so many nights while the people of Glenmirril dined and laughed and talked and threw bones to dogs. It was easy enough. He'd done it hundreds of times since his youth. Amy would have his things ready—he was sure she'd help, when he asked—and things would start to happen.

A humming sound caught his ear. He looked up to the source: pipes running along the ceiling. His eyes traveled from the pipes to the rest of his surroundings. Bare walls, like the monastery, but stark and pale, rose around him. A large wooden crate held costumes for some sort of mummery. Isolation engulfed him. He shook off the prickling along his arms. Nothing in this day and age compared to the dangers of his own. A tingle shot down his spine nonetheless. He started down the dim hall. He was quite capable of protecting himself. Just then, the lights flickered off, and he found himself in darkness broken only by the green glow of the EXIT signs far away at the ends of the hallway.

A dark figure emerged from a passage on his left.

Niall's heart quickened. "Who's there?"

"Lousy luck, the lights going off," said a hard voice.

Central Scotland, 1314

As morning sun flooded the dirt street, brightening the few cottages, the captain of the guard pushed his foot against the two English soldiers. Their heads lolled on one another, their backs against the stone wall of a small cottage. A red stain dribbled down the older man's white tunic. The empty wineskin hung from his hand. Gentle snores rose from the scarred man. Far away in the hills, a cow lowed.

"Fine guards Edward has!" sneered the Scot.

"Wake up!" the captain barked. He swatted the older guard with the flat of his sword. The man jerked on the bench and straightened himself, blinking. "What do you mean, sleeping on duty!"

"*Drinking* on duty." The Scot spit into the muddy road. The scarred man stirred; both guards shook their heads, rubbed their eyes.

"On your feet!" roared the captain.

They leapt up, arms stiffening at their sides, chins up, and looked almost like England's finest in the pink rays streaming over the eastern hills. "'Twas a long night," the scarred man defended himself.

"'Twas a cold night," said the other. "We but tried to keep warm."

"Hold your tongue! You drank on duty and fell asleep. Suppose the Scottish traitor came through, sneering at Edward's men as he danced by."

"We stayed awake through the night," protested the man with the wineskin.

"No monk came through," added the other.

"How would you know?" demanded the Scot. "Did ye think a wanted man would wake you to announce himself? Did you patrol the village as ordered?"

"Aye," said the older man. "We checked the forest and circled the village. We went to the top of yonder hill each hour."

The Scot's face darkened. The captain of the guard appeared likewise skeptical. The soldier with the wineskin suddenly brightened. "There was a minstrel, my lord."

"A minstrel?" queried the Scot. "Why did you not say so at once?"

The men squirmed. A bird trilled in the silence. The captain spoke for them. "They were told to look for a monk."

"Aye, that they were." The Scot glowered. "But you knew 'twas Niall Campbell we sought. Tell me about the minstrel."

"He wore a plumed hat," said the older man.

"Naturally." The Scot spoke dryly. "And mayhap colorful trews as well?" He slapped the side of the man's head. "Tell me something helpful. What instrument did he carry?"

"The harp, my lord." The man rubbed his temple. "He played the harp for us."

"The harp." The Scot's face turned red, inch by slow inch. "But his harp is still at Glenmirril."

"My Lord?" The captain inquired. When the Scot did not speak, he waited, a statue, for his orders. The soldiers shifted from foot to foot, looking anywhere but his face. More birds began to sing as they waited; sheep bleated on the hill.

"He can't have another harp," the Scot muttered. "Nor could he have eluded me in the Glen. And yet...." The Scot made his decision. "Gather your men," he snapped at the captain. And to the soldiers: "Which way did he go?"

Inverness, Scotland, Present

Green lights shimmered off white-blond hair. Niall let out his breath. "Rob."

"Yeah, Rob. Or do you call me the Stooge when I'm not around? Or Good Old Rob Who Will Do Anything? Rob Who Can Be Sent Fishing."

Niall edged toward the exit sign. He didn't wish to fight Rob. Every sense told him that was what the man wanted.

And Rob would get hurt.

Rob stepped farther out, blocking his way. "Rob." Niall held up a hand. "I don't know what I've done to you." The smirk, back by the bus yesterday had been unnecessary, Niall chastised himself, but that seemed poor reason for Rob cornering him in the dark.

"Bullshit, Shawn," Rob snapped. "I know all your tricks. This is just one more, pretending you don't remember anything. Did you hit your head on purpose, or are you just taking full advantage of the situation like always? Either way, you've fooled them all. You've pulled off another coup. Isn't that enough?"

"Enough what? Let's talk outside."

He stepped to his right. Rob's shadowy figure stepped with him. "Out where you can play Saint Shawn for all your new admirers? You know I won't say what needs saying in public."

Niall was confused. "Why not?" He stepped back to the left.

Rob moved with him. "You don't care about Amy's reputation, but I do. You know everyone's weak spot, and you use it."

"This is about Amy?" Niall relaxed. They were on the same side.

"Damn straight it's about Amy. You have everything, Shawn. *Everything!* Money, talent, fame, all the women you want. Why Amy, too? Let her go."

Niall struggled to understand. "Rob, I don't remember. What did I do?"

"It's what you're doing now!" Rob moved forward, menacing. He seemed taller than Niall remembered. Bathed in the green glow, his face darkened with anger. The exit signs turned his hair the color of a dying fish. Niall backed up a step, glancing toward the exit, far down the corridor. He would not run. "Turning on the charm again. This ridiculous accent." Niall made a note to copy their speech more carefully. "Getting the ring back. You only did it to reel her in again. How long is it going to last this time?" Rob pointed a finger in Niall's face, backing him up a step. "Damn it, Shawn, she's a real person, not your toy. Quit playing with her."

Niall couldn't make promises he might not be there to keep. He edged away from Rob's jabbing finger. "Rob, listen to me."

"Listen to you! Everyone listens to you! Look where it gets them! Look where it got Amy. First the abortion!"

"What's abor..." He didn't know the word. "What's that?"

"What the hell are you playing at, Shawn? I don't buy it." Rob punched his arm. Niall jerked backward. "You know what it is. *You* took her there begging and crying. She didn't want to do it."

"Do what?" Niall fought the edge in his own voice.

"She was afraid to go against you, you were so angry. Like you had nothing to do with it! And now she's pregnant again."

"She's with child?" The shock hit Niall like the loch's icy waters in early spring.

"With child!" Rob sneered. "Yeah, she's 'with child.' She didn't tell you? I bet she was afraid to after the last time." Rob punched his arm again. Niall flung his hands up, too late to ward off the blow. "Don't you know what that abortion did to her? Don't you see the look she gets around babies? You're supposed to love her, but I saw what you couldn't. June sixth. Oh-six-oh-six. I saw her change that day. That's the day it happened. Sometimes, I see those numbers written on her things."

"I don't understand," Niall said. "She wanted a baby?"

"Of course she wanted it." Rob swore. "You don't *want* to see, do you? You wear selfishness like a badge of honor. Nice guys finish last. That's your motto, isn't it?" He pushed him, hard. Niall stumbled backwards, up against the wheeled crate bulging with costumes. It rolled an inch under his impact, striking another wall.

Niall caught himself with one hand, twisting off the crate.

Rob slammed his palm into Niall's chest, backing him up a step with each beat. "You are selfish *slam* and self-centered *slam* and cruel *slam*. She begged you!" *Slam!*

"Listen to me," yelled Niall.

"I'm *done* listening to you. Let her go, Shawn!" *Slam*. Niall threw up a hand in defense. "She'll never leave you when you act like this, but I know you." *Slam*. Something caught in Rob's voice, and Niall saw, in the dim light, two dark streaks running down his face. "I *know* you. You'll lead her on and then abandon her again." His voice caught again. "And just when she's ready to really leave you, you'll turn on the charm and reel her right back in." *SLAM*. The wall crunched into Niall's spine and the back of his head, jarring him.

He shoved himself off the wall. "Listen to..."

Rob wiped his eyes angrily. "Cut her free, Shawn. I love her. I'd take care of her." A sob came from deep in his chest. He punched Niall, a closed fist this time, throwing him backwards. "I would have taken care of her last time. I would have loved that baby like my own. I would have done that, I would have done *anything* for her sake, but you just keep reeling her back in. You have to have everything, don't you?"

Niall held up his hands. "Rob, we're on the same side."

"I would love this baby like my own. We'd be a family." Rob shoved him up against the cinder block wall, gripping his shirt. "Let her go, Shawn!"

The name grated on Niall's nerves. All the hatred of Shawn flooded back, a blaze of red anger behind his eyelids. "Stop calling me Shawn!" he roared. He threw his hands up, throwing Rob off, and shoved back. *"I am Niall Campbell, heir to Glenmirril!"*

Rob stumbled back, crashing into the opposite wall. A mad bellow erupted from his mouth, and he threw himself forward. One fist powered into Niall's jaw, shooting his head backwards. A jolt of pain ripped through his head, his neck, his eyes, dazing him. Red shots of anger flashed before his eyes.

Niall dropped to one knee, feeling for his knife.

Chapter Fifteen

Central Scotland, 1314

Birches and firs engulfed Shawn; rocky outcroppings and boulders jutted up around him. He wondered that Allene threaded her way so surely among them. "You know where you're going?" he asked.

"Surely," Allene said. "And before your injury, you did as well."

They fell silent for several furlongs, their energy going into pushing through dense underbrush. Brother David tried to hide the limp that held them up. Shawn wrapped an arm across his back, helping him along. "Wouldn't it be easier where there aren't so many trees?"

"We may as well play a trumpet to signal Edward's men," Allene said. "D' ye remember naught? They'll see us for many furlongs, out in the open."

"They're looking for a monk," Shawn reminded her.

"Aye, they were," said Brother David. "But it's someone who knows you. When the soldiers say they saw a man playing harp, they'll begin looking for a minstrel in a plumed hat."

Shawn's insides turned a peculiar shade of cold. His throat became stiff, though he tried to swallow several times. He stopped, unable to move.

"Och, Niall," Allene said sadly, placing a hand on his forearm. "You're yet so changed from who you were. I thought ye'd see that immediately. Come, we can scarce afford to stop and be fearful, now."

"But...." Shawn managed a step, and stopped again. He yanked the green-feathered hat off his head, and threw it on the ground. "But I look like a peacock!"

Allene snatched it off the ground, horrified, and stuffed it in her robe. "We canna have them finding it, now!"

He gestured at his jewel blue and poppy red tunic. "I look like a neon sign!"

"Knee...what?" said Brother David.

"I glow in the dark!" Shawn snapped, his anger building with his fear. "It's fine for you two, all in brown, but they'll see me for miles even in this forest! Why didn't you tell me they'd still be after us!"

"Sh, now." Allene squeezed his arm. She pushed a branch aside, pulling him through. "I thought ye knew."

"Then what's the plan?" Shawn asked. "I have to get out of these clothes."

"I've naught else for ye to wear," Allene said.

"Then we *find* something else. Is there a town, a village, anything where there might be people who wear—" he gestured wildly at his bright minstrel colors, "—who wear anything other than peacock feathers!"

"The town is north," said Allene. "'Tis the wrong direction."

"And I'm wearing the wrong clothes." Shawn spoke low and clear —the Shawn who ran an entire orchestra and everyone in it to his liking. His eyes shot darts. A birdsong stilled, and its singer lifted in flight, fleeing the tension.

Her jaw came out. "We'll go as planned."

He pushed his face close to hers. "Plans changed when they saw me dressed like this."

They stood in the forest, staring one another down.

"Come now," Brother David tried. "We've no time for this."

Shawn ignored him. "The soldiers saw which way we went. They'll go that way, not toward the town."

Brother David's arm flashed up suddenly, yanking Shawn down in the underbrush. Shawn twisted, yelling. The monk's hand clamped over his mouth. "We're not alone!" he hissed.

Shawn became still, the smell of the vegetation twisting into his nostrils, hot and heavy. A spider dangled before his eyes, dropping to the earthen floor on its web. And he heard the voices calling, far off. They listened, pressed on the forest floor, not breathing. Allene's eyes, close to Shawn's, grew big with fear. Her arm, touching his, trembled. The voices came nearer. "Take us to the town, Allene," Shawn whispered. He covered her hand with his. She nodded. Slowly, she raised her head, her hair once again covered by the brown hood.

After seconds, ticking by each like an hour, she motioned, and started inching through the underbrush, slowly, so slowly. Shawn's heart pounded, a timpani out of control, banging in his bruised chest. He kept his breathing shallow and silent, straining to hear the soldiers. Thrashing and swearing told him they were to the left, far off, but still close enough to make the sweat prickle on his back. He crept behind Allene, listening the whole time. They inched—paused—listened— inched.

"Campbell! Give yourself up!"

The voice bit into his being, stopping his heart. He froze.

Inverness, Scotland, Present

Niall's hand grazed the rough jeans. He remembered: he'd stopped carrying his knife. He sprang to his feet, fists up.

The hall was silent.

At the far end, Rob strode away, his shoulders bunched in anger. Niall's nerves screamed for him to finish the fight.

He took a deep breath.

It wasn't worth it. He squeezed his eyes shut, fighting rage, not at Rob, but at Shawn, for being such a scoundrel and wastrel. Shawn deserved the pounding Rob thought he'd just given him. Niall wanted to, himself, and he'd never even met the man! Leaving Amy with child! Abortions! He leaned against the wall, the anger draining from him.

At the far end of the hall, Rob slammed through the door. It flashed a beam of light, then swung shut with a thump, shutting Niall in darkness again, broken only by the green glow.

Pray for him!

Niall raised his head. He shouted out loud at the empty walls: "He doesn't deserve it!" His voice echoed back.

Now!

Niall dropped his head in defeat. He slid down the wall and sat, head on knees, in the dark, ashamed of his hatred. "I think he deserves what William Wallace got. But for some reason, You don't." His rubbed his aching jaw. Shawn was most likely with Allene, hunted by English soldiers and a castle traitor. "I pray for him, then. Guide him, protect him."

His pulse raced. They were surely in danger. His hands gripped each other in white-knuckled prayer. *Aves* and *Paters* poured out of his mouth. He didn't look to see who was playing the flute this time. He knew he was alone.

Central Scotland, 1314

"Campbell!" The voice shouted from far off.

"They're bluffing," Allene whispered. But her voice shook. They crouched on hands and knees in the rich vegetation. Her fingers clenched Shawn's hand till he thought the bones would break.

"Campbell!" The sound echoed through the woods. A squirrel stopped chattering, paused, and darted up a tree.

Allene's face, close to his, drained of color. "Doona do anything foolish, Niall. Ye canna fight so many."

"Are you insane?" he hissed. "What makes you think I plan to fight them?"

Her fingers relaxed a fraction on his hand. "Ye've been known to be over-confident," she murmured.

"I'm all about running. Cowards live longer," Shawn whispered back. "Go!" He felt for his hat, remembered she'd taken it, and pushed after her on hands and knees. Brother David rasped at his heels. Shawn hoped the man would survive the nightmare journey. They inched along, ferns brushing overhead, hearing the soldiers' calls.

At the bank of a small creek, Shawn grabbed Allene's ankle and gestured. She shook her head. He paid her no heed. Listening first for the searchers, Shawn crept from the cover of the brush. He scooped handfuls of mud from the shallow creek to cover his face and bright clothes, wherever he could reach, before inching back into the forest growth. The squirrel jabbered above, making him cringe.

"Campbell, come out! We know you're there!"

Allene jolted in fear, but gave her head a hard shake, assuring him they knew no such thing. She inched forward again, all but on her stomach. Shawn and Brother David followed.

An hour passed, Shawn guessed, with the calls and thrashing of their hunters behind them. He hoped Allene knew where she was going. He hoped the mud covered the worst of the light-house signal of colors of his clothing. He hoped....

A shout rang out, far behind. Allene wiggled faster, rising to hands and knees for speed.

"I found his hat!" Cries went up throughout the forest.

Allene looked back at Shawn, her lip trembling. "Stay down!" he whispered. Every tremble of tree or bush might be the enemy. He fought blind panic, while she patted her robe frantically, but he knew it was his hat they'd found.

Far back, the soldiers' tramping and thumping raised forest birds, screeching at the intrusion, into the air. "Faster!" Shawn snapped. "They're making too much noise to hear us." They scrambled to their feet, running, crouching, through the thick vegetation. A grunt of pain escaped Brother David. Shawn grabbed his hand, dragging him along. Allene crested a wooded hill. They sprinted down the other side. Behind them, the English yelled in excitement. "How far to the village?" Shawn panted.

"A dozen furlongs," Allene gulped. Her feet slid suddenly on the damp slope, flying from under her, and she tumbled down, grabbing at trees as she flew head over heels, her robe tangling around her, shouting.

"Open ground!" Brother David pointed, panting, to the bottom of the hill. They plummeted behind her, hurtling, stumbling, sliding, over thinning underbrush. A quarter mile ahead, the forest ended, and a field raced toward another rock-strewn hill.

"A dozen furlongs?" Shawn yelled after Allene. "What is that, a dozen miles or something? We can't run twelve miles!"

"Miles? Aer ye mad?" Allene jolted to a stop at the bottom of the hill and clambered to her feet, yanking at her robe, jerking her hood back over her tell-tale hair. "We've no choice!" Shawn and Brother David skidded to a clumsy halt beside her, bumping into one another.

Brother David limped ahead. Allene and Shawn gave one another one last, sharp look, and raced after him. Shawn swung an arm around his back, and they loped along, slower than Shawn could have gone, but faster than Brother David could on his own. "Where's the town?" he asked Allene.

"Straight over the next hill," she said.

"Run!" he ordered.

"I canna leave you!"

"Run!" Shawn barked. He slung the harp off his back and pushed it at her. "Hide this. Clothes for me, a hiding place, anything!"

Her lip trembled. But she took the harp and hiked up the robe. Her legs flashed as she flew across the field, up the next hill. Shawn threw a glance over his shoulder—the soldiers had not crested the hill—and dragged Brother David as fast as he could. "Leave me," Brother David said. "Get Hugh."

"Save your breath," Shawn muttered. He dragged the monk at a hobbling half-run. Brother David grunted in pain with each jolt, but made no further protest. They struggled to the top of the rocky knoll.

A shout rang out behind them. Shawn grabbed Brother David in a crocodile hug, throwing them both down the slope, rolling one over another. Heather and gorse scratched. Stones gouged. The young monk groaned and cried out the whole way.

"Sorry," Shawn gasped, rolling up for air. "This..." He rolled under Brother David's weight and up again. "...or...die."

Crashing into a boulder at the foot of the hill, he leaned in, scooped the other man over his shoulder with strength he'd never had, and ran, jarring the monk with each step. The town appeared ahead. A more beautiful sight he'd never seen! Already, his chest heaved for air. His legs screamed for mercy. He couldn't look back. A stitch ripped through his side. Shapes formed ahead as he closed in: crowds! His salvation!

The merry sounds of a festival reached out to him. He pushed himself, Brother David's abused body slamming into his back, his moans filling his ears, and reached the edge of the throng.

Jugglers in harlequin clothing danced around him, spinning balls in the air. He gripped Brother David's legs, batting at the jugglers with his free hand, fought his way through to a booth laden with vegetables.

"Turnips, tasty turnips!" bawled an old woman, grabbing his sleeve. He spun his head, searching for Allene. Now there were more stalls, musicians strolling the street, a man with a monkey. He reached the outlying buildings of the town, his head twisting side to side, hunting for a hiding place.

"Your fortune for a penny," cried a scarved woman in front of a painted gypsy caravan.

"Breads, buns, rolls!" bellowed a fat man draped in white.

Shawn pushed through a gaggle of giggling children. Brother David grew heavier. Shawn's legs trembled under the weight. Stone houses and merchants' stalls rose around him.

"Fruits!" a young girl shrilled in his ear, snatching at his sleeve. "Five a penny!"

He took another step, twisted to peer down a dank alley for a hiding place.

An acrobatic team strolled by on their hands, pointy shoes waving in his face. A boy led a string of ponies, brushing against him, making him stumble. The smell of cheeses and fruits and meat and animals filled the air. Shawn spun, the weight of the monk on his shoulder growing; seeking sanctuary. People called and laughed. Colors spun in and out. His legs weakened under Brother David's weight.

"Alms!" cried a toothless beggar, stretching a bony hand from among rags.

His knee buckled. He grabbed a stone wall to steady himself.

Something gripped his elbow. He spun, yanking his arm back, and staggered with relief to see Allene's red hair and pale face. Wordlessly, she pulled him into a small, empty room, with stone walls and a rough, wooden floor. "Change!" She pushed a bundle into his arms, and reached to ease Brother David off his shoulder, onto a straw pallet in the corner.

Shawn asked no questions. He rinsed his muddy face in a water bucket by the fire, then stripped his torn and muddied clothing down to his Hanes. That Allene might question his underwear was the least of his concerns. But she was occupied, dressing Brother David in his own new outfit. Shawn fumbled with his clothing, hopping on one foot.

"Tights, you got me tights," he muttered, dragging the forest green apparel over one foot. He toppled onto the floor, cursing, yanking at the leggings, trying to remember how Caroline, Celine, Amy, any of them, pulled on nylons. He struggled to his feet, yanking them up around his waist, and snatched up the voluminous linen shirt. Next came a dark-green tunic. He twisted it once, twice before finding the right way to slide it over the shirt. "Who am I now?" he grumbled. "Robin Hood?"

"Dry yer eyes," Allene said. "Ye're in better shape than poor

Brother David."

Shawn picked up a pointy green hat. "Yes, how is Friar Tuck?" he asked, jamming it on his head.

She turned from the bed, gripping her knife.

He jumped back. "It was a joke!"

"The hair," she said.

Shawn put a hand to his hair, shocked at her intention. It was as bad as stabbing him. Worse. "No." He stepped back, holding up his palm.

"It has to go," Allene reasoned. "We canna stay here. I know not when the owners will return. Haste!"

"You don't touch my hair." Shawn pushed his face up to hers.

"An I doona touch your precious locks," she said, "they most certainly will. Come here, you bampot."

"I am not a bampot," he snapped. "What the he...what's a bampot?" The shouts of the crowd outside reminded him it would be the shouts of the soldiers soon. He turned to the door. Allene flashed forward, grabbing a hank of his hair. He yelped, clasped his hand to his head. "That's my signature!" he yelled. "That's how people know me!"

"You wish the English to know you?" Allene snapped. "Doona be foolish."

"Braid it," he said. "Quick!"

She heaved a sigh. Her fingers flashed, pulling his hair so tight he thought his skin must be stretched across his skull. She yanked a length of leather from a shelf, and knotted it at the bottom of the short braid. "We must go," she said. She bundled the used clothes under her robe, becoming a portly hooded figure. "I'll take Brother David." She helped the man to his feet, dressed in an outfit similar to Shawn's. Nobody would take him for a monk or a minstrel. She hefted the harp on her shoulder. "Meet us at the tinkers' caravan. Mayhap they will help us."

"Wait, why can't I go with you?"

"The soldiers at Fergal's Inn saw three. Such will they be looking for. Now go! Doona attract attention." She wrapped her arm around Brother David, leading him out.

Shawn slipped out the door, trying not to look furtive. *You're a performer,* he reminded himself. Everything in his being screamed to run. But he straightened his spine. He thought of every Robin Hood movie he'd ever seen, and put on a jaunty fair day smile. He had no idea where the tinkers' caravan was. He wasn't even sure what a tinker was.

A caravan, he remembered, was a wagon of some sort. He looked around. Dozens of wagons leapt out at him, wagons with children, wagons with wool, fruits, turnips and woven goods. Small, broken-down wagons running like medieval rickshaws on two wheels, and large rugged

.

ones on four wheels, pulled by behemoths with feathered hooves. He sauntered through the fair, hefting vegetables, inspecting sheep, and asking where the tinkers might be found.

Outside the inn, a group of men sang. *Sumer is icumen in, Lhude sing cuccu!* Shawn groaned. Of all the songs to run into. But he stopped, fascinated. Sung in a holiday atmosphere, it wasn't such a bad piece.

He joined in. "The seed grows and the meadow blooms, and the wood springs anew! Sing cuckoo!" They smiled, welcoming his bass. When the song ended, they clustered around, inviting him for a drink. A busty girl hung out the window, spilling bountifully over the top of her blouse. Shawn smiled, thinking he might.

The acrobats strolled by again, one man balanced on the shoulders of the two below. "We found the tinkers, over at the far end of town," called the man at the top of the pyramid. He leaned down, nose to nose with Shawn, placed his hands on the other men's shoulders, and turned himself upside down, feet in the air far above. A boy raced up, vaulted into the hands of two more men, and flew into the air, landing on the upside down man's feet. Laughing, he streamed a multi-colored scarf from his mouth, yards and yards of it trailing down to the giggling village children.

Shawn smiled. He winked at the girl still beaming in the window. It wasn't such a bad time when people weren't trying to kill you.

But—they were. He set off toward the far end of town, stopping to haggle over a pony with a merchant. He inspected the animal's teeth as he'd seen done in a movie, and turned away.

He stopped short, face to face, chest to chest, with the soldier he'd played for in the village. The scar pulled his lip up and his eyelid down.

You're a performer, Shawn told himself in the nano-second after recognition. He kept the cold wash of fear inside, behind a large show of teeth. The man had been drinking that night, after all; he might not even recognize him. "Fine animals," he said, jerking a thumb at the ponies. "But he's asking too much."

The man stared, his one good eye open wide.

Then he opened his mouth.

"Niall Campbell!" he screamed. "Captain! Captain! I've found him! I've found Niall Campbell!"

Inverness, Scotland, Present

Niall crossed the broad castle lawn, toward the gardens. From his room, high above, the gardens had been clearly visible. From the ground, he saw only high stone walls. Like life, he thought—change your position and things look different. Amy's pregnancy changed things. Maybe the peaceful gardens would give him a fresh perspective. He prayed desperate *Aves* for Shawn and Allene. But he questioned their value. Shawn and Allene's fate had been sealed seven hundred years ago.

The taste of blood welled in his mouth; he wiped at it and rubbed his jaw. Rob's blow would leave a nasty bruise. He hoped there wouldn't be too many questions.

He followed the garden wall to an arched opening, with wooden doors flung wide in welcome. A path drew him in to solitude. Gone was the noise of cars. Gone were the voices of Rob and Amy and Conrad. Gone were the soothing scales and melodies to which he'd become accustomed. He looked around. The path of crushed shells and stones wound through a vivid blaze of crimson, saffron, and sapphire blooms he couldn't name, into a shady arbor of towering oaks. The stones and shells crunched beneath his shoes. The gardens stretched for acres; he thought again what lives of luxury these people led. But that had no bearing on his problems. He must set his mind to it, and see what he could sort out.

He made the sign of the cross, clasped his hands, and with lowered head, followed the oatmeal shells. "God in Heaven, my Father," he prayed, "I thank Thee—I suppose I should, at least—that I've quit carrying my knife. I'd ha' killed Rob. I think that may be more of a problem here than in my own time." He kicked a shell, and kept walking.

"I'm lost," he said. "I doona ken why You sent me here." His eyes picked up a burst of indigo, running rampant along the edge of the path. He stooped and picked a handful of bluebells, their blossoms dangling gracefully. He lifted them to his nose and breathed in, seeing Allene in the tower, angry and impetuous and determined. And no doubt alone in the wilderness at this very moment, with that monster, Shawn. He squeezed his eyes tight, suffering his own personal hell at the thought.

"Allene and Scotland need *me*," he whispered fiercely. "Not that weak excuse for a man. Why did You give me the answer to turn the battle, did You not intend me to use it?" Surely God would look with favor on his plan, and take him back.

He opened his eyes. A black garden snake slithered from the blossoms. It paused, its black eyes glittering, before undulating across the path into the bluebells, drawing his eyes to the peace and beauty there. He scanned the resplendent hues of the sanctuary. There seemed to be no war here, only making music all day. Still, Amy needed someone. Could it be God's intention that he care for her? Even if Shawn came back, he wouldn't.

Niall rose, entering the oak arbor. The sun dimmed, as leaves twined overhead. If he were caught in this time, it wasn't a bad existence. He could do so much for Amy. *My burden is light*, said Jesus. He'd been torn from family and friends, knowing he'd failed them, feeling the coward, safe here while they suffered their fate, even if it was beyond his control. But there would be Amy, and music.

He emerged from the arbor into an alcove, hemmed in by towering box hedges. A marble bench, with round stone balls for legs, faced the hedges. A stone statue of a nude woman danced in jets of water shooting from a fountain. He'd heard of such things in Florence, but the rugged Highlands had nothing like it.

He dropped onto the bench, contemplating the woman, every inch of her, while the melody and movement of the water mesmerized him. He thought of Shawn and Allene. The past had already happened. Maybe, as the time travel sites argued, history couldn't be changed. But he could help Amy here and now.

His mind drifted, imagining his life in this place: playing the harp, sleeping in luxurious beds, marrying a kind and adoring woman. Travel—he'd dreamed of traveling farther than the Laird, but had never thought he could, with Scotland's troubles. Women. He blinked. Women? That didn't happen under the Laird's watch. But here, Shawn's exploits had put ideas into his head. More than ideas—possibilities. He crossed himself. He would not become Shawn.

He stared at the woman, dancing under the stream. Her hand stretched out to him. There was no guarantee he could change history. He might be returning to find his people slaughtered, dead, and gone. He might be sacrificing Amy for an unalterable past. He yanked an apple from the tree limb above him, and placed it in the stone woman's hand.

"God, place your angels beside Shawn," he said. "Be with my Allene." His shoulders sagged. He felt less sure of his choices than before he'd entered the garden.

Central Scotland, 1314

With cries of *Niall Campbell!* ringing in his ears, and the scarred soldier gripping his arm, the cold wash of fear turned to ice in Shawn's stomach. It brought with it cool logic. Niall would fight or run. *So I can't do either.* Shouts and cries rang out. The acrobats tumbled to the ground and somersaulted away. The boy dragged his braying, protesting ponies off as quickly as they'd move. Yelps sounded through the crowd as children and dogs were shoved aside. A phalanx of soldiers in white tunics and round, metal helmets surrounded Shawn.

He pushed away the terror, and pulled his natural arrogance back to himself. A cow lowed. His mind flashed to milk, and he let out a laugh, such as he'd let out at his parties. "I don't know any Niall Campbell. My name is Carton." A name jumped to mind. He ran with it.

"Sydney Carton." Must be someone he'd known in school.

The captain of the guard stepped forward, chest to chest with Shawn. Shawn pictured Conrad, and stared back with the indolent smile that always got him off the hook with the conductor. The captain hesitated. He turned to the soldier. "You saw him, I didn't. What makes you so sure this is Niall Campbell?"

"He looks just like the minstrel, sir."

Shawn didn't part with his grin. He vowed they would not hear the thudding of his heart. "I look like who? Who do I look like now? Someone really ridiculously good-looking, I hope?" He turned his two-hundred watt, village-idiot smile back and forth between the two like a giant friendly dog. He let out another boisterous laugh, throwing his head back, and hee-hawing. They'd think he was too stupid to be Niall Campbell. Right now, he assured his inner Dr. Phil, that worked for him.

The captain looked doubtfully at the soldier. "If it were him, don't you think he'd be running instead of laughing like an idiot? And wasn't Campbell wearing red and blue?"

"Sir, it's him," the man protested.

"It's hard to tell one man from another when you're drunk," the captain said. He studied Shawn, up and down, from his pointy green hat past his olive leggings to his leather boots. "I hear Niall Campbell is a deeply religious man." He snapped his fingers high in the air, his eyes locked on Shawn's. A soldier appeared beside him, pulling a crucifix from his neck. "Put your hand on it. Swear you're not Niall Campbell."

Shawn laughed again. Thank God Niall wasn't here. He, Shawn, had no qualms about swearing on a crucifix. Especially in the rare instance he was actually telling the truth. He placed his hand on it; indeed, held it high, turning and playing to the gathering crowd, to dirt-streaked boys and fresh-faced girls and old men, and said, "I swear before God and all the angels and saints,"—that phrase rang nicely in his ears—"that I am not now, nor never have been, Niall Campbell." He lowered the crucifix, and cocked an eyebrow at the captain. "My *name...is Sydney Carton.*"

The crowd clapped. He wiggled his eyebrows at the ladies, making several of them blush, and bowed deeply. They clapped again.

"I wasn't drunk," the soldier insisted. "I watched him for ten minutes. He sang, he and the other one."

Shawn looked around. "I'm the only one here." He turned to the crowd for approval. His own conviction that he'd said something unerringly clever washed over them. They laughed. He played it up. "Don't see any more of me, 'cept for those times I'm beside myself." The crowd, chuckling, inched closer, losing its fear of the soldiers. The guard's ears turned red. "He played the harp, sir."

Shawn held out empty hands, pretending to play. "Always sounds good with a skin of ale in me, too."

The crowd roared. A man slapped his knee. Shawn grinned. The soldier glared. The captain looked back and forth between the two. "Hold him," he snapped, and stepped through the crowd.

Shawn's heart began its snare drum tattoo. Streaks of panic shot up and down his arm where the soldier gripped him. He'd thought he'd done it. He breathed deeply, as he did before a concert, calming himself.

"No hard feelings," he said. The soldier scowled. Judging by the man's vice grip on his arm, the feelings were hard indeed. Shawn forced a shrug more careless than he felt, and rose on his toes, scanning the crowd—old women in kerchiefs, girls in braids, boys with wooden swords, all staring at him—and willing his heart to slow. He spotted the captain consulting with a hooded man. His gut told him this was bad—very bad. His insides turned watery, but his brain churned. The sound of a flute, from the small ensemble playing at the other end of town, drifted to him.

He waved his free arm suddenly at the captain. "I've never touched a harp," he shouted. "I play the sackbut. Can Niall Campbell play sackbut?" He didn't know what made him do it.

The captain and the hooded man stared. His heart slammed roughly in his chest. The faceless figure nodded. The captain charged, shoving villagers aside. He grabbed Shawn's arm, yanking him from the soldier's grip. "We're calling your bluff, Campbell. Tell the truth now and die quickly; play with me and die like William Wallace." He dragged Shawn through the crowd, now scrambling out of the way, to the far end of town, where a small orchestra performed.

"Stop playing!" he shouted. The men lowered their instruments, looking fearfully at each other. "Last chance," the captain barked at Shawn, yanking him nose to nose. Foul breath singed Shawn's nostrils. "You do know how William Wallace died, don't you?"

"I do, sir," said Shawn. Anger wrestled with fear, giving his voice strength. "And when you see I speak the truth, I'll not die at all. I have your word?"

The captain, unnerved by Shawn's confidence, turned to the hooded figure, behind the musicians. He nodded. "You have my word." He scanned the musicians, and pointed. "That thing?" Shawn nodded. The captain snapped his fingers at a gangly man. He came forward, trembling.

Shawn bowed to him; then accepted the sackbut, the feel of it strange in its lightness, yet familiar and beloved. He ran a hand down the smooth brass slide, and over the slight flare of the bell.

"Play!" shouted the hooded figure. His hatred streaked over the orchestra like sheet lightning, crackling around Shawn.

Shawn blew one long, golden tone, settling his nerves. His gaze drifted over the orchestra, to the hooded man who wanted Niall dead.

"Anyone can do that," the captain snapped. "Play, or you're dead."

Shawn scanned the crowd. He spotted Allene far back, pale as an albino rose and straining against Brother David's arm. He turned from her, winking as he did. He started a scale, getting a feel for the instrument. He played some lip slurs, jumping octaves faster and faster, as a boy skips stones in a river.

"Anyone can do that!" the captain roared.

"Want to try?" Shawn offered the instrument. An easy smile curved his lips.

The captain glared. His eyes narrowed. His voice dropped to a deadly whisper. "Play a song, *Sydney*. I'll cut your bowels out myself for playing me for a fool."

Their eyes locked. Shawn read bloodlust. Once more, his heart took up its pounding. This man did not want to be convinced. A moment of doubt assailed Shawn. But he swallowed hard and stepped boldly into his fate, as he always had.

He raised the instrument, paused for effect, meeting the eyes of several in the crowd: the dark-haired woman with child; the apron-clad apprentice. He let out a single note, tripped a half note up and back down, and slid an octave higher. He dropped in a couple of effortless grace notes, and drifted into the sweetly poignant melody of *Czardas*.

A gypsy women near him swayed, her long black hair, like Amy's, swinging, her skirts swirling around her ankles. A couple of sixteenth notes floated from the bell, and she twirled. People stepped back, giving her space. He slid into a lively melody, the slide flying, notes tumbling out in revelry. The woman threw her head back, laughing; spun, twirled, raising her arms over her head, her feet skipping to his sparkling music.

He smiled behind the mouthpiece; his eyes danced with hers, then skimmed out over the crowd. He found Allene, leaning against Brother David. The gypsy's skirts spun in a magnificent circle, flashing layer after layer of kaleidoscope petticoats. Young girls swayed to the music. His arm flashed in and out, his tongue clicked out the tu-ku tu-ku tu's needed for notes this fast. He leaned toward the gypsy, their eyes met, and they circled one another, the sackbut singing, the slide flying, her feet dancing, gold earrings flashing sunlight. Shawn skipped and danced as he played, the notes skimming out in joyous revelry.

Villagers gaped. The sackbut player gaped more. Shawn slid back into the poignant melody, and the gypsy laughed again, showing white teeth and joy in life, and slowed back into the swaying, matching his music beat for beat; a bright crimson kerchief floated from her hands. The last note drifted from the bell, shimmering in the summer air. Shawn lowered the instrument, beaming, bowing. The crowd cheered and clapped. They shouted. A girl threw blossoms, whites and blues and pinks showering his feet. He blew her a kiss. He grinned from ear to ear. He turned to the captain.

The man's face glowed crimson.

The words *Can anyone do that?* froze on Shawn's lips.

For once, he recognized a man humiliated, and had a diplomatic urge. He threw his arm around the man's shoulders, ignoring his tension, and the hand clenched on his sword. "Thank my friend!" he bellowed. The crowd cheered. "This man insisted I play. He procured this fine instrument. A drink! Who will buy a drink for my friend?" The innkeeper bustled off for a flagon of ale. The captain's hand slipped off his sword; his muscles relaxed. Shawn pressed his advantage. "Not only is he a military man of the highest caliber, he has a fine ear for music. He is the best of men!"

He doffed his cap to the captain, who now glowed red with pleasure under the crowd's admiration. He'd no doubt never experienced such adulation before. Shawn knew too well what a powerful drug it was. He offered his hand to the captain, who removed his heavy glove to shake. "I'm most sorry I didn't realize how serious the situation was." Shawn leaned in confidentially. "It must be a real villain you seek."

"Aye, the worst of men," the captain confided. "A traitor raising men against England."

Shawn put a look of disgust on his face, spitting to reinforce the opinion. "Praise be to God above we've men like you to guard us! To Edward," he said. "To the king. Is there aught I can do to help?"

The captain slapped him on the back. "Fine men like you almost redeem this dread country. Get yourself to Stirling for the battle."

"That I will," Shawn agreed. *If I can't find a way out of it,* he added to himself.

"I shall see the king rewards your loyalty. What's your name again?"

Shawn panicked. Little John? He remembered the captain spitting it out. "Sydney." He searched desperately for the last name, and remembered the cow. "Sydney Carton."

"Ah, yes, that was it. Keep playing."

Certainly Niall couldn't do any such thing on a sackbut, but Shawn raised the instrument and started the Davison *Sonata*. At least it was a pleasure to play, and work an audience again.

* * *

"My lord," said the captain. He and the hooded Scot stood under a tree, watching the man playing sackbut. Soldiers ringed the crowd. "Would Niall Campbell swear a falsehood on a crucifix?"

"He'd have run. Or more likely, fought. He may have lied at first, but faced with a crucifix, he'd have gone pale and sought an excuse."

"He does not speak like a Highlander."

The Scot scowled. The summer breeze rippled the edge of his cowl. "Niall was ever a clever mimic. He speaks as he pleases."

"He is not wearing what Campbell wore in the forest. And the sackbut. Can he do such a thing?"

"Impossible," murmured the Scot. "Niall is clever, but not so clever as to have fooled me all these years. He'd no reason to." His jaw clenched. "But he looks exactly like Niall."

They watched the man playing the sackbut, with precision and ease that spoke of years of practice. The captain gestured at him. "My lord, I ask again, can Niall Campbell do that?"

"No," admitted the Scot. "He canna do that."

"Then it is merely a man who looks like him. Is that so strange, with your clans being so close and marrying one another?"

"Still...." The Scot issued instructions, and stalked away.

Ten minutes later, the musician had regained his sackbut, staring at it in wonder. Shawn waited in the tavern's upper room that struggled to pull sunlight through one small window. "Take off your shirt," the captain said.

Shawn kept his wisecracks to himself. But wary relief crept in. They were looking for Niall's scarred back. Still, if *Czardas* had not convinced them, would his unblemished back? He pulled off the tunic and shirt, waiting with growing distaste in his mouth, and considering whether he could take on the two of them. He looked out the small window, across the field. Allene watched the tavern from behind a tree. He hoped she wouldn't give them away, try some ridiculous diversion or something.

The man in the cloak circled him, a faceless grim reaper. He pushed Shawn's hair off his temple. Shawn stood still, disliking the man more with each invasion. The man dropped the hair back in place and pulled the captain across the room. Shawn's heartbeat slowed gradually to something like normal.

The captain returned swiftly. "My lord offers his apologies, and bids you well." He held out a small leather bag. Shawn took it, surprised at its weight. "Our apology, Sydney," the captain explained. "Godspeed."

The realization dawned slowly: he would see the sun sink in the west tonight. With the end of danger, the trembling began. Hatred burned like bile in his stomach. He steeled himself, turning to the hooded figure. The man had withdrawn into a shadowed corner, a swath of brown wool, nothing to identify him. He'd said not a word.

"No worries." Shawn pulled on the shirt and tunic, buckled the belt, and tied the pouch's drawstrings into it. He headed out into the fair, relieved and shaking, and ambled about, inspecting sheep, buying a turkey leg, talking with the sackbut player. Only after the soldiers gathered and marched out of town, did he turn to the tinkers' caravans.

He found them on the far edge of town in the clearing of a grove—a cluster of gypsy wagons with rounded tops, brightly painted wood, cheerful blue curtains fluttering in the evening breeze. The woman who had danced sauntered from behind one of them. She rounded the campfire, swirling her skirts within inches of the dancing flames, smiling. Black ringlets tumbled down her back. Her red-nailed hand came to rest on his chest, and she stood on tiptoe to kiss him full on the lips. He caught his breath. All the familiar feelings burst to life. She spoke, a low, husky melody, in a language he'd never heard.

A proposition in any language, he found, was not hard to understand.

As he stared into her black eyes, the weight of his situation settled on him. He was trapped in the wrong time with men who wanted to kill him and no idea how to get back where he belonged. He'd been a long time without a woman—more than a week.

And he did not want this woman or her red nails.

He wanted Amy, sitting on the hillside. He wanted to be in Amy's apartment, handing her tickets to visit her mother, talking half the night; or beside her, arguing about chord structure in a new arrangement. He wanted Amy sleeping against his chest, as Allene had, confident he would protect her.

He wanted Allene's respect.

He stared into the depths of the gypsy woman's eyes, eyes that waited, eyes that promised. "This can't be me," he said, and sadly shook his head.

She laughed, none of her joy lost, and led him to another wagon, where Brother David rested with help from the gypsies' healing herbs. Shawn dropped on the pallet beside him, confident Allene was also being cared for, and sank into deep sleep.

Inverness, Scotland, Present

Niall trailed slowly back to the castle, his mind nowhere near as settled as he'd hoped. His jaw ached. Either choice, as far as he could see, might be God's plan. It might be a miracle that had brought him, meaning he should take care of things here. Or it could be devilment, such that he should fight his way back to his own time. One thought dominated: *could* the past be changed? He might be abandoning Amy, whom he could help, for an unalterable past, for slaughter and death he could not prevent. He looked up at the sun's decline, and quickened his step. They'd be serving dinner at the castle.

In the great hall—the dining room, he corrected himself—a group he vaguely recognized as some of the percussion and brass players hailed him. He carried his plate to their table and seated himself.

"That's quite the bruise!" The older man at the table stared. "What happened?"

Niall touched his jaw. "A mishap," he said.

"Must have been some mishap," said the woman.

"You don't mind joining us, the holy rollers?" the young percussionist asked.

"Of course not," said Niall, seating himself. *Holy rollers*...would he ever understand these people's speech? "Why should I?" Indeed, it felt good to be welcome, despite their open looks of curiosity at his bruised jaw.

The group exchanged uncomfortable looks. Niall raised his eyebrows. Understanding washed over him. These were Shawn's detractors; those he'd sensed giving him disapproving stares the first day. They were, then, Niall thought, most likely exactly his type. He smiled a friendly overture, and used his standard excuse. "I remember nothing before waking in the castle. I'm a new man. I hope we can start anew." Relief sprang up like spring blossoms around the table, skipping from one to the other. All their faces lightened. "You'll forgive me if I ask your names?" Niall said.

Looks of open curiosity shot around the table this time. "So it's true?" asked the woman.

"Excuse me?" Niall bit back the *my lady*. "Is what true?"

"Amnesia? You really don't remember anything?"

He nodded. "I know nothing of the man you knew, but what I've been told."

"You don't remember the hotel in Edinburgh?" The percussionist spoke doubtfully.

The others shushed him, while Niall confirmed he really didn't. "He asked for a fresh start," said the older man. His white mustache quivered as he spoke. "I will be the first to give it to him." He leaned forward, pressing his large belly into the table, to shake Niall's hand. "Jim."

"Ni...Shawn."

They laughed. "We all remember *you*," said the percussionist. He held out his hand. "Jason, percussion."

Niall nodded. "Yes, I've seen you behind those big drums." Looks flashed around the table again. He wondered what he'd said wrong this time.

The old man spoke again. "You really don't remember me? It was my chair you took."

Niall's eyebrows furrowed. He glanced at his dinner, hungry, but he hadn't prayed. "I took your chair?" Why would Shawn take an old man's chair? He really was despicable, Niall thought. How had he ever found that glimmer of compassion for the scoundrel? An old man needed his chair, after all.

Jim looked equally confused. Perhaps, Niall thought, in this time, old men didn't need their chairs so much? "My chair," Jim said. "You know, first chair." At Niall's continued lack of comprehension, he tried again. "I'm now second chair? Never mind," he said. "It doesn't matter. Personality conflicts aside, I've always said you're a fine player, and I hope you can play again, or the world's lost something."

Jim waved to Amy, leaving the buffet. She joined them, seating herself beside Niall. He studied her, the newfound knowledge of her pregnancy swimming in his mind.

"Shawn," she whispered, leaning close. "What happened?"

"Nothing," he said. "A mishap."

"It's..."

"Later, Amy." He leaned close, shaking out his napkin. Her eyes flew to Rob, at the buffet. "It was nothing," he said again. "Leave it." But he found his own gaze resting on Rob.

"Mike," said the man to Amy's left, continuing the introductions, and Ronda, Matt, 'Still Jim,' Chuck and 'Still Jason.' Niall repeated the names in his head. From the buffet, Rob glared at him. Niall rubbed his jaw.

"We're dying to ask you something." Jim's voice drew his attention back to the table.

Niall's stomach chose that moment to rumble loudly. He touched his stomach. "If you'll excuse me a moment?" He waited for their nods of assent before bowing his head, crossing himself, and praying. He included one for Amy. And another for Rob. Rob would not like his plan. One for Shawn, and several for Allene. Crossing himself again, he smiled around the group before sampling his Atlantic salmon.

There was a moment of stunned silence. Niall looked up to see them all gaping. "That's just it," Jim burst out. "Prayers before meals, the crucifix...." He waved at Niall's throat. Jim gestured, moved his mouth, failing to find words.

"When? Why? How?" Ronda blurted. "You never wore a crucifix. What happened in that castle? Someone shot you, clubbed you, and put a crucifix on you? Where did you even get it?"

"The pawn shop." Niall thought up a story quickly.

"You put that crucifix on the wall." Amy's eyebrows furrowed.

"I bought this one as well," Niall said.

"But why now?" Jim persisted. "Not that we're complaining."

A rush of agreement raced around the table. "The change in you is great," Mike said. "We're burning with curiosity." All of them nodded.

"I can't explain." Niall cut his potato, hoping they'd drop it.

"Were you always Catholic?" Ronda asked.

"Will you be going to church?" said Matt.

"Do you have a favorite saint?" questioned Mike.

The questions flew, till he laughed and held up a hand. He saw no way to reconcile any possible answer with the real Shawn, or even with the supposed amnesia. "I remember nothing," he reminded them. "The crucifix caught my eye. The prayers—I just do. I can't explain."

"You were raised Catholic," Amy suggested.

Niall hoped that would satisfy them. How, if they asked too many questions, could he possibly explain parading as Shawn, much less what had happened to the real Shawn? He wasn't sure, himself. "Help me re-learn all I've forgotten. Tell me about yourselves. Who are your favorite saints?"

"There's an interesting local saint," Jim said. "Margaret Morrison."

Niall set his fork down abruptly. "She's a *saint* now?"

Amy turned to him. "What would you know about any Margaret Morrison and why shouldn't she be a saint?"

"I, uh, I—read about her. On the internet. She didn't start out so saintly." He swallowed hard, hoping they'd buy it. He didn't dare ask what had become of her sister. They all stared at him much as he'd stared at Lord Morrison's identical daughters the first time he'd seen them. Margaret had taken advantage of his surprise to drop a fish down his shirt.

"Well, I'm not Catholic." Ronda broke the momentary silence. Niall wondered what she was, if not Catholic. The Laird had spoken of wild hordes in the East who were not Christian, but Ronda looked nothing like what he'd described. "But I've always admired Peter. All the early disciples, really. Put yourself in their place. If I'd seen Jesus die on a cross, I might still be hiding in the upper room."

"St. Francis," said Chuck, pausing with a forkful of potatoes in mid-air. "Everyone loves St. Francis."

"Yes!" Niall feigned enthusiasm. He'd never heard of the man. "What do you love best about him?"

Amy set her glass down, staring in amazement. "I wouldn't have guessed you ever even heard of St. Francis, Shawn!"

Niall smiled at her, shrugged, and savored his salmon while the others enlightened him.

"His love of animals," said Ronda. "I have his statue in my garden, with a bird feeder, and a salt lick for the deer."

"His humility," said Jim. "Francis is my confirmation name. He loved and accepted everyone, no matter what they were like."

Across the table, Mike put down his fork and leaned forward, obviously relishing a favorite subject. "St. Catherine of Sienna. Fascinating woman!"

"Definitely a Catholic saint," said Jason. "I never heard of her."

Niall took another bite of salmon, wishing Glenmirril's cooks could make the loch's fish taste so good. But his thoughts returned quickly to the conversation, equally succulent. He'd never heard of Catherine of Sienna, and didn't know if he should have. He phrased his question carefully. "What do you learn from her?"

Mike gestured with his hands, nearly hitting the serving woman who approached with a jug of water. *Ewers of glass!* Niall couldn't take his eyes off it, despite several days' acquaintance with such things, and missed the first of Bob's words. Amy nudged him. "It's just a pitcher! Are you okay?"

"Fine," Niall said. "It's just—beautiful." He pulled his eyes back to the others. Several of them glanced from him to the jug, frowning.

"...saw Jesus," Mike was saying. "He appeared in the flesh and offered her two crowns—one of roses and one of thorns."

Niall stopped eating and found himself leaning forward with the others.

"Which did she choose?" asked Ronda.

"Which would you have chosen?" Mike asked.

"Roses." Ronda set down her water glass. "Being a saint means you're doing everything right, right? So He was honoring her. Isn't Mary always shown with roses?"

"Roses signified Him granting her a good life," Mike said. "She took the thorns."

"Signifying a hard life," Niall mused. The roses in the garden filled his mind. Catherine's choice illuminated his own soul and desires.

"She wanted to be like Jesus in all things. He didn't have a life of ease, so she didn't want one, either."

Niall stole a sidelong glance at Amy, eating her salad, and wondered which crown he'd really hoped for, in the garden.

Chapter Sixteen

Central Scotland, 1314

Shawn, Allene, and Brother David slept briefly, buried in deep underbrush. The gypsies had carried them many miles in bumping caravans, giving them a much-needed rest, and hot food. The black bruises ringing Brother David's eyes had faded to mottled yellow, his breathing had eased, and the limp was almost gone. They slept by night, short as that was, and traveled by day, with less fear of Edward's men, and greater difficulty seeing at night, in the thickest forest they'd yet encountered. Nestled in his mossy bed, with Allene curled in his arm, and her hair brushing his nose, Shawn reviewed his situation.

He'd been switched in time, impossible as that was to believe. Glenmirril was his best—perhaps only—prospect for getting back. Yet he was following Allene away from his only hope. He traced events, from his moment of realization in the cellar. He couldn't very well have insisted on leaving the village the wrong way, with the soldiers looking for him. He didn't know his way across the moors, or anywhere in Scotland, for that matter, so there'd been little choice but to follow Allene. So here he was, in a world over which he had no control. If Niall had been thrown into the twenty-first century, if he was smart, Shawn thought, he'd stay away from Glenmirril and any chance of a switch. Who would willingly come back to this brutal time? *Does that mean I'm stuck? Or will the tower cause the switch without Niall?*

He twisted in the dark underbrush, trying to get comfortable. Despite promising to get Allene safely to Hugh, it was she and Brother David guiding him, finding food and water. He'd fooled himself, thinking she'd felt protected in his arms, down there in the cellar. Moreover, shame stirred at his helplessness. He felt...hardly a man.

"What happens if Edward wins at Stirling?" Shawn asked. Somewhere in the dark, a brook bubbled over rocks.

"The Scots are destroyed," Allene said.

"He knows well he is not regarded as the king nor the man his father was," Brother David elaborated. "He is weary of being mocked. If he wins, he will slaughter every man on the battlefield. Then he'll send his armies throughout Scotland to kill the old men, women, and children of every clan that stood against him."

"He'll kill children?"

Brother David spoke softly over the hum of night insects. "He'll no give them the chance to grow up and avenge their fathers' deaths."

"How does he kill children?"

"Surely you remember the massacre after Falkirk!" Allene exclaimed. "Some were stabbed with dirks or cut down by men on horseback as they fled to the forest. Some were hung beside their parents. Babes were torn from their mother's arms and thrown from the tower."

Shawn shuddered. "Sorry I asked."

"He'll kill livestock or take it for his own," Brother David continued. "Anyone who survives his slaughter will starve. He'll take back castles and give every bit of Scottish land to his nobles and those Scots who fought with him."

Something rustled in the brush. They fell silent. Shawn's insides tightened, wondering if Edward's men had found them. Allene became still. Soft footsteps crept nearer—something large, something heavy, moving with delicate deliberation.

Branches whispered against a body. Immediately behind him, a footstep fell, brushing his back. Shawn jackknifed to his feet, spinning and wrenching the dagger from his boot. His breathing came fast, searching for the soldier in the dark. He saw none.

Then ragged, stinking breath caught his nose. He searched downward, and met yellow eyes glinting in the moonlight. Allene screamed. He heard a scramble of branches as Brother David dragged her from harm's way.

Arrrgh!

A guttural battle cry erupted in the night; Shawn stiffened for battle, before realizing it was he, himself, bellowing at the wolf. The beast growled deep in its throat. Shawn's world shifted into slow motion; his senses heightened. Moonlight glinted silver off the wolf's fur. Its haunches lowered, bunched; its lip curled, baring yellow daggers in a frothing mouth; its eyes gripped his. The haunches sprang, rocketing the wolf toward his throat.

Shawn threw himself back at the animal, snarling. His right hand shot up, digging the knife into the animal's ribs, blade scraping bone. He jerked back. The wolf breathed heat in his face; incisors the size of fingers slashed at his eyes. He stumbled under the animal's weight, falling in thick, jabbing brush; the wolf on him, lunging for his throat.

Allene screamed.

He yanked back on the knife. It came free, but his hand was

pinned between himself and the wolf. His left hand caught its throat; pushed, trembling with effort, squeezing the jugular. The animal thrashed, snarled, scraped its front paws, scrabbled with its hind legs for footing. A claw tore down Shawn's thigh, ripping a bloody trail the length of it. Shawn arched, screaming, glaring into the ugly face, pushed his foot back and leveraged both their bodies into a roll.

His knife hand came free. He jabbed, yanking back swiftly. He fought to grip the wolf's throat, through slippery, sticky streams of blood. He stabbed again, over and over, quick, sharp thrusts to ribs and belly. Hot blood soaked his shirt, and flowed down his legs. The wolf clawed again, digging deep.

He snarled, furious, blood pulsing through his temples, gave a hard thrust with the knife, and heaved the wolf off with a powerful thrust of his left arm. It sprawled, still fighting, in the vegetation a foot away. Shawn bellowed a murderous cry and launched himself on the thing, stabbing and stabbing and stabbing and stabbing, till Brother David's voice broke through.

"It's dead."

"You'll ruin the pelt," said Allene.

He fell off the animal, kneeling beside it panting and furious, no longer himself. He turned to her in disgust. "It tried to kill us! You think I care about the pelt!"

Allene fell back a step, a glimmer of fear and doubt in her eyes. "Only that it will keep someone warm of a winter night."

"What! We're taking this thing with us?"

"'Tis good meat for Hugh's men," Brother David said. "And good fur. Give me the knife. I'll skin it. My lady, gather leaves to wrap the meat."

Shawn braced his hands on his thighs, gripping the knife in his bandaged hand, head down, breathing hard. The wolf twitched, death rattling in its throat.

The adrenaline subsided in Shawn. He settled back into himself. What animal had risen in him, screaming blood curdling cries like a man demented?

He studied the wolf now lying motionless before him. He prodded it with a fist. It must be a hundred and fifty pounds of murder he'd just fought off. His pulled his hand away; his arms began to tremble. Stinging pains screamed down his thigh.

Brother David took the knife from Shawn. "'Twould be better if you could help me drag it to the river to work," he suggested.

Shawn did not move. He did not speak.

"You are hurt," Allene murmured. New respect lined her voice like velvet. She dabbed at his cheek. He winced, jerking away. "Without you, he'd ha' killed us," she said. "I canna fight a wolf, nor can Brother David with his injuries."

Shawn said nothing.

Allene's hand fell on his shoulder. "You saved our lives."

He suddenly threw his head back and laughed; huge, belly-shaking, hysterical, bellowing laughs.

"Niall! Niall, stop it!" Allene yanked her hand away, then moved in again, trying to dab at the blood on his face. "You're making it bleed more. Let me tend it."

Shawn laughed again, looking at the wolf. He'd done it. He'd fought the bastard off. He'd done something good.

"Leave him be," Brother David said.

Shawn vaguely noticed him pulling Allene away. The two of them began tugging at the wolf, inching it down to the stream. He laughed and laughed till he cried, tears streaming down his cheeks until he sobbed openly, thinking of Amy and all the rotten, lousy things he'd done to her, the way he'd pushed and pushed till he got his way with her, all the times he'd lied and cheated, and the ring he'd stolen for his own selfish reasons.

...the baby she'd wanted so badly. He'd all but dragged her away to rid himself of it. He thought of the children ripped from their mothers' arms and thrown from the towers. He was no better.

His head sank to the ground, where the wolf had lain. The earth was warm from its body and wet with its blood. He pushed himself up, tore the bandage from his hand, and stared at the jagged reminder of Allene's knife.

He'd deserved so much worse.

Amy.... He remembered now. He'd been drunk, he'd told her all about his father. Heat flushed his face even now, remembering that night. She'd held his head, cleaned the vomit, wiped his forehead and cheeks time after time, and never said a word about it.

Amy had deserved so much better.

Inverness, Scotland, Present

Amy, Niall vowed, would be cared for as she deserved. Still forming his plans, he rose from his early morning prayers beside the curtained four poster bed. He found a serving woman in the hall, who went to fetch Amy. While he waited, he paced the sitting room, under blue-toned paintings and cornflower walls, past the periwinkle cushion in the window seat, and around the high gloss of the wooden table.

He needed the money from the walls, but only one of thousands of numbers would release Shawn's wealth. He pressed the heels of his hands into his eyes, seeking a solution, but none came. And time was slipping away. The concert and battle were fast approaching. He had to at least try.

She arrived in his rooms, her cloud-white shirt and knee-length jeans complementing the paintings and wallpaper, only after he'd paced it several times, considering and dismissing multiple solutions.

"I need the card that takes money from walls," he said, abruptly. "I need to know the number."

"It's your card." She pulled it from her back pocket, and flipped it onto the table. It skidded across, its shiny colors contrasting with the wood. "How would I know?"

"Only four numbers, right?" He snatched it up, waving it in her face. Spewing his frustration on her was unjust, but he felt powerless to stop. "There are always patterns. What kind of patterns do people use?"

She backed away, eyes narrowed. "Back to your same old arrogant self? Why are you angry at me?"

Niall sighed, his body deflating. He lifted his gaze to the frescoed ceiling, hands on his hips. "I'm sorry." He met her eyes again. "I'm not angry. I'm frustrated. I need to get at hi...at my money, and I can't remember. What patterns do people use?"

"Patterns." She tested the word. His apology had mollified her. She took the card from him, studying it as though it would give her the answer. "I don't know. Sequences, four in a row. Everyone says not to use them, but some people do anyway."

"No." It didn't sound like Shawn.

"No? What, you remember now?" she demanded.

"No. He just wouldn't do that."

"He, who? You picked the number."

Niall pressed his palm against his forehead, screwing his eyes shut. He couldn't slip back into talking about Shawn as if he was someone else. "The Shawn you've spoken of seems like a different man to me. I don't think he'd do that. What other patterns do people use?"

"Dates. Years or dates that are important to them."

"Show me," he commanded. He yanked paper from the printer and thrust it, and a pencil, at her. "What dates were important?"

She took the pencil, keeping the table between them. "We already tried your birthday. Your mother's?" She jotted a number. "The year you graduated from high school? From college? No, anyone could find that in Wikipedia."

He almost asked *wiki-what?* But it didn't matter. "Write it down. What else?"

"The date of your audition? Shawn, I don't know. I'm completely guessing." At his commanding look, she wrote it down. "You know, you can just get a new card when we get home."

"No. I need it now."

"What's going on? What's the money for this time?"

Niall sighed. His frustration drained. "Sit down," he said. Amy perched on one of the dainty chairs, on the edge of the needlepoint seat as if waiting for her doom to be announced. He pulled a chair up, facing her, and sat knee to knee. "Amy, I talked with Rob."

Her face drained. Her gaze flashed over the bruise on his jaw and darted away. She licked dry lips. "I was going to tell you." She twisted her ring. "How does he know?"

"Rob fancies you. He sees everything."

She reached up, brushed her fingers against his bruised jaw, sending flutters along his skin, then dropped her eyes and bit her lip. "I let him think.... Well, I meant it, I wasn't leading him on. That's why he hit you, isn't it? I told him it was over between you and me, unless you finally proved you were really the man I thought you were. Now he thinks you've taken me from him. I didn't know...I would have been more careful if I'd known he felt so strongly."

"Don't blame yourself." Niall pushed himself off the table and dropped to one knee in front of her. "About the baby. I'll take care of you, Amy. I can't make promises for a week hence, but now, today, I'll do what I can. But I need your help." He wrapped his fingers in hers, wondering what the future held for them. "Don't ask questions. Just do it, while I take care of some things before the concert."

She listened as he listed off what he wanted, shaking her head. "This makes no sense," she said. "I don't understand." Her fingers lay still in his; her eyes scanned his doubtfully.

"I'll explain after the concert. Trust me until then."

"Conrad will have a fit," she said softly.

"Don't tell him. As soon as possible after the concert," Niall insisted.

She took the pencil he held out to her, hesitated briefly, then wrote the list, biting her lip as she did. He handed her Shawn's wallet, sliding his fingers around hers.

She met his eyes, rested her lips against his fingers. He leaned his forehead on hers, touched her hair and cheek. Two futures hovered before him. Only one would happen. He let his hand slide from hers, and headed for the door with a backward glance.

Central Scotland, 1314

Allene turned sharply at a stone roughly in the shape of a horse's head, and pushed from the dirt path onto a trail hidden amongst the foliage. The trees seemed a mile tall, dark and glowering overhead, shutting out all but patches of the western sun. Thick ferns rose to their waists. Berries and sprays of wildflowers splashed color over the palette of forest greens. Mosses and animal musk and the meat they carried gave a rich, humid scent to the air. Despite Allene's efforts at bandaging his leg, the deep wounds left by the wolf stung with each step. His Robin Hood tights hung in shreds under his tunic.

By unspoken agreement, they fell silent in this dim sanctuary. They heard only the rustling of branches as they passed, and occasional birdsong. Their soft leather boots fell silently on the humus rich earth.

Shawn's spirit soared: they needed him. He trekked through the forest cathedrals, past streams and over boulders, hour after hour, with energy he'd never felt. He would see them to Hugh and then, somehow get out of fighting this lost-cause battle and back to the castle. The injuries from the wolf ought to excuse him. They'd see he couldn't fight. Allene would be safe with Hugh. And he'd go to the tower and wake up in his own time, find Amy and ask her, beg her, to give him another chance.

The forest thinned. They left it behind to climb a boulder-strewn monroe, pausing at the pass in exhaustion, breathing heavily. Heavy mist clung in their hair and obscured what might have been an expansive view. They crossed another stream on the way down, and entered another forest silver-green with mist. Shawn chewed his tongue to keep from making a sound at the pain shooting down his leg.

"Are we there yet?" he whispered, once. The stillness and sense of hidden danger kept every sense alive. Allene and David glanced back dismissively, returning him to monastic silence; but even without their looks, he felt he'd violated something sacred, attempting levity in this place. He gazed up at the soaring pines. He breathed in their heady scent. Amy would like it here. He wanted to wrap her long, thick hair around his hand, draw her close and kiss her here under these trees, in this mist. He had an image, an insane image of the two of them, a boy on his shoulders, hiking these hills.

Maybe a child wouldn't have been fun.

Maybe it would have been something better than fun.

They pushed another mile through thick brush. His hand flew up more than once to fend off a branch snapping back behind Brother David. Midges swarmed the leaf-wrapped meat, and up around his face and the blood-seeped bandages on his thigh. He wondered if Amy missed him. But of course, Niall may have woken up in his place. Would she actually think Niall was him?

He stopped, his stomach turning! What if she'd gone to bed with Niall? Sure, he was a Boy Scout, but maybe only because Allene would stab him. Amy wouldn't. And Amy was beautiful.

Allene and Brother David forged ahead. He'd be lost if he didn't keep up. He limped after them, slapping a little too roughly through the forest, burning with the thought that Niall might have taken advantage of the situation. In *his* four-poster bed! Glaring, Shawn slapped at a midge circling in front of his eyes, and bent to brush at those around his legs. He straightened and slapped at the new swarm in front of his face.

His hand grazed, instead, cold steel.

He stopped. He touched it gingerly.

Something snaked over his left shoulder and across his chest, pulling him back against a rock. His heart struck up a frantic tempo. Synapses spread alarm up and down his arms. Cold sweat burst out on his forehead. He lowered his hand to the hairy arm clamped across his chest.

Allene and Brother David plunged into the darkening forest, leaving him behind, in the grip of someone unknown.

Inverness, Scotland, Present

Among the morning throngs on the sidewalks of Inverness, with his jaw aching and full-blown purple now, thanks to Shawn's misdeeds, Niall's view of Shawn swung full throttle back to its original, ugly impression. So he'd lost a father! *So did I*, Niall muttered, *and I don't behave so!* He rubbed his jaw, conscious of the stares it drew.

He passed one of the paintings of Shawn, ragged around the edges now. Shawn wore a plaid and the grin of a town fool, astride a shaggy highland cow, with two buxom lasses staring moon-eyed up at him. *Scotland's best* indeed! Niall seethed. The man was a scoundrel and wastrel, his moments of kindness and humor mere feints to get his way. He'd probably finagled this whole switch somehow just to escape the consequences of his many misdeeds.

He was most likely with Allene right now and if Niall's plan succeeded, he'd be back with Amy, pressuring her into ridding herself of the child, or abandoning her to raise it alone. And all Niall had said and done these past days would appear another of Shawn's insincere jokes on good-hearted people. He scowled, storming down the street toward the money wall.

"I pray for him, anyway," he muttered, irritated with his own hatred. He'd found it so easy to follow the monks' teachings, and God, before he'd known a man like Shawn. But Amy, he vowed, *would* be taken care of, to the best of his ability.

Reaching the money wall, he pulled Shawn's things from the back pocket of his jeans, and shuffled through the plastic cards. He found the proper one, and Amy's list of numbers. He studied it, drawing on everything he knew of Shawn, every word he'd heard of the man, every scrap of evidence left in his rooms, trying to guess. What was important to him? Which number held significance?

He lined the card up according to the picture on the machine and chose the first number: Shawn's mother's birthday. He'd tried to buy her a house. Scoundrel though he was, he loved his mother. Niall punched the numbers. The machine beeped angrily. He groaned, realizing the futility. There were thousands of combinations. Amy had warned him he only had three tries: two more before he lost the card forever in the wall.

He crossed himself, staring back at a passerby who gave him a disapproving look.

"Praying ye didn't drink it all last night?" she sniffed.

He shook his head and looked to Heaven—these people made no sense—and turned back to the machine and his knowledge of Shawn. He'd stayed with Amy, and Niall, too, had begun to wonder why. Caroline seemed more suited to him. Maybe Amy was right and there was more to Shawn? Might he have some feelings about that baby he'd rid her of? He felt a rush of excitement, remembering the numbers Rob said Amy wrote sometimes. He knew! He'd prayed, and the answer had come to him! He punched the numbers quickly: oh-six-oh-six, wondering how to get the money, once he got access.

The machine beeped.

He stared, shocked. He'd been so sure. His shoulders sagged. He had only one more try.

"Other people need that," a peevish voice snapped. Niall scowled at the woman behind him. She blinked, hard, and hurried along.

Niall turned back to the machine. He had one try left. He shuffled through the plastic cards, seeking inspiration. Among them, was the photograph of Shawn and his father. Niall studied it, wishing Shawn had not left him with such a mess. He wondered what it was like, the two of them together. He turned the picture over, thinking of the day Shawn's father had died; imagining the shock of a young boy hearing of his father's murder. That one event had changed Shawn and all the lives around him.

Slowly, Niall lifted his hand and punched that horrible day into the machine.

Central Scotland, 1314

"Halt!" roared a guttural, Gaelic roll of thunder. It peeled back Shawn's eardrums. He swore several trees swayed under the impact of the Voice. Rustling in the brush suggested the man had brought friends. Shawn stood motionless, sweating under the weight of the man's arm clamped across his chest.

Laura Vosika

Allene and Brother David turned—silently—in slow motion. David's eyes widened, his mouth opened. Allene's cowl hid her face. Birds fell silent. Shawn's every synapse trembled, hyper-aware of the cold blade. He swallowed. He wondered how much it hurt, having your throat cut. He thought of Amy, alone with the child, and wanted to be with her, with them.

"Naeme yerselves," the Voice bellowed. Shawn closed his eyes; his knees weakened. He prayed these were the men Allene sought, not the men seeking him and Allene.

Allene threw back her cowl. Her hair blazed in the evening light. She lifted her chin. "We seek Hugh MacDonald."

Silence stretched around Shawn. Fire ran up the wound on his thigh.

Cold steel brushed across his throat...

...and fell away.

The huge arm released Shawn. He sagged, stumbled, then caught himself.

"My lady! Hugh will be joyed to see you! Come quickly ere the sun sinks. Niall, you're ever welcome." Shawn was spun around, to face a giant of a man. He winced as a large hand crushed his injured palm in enthusiastic greeting. The man pulled back. He noted the bandage, filthy gray despite his attempt to clean it in the river after his fight with the wolf. "Trouble on the way?" he asked.

Shawn trembled. This man was taking them to the brother of the Laird who'd threatened bodily harm. He swallowed. "I...uh...made...."

"He fought a wolf," Allene interjected. "He saved our lives."

Shawn's eyes met hers. In the dying sun, Allene's lips curved into the smallest smile. She gave her head a small shake.

The man jerked his head at the monk, who carried the wolf's pelt. "Who's he?"

"This is Brother David, a man of God who was mistaken for Niall, and beaten nigh to death in the Great Glen," Allene answered. "He's been our companion. I beg your leave for him to come to camp and fall under Hugh's protection."

The three men sized Brother David up, and the leader nodded. With a beckoning hand, they turned and tramped deep into the brush.

Inverness, Scotland, Present

Niall braced his hands on either side of the money machine, holding his breath. It whirred and the words, *Hello, Shawn,* appeared on the screen.

He closed his eyes, breathing thanks to God. Five minutes later,

283

the sporran hanging from Niall's jeans bulged with all the cash the machine would give him. It seemed a vast treasure. In his time, only kings thought in thousands. But considering what he'd paid for the meal at the Two-Eyed Traitor, he guessed it wouldn't last so long here.

He debated only briefly, before starting down the street toward the seedy alley of the pawn shop. He'd promised Amy, and he would get as much money for her and the child as he could. He pulled the crucifix from under Shawn's *polo shirt,* studying it only a moment. Then, before he could change his mind, he rounded the corner, past bits of trash swirling in the breeze as the mist did outside the castle of a morning, and pushed into the pawn shop. Bells jingled on the door. *May things go as well here,* he prayed. The old shopkeeper shuffled out from the back room. "Ye're up and aboot airly," he said.

Ignoring the cry of grief inside, Niall came straight to the point. "I'll sell the crucifix."

The man's face lit up. "How much?"

"Five thousand."

The man shook his head. Niall leaned forward, planting his hands on the counter. The crucifix swung forward, catching the old man's lascivious eye. Niall stared him down. "It dates from 1297, made by the monks of Monadhliath. 'Tis in perfect condition." He'd researched his options, late the previous night. "If you don't want it, a university or museum will be glad of it."

The man planted his hands on the counter, mirroring Niall, and stared back.

Niall turned for the door.

"Two thousand."

Niall turned. "Six thousand."

"Ye canna raise the price," the man huffed. His belly and mustache quivered in outrage.

Niall stepped back to the counter, nose to nose. He slipped the crucifix over his head and laid it softly on the counter: his future and his past. It was the last thing his father had given his mother, before heading to Falkirk to lay down his life for their safety. It was his gift to Allene. He'd dreamed of the day he'd marry her and slip it over her head, and see it passed to his own son. He stared at the man on the cross. *Care for the widows and the orphans.* That described Amy and her child, as Shawn had left them. *Sell all you have and give it to the poor.* It was all he had. He would not sell it cheaply.

"Raising the price is not how it works," the man insisted.

Niall raised his eyes from his memories and hopes, waiting on the counter to be sold. "Sixty-five hundred. A museum will give me more."

"Three thousand."

Laura Vosika

The air crackled with tension. The store owner stared with salacious desire at the piece. Niall watched him steadily. A museum would treasure it as he did. He swallowed hard, his eyes hot and dry.

A muscle twitched under the man's eye. He blinked rapidly, and blurted, "Thirty-five hoondred!"

Niall picked up the crucifix and headed for the door.

The shop owner scurried around the counter, waving his hands. "Four thousand!"

Niall paused. He should take the money. He gripped the crucifix, the figure of Christ biting into his palm. Maybe he could get more. He pushed the door open, flooding the entryway and his eyes with blinding morning sun, still berating himself to take the money. But he couldn't.

"I canna go tha' high!" the man wailed, from the dim interior.

The door slammed shut. Niall left the trashy alley behind and turned down the cobbled street to the museum. It loomed, suddenly, a large stone building on his right. He quickened his step, smoothing the shirt and jeans. A lock of dark hair fell over his forehead. He pushed it back, hoping he looked presentable. He crossed himself, and breathed a prayer as he climbed wide stone stairs.

Seeing someone with authority proved difficult. The museum staff sent him from one office to another. But in the end, Shawn's name got him things mere mortals didn't get. The curator hastened to meet him, pumping his hand and enthusing about the upcoming concert.

"Thank you. Pleased to meet you," Niall said, copying a greeting he'd heard. "I have something your museum would like."

Moments later, the man was fingering the crucifix lovingly. "It's as authentic as anything I've ever seen," he said in amazement, "but we'd have to verify it. And that takes time." He turned the crucifix around, studying it front and back. Niall could see the longing in his eyes. The man looked up. "You understand my problem?"

Niall nodded. "Do you have any other suggestions?"

"A couple weeks, and I can do it." He caressed the cross.

"I'll not be here in a fortnight," Niall replied. "I am leaving in a matter of hours."

"Well, then, here's my suggestion." The man outlined his ideas, while tapping on one of the *computers* that seemed to be everywhere. The printer behind him whirred, and he spun his chair to take two sheets of paper from it. He handed them to Niall. "Try these. Best of luck to you, and I do hope we see your friend."

"Thank you." Niall dropped the crucifix back over his head.

"You wear it?" the man asked in surprise.

"Sure, an' what else would I do with it?" Niall asked. He shook the man's hand, thanking him for his help, and took his leave.

285

Chapter Seventeen

Inverness, Scotland, Present

Niall paced the green room.

The *tuxedo*, buttoned to the throat, the tie and cummerbund Amy had fastened, chiding him that she'd been doing this for him for over two years, and wasn't it time he learned to do it himself, the cuffs and collars and sleeves, all clung, hampering his motion.

Some musicians paced, the men in their tuxedos and women in black; some sat, eyes closed, removed from the world; some conversed; some warmed up. Violins hummed, their owners standing with heads bowed over their instruments. Flutes trilled, the tuba rumbled. Niall could name them all now. He yanked at the cuff one more time. He couldn't play in this ridiculous, confining get-up—he couldn't imagine how all the others did it—and made his decision.

He pushed through the hundred musicians, to where his bag waited, ready for after the concert. He snatched it up and marched to the bathroom.

"Where you going, Shawn?" Jim called.

"I can't play in this," Niall said.

"Show time!" someone hollered. The hummings, trillings, and rumblings stopped, one by one. Instruments lowered, women rose from couches, and musicians rustled toward the door in pairs and groups. Niall threw open the bathroom door. He'd miss these modern bathrooms, with their fresh smell. He tore off the jacket. He had no time to worry over bathrooms! He yanked at the tie. It wouldn't budge. He stuck his head out the door.

Musicians surged past. "Let's move, Shawn!"

Dana touched his arm, clutching her golden horn against her black blouse. Her short hair jutted in wild angles from her head. "Come on! It's your big day!" She hurried on.

"Amy!" Niall bellowed over the heads moving past him.

A couple of people looked at him. "Don't get her mad," someone said. "She'll punch you again." Niall rubbed his jaw, grimacing. A woman had tried to cover the bruise with something called *make-up*, but it had not stopped the ribbing and stares. Several of them shouted for

Amy. He saw her, far ahead, pushing back against the flow of musicians, holding her violin high above her head.

"What do you want?" she asked, when she reached him. "We're going on."

He wanted to laugh! He wanted to kiss her. He'd miss her, and he couldn't wait to see Allene. If he could just get this playing thing over with, then she was taking him—hopefully—home! "Get these things off me." He gestured at the tie and cummerbund. "I can't play with my arms all bound up and a corset and a noose around my neck."

"You can't change now," she said.

"I'll get it done faster if you help me," he replied. "I'm not playing like this."

"Same old Shawn," Amy muttered. But the words sounded affectionate. She yanked at the tie and cummerbund and they fell off.

"The sleeves." He held out his arms. She worked the cuff links loose, and helped him with the buttons running down the shirt. He laughed, freed, and grasped her face, kissing her.

She gasped. Then her face lit up, and she kissed him back. No laird to care! He was crazy to go back, he thought, but he wanted Allene.

He pulled back, studying her face, her cobalt eyes. "Thank you, Amy," he whispered. "You'll never know how much you've done for me! Go now!" She nodded, gave him a tight hug, and hurried to catch up with the orchestra.

A glow from the kiss hung all around him. He grinned, a crazy, unstoppable grin. It felt good, as good as slipping back into the linen shirt and tunic. He took a deep breath, swearing he could smell fresher air and heather and bluebells already. He pulled on his leather boots, elated to have his feet free at last of the confining *dress shoes*. Lastly, he pulled his dirk out of the bag and pushed it into the top of his right boot. It was time to be himself, not the man they expected him to be.

He took a moment to revel in the freedom of his own clothing, stretching his arms and grinning like a boy just before he got caught behind the oven kissing the chieftain's daughter. He saw himself playing Celine's magnificent harp as he'd played at Glenmirril. It was not just the discomfort of the tuxedo he'd shed, but Shawn's persona. He was leaving tonight. He wanted, just once, to be himself with these people.

He took a deep breath, left the bathroom, and crossed the short hall to the stage door. One of the servants grabbed him with a shout of *Mr. Kleiner, your microphone!* and clipped something to his shirt.

With a last glance at the white-washed brick walls, Niall opened the door and stepped through, from the dismal monochrome of backstage into blinding, glaring color. Edging the stage, blue velvet curtains soared as high as his beloved heathered hills; white walls rose behind the musicians, all of them seated and waiting for him. Even their black clothes blazed with vibrant life and rich textures.

A barrage of thunder greeted him. A girl screamed. He jumped. "Shawn! Shawn, I love you!" Something hit his knee. A rose fell at his feet. He stared, dumbstruck, into the stage lights. They blinded him. He blinked hard, shielded his eyes, and looked again. Hundreds, thousands, of faces filled the seats of the hall, seats climbing all the way to the ceiling, every one filled with people clapping and beaming. They stopped clapping, one by one, and stared, waiting expectantly.

"Shawn." Conrad spoke dryly, from the podium. "Thank you for joining us." His words boomed out from giant boxes around the hall. The audience laughed. Niall started at the sound, but bowed low before Conrad. This set the audience off again. Niall's mind raced. Thousands! It could be the whole of the Bruce's army!

"You changed," Conrad said. "You didn't approve of the tuxedo?"

"Aye," Niall agreed. His own voice boomed back from the boxes, startling him again. The audience cheered as if he'd flung forth a pearl of great witticism. Where were the tables and servants? "I thought I'd be more comfortable in this." Again, the applause, as if he'd spoken quite cleverly. He found it annoying, and wondered what they'd do if he flipped his tunic up at them, as he'd done to MacDougall. Their unnerving adulation made him almost grateful MacDougall had merely shot an arrow in his arse, rather than laugh, clap, and cheer. Bampots, the lot o' them!

"Well, it's appropriate," Conrad mused. "Wish I'd thought of it. Where's your trombone?" This part, they'd planned.

"I thought..." Niall's knees shook, as the realization took root that these people intended to do absolutely nothing but stare at him the entire time he played. "I thought..." He couldn't remember his line. At Glenmirril, they'd supped and clapped for servants and tossed bones to dogs and talked to each other and listened to him now and again as they chose. These people, this force the size of an army, they were going to just sit. And stare. At him. His stomach quelled. "I thought I'd play harp tonight." It wasn't the clever line he'd been given. He had a sudden fear this would stop him carrying out his plan, that he'd ruined the concert by giving the wrong line. "I hear it's a traditional Scottish instrument." His voice echoed around the hall.

Silence fell. Then someone laughed. The laughter swept across the auditorium, up into the balcony seats, and applause broke out again. They didn't believe him, of course. And suddenly, the performer in him took over, eager to spring the surprise.

He turned, searching the orchestra. "Where's the harp?" He strolled to examine a cello. The cellist shook his head, smiling. Niall shrugged, and stood on tiptoe to scan the percussion at the back. "Is there a harp there?" he shouted.

"No harps here," Aaron called back. "Try that, at the front." Niall turned and started, deliberately exaggerating his reaction, at the size of the harp. It was easy, remembering his first sight of it. The crowd roared with laughter again. He played it up. He strolled to the harp and tried playing from the wrong side, his arms wrapped around the front pillar, and his back to the audience. "'Tis not yer faither's clairsach," he said, letting his own natural accent creep back into his voice. The musicians and audience laughed. He had no idea why the orchestra found this line so funny, but Conrad had insisted. An old car ad, he'd explained, whatever that meant.

"No, no, no, *no!*" Conrad shouted, parodying himself. People chuckled. "You told me you could do this. Are you sure you don't want to play trombone?"

"Is this wrong?" Niall asked innocently. "No, I want to play the traditional Scottish tunes on a traditional Scottish instrument. They deserve it." The crowd roared their approval, hands pounding together. "Just give me a minute to get the hang of it."

Conrad tapped his foot while Niall played an ill-sounding melody laden with sour notes. He tapped his baton against the podium. He glared at his watch. The crowd chuckled.

"Celine," Conrad finally called over the heads of the orchestra. "We could use some help."

Celine appeared, her white-blonde hair flowing down the back of her black blouse, and made a show of placing Niall in the correct position.

"And what would the red strings be for?" Niall asked. His voice ricocheted around the hall. He plucked another few, drawing more laughter. Whatever else Shawn had been, Niall thought, he'd convinced these people he was inerrantly funny. They'd laugh at anything. He rather appreciated that in the man. But it was time to end the joke. His performer's soul relished the moment. He struck a particularly bad combination of notes and nodded approvingly. "I think I've got it!"

He stood, faced the audience, and became serious. "This concert and this night are momentous occasions for me. I love Scotland."

Applause broke out, whistles, and cheers. No laughter for this solemn profession of love that the audience shared. He waited, his natural command of a crowd shining through. They hung on his next words.

"Tonight, I am not Shawn Kleiner." To his left, Conrad gave a start. Niall drew himself to his full height. His chin lifted as it did when he spoke with the lords or instructed his men before a raid. "I am Lord

Niall Campbell, born in Glenmirril Castle on the shores of beautiful Loch Ness in the year of our Lord, 1290." He saw the loch in his mind, surrounded by hills and groves, the castle rising strong beside it, and missed it so fiercely, that, for a moment, his heart clenched in his chest. "I am wearing what I wore in 1314: trews, shirt, and tunic. My boots," he slid a foot forward for inspection, "are made by our cordwainer Owen MacDonald. I am a soldier, a patriot, and the next laird of the castle. It is a much harder life than you lead. And I have long loved to bring joy to my people with my harp, of an evening."

Whispers rose behind him. He could sense heads turning as the musicians wondered at this unplanned speech. Several in the audience chuckled. Others shushed them. He could see them, beyond the glare of the stage lights, straining forward to listen.

He turned to meet Amy's eyes, and in turn, Aaron's. "This is who I am." Aaron frowned, looking thoughtful. Amy tilted her head, unsure what the joke was.

He turned back to the audience. "And how I come to play harp. Tonight, I take you on a musical tour of Scotland's history and people."

Massive applause broke out. People pounded their hands together. He smiled, bowed low, and seated himself behind the harp, lifting his hands into position with the drooping fingers Celine had helped him perfect over the past days. He glanced around the hall. Maybe having everyone stare at him wasn't so bad. He might miss this, too.

The applause died as people saw he was ready. Conrad lifted his arms. The slightest rustle behind Niall told him instruments were being lifted. Conrad's eyes met his. Niall nodded. Conrad's arms flashed down, and Niall pulled a rich chord from the now-familiar strings of the harp leaning on his shoulder.

He sang of love and outlaws and wars. He recounted histories and stories, as Conrad stood back in surprise. He played with singers, bagpipes and uilleann pipes. He finished the first half with *Blue Bells of Scotland*. The audience clapped its approval of each piece, twice as loud after *Blue Bells,* though it was simpler than Shawn's signature version.

The orchestra took a brief intermission, in which Conrad quizzed him in the green room. "How do you know all this?"

"My father, the reenactor," Niall said, drawing on his knowledge of Shawn. He hoped Conrad wouldn't ask him to elaborate. Forestalling the possibility, he winked suddenly, grinning. But he spoke solemnly, shedding the accent he'd copied. "D' ye no believe I am Lord Niall Campbell, heir to Glenmirril?" He exaggerated the roll of his R's.

Doubt flashed across Conrad's face. Then he laughed, though uneasily. "A story only you would think up, Shawn! It's hard enough to believe what I saw out there." He studied Niall's garb. "Although I must say, you do *look* as if you stepped out of the fourteenth century." Niall laid his hand on the man's shoulder. He did not smile. "I read something on the internet. I believe 'tis a common saying among your people. Truth is stranger than fiction."

"But not that strange." Conrad cleared his throat, coughed, and put a smile on his face. "They love you even more than they did. I didn't think *that* was possible! Let's finish this up." He raised his baton, marshaling his troops, and the musicians flowed back onstage.

Niall took his place behind the harp, flexing his fingers. He'd mostly forgotten the audience, and when he remembered them, enjoyed their rapt attention. He played ballads, dances, and battle tunes. The auburn-haired woman sang of young Ian's betrayal in his swirling, crimson cloak.

After the last piece, after the applause, the bowing of the orchestra behind him, Niall announced he had one more. Conrad, smiling, stood back. The crowd fell silent. The musicians behind him fell silent. He touched the harp, paused with his head bowed alongside the strings, summoning all the emotions the song drew forth; then ran his fingers up a graceful arpeggio. He played a verse, and opened his mouth to sing the piece commemorating Falkirk, in the rich bass that so pleased the laird. He wished Iohn were here to sing with him. He sang in English, played a verse on its own, and sang again in his native highlands Gaelic. When he finished, the crowd roared with approval.

Conrad gestured frantically, and he came to stand at the front of the stage and bow, again and again. Hands clapped. Men whistled. A girl screamed. "Shawn! I love you! Shawn!" Bluebells landed onstage.

A commotion arose at the side of the stage, as a girl with wild blonde hair burst from the wings, skipped around the cellos, kissed Niall on the lips, and clung to him in a tight hug, screeching in his ear and stamping her feet in the most ludicrous fashion. Niall struggled to breathe, pushing at her. No doubt the real Shawn would love it. Two guards rushed the stage and pulled her off, kicking and still screaming "I love you, Shawn! I love you!"

He gathered his dignity and bowed to the audience. The cheers continued, so that Conrad had to push him back onstage several times. *Curtain calls*, he said. Niall flushed with victory. Who would turn their back on such adoration! *He didn't have to go.*

Backstage, with musicians and well-wishers pressing everywhere, Amy wrapped her arms around his neck and kissed him, long and clinging. *It'll be too late, anyway.* Excitement caught him in its grip. He kissed her back, his hands pressed on either side of her face. His pulse raced. *He couldn't change history.* He came up from the kiss with a grin.

Men hooted, and clapped his shoulder. "Won her back, Shawn?" *Allene and Shawn could never have made it.* He separated from Amy, their eyes locked. *He could stay here, care for her and her child. Play the harp.*

"You were incredible," she whispered. "When we get to Stirling...." Her eyes shone. Niall knew what she was promising. Blood raced through every inch of him. His breathing came fast. Life was good here. *He'd be going back to bloodshed and death, too late to save anyone.*

A girl edged through the crowd, waving. Red hair tumbled down her back, like Allene's. He shook his head sharply. What was he thinking! He had to get out of here fast, before the drug of adulation changed his mind. He had to at least try. He strained for a last glimpse of the blue and white decked stage through the open door. He wanted to imprint this euphoric moment on his soul, forever.

"Let's go." He spoke harshly to Amy. He didn't want to go.

"I'll get your things," she said. "Meet me at the stage door." She disappeared. Crowds swarmed him, blocking his way. He gritted his teeth at the handshakes and back slaps, but smiled graciously; said *thank you, a pleasure, wonderful to meet you.*

The redhead sidled up to him. "Is there another party?" she purred. He shook his head, trying to pull his hand away.

She held tight, all smiles, and batting eyelashes, leaning her body against his. "Join me at the Blue Bell anyway."

"I have plans, thank you." Niall tried to dislodge his hand from her velvet grip.

"Me, too." She ran a finger down his chest, where the shirt gaped. He jumped, smiled awkwardly, and yanked his hand away, turning and bumping into Amy. "Are you ready?" he asked. The smiles-for-strangers dropped from his voice.

"But we had so much fun last time," the redhead pouted.

"Ready," Amy said. "I got it." They moved as quickly as they could, edging through the narrow, crowded, hallway, Niall clutching her hand behind him. They reached the stage door, greeting several more people with plastered-on smiles, and pushed out into the cool summer afternoon, onto a narrow, metal walk hemmed on three sides by the theater's stone walls.

Niall glanced behind, sealing in a last memory of the laughing musicians, before the stage door slammed.

Then Amy screamed, yanking his hand.

He spun. A huge man with a bristling red beard stood at the bottom of the short flight of stairs directly across from the stage door, blocking their exit. Another man stood beside him, arms across his burly chest. They were Niall's height. Each outweighed him by a stone. Niall was sure they did not want to shake his hand. His whole body, maybe.

He edged Amy behind him, shielding her.

"Looky, looky," drawled the man with the beard. He planted a foot on the first stair. "What have we here? Remember me? Jimmy from the pub." He leapt up the last two steps and bunched Niall's tunic in his hand. "Someone passed me some funny money, mate. Who might that ha' been?"

Niall's heart skipped a beat. He didn't have time for this! There was a train to catch. The linen shirt scraped his chest. Amy's breath came in fast, shallow bursts. He squeezed her hand, behind his back.

"Let go, and we'll talk," he said to Jimmy.

Below, the friend climbed two steps, gripping the rails. Jimmy pushed his ale-tinged breath in Niall's face. "I let you talk once, an' you cheated me."

"What did you do, Shawn!" Amy hissed. "How could you!"

He gave a sharp motion of his hand, waving her away. To the men, he said, "Meet us at the hotel. I'll give you your money."

"Not this time," growled Jimmy. "This time, I beat the stuffin' outta ye." He dropped Niall's shirt, and swung. The friend jack-knifed up the stairs, and they both descended, swinging. Niall's arms flew, blocking one and then another.

Amy screamed. "Go!" he shouted at her. "Get out!" He turned to see her scramble safely down the stairs, and a fist slammed into his temple. He staggered. Bells pealed in his head. He caught the rough stone wall and shoved himself upright. A flurry of fists came at him, driven more by anger than intelligence. He weaved, dodged, and blocked their mindless flailing.

"It wasn't me," he yelled. "Stop!"

"'Twas you gave me the money!" Jimmy shouted. He aimed a ham-sized fist at Niall's gut. Niall's stomach sucked in, under the impact. He spit blood, coughing.

"Stop," he shouted. "I don't want to hurt you."

"'I don't...want to...hurt you,'" mimicked the friend, gasping for breath. "You're the one...gettin'...gettin' hurt, mate."

"Last chance." Niall sidestepped a vicious swipe from Jimmy. The rough stone wall pressed into his back.

"Last chance, my hairy arse," jeered Jimmy. He stepped back, lowered his bullish head and charged.

Niall almost laughed. Without horns, this was easy. He danced to the side, locked Jimmy around the neck, doubling over as he did, and yanked the dirk from his boot. He came up sharp, flinging Jimmy back against the rail. A wicked gleam shone in his eye. Sunlight flashed off his blade. Amy screamed, a short, sharp sound. She cringed against a brick wall, down in the parking lot, her hands over her mouth. Niall's eyes cut back to Jimmy and his friend.

"Foul!" cried the friend, scrambling backwards. The metal walkway clanged under his frantic motion. "Jimmy, 'e's got a knife!" Jimmy's fists shot up, but he jerked back, heaving for air.

"Foul," rasped Niall. "Two against one, ye cowards." Jimmy's fists wind-milled. He stepped in. The knife flashed. Jimmy yanked away, his face red, breathing hard. "Are ye goin' to listen now?" Niall growled. Jimmy lunged. Niall rammed the hilt hard on his thigh. Jimmy bellowed and collapsed, rattling the metal walk as he fell, clutching his leg. His friend crouched, ready to spring.

Niall spun the knife between nimble fingers, his eyes boring holes in the man. "Next time, it's the blade," he whispered. He eyed Jimmy, sniveling and clutching his leg. "'Tis sorry for yer troubles I am, but I'm not Shawn."

"You take me fer a fool!" Jimmy shouted. His face deepened several shades of red, till it matched his beard.

"I take you for a man who was wronged," Niall said. "Could I make up what Shawn did, I would. But now your friend's goin' to let me pass, aye?"

"I want me money!" Jimmy bellowed. His face flamed with rage.

"You have the wrong man," Niall said. He inched toward the stairs, his left hand raised as a shield, his right hand wielding the weapon. The friend backed up a step, but made no sign of letting him through. "Do you move, or do I hurt you?" Niall murmured.

The friend glanced at Jimmy, then stepped aside. Niall watched warily as he squeezed between him and the iron rail, brushing the other man's garments. He spun quickly, backing down the stairs toward Amy and freedom. She screamed again as the man leapt down two steps.

"Get him!" Jimmy screamed. "Get the limey bastard!"

The friend hesitated, eyeing the knife. Niall eyed the friend. He grabbed Amy's hand, backing away.

"Get him!" Jimmy bellowed.

"'E's got a knife!"

"Get him!"

Jimmy's friend spurted forward. Niall's knife flashed; the man fell back, screaming, blood streaming down his arm.

"I gave ye fair warnin'," Niall said. He turned and, pulling Amy's hand, ran.

* * *

294

Laura Vosika

They raced around the Bishop's palace, past the cathedral's soaring spire, and north, their feet pounding the footpath, away from the theater's steel and glass. The silver ribbon of the River Ness wound along on their right. Inverness Castle rose ahead, a solid dominion of red stone across the river. Amy struggled to keep up, lifting her long black skirt as she ran. "The bridge is ahead," she shouted at his back. She could see it, flat across the top and supported by concrete arches. She hadn't run since her required mile in high school gym. But fear of Jimmy and his friend spurred her on. Maybe Jimmy would find himself a knife.

"The bridge? This one?" he yelled.

She nodded, remembered he couldn't see her, running behind him, and choked out, "Yes! Go!" They skidded past a girl who gaped at his tunic and trews, onto the pedestrian path over the bridge. A boy in a black kilt and jet black Mohawk jumped aside. The river shimmered below. A stitch bit into her side. She didn't want to feel a knife in her back.

"Come on, come *on!*" Shawn shouted. Only, she realized, with a start, she didn't see Shawn. She saw a man named Niall. She shook the thought aside. Her lungs burned. Her legs slowed, a nightmare dream where she couldn't run, where people swirled around them, slowing her even more.

"Hurry!" he barked. He spun to face her, stooped to push the knife into the top of his right boot, and as she reached him, grabbed her hand, pulling. "Did you no say 'tis but a mile?"

"Yeah, a mile," she gasped. "I can't!" But she made it halfway across the bridge before even fear couldn't push her another step.

"We must get the train."

"We won't...." She stopped cold, leaning with one hand on her black-skirted knee, the other gripping her side, in the billows of her concert black blouse. "We won't make...the train...if...." She took a deep breath. "If I die." She stared at the concrete. Cars rushed past on her left. Afternoon crowds surged around them. Water drifted below, *slap, slap, slapping* softly against the pylons. She fought the cold burn racing up her lungs. "He's going..." Where did Shawn come by such stamina! "...to kill us! Where did you learn...to fight...like that?"

The man in front of her—Niall, Shawn, she saw them both—danced in place. "He'll no be roonin' on tha' leg. Are you aw' right?"

Amy lifted her head to gape. "All right?" She tried to slow her breathing. "I can't...guess what is going on...around me." A woman with a stroller pushed past them, staring hard at his tunic and boots, and at Amy all in black.

He tugged her hand. "We must go!"

"You're not even breathing hard," she said. "How are you in good

295

enough shape...?"

"On the train," he said.

"Promise!" She clutched her side with her free hand.

"Hey!" Their heads jolted up. Across the bridge, Jimmy's friend shouted. He began a stilted jog, clutching his arm, and yelling, "Cops! 'E stabbed me!" People turned, searching the crowd for a knife-wielding villain.

"Come on, come on, come *on*," he yelled, dancing in agitation.

She drew in air, and shoved herself upright. "I can do this," she gasped. They jogged across the bridge, through the shops of High Street, darting in and out among the crowd. The man's shouts faded behind them. Ahead, something screeched.

"It's the train," she shouted. "It's leaving!"

"Did ye no say there air many?" he demanded.

"But only one to Stirling." She stopped, staring hard at him. "You're speaking with a Scottish accent again."

Central Scotland, 1314

Hugh stood well over six feet, two hundred and fifty pounds, with a broad smile, hearty laugh, and weapons not to be messed with. "Niall Campbell!" he bellowed when the travelers pushed through the last of the maze of thickets and hidden paths. It was a wonder, thought Shawn, that he could remain hidden, if he routinely put out that kind of volume. The volume, however, paled in comparison to the bear hug with which he nearly crushed the life out of Shawn. He shook Brother David's hand with a modicum of restraint and lifted Allene clear off her feet, swinging her around. "How's tha' brother o' mine?" he demanded.

A fire blazed in the clearing, roasting wild turnips. Hugh dragged them to the center of the camp, dominated by a gleaming white wall of rock shooting twelve feet into the sky. "You remember The Heart of our camp," Hugh said, patting the rock fondly. Shawn stepped back and saw that the rock held roughly the shape of a giant valentine. A man in a ragged tartan scrubbed it with a pinecone. "Found Adam napping in the woods on watch," Hugh told Allene.

Men closed in around them, ragged men, men with scars, men of joy. They greeted the wolf meat with enthusiasm Shawn had last seen in his young groupies. They shouted and laughed, and whisked it onto the fire. Shawn's stomach rumbled, anticipating the meal with gusto he'd once reserved for fine restaurants and women. He soon found himself enjoying the company of these men with deeper satisfaction than he'd ever enjoyed his drunken soirees, while Allene gave Hugh a brief account of their trip. He sat back against a tree in the cool evening, listening to their Scottish lilt. It no longer sounded foreign to him.

"Ha' ye a song, Niall!" called Hugh. "I see ye've brought yer clairsach!"

"He traveled as a minstrel till recently," Allene said.

"Clever, though the traitor will note 'tis missin.'"

Shawn looked to Allene.

"Ye sadly underestimate yer brother," she told Hugh. "He built its match months ago, staying up nights when all slept. 'Tis hanging even now on its peg so none will miss it."

"Much good it did," Shawn said. "They figured it out."

"Aye," said Allene, "but it took that much longer. It may well ha' saved our lives in the village. Not to mention, ye never told me...."

Shawn frowned, giving his head a sharp shake. These men loved Niall. They were large and carried heavy weapons. He didn't care to have their suspicions roused with her story of the sackbut. He meant them no harm, but they had no way of knowing that, should they discover he was an imposter.

Hugh roared with laughter at his brother's forethought. "He always was a clever one. The Sassenach will no find ye wi' him lookin' out for ye, laddie! He'll die himself ere he'll let hairm come to ye. Sing for us!"

The men settled around the fire. While the meat sizzled, Shawn began his stand-by. Brother David harmonized, and the men joined in heartily.

He's gone with streaming banners
Where noble deeds are done,
And it's oh in my heart,
I wish him safely home.

He thought of Amy. Self-pity brushed his heart. He lapsed into silence, while the men sang to his harp. She'd sing no such thing for him. She might throw her own party at the Blue Bell, if she realized he was gone. Peter would go, and Jim, and Aaron. He could hardly blame them. He'd had great fun, at Aaron's expense, played cruel pranks on Jim, and treated Peter with the same disregard as he had Fergal. He would have sunk into moroseness, reflecting on it, but they called for more. Niall, he thought, would be cheerful. He smiled and began a tune he'd played in the last concert. *"Where ha' ye been so fine, lad? Where ha' ye been so brankie-o?"*

Brother David did not join in. Nor did the men. They stared at him, eyebrows furrowed. One man scratched his head and whispered to another.

Shawn sang the second verse somewhat more hesitantly. *"An' ye had been where I ha' been, Ye wouldna been so jolly-o."*
These men had probably been far worse places than he'd been. Realization rushed upon him. He drew to a finish with a full chord. "No one knows this one?" Heads shook all around.

"I ha' heard o' Gilliekrankie," said Hugh, "but naught ha' happened there o' which to sing."

"The battle..." Shawn began. He looked around the blank faces of men who must surely know their battles. Awkward silence followed. Perhaps no battle had yet happened there. He wondered how he would explain this.

"Weel then!" cried Hugh. He clapped his beefy hands with a crack that set several evening birds to flight. "The neeps are cooked!" The men dug in, stabbing chunks of meat with their dirks. "Tell me why my brother has risked sending ye, and with his daughter no less!" The men turned to Shawn.

"Edward is sending troops to Stirling," he said. "Your men are needed."

The men waited expectantly. The sun glowed pink and orange behind the hills. Fire threw flickering shadows across tough faces, and flashed off golden-red beards.

"They're needed very badly?" Shawn added. He looked from one to another, wondering what else they wanted.

"Ye've become a man o' few words, ha' ye not, laddie!" Hugh said with mirth. "When is the Sassenach fool due to arrive at Stirling?"

Shawn looked helplessly at Allene, who bowed her head. Brother David spoke. "Midsummer's day. They say his army will shake the land as it passes, and that he will destroy Scotland once and for all."

"The Laird is on his way," Shawn added, "to train his men with Bruce. He begs you to join."

"So," said Hugh. He gazed around the campfire. So did Shawn. The trees had darkened to black shapes with silver-gray leaves, rising around them in the night. Thin wisps of mist trailed close to the forest floor. Flames lit and shadowed the faces of dozens of men. They sat in tartans and tunics, chewing meat and turnips, swatting now and again at midges. And every one watched Hugh. Hugh himself stared silently into the flames. Beside him, Allene tensed, looking to Shawn with worried eyes.

Shawn lowered his meat, clinging to the end of his dirk. "You can't leave them to fight alone!" The words flew from his mouth. It had not occurred to him that Hugh would not immediately agree. Even less had it occurred to him that he would care.

Hugh lifted his eyes from the fire, to Shawn. For once, he didn't

smile. "The greatest army ever? Thousands upon thousands? We can field but a fraction o' that. 'Twill be slaughter."
Murmurs whispered around the campfire. A breeze rustled the black leaves above.
"If you don't come, it will be," Shawn said fiercely. "The Laird, your brother! Will you leave him to be slaughtered when maybe you could have made the difference?"
"*Can* we make a difference?" asked a little man with a missing tooth. "Would it no be better to wait here that we may yet fight another day?"
Shawn leaned forward, his eyes darkening, biting each word. "There will be no more fighting, if they are not stopped at Stirling!" The men around the fire leaned close to one another, speaking in low agitation. Hugh conferred with the men on either side of him.
Shawn's heart hammered, waiting.
Hugh stood, commanding silence.
Shawn drew in a breath.
"We'll aw' most likely die, an we meet Edward at Stirling," Hugh said.
"An what are we to protect our skins for?" shouted a man with coarse black hair springing up in wild curls from his head. "To continue hiding? Better to die for the chance of freedom, than live forever this way." He stood, fixing an iron gaze on each man around the circle, one by one. "Is it no for just such a moment we've waited?"
Some men muttered. Some nodded. Hugh held up a hand, and silence fell. "It seems as ever my big brother needs me to save his skin! Imagine fighting an army so large!" He gave a hearty laugh. "Perchance 'tis time to leave our mountain retreat and remind the Sassenach whose country 'tis." Shawn held his breath. Hugh's smile fell, his eyes turned black. "Or perhaps it is not yet time. "MacGregor, what say ye?"
The little man with the missing tooth stood, his face solemn. His few men rose beside him. "To Stirling, my lord."
"Clan Grant?" A cry went up from the far side of the fire. Three lanky young men leapt to their feet, shouting, "To Stirling!"
"Chisholm? MacLeod." Two more men stood with their groups, and with each name on the roll call of the doomed, Hugh's voice grew stronger. "Fraser. Mackenzie!"
Again and again, cheers went up, signaling the assent, each of dozens more men, to their own slaughter—to their chance at freedom, self-sacrifice for their loved ones.
Shawn's skin tingled. His heart raced. Hugh's voice beat a quickening tattoo: "Sutherland! Gunn! Munro!"
Now the whole camp stood, bellowing to meet the Sassenach.

The men demanded a song from Shawn, bawling out the lyrics of war and victory. They downed ale and raised cheers to driving the Sassenach into the sea.

Finally, sated with meat and music, with the light dying in the west, they drifted to their corners for a night's sleep. Hugh and the clan leaders gathered around the embers of the fire and murmured with the chirping insects. Their beards close together, they chose runners and messengers and laid plans to gather another thousand to war.

Inverness, Scotland, Present

They burst through the sliding glass doors of the train station into a white, high-ceilinged chamber with bright banners and streaks of color everywhere. Amy stopped for only a minute, a minute in which people turned to stare at them both. "Dress up day?" someone said.

At the far end, the station opened to the outside. Long, slithering behemoths faced them, each staring with a large, single eye. "This way," Amy said. They jogged toward the things, Niall with impatience and energy to burn, Amy lagging with exhaustion. Niall looked around in confusion. Half a dozen of the chutes ran into the station. "Help me out here," she said, but Niall had no idea how. He stared at the huge metal contraptions littering the area, some in hues of forest green and others sporting bold splashes of bright, unnatural colors. These must be the *trains* of which Amy had spoken. "This way," she said. A rumble filled the air. She grabbed his hand. "It's leaving!" Niall jogged after her, lost and helpless. "What if he followed us?" she panted.

A man waved frantically from the door of one of the metal beasts. The thing snorted. "Wait!" Amy yelled.

"Hurry!" the man called back. He braced one hand against the door, holding the other out to them.

Niall got there first and jumped in. The man shoved him through, and reached for Amy. The train shuddered and trembled.

"Hey, you!"

Amy looked back, one foot on the platform, one on the train, and went pale. Niall's heart leaped. Jimmy's friend shouted from the station doors. Niall yanked her hand. She stumbled into the train, catching herself against a wall. The doors slid shut. Niall looked out the windows. The platform was moving, at a nauseating pace, away from the train.

* * *

Despite his stomach lurching at this bizarre contraption's motion, and his mind screaming to flee, Niall led Amy to the most isolated seats.

She dropped into one near the window, clenched her hands in her lap, and closed her eyes. Her face was pale, bone white against her jet black hair and black clothing. He pushed aside his own nausea, thinking of the child she carried. She didn't need this strain. He wished he hadn't brought this on her. He could have asked Aaron. But he'd had his reasons.

He took her hand. It trembled in his.

Gradually, she relaxed, and her hand became still. A little color—not much, but a little—crept back to her cheeks. She opened her eyes and turned to him. "Tell me what's going on."

He searched for words. Maybe he'd start with the good news. He pulled the crucifix from his tunic, over his head.

She stared, uncomprehending. He wanted to yank it back. "Take it," he said. He pressed it into her hand, closing her fingers over it. Then he dug in the sporran, for the roll of bills he'd collected from the wall. "It took some time." He smiled ruefully at his own ineptitude in this era.

She sucked in her breath, thumbing through it. "It must be a thousand dollars!"

"Much more. After a bit, it wouldna let me take more. Here's the card. The code is zero-eight one three, the day his father died." Trees flashed past the window, giving him vertigo. He tried to focus on her.

Amy bit her lip. "You were walking around with thousands of dollars in cash?"

"How else was I to give it to ye?"

"Someone might have stolen it!" Amy's eyes widened as she fanned the money. "Is *this* what that was about, behind the theater?"

Niall shook his head. "I doona think so. Someone gave him bad money."

"You were gambling. Did you have anything to do with it?"

Niall sighed. His stomach heaved at the rattling and swaying of the *train*. "I did not."

"Well," she said, "Why? Why are you giving me all this?"

"To care for yourself and the child." He nodded at the crucifix. "I couldna sell it so fast, not for what it's worth. Keep it, an' you need more, sell it." His heart cried out, seeing his last remnant of his father slip away. He wanted to see it around Allene's neck. But Amy needed it. And Amy would not see what it cost him to let it go. She would refuse, if she understood. "'Tis from 1297." He kept his voice steady, tearing his eyes from his memories. He reached into his pouch for a folded sheet of paper. "I've written the history here, and places that will give ye a good price."

Amy looked from the paper, to the crucifix, to Niall. "I don't understand. You said you got it at the pawn shop." She started to say more, but her mouth moved wordlessly. She lifted her hand, trying to speak. Her eyes became damp, and she said, "This means you're leaving me when we get there." He heard resignation in her voice. "Is it guilt money?"

His heart sank at her grief. "'Tis doing the right thing. I doona ken if I'll be back." The train *chick-chick-chicked* under him. He felt as green as those fish Lord Darnley used to throw on the banks of the loch. Thoughts of Darnley brought on another ill feeling. He wondered at the ease with which Amy accepted this jolting, rumbling machine in which they were trapped. "Amy." He took her hand again. "You must see what you already knew, deep down."

"You're not Shawn." Her voice came out thin and gray. Her eyes met his steadily. But something in them looked as ill as he felt. "You understand why I haven't believed it, don't you?"

"Aye. But you knew Shawn better than anyone."

She was silent a moment, studying him, before saying, "The handwriting. The scars on your back. I tried to believe they were from trees, but they're old, aren't they?"

He nodded, with a slight smile. "The laird caught me kissing his daughter."

"They still do that in the Highlands?"

Niall shrugged. "Some would do worse."

"The way you speak," she added. "And you're kind. Always." The train rumbled under them. She stared out the window into the evening. "I wanted to believe it," she said. "That the Shawn I'd believed in really existed." He watched her reflection in the glass, superimposed on the trees racing by, until she turned back. "And it's too strange that someone who looks just like him showed up exactly where I left him."

"I canna explain that." Niall spread his hands in apology.

They sat in silence for several minutes before she asked, "So who are you? Where is he? Did you do something to him? I can't imagine it, unless he attacked you. I saw in the alley you can take care of yourself."

Niall held up a palm, stopping her. "You misunderstand. I never met Shawn. I doona ken where he is. But I think he took my place."

"Took your...?" She searched for words. "What does that mean, your place?"

"Glenmirril."

She shook her head, eyes shut tight. "No!" Her knuckles turned white around the crucifix in her hand. She opened her eyes, sitting upright. "No. Nobody lives in that castle. I searched it that day. I called him, over and over. There was only you!"

He touched her shoulder. "You doona understand yet, d' ye?" he said softly. "He *was* in the castle. At least I believe he was, in the tower."

"I looked there. I went all the way up."

"But you couldna see him, for he was in 1314."

She became eerily still. She closed her eyes and clutched the crucifix to her chest. "Please don't start this again," she whispered.

"D' ye no think 'twas a shock to me?" he asked. "It still is, every moment, to think I am seven hundred years from my own time." He tried to keep his eyes off the crucifix. "D' ye ken what was happening in June of 1314?"

For another minute, she didn't move. He wondered if she'd heard him. She opened her eyes. "The Battle of the Pools," she guessed, her voice flat and frightened. "It would explain why you didn't understand the internet. Why you ordered so much food. You weren't just being arrogant like Shawn." The crucifix shook in her hand. "You know this is impossible, don't you?"

He nodded. "Aye. And yet, here I am. I went to sleep in 1314 and woke to find you and Rob on the shores of my loch. I was meant to go for a man named Hugh." He told her of the journey he was supposed to make, of the Laird's knowledge of a traitor in the castle, of England's aggression.

"That's why you wanted to know so much about the Battle of the Pools. And that means..." She bit her lip and suddenly pressed her fingers against her mouth. Voices chattered around them. She lowered her hand. "If Shawn woke up in your time and they thought he was you—*he's out there somewhere!*"

Heads turned at her sharp words. Niall touched her arm. He didn't know what to say. His heart bled at sight of her fear for him. He didn't mention Allene would guide him. It would be small consolation to her. To him, it was worse than none.

"And someone wants to kill him."

Several people sitting nearby turned once again. Niall thought it best not to mention wild boar and wolves in the forest. "The Laird will have provided well." He needed to convince himself as much as her. The train chugged beneath them. Its mournful whistle stretched out behind.

Amy buried her face in her hands, shaking her head. "This can't be real. If it weren't for the scars, the accent—if you didn't know so much about the Pools...."

His voice rose with excitement. "I know what went wrong."

"They were outnumbered," Amy said. "Badly outnumbered. Can Hugh change that? Does he have that many men?"

"Nay." Niall leaned forward. "But it doesna matter. We were outnumbered five to one at Stirling Bridge and won. Routed them! I know what really went wrong."

"It doesn't matter!" Amy's voice rose. She glanced quickly

around the train, and lowered her voice to a hiss. "You're seven hundred years too late. I mean, you would be, if this were even true."

"'Tis true," Niall assured her. "If I can get to him, if I can reach Shawn and change places again, I can save the battle for the Scots!"

Amy bit her lip, staring at the Medieval-styled Jesus on the cross, and forcibly slowing her agitation. "So what happened?" she finally asked. "In stories, it's always an evil witch or sorcerer...."

Niall laughed. "There are no witches. My betrothed..."

"You're engaged?" Amy's head snapped up.

Niall's eyes twinkled. "Are ye jealous?"

She narrowed her eyes at him. "You *are* just like Shawn!" She leaned back, closing her eyes. "I kissed a man who's engaged. You kissed me. I'm no better than Caroline."

He put his hand on her arm. "Ye dinna ken. I got carried away. You're bonnie. And Conrad said I'd be fired."

"Fired for not kissing me?" She opened her eyes, confused.

"For being an imposter. I've no wish to burn before I can reach Hugh."

"Burn?" She stared. Then her eyes widened. "You thought he was going to burn you, what, at the stake?"

Niall fell silent, hoping the heat on his face didn't show.

She laughed. "All it means is losing your job." Her smile fled. "If I'd known you were engaged, I wouldn't have...." Warmth climbed up her face. "I'm sorry. Forget it. What happened in the tower?"

"Allene met me there."

Amy nodded, understanding beginning to dawn. "She brought you bluebells, didn't she? You had a fight."

Niall looked surprised. "How d' ye ken?"

"When Shawn and I went up in the tower that night..." She paused. "This can't be real."

"What happened?" Niall asked.

"I smelled bluebells at the top of the tower!" Excitement laced her voice. "I *knew* the smell was unusually strong! And I felt tension! I told Shawn, and he laughed at me."

"Yes," Niall said. "She brought me bluebells. And we fought."

"We brought bluebells, too," Amy said. "We had a fight and I left him there." She sank back, suddenly, against the train seat. She dropped the crucifix in her lap and pressed the heels of her palms tightly over her eyes. "This is impossible. You know that, don't you?"

"Am I Shawn?" he asked quietly.

She dropped her hands and studied him. "No. But you can't be from 1314." She shook her head, and whispered, "That just can't happen."

"Do people get shot with arrows today?"

She shook her head. "Not generally, no. Maybe you're crazy. Maybe you just think..."

"Someone shot me with an arrow," he said. "Someone whipped me and left scars on my back. Ye've seen it with your oon eyes." She said nothing. He touched the back of her hand. "Have I acted any time since you met me like a madman?"

"No," she admitted. "Well, I mean, apart from saying you're from 1314."

"I am who I said I am at the concert. Niall Campbell, born in 1290, future Laird of Glenmirril. I doona ken what will happen when I go into that forest or who will come out to you."

"What will you do there?" Fear shook her voice.

"Find Hugh's camp and hope being in the same place will switch us back."

"So Shawn could be up there, and find himself suddenly back in his own time?"

"I doona ken," Niall confessed. "I doona ken if he made it to Hugh's camp."

"How could he have?"

"Allene would have taken advantage and gone with him. I know her well." He smiled sadly. "If naught happens there, I'll follow Hugh to the Pools."

"You think Shawn will be at the battle?"

"I hope," Niall confessed. "If Allene took the chance to guide him, he will be expected to go to battle with Hugh. I have prayed and hoped and prayed some more, but 'tis only guesses."

She nodded, once more at a loss for words. He slipped his hand around hers. "There's a reason I tell you this, Amy." The train gave a whistle and the beast slowed beneath him. His stomach shifted uneasily. He looked out the window, reached for his bag.

"Not yet," Amy said. "We have lots of stops before we get off. It's a three hour ride."

They waited silently while people collected bags and left the train. Others filed in. Niall held his breath, hoping no one would sit near them. Amy tucked the money, papers and crucifix into her backpack. A young couple seated themselves across from Niall and Amy. The man eyed Niall's medieval garb up and down. The girl glanced at Amy's concert black with a quick smile.

Niall sighed in frustration. The train picked up speed.

* * *

Amy leaned back, eyes closed, against the seat. She looked pale. Niall pulled out his papers and let her rest. He spent the next hour studying maps of everything between Stirling and the forests west of it. The man leaned forward. "Going hiking?" he asked.

"Aye," agreed Niall. "Do ye knoo the forest?"

"Been there lots of times." The man reached for the map, and they held it between them, companionably, while the man told all he knew of the area.

"The wolves," Niall said. "Are they bad this year?"

The man laughed. He nudged the girl. "Hear that? Wolves, he says!" He turned back to Niall. "There haven't been wolves in Scotland for hundreds of years! Where you been?" His eyes skimmed Niall's outfit again. "Fifteen hundreds?" He laughed, such a good-natured laugh Niall couldn't take offense.

"Thirteen hundreds," he corrected with a smile.

* * *

The young couple climbed off at the next stop, with fond farewells and last words of advice for their new best friend. Amy slept on. Niall shuffled papers, made marks, and studied the *satellite* pictures she'd printed for him.

After another stop, and another shuffling of passengers, Amy stirred. "Thanks for letting me sleep," she said, rubbing her eyes. She looked at the maps spread out in front of him. Her eyes met his. "You're serious, aren't you?"

"Are ye startin' to believe me?" Niall asked.

"You can understand it's hard to believe."

"Aye."

They sat in silence, while the train gathered speed again. "Tell me about medieval Scotland," Amy said. "If this is true, you'd know it well."

Niall wrapped his arm around her, closed his eyes, and told her: training and education with his tutors, the Laird and how it amused Iohn to hear Niall imitate him, fishing with Lord Darnley and William, Allene with her red hair and temper. He told of dinners in the great hall, the mute servant boy, the Black Friars of Inverness' visit to the castle, the Monks of Monadhliath across the loch, his mother and her friends. He described the tapestries on the walls, raids to retrieve their cattle, the Morrison twins.

"The one who's a saint now?" Amy asked.

"Aye, the little wretch dropped a cold, dead fish down the back o' my shirt, the first time I saw her." He chuckled, remembering.

Amy laughed. He spoke of the bridge he'd known crossing the

River Ness and watching, with Iohn and William, as Bruce's men tore down King David's castle; sneaking out through the Laird's secret dungeon tunnel with Allene, into the heathered hills outside.

He told of Hugh's camp hidden in the forest, with its giant white rock, in whose gleaming white surface Hugh took such pride. Niall laughed. "He threw a man in stocks once for making a small scratch at the base."

"It's an unlikely story, to say the least," Amy finally said. "But it all fits. You said you told me for a reason."

Niall paused. His insides turned trembly and fluid, as they did before battle. He started off on safe ground. "Amy, I doona ken who will come down from the mountain to you. If he comes down, I've provided for you and the child to the best of *my* ability. Take care of what I have given you, and doona let him get his hands on it."

She twisted her ring. "You waited two hours to tell me that?"

Niall drew in breath and let it out slowly. He chose his words carefully. "If I come back down, 'tis God's will for me to stay. I doona ken what to do, then. Stay here and live Shawn's life?"

"I don't know," Amy said, her voice thin. "I guess. I mean, you have to make a living." She laughed more from nerves than humor. "You won't find many job offers for 'highland laird.' Especially in the States."

He smiled. "I am betrothed in 1314. If I'm caught here, I canna honor that."

"It would be hard," she agreed.

He paused, afraid of the words. Then he took her hand and spit them out, before he could reconsider. "I would ask for your hand in marriage, Amy, if I come back."

Her eyes widened. Her mouth opened as if to speak, but moved impotently, like the fish Darnley threw on the shore. A desperate longing to see Lord Darnley and Iohn swept over him. He spoke quickly, pushing the pain of Darnley's betrayal away. "I would provide for you," he said, "and give the child a name. I would treat you with love and kindness always."

Amy pulled her hand away. She lifted it to her mouth, put it in her lap, twisted her ring.

"Have I upset you?" Niall asked. "I'm not Shawn, but 'tis a good thing, aye? We get along well, you and I."

"I hardly know you," Amy said softly, lowering her eyes.

"Is that necessary?" Niall asked in surprise. "Have I not shown myself to be honorable?"

"You're serious." Amy met his eyes and laughed out loud. "I guess if this is true, that would be a surprise. Yes, it's considered necessary."

"Do you not wish to give the child a name?"

She blushed, lowering her eyes again. "That's *not* considered quite so necessary in our time," she said softly.

All the logic behind the decision swirled and dissipated like Highland mist in the morning sun. He'd expected she would be grateful. He'd expected she would readily agree. "I thought I was doing the right thing," he said. "Have I hurt ye?"

"No." Amy dared meet his eyes. "If you were someone else, I might think you asked out of pity."

"Who would pity you? You're strong and loving and giving." The words surprised Niall as much as Amy.

"That's one of the kindest things I've heard in a long time," she whispered. "It's just—I don't want to get married because it's the right thing. I want to get married because someone loves me, and I love him. Don't you love Allene?"

"Aye," Niall agreed. They sat in silence. A student, several seats away, laughed loudly, and began telling a bawdy story. The train's whistle blew, a long, mournful sound stretching back on the wind.

"I guess," Amy said, "it's like being widowed? You'll always love her, but she's beyond your reach, if you're stuck in this time."

"Aye," Niall said again.

"So you and I could really love each other."

"You're a good woman, Amy. In my time, people often wed without knowing one other at all. But we learn from the time we are bairns that love is how you treat another. And the feeling of fondness grows from that. I already feel great fondness for you."

Amy searched his eyes. "I feel—fondness—a lot of it—for you, too." A blush crept up her cheeks. "But I don't know what's real and what's mixed up with thinking you were Shawn." She turned to stare out the window, falling silent. Niall watched her reflection, wondering if he'd spoken poorly. A girl shushed the bawdy story, giggling. Several seats away, a child cried briefly and stopped.

"I want to do the right thing," he said again, finally. "I want to care for you and the child. I'd not want people thinking I abandoned you if I come back instead of Shawn." Amy wiped her nose, sniffing. "I thought about asking for your hand," Niall added, "without telling you. But if Shawn comes back, 'twould appear a cruel jest. I dinna wish to do that to you. I'm doing the best I can. Do you see I *must* try to reach Hugh?"

"Yes."

"But I want to be here for you."

"Yes."

"Then...?"

She turned from the window and took his hand. His heart pounded a heavy tattoo, waiting. "It would be insane to agree to this," she said. His heart sank. He realized with shock how much he'd come to plan on this future, if the switch didn't happen. "If you come back, we'll spend a year getting to know each other, and then decide."

Niall stared, stunned. It hadn't gone according to plan. His betrothal to Allene had been arranged by MacDonald and his mother. He'd known from the start that Allene wanted him as her husband. He'd never before risked himself like this with a woman.

But she hadn't said no.

She'd consider him! Elation tingled in his veins. A broad grin stretched across his face.

"You look just like Shawn when you do that," she said.

He leaned back on the seat, his arm around her and his face resting on top of her head.

He drifted to sleep. Two worlds and two futures twined in his dreams: Allene and war and living in MacDonald's chambers at Glenmirril one day; raising children with Amy, playing the harp for adoring fans, having pictures of his children and loved ones to carry everywhere with him, and never feeling death inching its claws around every corner.

Chapter Eighteen

Central Scotland, Scotland, Present

Niall and Amy alighted from the train. Crowds swarmed around them: Japanese tourists with cameras, Americans in slacks and tennis shoes, college students eager to take in the sights before hitting the pubs. A mother grabbed for a darting child, staring hard at Niall's tunic and boots. They surged with the crowd up wide concrete stairs and out of the station. Amy watched Niall, curious about his reaction to a Stirling much different than he would have known, if his story was true. He studied the scene briefly, his eyes sharp, then looked steadfastly ahead, neither left nor right. "Take me to the forest," he said. "I'll find my way from there."

Amy saw no point in reminding him yet again that Hugh was seven hundred years gone. "Night's coming," she pointed out, instead.

"The days are long. I can get a good start. I know these forests well."

She leaned in, conscious of the crowds around them, already staring both at his outfit and her concert black, and whispered, "You knew the forests *of seven hundred years ago* well." She glanced around at the business men hustling beside them, fearful of being overheard. "If what you say is true."

He squeezed her hand. "Take me to the forest."

Amy sighed. "The bus station is next door." They followed the sidewalk, under white beams of modern construction. Ancient church spires shot into the Stirling sky farther up the city hill.

"You really believe this?" she asked. She couldn't think of him as Shawn. But neither could she face the question of how he came to be in Shawn's place. His story, strange as it was, accounted for everything. He'd spoken, on the train, with such intimate knowledge of a time unknown to all but the most authoritative experts. He couldn't have faked the scars on his back or an arrow wound. Since the moment he'd stepped onstage for the concert, he had shifted back to a heavy Scots accent—yet unlike the modern ones all around her.

"Believe I'm from 1314?" He smiled. "O' coorse."

At the station, Amy found the bus headed west. She watched Niall. He stared at the bus much as she had stared at haggis, the orchestra's first night in Scotland. A muscle twitched in his jaw. He pushed his hand through his hair, exactly as Shawn would. He heaved a sigh, and climbed on.

They rode the bus for a time in silence, watching first the city, and then fields, race by. "It was all forest," he said, gazing at it. She touched his hand. He closed his fingers around hers. Thoughts chased one another through her mind—where Shawn was, who would come back to her.

...who she wanted to come back.

"Tell me again what he's doing there," she said.

Niall told her again, his best guess. Her fingers lay warm in his hand. Guilt flowed around her heart. Shawn was in danger, possibly dead, and she was holding another man's hand. She'd even given him a commitment of sorts. She closed her eyes, remembering times she and Shawn had been alone, the way he'd touched her hair as if caressing a rose, or gazed at her as if seeing an angel. That Shawn, she grieved and feared for and wanted back. But Niall was all the good things she'd believed were in Shawn. She felt safe with him. Even his insane story gave her no turmoil. It made more sense than Shawn's stories ever had. The pieces all fit.

Niall stared out the bus window, now and again checking his maps, and finally, several miles past a small town, said, "Here."

Amy rang the bell, and the bus pulled over. Looking green and holding his stomach, Niall gave a grimacing attempt at a smile to the bus driver, bowed briefly, and thanked him. They descended the steps, to the side of the road, near a picnic table. Beyond the small clearing, trees ascended a gentle slope.

"'Tis very different," Niall said. He studied the sun, still bright in the sky even in the summer evening, and the lay of the land; looked skeptically at the hiking trail for weekend woodsmen, and started up the path. "You'll come along?" he called over his shoulder.

A moment of panic hit Amy. She trotted after him, up the path. What if it really was Shawn, hit on the head and believing this craziness so well he'd sucked her in? What if she was letting a sick man wander into the wilderness alone, wearing a tunic and tights? "Conrad would never forgive me if I left you." Had she really just committed a year of her life to this man?

"I may be gone for some days."

"Days? You can't do that." The panic increased, a swift beating of her heart. He wasn't Shawn. She couldn't wander into the hills with a man she didn't even know. He could have made the whole story up. He could be anyone.

"Och, an' why not?"

"Well, you didn't bring camping equipment. You didn't bring food." She wished her words wouldn't tumble out so fast over each other, betraying her fear.

Niall stared with eyes open wide. "Does the forest no have berries and deer still?"

"You can't kill deer here."

"I'll no eat them alive!" Niall shook his head. "I must find Hugh. You'll be safe?"

"The bus will be back," she said. A battle raged inside her: follow him or stay. Whoever he was, she wanted to be with him.

He closed the distance between them, taking her hand. "Take care o' yerself an' the child," he said. "If I see you again, well...I'll not be sorry." His smile squeezed her heart. A surge of envy for the lucky Allene tore through her, racing alongside fear for Shawn. There was an awkward silence. "If not, thank you for helping me." He paused, then said, "'Tis glad I am we met." He kissed her fingertips, lingering a moment, and squeezing her hand. Then he turned abruptly and set off at a smart tempo, up into the forest.

Panic seized Amy. She took a quick step after him and stopped. He disappeared around a curve in the trail. She ran another four steps and stopped again. The forest loomed, trees towering over the path and shutting out the sun. In the moment's hesitation, fear overtook her. There might be wolves. She put her hand on her stomach, and took another step—this one, backwards, back toward the road, still looking up the path where Niall had disappeared. In space or time?

She shook her head sharply. People couldn't disappear in time.

She grabbed her cell phone and pounded Conrad's number.

Central Scotland, 1314

Shawn woke to the crackling of the fire. The smell of roasting meat made his stomach rumble. A diet of berries had left him looking forward to something more substantial. And maybe venison another night, he thought with satisfaction. Around him, men shouted and called, and moved about with purpose. He stared in fascination: could it really be possible these men had died hundreds of years before his birth? That if he knew the right history books, he could tell them each their own future? The sun blazed into the clearing, even at this early hour. Wooden staves smashed against each other as men honed their battle skills.

Allene poked him with her toe. "The messengers left hours ago, ere the sun rose, to raise their clans." Shawn rolled over, blinking in the bright morning. Her hair tumbled around her face, without her maid to plait it. "You're to be up and training with the men, Hugh says."

Shawn squeezed his eyes shut tightly, pressing the heels of his palms into them. The bandage on his hand scraped his skin. He wanted to ask, *Training for what?* But he'd be asking only to give himself a brief respite in his fantasy world, a world where he was not expected to fight a losing battle with medieval weapons that would gouge, tear, and maim. Maybe he'd wake up and find it was a horrible dream from too much beer; that Amy was sitting beside him, waiting for him to come around. Maybe he'd get lucky and remember something from the re-enactment camps with his father. Maybe he'd find a way to escape. He opened his eyes.

Allene stared down, blue eyes determined, red hair flying around her freckled face. "So be up wi' ye!"

Allene would follow these men to battle—she couldn't stay here—and be left with the camp followers behind Bruce's army. If the English won, there would be rape and murder, there on Coxet Hill. The thought of running crept, tail between its legs, from his mind. Allene's small dagger, handy as it was against a lout like himself, would not stop armed warriors. He could be one more man between her and the English.

He pushed an easy grin onto his face, not wanting her to follow his thoughts. "A shame you don't have a bucket of cold water."

She aimed a sharp-toed foot at him; he rolled and sprang to his feet, laughing at her. She scooped up a pine cone. It hit him in the forehead before he could move.

"Niall!" barked Hugh, as Shawn rubbed his head. "Ye've lain abed long enough to recover from yer romp wi' the wee hound!" The men laughed, wild and free in their hiding place. "Up and about, or ye'll be scrubbin' the Heart like anyone else!" He grabbed a broadsword from the cache leaning against a tree. His biceps, the size of a small oak, flexed as he launched the weapon across the clearing. It arced through the stream of smoke rising above the blazing fire. Morning sun flashed off the blade in a long bar of light. A dozen men turned with eager expectation.

Shawn's eyes widened at the weapon hurtling toward him. He threw himself to one side, hands over his head. The sword smashed into the ground where he'd stood. It kicked up a divot of dirt as it struck the earth, and toppled to the ground.

Shawn raised his eyes—shocked, startled eyes—from the fallen weapon to a circle of mouths open in disbelief. "You dinna spin and catch it?" Hugh demanded.

He and Hugh stared at each other across the sparking, spitting flames.

Then Shawn found his voice. Blood flushed his face. "Are you crazy!" he roared. "What the hell was that for? Are you effing insane?" "What the hell was divin' fer cover like a wee lass for?" Hugh roared back. The blast of air swayed the flames toward Shawn; the bushes behind him trembled. "Ye were meant to catch it as ye've always done!"

Shawn stared at him in disbelief. Niall played catch with ten pound, four foot blades? They expected *him* to play catch with one? He sagged against the tree behind him, and touched his temple. "The head...the injury," he said weakly. "I forgot." He forced a laugh. "Can you believe it?"

"Ah, the blow to the head," Hugh said with less power. "So you won't be helpin' train the men?"

"I'm supposed to teach them?" Shawn closed his eyes and slipped into that fantasy world, after all.

Central Scotland

Niall forged up the forest path as the sun sank in the west. How neat and civilized, how typical of the time, he thought, of the tidy path directing his feet where someone else had decided he'd like to go. Even a trek in the wilderness featured ease and comfort.

He looked at the bluebells, sprinkled under the trees; his gaze climbed higher up the towering firs. Pine scent hung heavily in the air. The branches of broad-leafed trees, bursting with the vibrant, lively greens of June, met overhead, keeping his world cool and shady. He wondered if any of these trees had existed in his time. He wondered if he'd set himself a fool's errand. It might prove impossible to navigate miles of forest without his landmarks—the fallen oak, the tree with the knobby trunk.

He reached for the crucifix; touching his bare throat, he felt, for a moment, abandoned. God was not in a wooden cross, he admonished himself, but all around, setting angels by his side. He bowed his head, praying for himself, for Allene.

For Shawn.

Opening his eyes, he looked around. The trees would be different, but hills, lochs and rivers remained. Giant boulders that had guided him with their distinctive shapes might be here yet.

As his leather boots moved silently forward, his mind turned back to Amy, scared at the bottom of the hill. He shouldn't have left her.

He stopped. But he couldn't turn from the search for Hugh and his own time. Still, he hesitated. She'd assured him the bus was coming right back. All the same, he'd left a woman alone on the edge of a forest.

But what if she crossed back into his own time with him? He couldn't do that to her, either. She'd assured him she'd be safe. He crossed himself, sending up another prayer for her, and turned regretfully back to the tree-lined path.

He listened, standing still.

Away from the cars, the forest sounded as it had in his time. A squirrel skittered up a tree. A moment of silence, and a bird trilled. Niall closed his eyes, focusing on the sounds. And now he heard it: a burbling rush of water, far off to the west.

He opened his eyes to the pleasant, dappled lane. A steep hill rose on his left, with a racing stream beyond. He smiled. He'd found it. He left the mapped and manicured twenty-first century wilderness and plunged through underbrush, up the hill. Leaves tore at his tunic. He pushed faster, willing away the irritation of many small stings of jabbing branches.

He found the stream and followed it west through the dusk. A few handfuls of berries, mountain stream water, and a squirrel—shot with a well-aimed stone and roasted over an open fire—served as dinner. As the sun sank, he prayed, bowing his head and thanking God for the heavy wool plaid Amy had bought him—the night was chill—and the maps she'd given him. He wrapped himself in the plaid and lay down, listening to the night sounds, the buzzing of midges and whisper of the stream, the rustle of leaves in the breeze high overhead.

Then another sound caught his ear: a heavy rasping breath. He rose slowly, the small fire guarding his back. The forest became still. He peered through the leaves. The yellow eyes of a wolf stared back.

Central Scotland, 1314

Under the trees edging the mountain loch, Allene dipped her cloth repeatedly in the cold water, damping blood off Shawn's thigh.

"It needs stitches." Shawn bit his lip at the sharp pain, and hated himself for even suggesting it. They wouldn't have anesthetic. He was offering himself up for more pain in lieu of the feel of Caroline's arms that should have been his.

He closed his eyes, sucking in his breath as her cloth stung again. He had no business thinking of Caroline. What if he'd appreciated Amy? What if he hadn't pulled that stupid stunt, gambling away his trombone? Heat spread up his face. To these men, locked in daily struggle with death, he would look a fool, gamboling down the street, drunk, swinging his bucket of money with Caroline.

And what if he'd taken Amy home when she wanted to go? Maybe he could even have listened, when she'd wanted to talk about...

the abortion. It hurt even to think the word. His face grew hotter, thinking of that day, and he wondered why he only now remembered her reluctance. If he'd listened, maybe he wouldn't be here. He'd be home, not with Caroline, but with Amy: Amy who had loved him through all his faults and mean tricks. Maybe even with Amy and a son of his own.

"Stitches?"

But he *was* here. He had a job to do. He swallowed, dreading it. "It won't heal like this. You need to sew it together." Shawn studied the raw, gaping wound. Each time he drilled with the men, what little healing it had accomplished overnight tore open.

"Hugh will see that you canna fight, and station you on Coxet Hill. You'll be *safe*, Niall."

Shawn knew what the English would do to the people of Coxet Hill, if they broke through the Scots. "I'll fight," he said.

They stared at each other for a long time, Allene's jaw set. Certainty settled on him. "We've had this conversation before, haven't we."

"Aye.

"Is that who you want me to be, Allene? The man who hides on Coxet Hill?"

She lowered her eyes. "I'll get Brother David." She gathered her skirts and climbed to her feet.

"Put the needle in the fire, first!" Shawn shouted after her.

Brother David followed her back through the trees, needle and thread in hand. He handed Shawn a tough piece of leather. "Bite it," he said. Allene took his hand.

"What am I doing?" he muttered, looking at the needle. He closed his eyes; tensed, waited.

Brother David's hands clamped down on calf and knee, holding him tight. The needle dug in, sending shards of pain shooting like slivers of broken glass up and down his leg. He jerked against Brother David's grip. He gritted his teeth as the coarse thread tugged his skin.

She poked again, whispering, "I'm sorry, Niall, hush now, I'm sorry." She tugged and stabbed, stabbed and tugged. Sweat prickled his forehead. Against his will, he imagined red, raw flesh being stitched and drawn together. He tried to slow his breathing and stop the shuddering intakes of breath, each time the needle pushed through his skin again.

"Bite the strap," said Brother David.

He bit the leather, eyes squeezed tight, as the needle gouged in again, determined not to sully Niall's name, in case the man ever came back to reclaim it. "What am I doing?" he muttered. "I could have stayed on Coxet Hill."

* * *

Allene covered the eighteen stitches with salve and wrapped them tight in clean linens. Shawn sat on the edge of the field the rest of the day, watching the men drill. He rehearsed each move in his mind. *Thrust. Jab. Parry.* He copied their moves with his arms, slowly, then faster and faster, exactly as he'd learned *Blue Bells* so many years ago; exactly as he'd learned the pieces on harp. *Thrust. Jab. Parry.* He watched every move they made, rehearsed it slowly in his mind, and made it his own.

Twenty-four hours later, rested and bandaged, Shawn limped onto the field, hefting a sword. He swung it, slowly, as he'd watched them do; as he'd rehearsed in his mind. He swung it again, in the arcing patterns he'd memorized, *adagio, moderato, allegro.* The thought of the English swarming Coxet Hill gave power to each swing; his jaws gripped together against the pain in his leg and the blisters rising on his palms, as he perfected the motion and built his strength. *Allegro, presto, vivace,* he increased the tempo of each pattern till they became part of him.

Central Scotland

Streaks of pink and coral silhouetted black hills undulating in every direction. Trees towered around Niall, a sparser forest than he'd known, but still thick with oaks, and silver-barked birches. White mist curled around the trees, turning them a mystic gray-green, and softening every edge.

He squatted on the rocky bank of a stream and drank, energized by the shock of cold; he straightened his tunic, and checked that his dirk was snug in his boot. The morning air defied his discouragement, with its crisp energy.

Despite the wolf, a wolf which the man on the train said did not exist in present-day Scotland, the trails and trees he'd expected had not materialized through yesterday's full day of hiking. He wondered if he could be in the wrong place. The landscape had looked very different in the future Scotland.

Hugh's mountain should have been distinctive: a pair of sharp crags with a small rounded sunrise of a hill dawning behind them. But though he'd searched the southern horizon, hour after hour, the rising sun formation did not show itself.

He rose from the stream. "Am I on a fool's errand?" He shouted it into the forest. His voice echoed back, faint as a lost soul. Shawn might have stayed at the castle. He and Allene might have been killed on the way or taken to an English castle for sport. Niall crossed himself and

317

whispered an *Ave.* Even Shawn didn't deserve that.

Or the time switch just might not happen again, even if they brushed shoulders in space.

He dropped to his knees as he had every morning of his life, this time on the forest's earthy floor. Discouragement crouched on his shoulder like a gargoyle. Immediate, clear-cut answers, always rare, had been in especially short supply lately. Nonetheless, he imagined Jesus, walking the shores of Galilee, perhaps misty at dawn like his own forest, and prayed, "In the name of Christ Jesus, crucified, I arise." He conversed for half an hour, while birds chirped around him. He asked for guidance, for protection of his loved ones, for anything else that would delay the moment of standing up and facing his hopeless task.

...of facing the truth that God was not conversing back.

His stomach rumbled, dragging him to his feet. He brushed at his knees. "Give us this day our daily bread," he said ruefully, straightening up. He crossed himself, looked around, and added, "Or berries." He took a handful of blackberries from a bush and pressed his toes, in his leather boots, into the forest floor, enjoying it after the boxy *tennis shoes* and the city sidewalks.

He walked back to the stream for a last drink, hoping to spot a squirrel or some breakfast heartier than berries. Mist swirled around his calves, touching the edge of his tunic before drifting away. A pine marten froze on a rock by the stream, front paws planted, head stretched up and cocked, its white chest blending with the mist. Its round, black eyes fixed, unblinking, on Niall, hoping not to be seen.

A corner of Niall's mouth twitched upward at its delusion of invisibility. He reached for his slingshot. The cat-like creature darted away, scampering up a tree. Niall's gaze followed, higher and higher, skimming over the bark. The marten disappeared into the new June leaves. He squinted upwards, slingshot poised. The tremble of a shadowy branch suggested where the animal had leapt from the limb. It had escaped him. Defeated, Niall's gaze skimmed down the mist-shrouded tree, past the silhouetted mountains to the north, more rounded shapes, more sharp peaks, stretching like a green, rolling sea as far as his view could reach.

A squirrel chittered somewhere above him.

He reached for another handful of berries and chewed slowly, studying the formation to the north: a hill rose gradually to a plateau, before sloping down again. Behind it rose two peaks, one on either side like horns on the helmet of the Northern invaders of years ago. It niggled at his mind. Why, he couldn't say. He'd never seen that formation.

Central Scotland, 1314

Deep in the woods, Shawn dropped his end of the great buck on the forest floor, and collapsed onto a giant fallen oak. Every inch of his body begged for rest. Men plunked down around him. Roger dug flint from his sporran and sparked a fire against the evening chill. They had been hunting since dawn, before daylight chased the thick mist from the ground.

Over the last days, with his leg on the mend, Shawn had drilled for war and helped prepare weapons, food, and animals for the journey to Stirling. It had been a trick, learning what Niall should know without revealing the full extent of his ignorance. Memories from the re-enactment camps helped. Still, Allene raised her eyes often enough over sewing, concern creasing her forehead. Some of the men looked surprised. But they accepted the explanation of the head wound and did their best to help him.

He did his best to learn: shooting, skinning, lunging, feinting, leaping, jabbing. They drilled twice a day. Those who fell short scrubbed Hugh's rock, The Heart, with pine cones and leaves.

They practiced everything except running, for if they ran, no one would stop bloodthirsty England's attack on their sons and daughters. Those who didn't drill with energy and vigor scrubbed Hugh's rock.

Every night, Shawn and Brother David sang songs of valor and victory. Anyone who did not sing with courage and gusto scrubbed Hugh's rock.

Not once did Shawn scrub the Heart.

But in the quiet of the nights, with midges dive-bombing his plaid, he felt separate. None of them seemed concerned about killing or being killed. It gnawed at him: could he swing the sword with killing force into another human being? He would do what he must, he told himself, to prevent the Sassenach doing worse. It did no good to fret.

Now, on the log in the forest, Shawn swallowed deeply of the ale in his skin, and ran his sleeve across his mouth. One of the men clapped him on the back. "Nice shot on that buck, Niall."

"That's our Niall!" An older man chuckled. "Takin' it down even as it charges him."

"'Twas naught." Actually, he'd never even seen the buck streaking toward him. The arrow had sprung from his bow when he tripped on a root. It had been sheer luck, both good and bad, that had landed the arrow in the animal's foreleg. Still, he couldn't stop a smile of smug satisfaction.

"You slowed him so Roger could take him down."

Roger, by the fire, grunted. The other man took a swallow of his own ale, and they sat silently, shoulder to shoulder, watching Roger nurse the newborn flames into blasts of heat. Several men busied themselves with the carcasses. Shawn turned to watch. He should help. But he didn't know what to do, any more than he'd known what to do when they'd bled and disemboweled the animals. He watched them bind the buck's hooves, and jumped up to help hoist it into a tree for the night.

"Goin' to ha' another bairn by the time we get home, aer ye?" Roger spoke into the silence.

All the men looked at Adam, with the missing tooth. He grinned. "Aye, I 'spect so. A wee braw laddie this time, I told the wifey!"

The men chuckled. "After seven lassies, mon? D' ye think sae?" asked one.

"There be no more bonnie lassies in the Highlands than mine," Adam said. "Yer own lad thinks so," he added, with a wink at James.

"Aye, another year or two, an' they'll be merrit." James thrust a dagger laden with meat over the growing fire, slowly rotating it. Shawn copied him. The fire sizzled and spit as the juices fell into it; the smell of roasting meat revved up the hunger in his stomach. His mouth watered.

"An' they'll ha' their ane braw bairns."

"Would we are there to see them," said James.

"Some of us will be," spoke the oldest man, a veritable bear wearing a cloak. "But I'll gladly die an' it stops Edward."

"Your wife'd sore miss ye, Will."

"I'd sore miss her. Better still that I die than she should fall into the Sassenach's hands. An' I doona come back, tell her I'd die a hoondred times in front of Edward's chargers ere I let 'em at her. We all know what they've done to our women and bairns." Nods went all around the circle. Shawn nodded as well. It seemed judicious.

"An you, Ralph." James spoke again. They turned as one to a tall young man, who would barely be out of high school, in Shawn's own time. "Just merrit." He shook his head.

The young man pulled his dirk, the meat brown and dripping, from the fire, and began to chew. "If I die, I thank my good Lord I had the time wi' her. 'Twould be greater sorrow to die wi' none to mourn ye."

In the flickering firelight, while the men spoke in hushed tones around him, Shawn ran his free hand down the steel length of the sword Hugh had given him. Hugh's words resonated in his heart: "Ye've ever been a man of honor and valor, Niall. I'll be proud to call you kin. I'm proud to fight beside ye."

His boding sense of failure now came from Allene's repeated question: *Who else knows the way through the Great Glen? We must know who is betraying us, ere we reach Stirling.*

And from his thoughts of Amy. Shawn pulled his dirk from the

320

fire. He eyed it warily and stuck it back in the fire, settling his mind on the meat, rather than think about what he'd done with his time with Amy. Or who would mourn him.

Central Scotland

Niall jogged steadily northwards, crashing through forest undergrowth. His excitement mounted. He'd made a mistake! Never had he felt such elation at making one! His heart pounded in his chest, strong and sure. His legs drummed a steady rhythm, his leather boots skimmed leaves and pine needles and soft soil. His tunic batted his knees, swishing as he ran; his cloak tore at twigs as he raced by. He'd gotten off the bus too far south!

What appeared, looking down from the northern highlands, as a sun rising between two small crags, seemed, looking up from the flatter south, to be a horned Norse helmet. On the other side of that rounded hill, was Hugh's camp! He was sure of it. The wolf had been real. *He'd been in the wrong place, not the wrong time!*

Niall picked his way, sometimes quickly, sometimes more slowly, sometimes losing sight of his target, throughout the day. He drank from streams when he found them, ate berries, and managed to trap a trout in a small loch. He dug flint from his sporran and built a fire on the rocky bank, to fix it. His insides churned at the delay.

He prayed constantly as he ran, exhaling *Aves* and *Paters* in rhythm with his running feet. His certainty grew with each long-limbed stride. He was headed toward Hugh's camp, toward Allene.

He stopped on a high ridge, listening. A dull drone reached his ears. There, to his left: his heart sank. Had he really seen a wolf? Or had the man on the train been wrong? Because there, far below, ran a gray ribbon of twenty-first century highway. Two cars sped along, flashing blinding glares of sunlight into his eyes.

Central Scotland, 1314

Shawn lay awake the last night, one among many sleeping under cloaks, long after the fire had died to embers. He imagined the headlines. *Dateline 1314: World-Famous Musician Marches to Hopeless Battle.* He would most likely die. He pondered his life, itemizing what he'd left behind.

One: A pile of articles, posters, and programs—about himself. They didn't matter here, seven hundred years before his time, and, he realized with a sad jolt, they wouldn't matter seven hundred years after his time, either. Not in a hundred years would anyone care about those articles. Not in ten. He put his hands behind his head, staring upward. Trees swayed above, dark shapes blotting out a riot of stars.

Two: His recordings—solos, combo, quintet, and orchestral; Christmas, hits of various decades, ska, jazz. His world had been awed by the speed with which he arranged and recorded his albums. They didn't seem important next to what Hugh and his men were setting out to do. They were nice, the CD's. But recording them had taken no courage or nobility; no risk. They wouldn't change the course of history. Indeed, what he mostly remembered now was the look of pain in a young man's eyes—one of the drummers hired to play on the CD—as Shawn sidled next to his girlfriend and lured her away. Insects chirped a deep night symphony around him.

Three: Caroline, the red-head, a dozen others, Amy. But no wife to mourn him. Caroline, he knew, would find some rising star to replace him rather quickly. Amy had tired of him. He wondered if she'd even come back to the castle for him. Nearby, men rustled in their sleep. Allene rolled, suddenly, close to the embers. Shawn sat up, alone among the sleeping men. He reached under her shoulders, eased her safely from the fire, and lay down again, wondering what else he'd left behind. It took him several minutes.

Four: A few students he'd taught, occasionally. They'd find other teachers. They wouldn't miss him or stare at his picture, as he stared at his father's; no child to carry on his name and legacy and what had been important to him. He thought about these men here in the forest, willing to die for their children. He had not been willing to settle down for his.

Central Scotland

Niall crossed the wooded ridge of the rounded hill, to the northern side he knew. His thighs and calves ached with a slow, dull burn. Crisp afternoon air reached through his long sleeves. Birches rose around him, pines before and behind, shading the bright sun down to a soft yellow haze.

A high-pitched *screeeeee, scree, scree, screeeeeeee* split the quiet. He shaded his eyes with his hand and stared at the sharp-beaked face of an osprey, perched on a branch high above. Sunlight stabbed down among the leaves behind it. Were osprey, like wolves, extinct in Shawn's time? Regardless, they lived near lochs. And Hugh's camp was near a loch.

He stared up through the trees at the sharp peak on his left; studied its twin to the east. They were sparsely forested, not the heavily-wooded crags he'd known.

Doubts assailed him. Had he spent a day jogging toward a fairy hill, a pot of gold? There were many lochs, and the osprey's loch was not necessarily Hugh's. Maybe the peaks looked different because he was still in the wrong place, rather than the wrong time. Maybe the switch could only happen with himself and Shawn in the same location, and maybe Shawn had already left. Maybe Shawn had never come. Maybe he and Allene were already dead. There was no reason to come back, if Allene was dead.

The osprey cried out, and rose, skimming up over the trees and out of sight.

He followed its flight till he could see it no more, then closed his eyes, the weight of the questions heavy on his shoulders and sour in his empty stomach. He missed his coffee. His knees sagged under him, hitting the soft earth; hands touched the ground and head bowed, too tired to go on. The ache throbbed in his thighs. *God*, he pleaded, *Can You give me any reassurance that Allene is safe? Give me strength.* He thought of Amy, scared at the bottom of the trail. Had he abandoned her for nothing? Or, if he had crossed back to 1314, would Shawn find himself in his own time, bewildered and lost in the mountain wilds?

He dragged in a deep, calming breath. *It is enough, oh, Lord! It's too much! I never knew how small I was. I have to trust you. And I'm not sure I do. Give me faith. Help me!*

He opened his eyes and fell back, sitting on the ground with his elbows over his knees. *Let's say you're in the right place.* He forced the thoughts through his weary mind. *You would hear a waterfall, and look for the rock like a horse's head and bigger than a man.* He sat still another moment. His head drooped on his chest. *God, I'm so tired and discouraged.*

But it must be done. He heaved himself to his feet, eyes closed, listening. A breeze rustled the oak leaves on his right. Birds warbled. A branch creaked. He opened his eyes, searching his lush green surroundings. A squirrel darted up a tree. A deer peered from a thick cluster of alder. There was no waterfall.

It would have been farther down the mountain, he thought, and set off down the northern face. Only after stopping to listen for the fifth time was he rewarded with the soft burbling of moving water. He broke into a run, pushing through pine branches that slashed back behind him, and frightening a red fox that darted away in a flurry of short legs and bushy tail.

The bubbling grew, his spirit soared, and he pumped his legs faster, till there he saw it! Hidden like a jewel among the thick forest, the water rushed over a series of stepped rocks, whites and blues a joyous sight amidst the greens. A smile broke out across Niall's face. His heart filled to bursting. He fell to his knees on the bank, splashing his grubby tunic and hands and face and chest in the water, laughing out loud. He threw his head back and shouted, "Thank you!" to God, somewhere above the soaring treetops. If he followed it far enough, he'd find the rock shaped like the horse head. He splashed across the narrow stream, heedless of soaking his boots, thrilling to the cool water on his aching calves. He bounded out on the other side, and down the slope, heedless of tree limbs tearing at his face. And there, where the land dipped, if he turned....

It was there! A bare rocky wall in the forest. It still bore the rough shape of a horse's head, though greatly softened around the edges. He remembered Hugh standing under it, even Hugh's great height barely reaching the top of the rock, and pointing to the entrance of the labyrinth that led to his secret camp. Niall closed his eyes for just a moment in silent prayer, tremoring to reach Allene, before bursting around the rock.

It was forest, just forest like all the rest he'd seen for days on end. There was no trail, no maze.

* * *

It didn't seem much of a legacy, Shawn thought, gazing into the night campfire. He didn't even know anymore what was important to him. He turned, tugging his cloak over his head and seeking respite in sleep, but none came.

After some time, he sat up again, staring into the embers, and turned, with limited hope, to itemizing how he would be remembered by those who knew him.

Great in bed. Well, Amy hadn't thought so lately. He wrapped his arms around his knees. The fire warmed his face despite the cool night. When had she begun to pull away and look reluctant? Was it a year ago?

Well, he was a great one for a party, anyway. He chuckled, remembering Edinburgh, the chandelier swinging crazily and the waitress. Man, he and Rob had had the time of their lives! Conrad had warned him about the orchestra's reputation; demanded he tone things down. Some people, he realized, might not miss his parties. Or him.

Arrogant. The word popped unbidden into his mind. He gritted his jaw. He'd ridiculed those who didn't join his parties, or play as well as he did, or laugh as loud, or drink as much. He'd had things to say about Aaron's seraphic longing and waiting for Celine, in a public bathroom on their tour in the south. They were clever, witty things, sly references to Shawn's own approach with Celine, and everyone laughed. Aaron emerged from a stall into their sudden silence, face dark and jaw tight, washed his hands and left without a word. Shawn and the men around

324

him had burst into laughter as soon as the door shut.

Was it his imagination, or did the fire grow several degrees warmer, till he could hardly stand the heat flushing his neck and face? But surely Amy didn't think that of him. She'd loved him, always, coming back to him time after time. He poked a stick in the embers. A spark shot straight into the air with a small sizzle, and died. He re-played their last night in the tower, and found no balm to his battered self-image. Amy had done so much for him, had had such faith in him. He deserved none of it. So many times, he'd chided and teased her into things she didn't really want to do. Never would she believe that he'd spent over a week alone with a woman without.... In the dark, staring at the stars, his face burned hotter still.

He'd never felt so small.

He had changed, but Amy would never know. Conrad, Rob, the world—they'd remember him as less than he'd become. If he must die, he wanted to be remembered as the new man he had become, not the old one he'd been. He wanted Amy to know he was sorry. If only there was a way to leave a message, some indestructible message that would cross seven hundred years. He wanted her to know her faith in him had not been in vain.

* * *

The lack of Hugh's labyrinth shouldn't surprise him, Niall knew. He hadn't been sure at all which time he was in. Still, it was another disappointment. He looked up through the branches overhead. Always dimmer in the forest, it would nonetheless be daylight for many hours yet, approaching midsummer's day. He closed his eyes, summoning up the lay of the trail, the markers. Some of them—boulders, streams— would still be there. He had to at least try. He pushed aside thick ferns and entered Hugh's realm.

Inverness, Present

"I don't know," Amy said again. Her body tensed in the window seat of Shawn's suite. Frustration rang in every note of her voice.

"You don't know or you don't want to tell us," the older policeman, Sergeant Chisholm asked yet again. "He told you he needed to go to the Trossachs so you just arranged the train ride, no questions asked, and left him?"

Amy bit her lip; she twisted her ring, glancing to Conrad, pacing the room, and Bill sitting, fuming, at the table.

"Why did he say he needed to go?" the officer pressed.

"I told you, he was looking for something. He didn't say what." She resisted the urge to touch the crucifix, hidden under her sweatshirt, and hoped God would forgive her the lie. "But it was so important to him. I don't understand. I haven't broken any laws, have I?' She looked to Conrad, raking his hand through his white hair.

Bill shook his head, the disgust evident on his face. "He was told not to leave town. You didn't know that."

Conrad stopped his pacing and turned to the police. "Is this necessary? She hasn't done anything. We know he's in the Trossachs. He said he's going to the re-enactment at Stirling. Find him there."

Sergeant Chisholm exploded, bursting out of his chair. "But it makes no sense!" He threw his notepad on the mahogany table.

The younger officer placed a hand on the Sergeant's shoulder. But his eyes lingered on Amy. She glanced at him, at his short black curls and ruddy cheeks, and dropped her eyes. "Clive, she can tell us no more. Let's go."

Central Scotland

Deep in Hugh's realm, as the sun faded, Niall found the abandoned castle ruins, jutting up rough and red among fresh green saplings. Ferns grew from cracks in the ancient stone. He walked through the arched entrance into an earthen-floored hallway; from there, into a courtyard open to the forest on the other side. Two large Celtic crosses, covered in white lichen, marked the long-ago burial of a lord and his lady. He ran his hand over the cool, rough stones, and turned back.

A tower jutted up, still bearing window arches. At its base were the cave-like remains of a small room. He wrapped the plaid around himself and crawled into what little warmth the lower tower offered.

He didn't want to think about the coat of arms and the name over the entrance: *Campbell.* The dates on the tombstones, perhaps thankfully, were obliterated.

Chapter Nineteen

The Trossachs, Scotland

With men snoring around him, embers glowing, and shame gnawing like a rat inside, Shawn fell, finally, into restless dreams.

It was his twelfth birthday. He stood outside the lesson room at Schmitt's, where his big-bellied teacher, his gray beard flowing down his chest, listened to a high school student play. Through the glass door, Shawn watched the boy's slide flash, golden, in and out, notes burbling and skipping like a gypsy's exuberant dance.

"I want to play that," Shawn announced, when the door finally opened. The older boy smiled tolerantly, as he snapped his case shut. The big belly of his teacher shook with mirth. "In a few years, Shawn. He's a very good player. He's in high school. You're not ready for *Blue Bells* yet."

"Let me try."

"Come on in and pull out your *Standard of Excellence.*"

Shawn gripped the money his mother had given him for his lesson. He narrowed his eyes, his decision already made. He turned on his heel, found a clerk to get him a copy of *Blue Bells of Scotland,* and walked home, swinging the heavy leather case in one hand while he held the new music open in front of him, already memorizing the first notes.

He quit lessons. He looked up positions on the internet. He sought advice on the trombone forum. He learned, a note at a time, a measure at a time, slowly, ever so slowly, playing first as half notes, then as quarters, as eighths, and finally as the lightning quick triplets and sixteenth notes Arthur Pryor had written. On his thirteenth birthday, he played it under his former teacher's window at midnight. At the second measure, a woman hollered to stop the caterwauling. At the fifth measure, a man threw a shoe. By the first variation, the entire neighborhood gaped silently out their windows. At the last note, there was a stunned silence; then they broke into applause, his former teacher with the greatest enthusiasm of all. He bowed, grinning at them all.

Shawn woke with a jolt, sitting up straight. He did have some redeeming qualities: Persistence. Patience. Determination. Dedication to what was important.

Leaving a message for Amy was important.

He studied the shadowy clearing, over the hulking shapes of the sleeping men. Ponies snuffled under the trees. The great rock, the Heart, shone in the moonlight. Food and weapons waited for the pre-dawn departure. He climbed quietly from his cloak, refusing to consider what Hugh would do, if he caught him.

Long before dawn, on the morning of departure, the men on night watch woke the others to the mountain mists. They gathered their food, supplies, weapons, and cloaks. Brother David led them in prayer. Beside him, on her knees in the mist, ready to march with the men, Allene clung to his hand as they prayed.

They tethered the ponies behind the men, and set off on their long trek down the mountains to fight for Stirling Castle and Scotland. By some miracle, no one saw what Shawn had done during the cold night hours.

Shawn sang with the rest, his heart light. He had left a message. It wasn't much, but somehow, he was sure, Amy would know.

Trossachs, Scotland

Niall woke in the gray before dawn, too keyed to sleep. He shook cold dew from his plaid and emerged from the small tower room into the misted forest. Gray ghosts of trees stood sentinel around the castle ruins. Wisps of fog drifted across the courtyard, wrapping tentacles around the tombstones.

After praying, he threw the plaid over his shoulder and turned north: past another waterfall, higher than it had been in his time. No sign remained of the maze that had hidden the camp. He closed his eyes, seeing his last trip here, the formation of the land itself, of rocks and jutting outcroppings and hidden waterways. More sure than ever this was the place, he broke into a run, through underbrush, past boulders, among trees, leaping streams.

And suddenly, the forest fell away.

He stopped, panting, on the edge of a clearing. The pines reached higher here than anywhere else, centuries-old cathedral spires stretching for God's face as they circled a floor of beaten earth. Their incense filled the forest sanctuary. Pale shafts of diaphanous emerald light shimmered through the stained glass of leaves far overhead, stabbing down into the cauldron of mist boiling in the clearing. He stepped in, gripped by the sense of age. It was utterly still, utterly quiet.

He knew what he'd find. He turned, staring in awe. It was unmistakable even with centuries of forest debris covering its white surface: the huge boulder, taller than Hugh, narrow at the bottom and five times again as wide at the top, the Heart of Hugh's camp.

His own heart pounded in elation. A smile tore across his face! He threw his head back, shouting, *"Deo Gratias!"* It echoed through the still clearing, as through an ancient ruin, calling life back to it.

"Hugh!" He touched the stone, Hugh's Heart, cool under his palm. Tingles dashed up his arm. "Adam!" Adam, with his missing tooth and seven daughters and a bairn on the way, had scrubbed the Heart almost daily, for sleeping on duty.

"Roger!" Niall spun to the center of the camp, where Roger had tended the flames. An indent marred the earth. Mist wreathed his wrist as he stooped to touch the cool spot.

"Owen? Angus!" They'd wrestled by the stream, till they landed in it, drawing the men's hoots.

There, through the trees, shining pink in the dawn light, was the blue shimmer of loch where he and Allene had sat under the not-so-discreet eye of her uncle's men.

"Allene! Shawn!"

He held his breath, waiting, and spoke again, more softly. "Allene? Shawn, I'm here."

Silence came back to him. Not even birdsong.

Niall's heartbeat slowed to the sluggish rhythm of disappointment. It was only a ruin, after all. There was no life here, and hadn't been for a very long time. Whatever had stared at him with yellow eyes, he was not in 1314.

He circled the camp, searching for he knew not what. A scrap left on a tree, a cooking pot forgotten, any evidence that they had existed and laughed and sung under the trees here, hiding from the Sassenach and biding their time.

He found nothing.

He came back to the rock and knelt, his forehead pressing its cool, grimy surface. *God, grant me wisdom; show me what I must do to help Hugh and my clan. Be with Allene.*

His gaze traveled over the clearing again, choosing his next step. Would falling asleep here bring him back? Did he and Shawn need to be in the same place for the magic to work?

Was Shawn here, even now? He stilled himself, trying to feel the spirits of the men who had been here in June of 1314. A breeze whispered past him; he imagined James' cloak brushing his shoulder. A sound boomed far away, and he fancied he heard Hugh's volcanic voice echoing back over the years. He opened his eyes to the empty clearing.

He sat back against the rock, deflated, trying to decide what to do next. But his mind stuck, like a boat caught in a current, on the mysterious Shawn who looked just like him. The man was a coward, a liar, a cheater, a ne'er-do-well. A genius, apparently. But a ne'er-do-well, all the same. What had he achieved of any importance in his life? What good had he done for anyone?

And if he was here, he had traveled alone with Allene. Niall closed his eyes, feeling the pale green sunlight shine through his lids, and tried to imagine how it must have been. The Laird had an intense need to reach Hugh, only Allene who knew how to find him, and only Niall—Shawn—whom he could trust to accompany her. He wondered, judging by Shawn's reputation, how long it had taken him to try his dirty tricks on Allene. Allene would have her knife. She would be safe enough, unless Shawn was not only a ne'er do well, but a vicious one, too. He didn't seem to be. God, he prayed again, what more can I do! Help me protect Allene.

By his calculations, it was now the twenty-first of June. The battle would happen in a matter of days. Time was running out.

He stood and stretched, touching the rock, and circling his hand over the old surface, wondering what to do next. A layer of dirt sifted off. It stained his hand and fluttered to the ground.

* * *

Furious with his failure, Niall attacked the Heart with the rough edges of a pine cone. It was foolish, but Hugh had taken ridiculous pride in keeping the stone shining, blinding, pure white in the sun. At the very least, in Hugh's memory, wherever he might be, it would be clean again as long as Niall was here.

He wore down the first pine cone. Dirt blackened his hands and caked his nails. Thirsty, he turned to the stream meandering around the edge of the clearing, and found himself looking into the face of a stag. It stared back, its eyes large and liquid with unnatural intelligence, still as the marble statues that graced the hotel's gardens.

Unnerved, Niall skipped his drink. He found another pine cone, and scrubbed more. He glanced over his shoulder. The stag still watched.

He turned back to his job. The boulder brightened to a murky gray. Years of dirt smeared under his hands, while he chided himself he ought to be finding some action to take. But there was none. He looked over his shoulder again. The stag had vanished without a sound.

He stripped off his tunic, and, doubling it over, filled it with water at the stream. A small puddle survived the short trip to the rock. He flung it on, and made another trip, and another. He used his hands and leaves and pine cones. He scrubbed in fury at his own failure to find a way back. He threw in all his anger at God's silence. He was out of ideas.

Finally, he stopped, breathing hard, his hands planted on the rock. It was white now, but scratches marred the beautiful surface Hugh had loved. He sighed. Hugh wasn't here to object. Whatever reward that noble and courageous man had gone on to hundreds of years hence was surely great enough he'd not worry himself about a rock.

Hugh's love of order, however, was not hundreds of years distant to Niall. It was last month. He touched the marks. They must have been deep and ugly long ago, but had softened with age. He ran his palm over them, and leaned his forehead on his hand, missing Hugh and Allene and MacDonald, and all of them. If wishing had any power, they'd burst to life around him.

The sun grew warmer as it rose to the tops of the pines. He went finally, in discouragement, to the stream for a drink. Maybe he'd lie down a bit, rest his aching arms, and decide what to do next. The place the stag had stood drew him. He waded across the burn, dropped to his knees in the same spot, and stared back into the clearing, curious what had captured the stag's attention.

And gasped.

The Trossachs, Scotland

Shawn marched with Hugh's men through the forest. Trees swayed overhead, cooling the air. Tunics swished, swords clanked. Ponies trotted behind, loaded with food and weapons, whickering as the men sang of victory. Now and again, deer flashed away from them, or a fox darted into the underbrush. Shawn felt tougher, stronger, fitter than he ever had, in body and spirit. In his mind, now, rather than music, he practiced battle skills.

Thrust, parry, feint, jab. Thrust, parry...

He made the sign of the cross and remembered a few words of the *Hail Mary* his father had taught him years ago. Edward would outnumber the Scots three to one, four to one, maybe more.

But odds didn't matter. They would fight, whatever the outcome. A bird trilled in song, and his spirit soared, inexplicably, with the notes. He'd learned his music sometimes two notes at a time; he would work his way through the English army one knight at a time. *....feint, jab.* He'd stop them reaching Allene. *Thrust, parry, feint....* And somehow, when he was done, he'd get back to the castle, and go up in that tower and wake up where he belonged, and find Amy and beg her forgiveness.

He had to believe that.

Hugh's Camp, the Trossachs, Scotland

Shawn K Stirl C 6-21-1314
A- so sorry
Iona J

The words jumped off the white stone now. What had been only a marred surface close up, spoke eloquently at a distance. The word *so* was underlined three times.

Niall's breathing slowed. The damp of the burn crept into his knees, barely noticed. He shook water from his hands, rising slowly. Shawn had been here, right here in this clearing, on this very date seven hundred some years ago. Why, then, had no switch occurred?

He scanned the clearing and the forest beyond, as if the men might materialize. The sun blazed high in the sky now. Only thin mist remained, ringing the trees and skating across the clearing.

No one appeared.

He turned back to the words. *Stirl C.* could only mean Stirling Castle. Niall's heart sang, seeing the deeper implications. Shawn had not only gotten this far, but had convinced Hugh to throw his considerable weight behind the Bruce. It improved Scotland's odds greatly.

A- so sorry

He waded across the burn, back to the rock, touching the marks. Seven hundred years! He stared in awe. They were dulled and eroded, like the carvings on old tombstones. How long must it have taken to do even this little bit?

He traced the letters of *Iona,* perplexed at Shawn's meaning. The letters were soft and rounded under his fingertips. They must have been deeply etched, to survive so long. And on Hugh's precious stone, under Hugh's very eye. He smiled slowly. It was an insane thing to do. Did he expect Amy to somehow find this rock, isolated and hidden even today?

A- so sorry

He must indeed have been sorry to have dared this feat, let alone managed it. He had hurt her, callously, over and over. The Shawn Niall had come to know would not leave such a message, and yet—there was no doubt this was from Shawn. Something had changed in him. Niall wondered what could have wrought such a miracle.

One way or another, he vowed, Amy would get the message. And he laughed out loud at the realization. Yes, it had been insane of Shawn, expecting Amy to get this message, hidden under layers of dirt in a deep wilderness. And yet, that's exactly what was going to happen! He crossed himself, offering a wordless plea that God would open a way for him to keep that vow. Amy deserved that much.

Till such a means appeared, he must do what he could to find Shawn and Hugh. He knew which way Hugh would take his men. But he could only guess whether Shawn had carved the message in the wee hours of June 21, or the last, waning ones.

Niall stood midway between the two. Had the men left early this morning, seven hundred years ago, or did their shadows move purposely about the clearing, even now, preparing for departure in the small hours of the morrow. He closed his eyes. His hand rested on the cool stone, the etchings clear under his palm, now that he'd seen them. *God,* he prayed, *lead your servant right.*

Shawn would have carved in the night, Niall decided, while Hugh slept and the night watch roamed the forest. It had been the wee hours, he decided, not the waning. The clearing felt empty. The men were gone. He knew it was nothing more than a guess. But he needed to believe something.

He searched the clearing one last time, for any clue at all. He saw nothing. So, with a last drink from the chirping stream, he girded his belt and set off east, across the mountain, listening for the ghostly echoes of footsteps that had fallen seven hundred years ago.

The Trossachs, Scotland

The woods echoed with bird song and the cry of the stag, the bubbling of the burn beside their trail, and the men roaring songs of valor as they had around the campfire, and talking of their loved ones at home. The ponies rustled behind.

But there was something else.

Shawn felt it, a shadow stalking them through the forest. He glanced over his shoulder repeatedly, peering into the brush. Could it be the English? Surely they couldn't be so quiet?

"A wraith followin' you, Niall!" shouted Will, clapping his back. "'Tis the forest spirits. Think naught upon it!"

"You're strangely nervous," Allene whispered, her hand creeping into his. "What is it, Niall?"

"We'll talk about it later," Shawn said, and she fell silent.

"'Tis but hours," shouted Hugh, from the head of the column, "and we'll be shoulder to shoulder with our kin, drivin' the English into the sea!"

A great shout went up, echoing up and down the mountain trail.

Swords and pikes waved in the summer sun, bouncing bright bits of light back in his eyes. Sweat streamed off the men in the warm day. As the sun tipped past its zenith, they chewed dried meat, or ate berries from the bushes. Rowan leaves hung heavy and still in the afternoon heat. Shawn looked behind again. Heat shimmered, forming a ghostly figure of a man that wavered and dissipated.

"Niall! Move, laddie! What ails ye!" Roger pushed him from behind.

Shawn felt a gentle breeze on his shoulder, and heard up and down the forest glen another echo. He swore it was his own name, carried back on the breeze again.

* * *

Niall raced through the pines and birches with the sureness of the stag. He leapt a small burn and kept running, flashing in and out of trees trying to stay near the path. Was he crazy, feeling he *knew* where it had been? They had many hours' start on him, he guessed. But traveling alone, he would move faster than the long, winding column of Hugh's men, snaking down through the forest trails, burdened with animals, weapons, and supplies. In mid-afternoon, he slowed long enough to pluck berries from the brush and gulp from a stream, to take his bearings and steady his course. Heat shimmered, columns of light stabbing down through the lofty trees. Ahead, something flashed the sun back into his eyes. But he could see nothing there. He closed his eyes and listened, still as the earth. At first he heard only the burn. Then the trill of a bird.

And the tramping of many feet.

"Shawn!" he called out, as loudly as he could. He dropped to his knees, palms on the ground, and tried to quiet the beating of his heart, listening intently. He raised his head, cupped his hands to his mouth and shouted again. "Shawwwwn! SHAWN! *SHAWWWWN!*" He braced his hands against his thighs, listening.

This time he clearly heard the tread of feet.

"You okay, man?" A pair of sandals crunched on a twig and stepped into Niall's field of vision: stocky, leather sandals with thick soles and brown, woolen socks. Niall raised his eyes from the feet, up past baggy short trews to a shirt bursting with wild red and blue flowers. A young man, his hair bound back in a long ponytail, round bits of glass in front of his eyes, and a large pack strapped over his shoulders, stared back, his head cocked to one side. Niall stared up at him; he conflicted bizarrely with what Niall had expected to see.

And yet—wasn't that his name, that he heard barked out, just now, across the stream?

* * *

Heat shimmered, dancing down green among the leafy overhead canopy, and dappling the narrow trail. Branches hung heavy and still in the heat. A squirrel darted, disappearing before the eye could catch it. Shawn glanced at the men to his right and left, marching in their tunics, and plaids swinging over each shoulder. Their fiery hair blazed even in the dim light of the forest. He looked back across the stream they were even now fording, and blinked hard at the American college student in Bermudas, Hawaiian shirt, and Birkenstocks on the far bank. He stopped in his tracks. Roger slammed into him, shouting, "*Niall!* Keep movin', laddie!" and shoving him forward. He stared back frantically. The college student was gone. A trick of a desperate mind.

* * *

"You okay?" the man asked again.

"Never better in seven hundred years!" Niall answered, and at the man's alarmed look, reassured him, "A jest, only a jest. Do I look that auld?" He climbed to his feet.

The man smiled, an off-kilter smile, unsure what the joke really was. He scanned Niall's tunic and boots. "If you need help," he said, "I've got a cell phone."

Ah, yes, the cell phones. "Can you call Amy?" Niall asked. At the man's doubtful look, he added, "Amy Nelson, with the orchestra."

"Do you have her number?" the man asked. "I remember an American orchestra. In fact," his voice rose in excitement, "aren't you...."

"The hotel," Niall said. "She's staying in Inverness, the hotel with the lions, the castle...."

"You're really okay? I know that hotel. My friend's in Inverness." He placed a call, spoke briefly, and hung up. In five minutes, five minutes of awkward silence and staring at each other amidst the ferns and moss and sounds of the forest, the phone trilled an old folk song. Niall looked at it in amazement. "*Blue Bells,*" the man apologized. "It seemed appropriate." He answered it. "Uh-huh. Yeah. Amy Nelson. He's right here. We'll wait. I think he'll wait." Niall nodded. "Yeah," the man confirmed into the phone. "He'll wait. Okay, in a sec, then." He snapped the instrument shut again. "He's at the hotel. He's got them looking for her. She'll call me."

Niall looked frantically down the mountain. Hugh couldn't get too far in the time this was eating up. Shawn had gotten Allene safely to Hugh, and had gone to great lengths to leave Amy a message. Niall would see that she got it. Who knew what would happen at Stirling. It might be the last message Amy ever had from him. From either of them.

The phone rang. A frantic, high-pitched squawking erupted from it. "Yeah, yeah, calm down," the man soothed. "He's right here. Says he's fine." His doubtful look at Niall's tunic and boots suggested he wasn't so sure.

"Amy." Niall took the phone as he'd seen others do. Her voice, coming out of the small instrument, amazed him. He pulled it from his ear and stared. The hiker looked at him quizzically, took the phone, gently turned it around, and handed it back.

He put it back to his ear, baffled by the man's look of pitying concern. "Amy." He stared desperately down the mountain after the ghosts of men long gone. "Listen to me."

Amy sobbed and gasped and chattered hysterically.

"Amy," he repeated. "I'm fine. I haven't much time." She quieted, amid several sobs and gasps, and he said, "Shawn reached Hugh. I found the camp early this morning, but he's already left." Her voice came over the line again, upset. "Doona ask how I ken," Niall insisted more urgently. "But he's heading down the mountain right now. I think I'm five minutes behind him." Five minutes and seven hundred years, he thought wryly. "He's going to Stirling. But he left you a message. Hugh's rock, the one I told you he loved to keep so perfect. He took a great chance, Amy, carving it under Hugh's verra nose. It said, *Amy—so sorry.* He's changed, Amy. He wanted you to know, and I want you to know, he's become the man you always saw in him. It says he's going to Stirling, it says Iona. I doona ken what that means. I'll get him back to you, if I can."

Niall handed the phone to its owner, thanking him, while Amy's agitated voice still flowed freely.

The man snapped the phone shut. "I just came that way," he said. "There's no one there."

Niall had already crossed the stream, soaking his feet, and plunged back into the forest.

Inverness, Scotland, Present

Amy pressed the *end* button. As her knees gave way, Rob eased her onto one of the lobby's overstuffed couches. Dana dropped beside her, comforting her. Musicians milled, eager for gossip, whispering Shawn's name. Rob patted her shoulder awkwardly. "They're calling the police," he said. "They'll find him." He thanked the young man and shook his hand.

"No prob," the boy said. He snapped his phone shut and ambled to a far corner of the lobby to pretend he wasn't watching curiously.

"I have to get out of here," Amy said. Her heart beat hard. Her body trembled, inside and out. Dana slid an arm around Amy's shoulder. "Come on," she said.

Trossachs

Ghostly sounds echoed among the trees: tack jingling, ponies whickering, gruff voices singing. Sometimes the sounds came from ahead, sometimes behind, sometimes all around, but always faint and far away, no matter how fast Niall ran. His frequent calls, hands cupped around his mouth, of *Allene! Shawn! Hugh! ALLENE!* went unanswered. In the late afternoon, thin mist gathered.

He stopped, breathing heavily, on a deer track. A cloaked shadow formed ahead, slipping amidst the silver birches. "Shawn! Answer me, Shawn!" The figure melted away. Silence came back to him, but for birdsong and the sudden *crescendo-diminuendo* of a car flashing around the curving mountain road below.

Anger swept through him, anger at Shawn for not answering, anger at God—likewise, for not answering. Anger at whatever dangled his own time before him, constantly snatching it away. He slammed his palm into a tree, his jaw tight, and ran, chasing mist and shadows. Anger surged through his legs, faster and faster. Late afternoon became evening. The fog thickened.

He burst from the forest, into a field. Sharp grass crunched under his boots. He swore he saw a big, shaggy man—Will!—off to his right, spun, and found it was only mist. Shaggy highland cattle bolted in their stiff-legged gallop and turned back to snort with wide, soft noses and luminous brown eyes. He ran again, tearing apart white ribbons of fog before him.

And suddenly, a stone circle rose, hovering above the boiling mist, in the middle of the field. He skidded to his knees in their midst. "Was it your sick magic!" he demanded. He pounded one with his closed fist. Pounded it over and over. "Take me back! Let me back to protect Allene!" He pounded till his fist hurt; till his arm hurt, till his eyes stung from tears a warrior would not shed.

He pounded till he had no energy left and dropped his head against the tallest stone, rising from the mist.

And the Lord was not in the earthquake.

It was one of the last verses the Laird had read before this switch happened. His earthquake subsided.

And the Lord was not in the wind.

The aftershocks trembled away. A gentle breeze curled through the stones.

Shawn was the whisper that came on the breeze. Shawn had changed, and he was there with Allene. A feeble flame of hope quivered in Niall's heart.

The tear worked its way from the corner of his eye and trailed, burning, down his face. He wanted to be with her. But Shawn—somehow—had gotten her this far; he would continue to care for her.

Niall climbed slowly to his feet. Mist arched like cats around his knees. His plan had been to follow Hugh to Stirling. There was still hope. He turned from the fading sun, and settled into a sad, but determined and steady jog.

* * *

Rob pushed at the gathering crowd. "Leave her alone," he said. "Let us through. Bill, tell Conrad to meet us in Shawn's room." He wrapped his arm around her waist. In minutes, he and Dana and Celine had her settled in the window seat overlooking the garden, a steadying mug of hot coffee—Shawn's mug with the golden trombone, the mug Niall loved—in her hands.

A knock sounded on the door. Aaron entered, seating himself beside her and Celine, keeping their silent vigil.

The days of questioning by police and Conrad and Rob and even Caroline tumbled inside her. They'd kept at her, sympathetic but relentless, till she broke down and repeated his story, hating herself for the fool she must appear.

Days of self-doubt gathered like storm clouds. How could she have considered such an insane story, even for a second? She touched the crucifix, hidden inside her shirt. She hadn't told them about it, afraid they'd take it. Had she abandoned a demented man in the forest when he needed help? But his eyes had been clear and rational, his voice steady; he'd understood her doubt. He'd spoken with such detailed knowledge of life in a medieval castle. Worry over Niall and Shawn sat, heavy as Wagnerian opera, in her stomach. Her breakdown in the lobby made her face flame.

"It's okay." Celine's voice fluttered like a butterfly. She held Amy's hand and patted it.

"You're not crazy," Aaron said. "He's not Shawn, and those coins you told me about, they came from somewhere." She slipped the crucifix from her neck, and handed it to him. They stared at each other.

Rob and Dana paced across the room, whispering to one another in agitation.

"He found where Shawn was," Amy said to Celine and Aaron. The dark clouds of self-doubt drew down into funnel clouds. She focused through them to the pinprick of light, telling them about Hugh's Heart, and the message, short as it was. "How much did it take to carve something so deep it lasted seven hundred years? Could he really have changed?"

She repeated the message. "*Amy, so sorry. Iona J.*" She looked from Aaron to Celine. "What does Iona mean?"

"It's the island where they bury the kings of Scotland," Aaron said. "It's on the other side of the country from Bannockburn. It has nothing to do with it, as far as I know."

She wrapped her hands around Shawn's mug, seeing Niall at the table sipping coffee by the hour, studying maps and mining the internet. She breathed in the specialty coffee Shawn loved. She'd always seen it in Shawn's eyes when he lied, though she tried to convince herself otherwise. And since the day she'd faced Niall and his dagger, behind the castle, she'd seen sincerity, always, in his eyes.

She believed him. He'd found a rock with a message from Shawn. Wherever, whenever he was, something had called forth in him the man she'd always seen. Her thoughts blew like tumbleweeds, fearing for Niall and Shawn both. She knew how the battle for Stirling would end.

Chapter Twenty

Stirling, 1314

Shawn's first sight of Stirling Castle made him stop and grab for another breath. It rose, a stern beacon of refuge, representing the safety and lives of so many. James, Owen, Adam with his seven daughters, all the men he'd come to know, stood, or sat on their sturdy Highland ponies. He knew a great deal about their wives and children and parents, waiting at home for word of them.

Allene curled her hand around his arm. All of them stared up at Stirling, stark and bold on the eastern horizon, etched against the evening sky. Sunlight glinted off what must be an archer's helmet or soldier's shield, on the ramparts. He imagined the English huddled inside, waiting for rescue Shawn prayed would not come.

"Aye, they'll be here," Brother David said. Only faint yellow bruises shadowed his eyes now. The gypsies' herbs, days of rest, and crisp mountain air all seemed to have returned his strength, though he still limped. "Edward fights not for Stirling, but for his name, which is scorned throughout England."

Shawn understood. He'd fight for Allene, he'd fight for survival. Even more, he'd fight to get back to Amy and redeem his name.

Up ahead Hugh shouted. The men pulled their eyes from Stirling Castle and wheeled south. A mile on, in the forest at the edge of the great bog, they found the Scottish camp. Dozens of clans had gathered from the highlands and the lowlands. Banners streamed. The biggest of all bore a red lion rearing on a field of brilliant gold-yellow. "The Bruce," Brother David told him, following his gaze.

Horses whinnied. Men in tunics and bushy beards, quilted gambesons and a variety of plaids, moved among the camps, hailing one another, trading jests and news, hefting pikes and comparing swords. The clash of steel on steel rang across the grounds as men tested each other's strength and trained in the final hours before battle.

Like a giant family reunion, Shawn thought, except these men were marching, not to a chicken dinner, but to their deaths. He'd heard enough of England's might. They didn't stand a chance. And he'd had a long walk to search his memory; he thought he remembered The Pools now, and felt sick. The word *slaughter* took on a pungent odor when it jumped off the pages of history, into his own life.

The scents of cooking and meat and turnips and horses and leather and sweat and heather and bluebells hung on the summer air, thick with anticipation. Amy filled his thoughts—how he'd failed her, the message he'd left. It was crazy, he realized, to think she would happen across that rock in their own time. Stark, sheer raving mad insanity, he berated himself. There was no reason she'd ever go into such wilderness. And his scratches would weather and fade over the centuries. Yet, he felt at peace. Niall was with her, and somehow, Niall would make it okay.

He moved to the edge of the forest that sheltered the Scottish troops. He looked east, over the field. Men in tunics and trews and rounded helmets worked the boggy carse. Evening mist rose around their ankles, making them float, ghost-like, over the ground.

"What are they doing?" he asked Brother David.

"This is where the Sassenach must come through. Bruce has chosen our ground well. See there, and there." He pointed to a hill on their right and a bog on the left. "They've only this narrow spit of firm ground to bring their great army through a bit at a time." He pointed to the men in the field the English must cross. "They've dug holes and filled them with spikes and covered them over. Now they're dropping caltrops on the ground, between the traps."

"Caltrops?" Shawn didn't remember the word from his re-enactment days.

Allene spoke. "They've sharp spikes that stick up, no matter which way they're dropped."

"Like a giant game of jacks," Shawn murmured.

"They'll pierce the horses' feet," Allene said. "The cavalry is the deadliest part of Edward's army. This will stop many of them."

"Hard on the horses," commented Shawn.

"Hard on our men, should the horses reach us," returned Brother David. He hefted the sword Hugh had given him. "Hard on the Scottish people and our country."

The evening mist rose higher, dancing over the field. Shawn startled at the sudden appearance of men in jeans among the tunics and trews. A bobby's helmet bobbed among the bassinets. He blinked, and they were gone. A trick of the evening light. A trick of a worn and exhausted mind, pent up with nervousness and anticipation over a coming battle he was in no way qualified to be fighting.

"*Shawn!*"

He spun. Beside him, Allene jumped, staring at him in concern.

He searched the faces, his eyes hard. He gripped his sword hilt.

Apart from Allene, no one paid him any heed.
No one had called his name.

* * *

Sunset found Niall atop a ridge, looking north across fields and hills, to Stirling Castle. Even from this distance, it inspired awe on its towering rock. It was good to see it standing strong, still.

The smell of campfires reached out beckoning hands. In Amy's time, he'd seen only electric lights. He ran, cantering and sliding down the hill. His faith, his hope, his persistence had been rewarded!

Sheep ambled out of his way, as he raced toward his own people, huddled even now around their campfires, toward Allene! The aroma of wood smoke grew heavier. Skirting another stand of trees, he splashed through a stream. His heart picked up speed. It had to be the Bannock Burn, on the southern edge of the battlefield. He bolted across a dirt road, the ground hard-packed under his leather-clad feet, and pushed through a hedgerow. A sharp escarpment rose before him. Trees sprang from its crown.

A string of campfires glowed at the top. They flickered far back into the woods. He could smell turnips cooking. Hope erupted! He scrambled up the hill, into a swarm of men and tents.

His heart thudded with excitement. He'd walked right back in time without feeling a thing! "Just like Aaron's stories," he breathed. Two bulky men in gambesons and trews slammed weapons against one another in practice. Sweat streamed down ruddy faces. Horses whinnied. He reached for his crucifix to thank God, touching bare throat. "Thank you," he whispered, all the same.

And out loud, he shouted, "Shawn!" He pushed through the crowd, shouting Shawn's name. But would he find him, or had Shawn simultaneously disappeared back into his own time? Was he, even now, wandering an empty field on midsummer's eve in the twenty-first century? He reached the first campfire, breathing a little harder. "Where is Hugh Campbell?" he demanded in Gaelic. And Lord Darnley, he added silently to himself. He must stop Darnley's treachery.

"Hold on there, pardner," the man in the gambeson answered. "Where's the fire? What are you sayin'?"

Niall stared.

These were not Highlanders. They were not even Scotsmen.

They spoke the same peculiar English as the orchestral musicians. His eyes opened wide with understanding. *These were reenactors.*

The full weight of the word settled on him.

From their rounded metal helmets past their tunics and plaids, to their leather boots laced to their knees, they were, every inch, medieval Scotsmen. He drew a breath, trying to settle his nerves, and asked, in English, "Where's Clan MacDonald?" Jim had raved about their accuracy. Perhaps there would be a unit where Hugh and the Laird had been in 1314. The man pointed. There, under a tree. A man sat, his back against the rough bark. Fiery shadows flickered over his harp.

Niall moved to the group, studying their faces. There was no Hugh, no Laird, no Owen or Angus or Adam or anyone he knew. He dropped to the ground against a tree, defeated, while the man continued playing the small harp. Niall had played the same song for the concert, though it sounded different under this man's touch.

The music washed over him. *Scotland the Brave.* But bravery wasn't everything. He had the knowledge which could turn the tide for those brave men, and he was trapped here, on the wrong side of an uncontrollable causeway between times. He leaned his head against the tree, staring up into leaves blackened with the dying of the sun. So many brave men had gone before him, fought and died; so many would march to their deaths on the morrow. And he couldn't use what he knew to save them. He'd done everything in his power and failed. He was out of ideas. There was nothing left even to try, despite all his prayers.

God had abandoned him.

The harp played, men sang, and he sank, bit by bit, into the gray, grizzled arms of the same Hopelessness that had met him, standing beside the messengers, when they'd told MacDonald of his son's death, when his mother wept for his brothers and father, when Gilbert lay ill.

Those times were tapestries woven from the same skeins. Messengers, women keening, pipes skirling. And the thing that kept a small flame burning through the dark nights of grief: each time, he'd comforted his people, and himself, with music.

The man finished playing.

Niall sat up, leaned forward. "May I?" he asked.

It was all that was left.

* * *

As the sharp fingers of the western hills pulled down the last coral streaks of sun, campfires began to glow, up and down the length of the ridge.

Shawn and Allene stood on the isolated fringe of the camp on Coxet Hill. Activity buzzed like night insects behind them, old toothless women and butchers and coopers, children, town folk of every variety, girls cooking on their campfires, mothers settling children for the night. "There must be hundreds," he said in amazement.

"A thousand or more." Allene turned, dismissing them. "They'll watch the battle from here."

"It's getting late," Shawn said. It was a poor substitute for all he needed to say.

"Yes, I must be off with the women." But she lingered, holding Shawn's hand. Together, they stared at the eastern sky, a rich, velvety blue. Now was the time to tell her. But she'd never believe him. Finally, he squeezed her shoulder and turned to face her. She reached up and kissed his cheek. His pulse pounded; he thought of Amy and his journey with Allene, and touched the side of her face.

"I'm sorry for everything," he said.

"'Twas not you, Niall," she answered. "I have always loved you, and I love you still. God be with you on the morrow." She threw her arms, suddenly, around him, and kissed him full on the mouth.

His eyes opened wide. His pulse raced, and every nerve stood on exuberant end. Caroline and Celine and Amy and every other woman swirled in his mind, and he wanted them all! He leaned in, kissed her back, but...he'd left a message for Amy. He'd meant it. He pushed Allene gently away, his face flushed, and his breath still coming deeply. He shook his head, said, "Whew!" and laughed in pleasure, surprise, and shock; not the least was his shock at himself for stopping her.

Her face fell.

"I know it's a surprise," he said. "You have no idea! We have things to talk about when this is over." He pushed away thoughts of how it might end. He'd deal with that when it happened. He pulled her close, held her tightly, his hand pressed in her hair, and said, "I'll do everything I can for you. And you'll pray and do what you can for the women there. And in case any Sassenach get through, you'll have shown them a few tricks with their knives, right?" He pushed a tendril of auburn hair from her face.

She laughed; then her lip trembled. She clung to him, shaking. "'Tis not funny, Niall!" He held her tight. He swallowed hard, wondering whether he'd die slowly or quickly.

He looked over the small band of Scots. The English would outnumber them severely. If only he could fool the entire English army the way he fooled so many others when it suited his purpose.

An idea sprang on him, crouched on his shoulder, whispered in his ear. It was ridiculous! But it touched the edges of his mind, pulled at him relentlessly, till he looked at it more closely. It would be in the midst of battle. How clearly did men think in the heat and dust and confusion?

It might work.

"Allene," he said abruptly. "You need to do something." He told her, his voice rising in excitement.

"'Tis crazy," Allene said. "You were ever over-confident."

He smiled. Maybe he and Niall weren't so different after all. "Would there be anything to lose at that point?"

"No," she admitted.

"Then do it. If anyone can convince them, you can."

As the eastern sky folded over them, chasing the last resisting streaks of sunset into the west, he pushed her away, and turned her, with a kiss on top of her head, toward Coxet Hill.

* * *

The man handed him the harp, a small one, like Niall's own. Niall touched the strings, and let the comfort flow into the night. He pushed lyrics over the swell in his throat. Something in the air echoed the music back strangely to him, creating harmonies not of his own making. He sang till the grizzled arms of despair loosened their grip; till an ember of hope reignited. He sang to those who could appreciate the authenticity of his music and his accent, and questioned him endlessly on his sources.

"An' do any of you know a Shawn?" Niall finally asked them, when he'd tired of their questions. "Shawn Kleiner? I must find him."

One of the men looked harder, and said, "Aren't you...?"

"No," Niall said. "But I expect him here."

Shawn's name was repeated around the campfire, and spread to the nearby camps, up and down the ridge: *Shawn, shawn, shawn*, like a whispered breeze ruffling the trees. But no one had seen Shawn.

Finally, Niall wrapped himself in his tartan, and fell asleep, hoping to wake to Hugh's men.

* * *

Shawn and Brother David threaded among fires, tents, and banners. Shawn's thoughts and emotions churned. He didn't want to think about any of them, especially the big one: could he change history? Because he didn't like the ending he thought he remembered.

From under a tree, Hugh's men beckoned. "Niall, Brother David, sing for us!" A cheer went up. Shawn grinned, pulled down the harp, and they sang and played one last time for the men. There were now hundreds more, all attached in some way to the men of Hugh's camp, and they still poured in, from north and west. The music echoed here, in a way it hadn't back in the hills, as if someone sang, just out of sync, with them. He wondered if someone was playing for another clan farther along. The men seemed not to notice. But then, thought Shawn, they weren't musicians.

As he played, a man rode a pony up and down the ridge. The rider stopped and raised his hand to Hugh, who, with all his men, rose, dropped to one knee and lowered his head.

A hush fell over the camp. Shawn saw the thin ring of gold circling the man's head, around fiery auburn hair. His fingers slowed and stilled on the strings.

"'Tis the man who will save Scotland," whispered Brother David. A cold chill crawled down Shawn's spine. He knew this man's future. He, too, fell to his knee. He lifted his gaze to meet the king's. He saw a face with fifteen years of age over his own, and a hundred years of wisdom, gleaned from hard living and the care of a battered nation.

But it was the eyes that jumped out at Shawn. He knew them. They were the eyes of his kindred spirit: the twelve year old Shawn, when he was told *You can't.* They were eyes that laughed in the face of the word *impossible* and announced, firmly, "I will."

Everything in Shawn reeled against the thought of how this man with the straight spine and fiery eyes would die tomorrow. He breathed a silent prayer, *They say You can do anything. Will You save him? Will You save us?*

"I hear something in your music," Robert said. His voice was deep and sure. Shawn looked all around the men, but it was he to whom Bruce spoke. "It is music that sees the future. Play for me."

"Sire." Shawn swallowed, bowed his head, closed his eyes, and touched the strings. He began one of the concert pieces.

> *Free from tyrant's dark control*
> *Free as waves of ocean roll*
> *Free as thoughts of minstrel's soul,*
> *Still roam the sons of Scotia.*
> *Down each green-wood skirted vale,*
> *Guardian spirits lingering, hail*

Hugh's men nodded, their faces shadowed in the dancing flames of the night, becoming serious with thoughts of home and the coming battle. Leaves rustled in the breeze. All around hung the heavy scent of burning twigs and peat. Fire glinted soft burnished glows off swords and helmets. Shawn fiercely wanted these men to live, forever, as they lived here, tonight. His heart and throat ached, knowing history said they would die tomorrow! All of them. He sang the second verse, his fingers strong on the chords.

> *Many a minstrel's melting tale*
> *As told of ancient Scotia.*

Wake, my hillharp! Wildly wake!
Sound by lee and lonely lake,
Never shall this heart forsake,
The bonnie wilds of Scotia!

He ran his fingers up a chord, and finished, his head bowed, falling in love with the country and vowing to save it, no matter what history said.

"Beautiful," said Robert. "A finer tribute to my brave men I've never heard. Give us another."

Shawn nodded, smiled to himself at the irony, and started his father's favorite, a tribute and lament to Bruce himself. His father had changed the words to reflect a battle won. It was unthinkable to sing any others, now. These men would fight bravely, and if he couldn't change history, at least they would die with hope roaring like forest fires in their hearts.

O King of Scots
The like we've never seen
That raised his people far and wide,
And stood against the English might,
And sent them fleeing home.

Men nodded, grunting their agreement.

The English came in storming droves,
And took our land and took our lives
But we are strong and we will rise.

As he returned to the chorus, men joined, a solid wall of confidence. Chills shot up Shawn's arms. Was he feeding them lies, or giving them the morale that would change their futures? It didn't matter. He sang with the rest, louder and stronger, and heard the words taken up at the next campfire, rich with tenors and basses.

And stood against the English might,
And sent them fleeing home.

And louder still, from more campfires, the treble voices of boys who should be in school, the creaky voices of men who should be fishing at their cabins, and the forceful voices of Hugh and dozens of powerful men who would ride their garrons or carry mighty lances in tight schiltrons tomorrow, against charging warhorses:

And stood against the English might,
And sent them fleeing home.

The song ended. Voices stilled, till only the chitter of insects remained, humming in the night. It was like the moment when Conrad stood frozen, arms suspended in midair; the moment when the orchestra finished, but the last notes reverberated invisibly, and no one was yet willing to break the magic. Hope crackled all around them.

The Bruce raised his head. "A man who sees the future, as I thought." He spoke gravely, softly. Then he raised his voice and shouted for all the army to hear: "We will indeed send them fleeing home." A mighty roar rose from the men, and spread to neighboring campfires.

"We'll send them fleeing home!" echoed up and down the ridge.

Robert the Bruce looked along the furlongs of his army, nodding in satisfaction. "I thank thee, Niall Campbell." He slid a ring from his finger. The gold and garnet glittered in the dancing flames: a garnet, like he'd taken from Amy. Bruce tossed it to Shawn. Shawn bowed deeply in thanks. When the king had gone, he slid it onto his own finger, stunned.

And somewhere in the camp, he heard a harp still playing.

* * *

With quiet falling, Shawn lay down, wrapped in his cloak. He was powerfully aware of the bog to the east, where he would fight and die. Unless his plan succeeded. Unless history could be changed.

Gentle night sounds drifted over him, a restless snort from a horse, the crackle of a fire, the shuffling of men, and, he swore, the sound of his name. He sat up and listened and knew he heard it, whispers of *Shawn, Shawn...Shawn?*

A chill shot down his spine.

Shawn Kleiner—the faintest whisper on the breeze, rustling in the leaves above. His breathing came hard. Fires flickered blood-red shadows over sleeping men.

The sounds drifted away, like a balloon floating over a hill. Though he listened for some time, they did not come again. He pulled his cloak tightly around him, the hair on his arms standing straight, and tried to sleep.

* * *

Niall woke early. Birds trilled and chirped in the gray pre-dawn. He knew instantly this was no real battle. Not a man stirred. Not a man prayed. For all they prided themselves on authenticity, they couldn't duplicate the fear and adrenaline that prodded men early on the morning of battle. Indeed, they only came awake, with good-natured grumbling at the early hour, long after the first red rays of dawn stretched dainty fingers across the daisy-covered field that would see battle, after he'd been praying on his knees for half an hour.

Disappointment consumed him. He'd hoped it would happen, as it had before, on its own, while he slept. He felt foolish, a boy believing in fairy knowes. What was he to look for here? How was he to tell a Highland soldier of the fourteenth century from a reenactor of the twenty-first?

The speech, he reminded himself. Their speech would be different. He wandered through thick knots of men in tunics, trews, hose, gambesons. He studied the men examining one another's weapons.

"Found this Shawn you're lookin' for?" asked a burly, bearded man in a flowing cloak. He handed Niall bread and a water skin. These men might lack the sense of impending battle that would make their playacting real, but Niall felt a sense of coming home, in the humble meal. "I haven't," he said. "Might ye know where the Bruce is, or Sir Keith?"

"The commander of the cavalry?"

"Aye, tha's the one," Niall said.

"The Bruce, you'd most likely find him on the right flank." The man pointed south. "Now, Sir Keith, I think the poor man was mismanaged all along, and you'll find his cavalry unit down south too, where they aren't as helpful as they coulda been. But we go with what history gives us, don't we?"

Niall smiled. "We'll see, tha' we will."

Chapter Twenty-One

Stirling, Scotland

The first sight of the English would inspire dread in the bravest troops in Christendom, it was later said. They covered the land like locusts, tens of thousands. Sunlight glinted off helmets, armors, spears. White banners, too many to count, snapped over them. Carnival-colored silken pennants flapped in the summer breeze. The earth shook under their heavy warhorses. Their columns stretched for twenty miles.

The Scots gathered, five thousand, for Mass, on the morning of the battle. They formed their lines with the trees and Stirling Castle behind them, facing the narrow stretch of the Bannock Burn over which the English must flow. The Bruce walked among them, marked as separate only by the thin band of gold circling his auburn hair and the suffering of leadership stamped on his face. "We are hopelessly outnumbered!" His voice rang like a clarion. "Any man who wishes to turn now and go to the aid and protection of his family may do so without consequence! 'Twill be held against no man, should he choose to walk away now!"

His voice carried clear and far.

The men heard.

The men held their ground.

* * *

The priests came before the Highlanders and lowlanders. The Scots fell to their knees as one, imploring Heaven for assistance and strength. From Coxet Hill, they peered down, eager and fearful, to see the production.

Edward of England, across the battlefield, watched the Scots fall, five thousand as a man, to their knees, and cried out, booming his line across the field: "They crave mercy!"

Edward's commanders, more experienced and less arrogant, saw what he did not: the Scots were preparing to attack. "It is of heaven, and not your highness," replied Sir deUmfraville, "for on that field they will be victorious or die."

"So be it, then!" Edward raised his mail-clad arm, tall and strong against the blue summer sky. Trumpets shot up in a straight row. Banners fluttered down from their lengths. Their sound rose, clear and golden across the battlefield, summoning England's chivalry to war. The English, surprised at the early hour, scrambled awake, bleary-eyed after a miserable night attempting to sleep in the soggy carse, and scurried for their armor.

Across the field, the blind old Abbot of Inchaffray, with bare feet and head, shuffled along the ranks of kneeling Scots, crucifix in hand. The bard from Clan Campbell held his hand, confessed his sins, and received absolution, breathing deeply of long-sought peace.

Edward of England paused his troops, staring across at the small band of Scots under the trees. His people thought him less a man than his father, did they? Today would change that.

His knights waited, brilliantly draped warhorses snorting and pawing, men in their matching liveries equally restless, hungry for blood and land. They had marched a long way in the summer heat over many days. But they were eager. Barons and earls clamored to get at the few Scots, to win easy glory and perhaps a fiefdom.

The Scottish skirmish line pulled back into the trees. The English clambered across the stream, leading their men into the narrow space of the boggy carse, between the Pelstream and the Bannock Burns, and up the rise.

One solitary figure remained, facing the might of England. He rode a pony, his back straight, with only the lightest armor, in full view of the English troops. Sunlight flashed off his copper hair. An arrow might fell him at any moment. His open defiance of fear and the Sassenach gave his men courage.

"It's the Bruce," went up the whispers of the Scots at the front.

* * *

The police gathered on the edges of the re-enactment. Crowds of tourists and locals surrounded them in shorts, visors, sunglasses, all the trappings of a summer day. Some soldiers laughed and joked, as Bruce trotted his palfrey before them. Others stood in character, spears stiffly at attention, faces set and hard. Amy, Dana, Rob, Celine, Aaron, and Conrad stood nearby, a tense contrast to the carnival mood. Children dashed by, swinging wooden swords. Pennants fluttered from tents selling crafts and food. Behind them rose the statue of King Edward II of England, astride his warhorse, on the spot he was said to have killed the last Scot, a looming, black silhouette against the blue summer sky. Amy eyed it, her stomach in knots.   Shawn and Niall were out there somewhere, sometime.

"We're looking for a man in a tunic and cloak." The police sergeant spoke dryly. He pursed his lips, surveying hundreds of men in tunics and cloaks, waiting for battle. To the south, Sir Keith's cavalry mounted their ponies. Across the field, English trumpets cried to the heavens.

"You have his picture," Conrad snapped.

"Look for clan MacDonald," Amy said. "That's where he'd go."

"Excuse me!" A heavy woman pushed by in a bright flowered dress, clutching a cardboard tray of fish and chips. Two boys with black curls scampered in her wake, lugging a picnic basket and a large blanket.

"Why MacDonald?" Conrad asked irritably.

"We haven't much time before it starts," said the sergeant to his men. "Everyone knows what Shawn Kleiner looks like. Spread out." They dispersed, the sergeant watching them.

Amy spotted him, from a great distance, only seconds before the production was to begin. He stood shoulder to shoulder with dozens of similarly dressed men, lined up and jaws set, looking for all the world as if they were marching into real battle.

"There! There!" She grabbed Conrad's arm, pointing.

"What's he *doing*?" Dana rose on her toes, straining to see.

"What the hell possessed him to join a re-enactment?" Conrad snarled. The sergeant shouted. Police snaked through the crowd toward Shawn.

Amy and Dana shouted and waved at him, bearded now, in his tunic and long cloak, his eyes locked on the man riding before the troops. Gold circled the man's head, holding down long, fiery hair. He seemed battered for forty years, a man accustomed to rough living. Amy began to push through the spectators, edging toward Shawn—or was it Niall? Suddenly, from the English side, a knight broke ranks.

* * *

Shawn strained to see, clutching his knife and sword. Bruce's crown flashed in the sun. Across the field, a knight rose in his stirrups, kicked his mighty warhorse, lowered his lance, and charged like dark thunder.

Bruce turned, almost casually, toward the powerful destrier. Behind him, his troops drew in breath. Tension snaked through the air like summer lightning. He held steady, making no move to flee, as the rider barreled closer. At the last moment, he twitched his bridle. The pony skipped nimbly to one side. Bruce rose in his stirrups. His ax arced up and smashed back down on the man's head. The blade drove through the metal helmet, cleaving the unfortunate knight's head in two.

A mighty roar thundered up and down the Scottish ranks. The ground shook with the stamping of feet. Shawn's ears and insides shook with the sound of it, and he realized a mighty bellow was erupting from deep in his own body.

* * *

The hapless English knight, Henry de Bohun, fell to the ground almost directly before Niall. One of Bruce's generals burst from the trees, remonstrating, "Bethink you, sire! The fate of all Scotland rests upon you!"

"I haif broken the haft of my guid battle-ax," declared Bruce, inspecting the damaged weapon, and expressing his only regret.

The Scots, audience and soldiers, cheered at his answer, and screamed battle cries, and Niall shouted with the rest, raising his fist and shaking it at the English. The roar echoed in his ears. He stared at the men around him, seeing their mouths closed, their eyes fixed like steel on the battlefield. The roaring sounded all around him. He closed his eyes, and opened them again. He heard his name shouted, and knew not whether it was Allene or Amy.

* * *

English trumpets screamed through the blood. Hairs rose on Shawn's arms. Sweat trickled down his chest and back, inside his padded gambeson. England's pennants snapped in the breeze, among the thousands gathered across the carse. His leg wept in pain from the wolf's claws. Back home, he'd be recuperating. Here, every man was needed. Old men with sunken cheeks and long gray beards, and fresh-faced pubescent boys, jaws firm, stood among the strong men of Robert's army.

His heart raced. He glanced back at Coxet Hill. His pulse pounded in his throat. He didn't want to be recuperating. The stitches would hold. They had to! His damp hand slipped on his sword. He wanted to be here, with these men and boys, between the English and Allene. *Thrust, parry.* He squinted against the sun, at the troops facing him, calculating how many he could kill before they felled him. *Feint.* He'd be grateful for three or four. The sun flashed in his eyes, bouncing off armor. The English charged. *Jab.* His heart pulsed furiously in his throat. He felt sick. He wanted to run. He squared his own jaw, awaiting orders.

The English sped, horses frothing and snorting in the summer heat, to the slaughter. Trumpets screamed; war drums pounded. The earth shook as huge Flemish chargers pounded toward him, with faceless visored riders gripping their backs. He braced his legs against the small earthquake, standing firm. Lances dropped, aimed at him. His legs screamed to run; he held fast, breathing hard, grateful now for Bruce's murder holes and caltrops.

They felled the magnificent, deadly beasts, one after another piercing hooves on caltrops. Proud war horses stumbled into the camouflaged spike-laced pits, or tumbled over horses felled before them. They crashed to their knees, with trumpets still screaming and war drums still pounding, and knights in heavy armor toppled helplessly from their backs, slapping at long tabards that tripped them as they clambered to their feet. Wounded horses screamed, reared, bolted, collapsed. Confusion spread among the English.

They charged again, and found that Wallace's immovable schiltrons had become aggressive, mobile fighting units. They advanced, prickly, impenetrable circles of spears allowing no entrance; slow and steady, unstoppable and deadly, grinding down England's nobility. Dust rose, an eerie haze around skewered stallions and unhorsed knights, from which rose cries of men and screams of horses.

Shawn surged with the Scots, slashing and hacking at downed knights. And the schiltrons marched on, step by bloody step. The English hurled lances and swords, furious and futile. The schiltrons marched on, step by heartless step, a slow moving glacier, grinding everything in their paths.

* * *

When the Scots surged toward the English, two men still chatting about last week's rugby match as they ran, Niall surged with them. He fought against the crowd to reach Robert Keith's standard. Hugh would have added his Highland ponies to Keith's cavalry.

It's not real, he reminded himself. A knight swung a sword at him. He blocked it, clanging and sliding his blade along it till he forced both points into the ground. From inside the visor came heavy, raspy breathing. Niall's biceps strained to keep the man's sword down, as he searched the chaos for Keith's pennant.

"Bloody Scots!" came from inside the helmet, muffled and harsh. "Die, Highland dog!" He yanked his sword from under Niall's, slashing at his knees. Niall leapt. The knight arched forward, a spear shooting through his side. The smell of hot blood washed over Niall. His heart raced with hope. He dodged and bolted.

"Where you going?" shouted a man in an authentic-looking tunic.

Niall recognized the drawl as *American*. He thought painfully of Amy. Another man erupted in front of him, barking, "Get back to your unit!" He had no idea if the wicked-looking dirk in the man's hand was authentically sharpened, or dulled for the reenactors' safety. He shoved his way south, breaking into a run. A schiltron bore down on him, the men scruffy and unbathed. Red stains flowed from their spears. They moved like they meant it.

Elated, he dodged and sprinted for Keith. He recognized his arms on the back of a tabard, and lunged from behind, grabbing the horse's reins. The great beast turned its head, snorting in his face. "Keith! Robert Keith! Stop the archers!" Niall spun to face the great cavalry leader. The horse whinnied in his ear. "Stop Edward's archers!"

Keith yanked his reins and shoved his visor up, revealing small round *glasses*. "What the hell are you doing?" he shouted down. "We don't stop the archers! That's why we lost!" He slapped his visor down and wheeled his horse round.

Niall backed up two quick steps, despair gripping him. He nearly tripped on a Scot, lying on the battlefield moaning in pain. He stared, shaken. He spun and sprinted for the edge of the field, more scared of interfering in a fake battle than he'd ever been of being killed in a real one.

Suddenly, a deep voice called his name. Conrad? Had Amy told them his real name? He scanned a sea of faces, his sword limp in his hand. His heart nearly stopped, then leapt in joy. Iohn burst from the woods, running.

* * *

Across the field, Amy saw him. Saw *them!* Shawn's eyes met hers, and she knew: this was Shawn, the real Shawn, neither the man she'd known for years, nor the man she'd known for the past week. Niall, in tunic and trews, ran toward him, shouting.

"It's started," the police sergeant snapped. He grabbed Amy's arm as she made to run toward Shawn. She yanked once. "You canna run ou' there!" the man said. "He'll be there still when it's over. Though what the devil he's doin' is beyond me!"

Amy bit her lip. She turned to Conrad. "We have to get him. Now!"

"He'll be there afterward," Dana said. The sun glinted off copper strands of her spiky hair.

Conrad patted her arm. "She's right, Amy. He'll still be there. But what the bloody hell is he up to? And what is *that?*" He cocked his head, listening.

"Is someone *singing*?" asked the sergeant. "Why the devil is someone singing?" He squinted, shading his eyes with one hand. "Summat funny's goin' on here." He waved for his men, circling the field, and pointed to Shawn, driving a sword through a man in a long tabard.

Amy's heart pounded. Blood poured down the man's back, surging around the sword. Her skin became clammy with sweat. "How do they make it look so real? Did he just kill a man?"

The sergeant roared for his men. "Get him off that field! What the devil is goin' on?"

* * *

Iohn was a hundred yards away. Surely, Niall thought, he was mistaken again. It wasn't Iohn's brown woolen cloak, after all, but a scarlet one, lifting behind him as he ran. Niall stepped closer. A horse whinnied. Was it a trained reenactor or a real one? A lance pierced its side. It reared, hooves clawing madly at the air and teeth bared in pain. Its knight rolled off in a clatter of metal, thumping on the ground and descended on by angry Scots.

"Niall!" Iohn's voice rang out again. Niall turned back to Iohn, raising a hand. But Iohn was looking beyond him. Niall turned. He gasped. He stared into his own face! He made a weak sign of the cross. It could only be Shawn.

But it wasn't the lying, gambling, womanizing Shawn Niall had come to know; the Shawn who smirked and laughed and left a woman with child, who spit life in the face and took nothing seriously. This man's jaw was set, his eyes fiercely scanning the fight around him. His tunic hung askew. Sweat streaked his dirt-stained face. Blood caked one leg; a long and ugly wound showed through the gaps in a ragged bandage. His feet locked in combat stance. He lifted a sword menacingly toward an English soldier.

Then Niall and Shawn both heard it. Over the clash of metal, the cries of wounded men, the shouts of commanders, rose a beautiful baritone voice in the words of his and Iohn's greeting. *The Laird's own bard to war is gone!* Those near him turned. Shawn slashed at the soldier, jab, thrust, and a lucky kill. Shawn raised his head, lifted a hand in greeting, and strode forward.

It hit Niall hard. "*NO!*" he roared.

His harp and sword at hand!

Niall charged. He dropped his body low, yanking a sword from the fallen knight as he ran. The knight clung to it, but Niall was faster, stronger.

To the fields of death he goes.

And he had seen the future.

He knew what would happen: he'd heard it in a song. The English near Iohn would gather. Advance on Shawn. Niall's leather boots tore up the field, speeding toward his best friend and mortal enemy. His face twisted in fury at the betrayal. Iohn started toward Shawn. His sword rose.

"No!" Niall bellowed. He'd promised Amy! He'd promised to send Shawn back.

Iohn spun; the cloak—the cloak immortalized in song as crimson —swirled out around him, a shimmering aurora borealis, hanging for a moment in time. His eyes met Niall's.

Niall ran, screaming, "Get back, Shawn! He's betraying us!"

Iohn stared from Niall to Shawn. The song dropped from his lips; lips that now formed a silent *no.* He shook his head in disbelief. He tried to lift the sword, but shock slowed him.

Niall skewered him.

Blood sprayed Niall's white shirt, warming his skin. Its scent filled his nostrils. Their eyes held, Iohn's in mortal shock, Niall's in grief. "Why?" Niall whispered, his voice hoarse. "You were my friend."

Iohn's mouth moved, but no words came out. Shawn skidded to a stop beside them, breathing hard. Iohn gripped his side. Blood spurted from his mouth.

"What the hell is going on?" Shawn demanded.

"I'm sorry, my friend," Niall whispered. He made the sign of the cross on the dying man's forehead, and yanked his sword. The tug of Iohn's body against his blade, before it suddenly fell and crumpled to the ground, sickened him. Tears stung his eyes. He clenched his jaw and barked at Shawn. "Get Hugh!"

"Aye!" Shawn sped, an arrow from a bow.

Niall dropped to his knee beside Iohn on the ground, cradling his head. "Why?" he whispered again. "I loved you like a brother."

Iohn tried, but no words came out. Another trickle of blood crawled from his mouth like an evil worm. His face turned chalky. Niall brushed at his eyes. Iohn stared at the sky. Niall yanked the crimson cloak over his face, and swiped the back of his wrist under his nose. Steel clashed all around him. Horses whinnied; men screamed.

One of the tough Highland ponies burst through the haze of battle, with Hugh gripping its flanks. Niall scrambled to his feet, waving his arms, yelling. Hugh threw himself off the pony, knocking Niall to the ground.

Niall's heart thundered. Not Hugh, too! He rolled, ready for action, as Hugh dispatched the English soldier behind him. Niall's pulse raced.

"How the devil did ye get afore me, lad!" Hugh roared. "You were behind me!" He turned, saw Shawn sliding off a pony, and spun back to Niall, gaping.

"Later," Niall snapped.

Hugh crossed himself, muttering, "Mary, Joseph, and Jesus!" He looked from one to the other, and stepped back.

Niall grabbed his arm, pointing wildly toward the carse's northern edge. "Archers!" Already, they were marching, wraiths in the haze, in long files toward the northern ridge. Their longbows rose, slender and deadly, above their heads.

"How dae...?"

"They'll destroy our schiltrons. Stop them!"

Hugh looked again at Shawn. "Do it," Shawn said. "That's Niall."

"Who are...?"

Niall yanked Hugh's arm roughly. "Now! Send for your cavalry and Keith's, ere Scotland is lost!"

Hugh shook himself, nodded, and leapt back on the hardy pony. He dug his heels in, screaming, "Hiya!" The frothing animal snorted and bolted, kicking up dirt.

Dust and cries swirled around Shawn and Niall. They stared at each other.

Niall laughed, suddenly, and clasped Shawn's hand, pulling him into a hug, slapping his back.

"Niall Campbell, I presume," Shawn said. A wide grin spread across his face. "I've heard about you." A horse draped in blue and white charged past them. The first row of archers was in place.

"Aye." Niall grinned, too. Before he could say more, an arrow whined. Shawn grabbed for Niall, the two of them rolling for shelter behind a fallen horse. The animal's chest heaved in sharp strokes under its green and gold trappings; foam flecked its side, its eyes rolled.

Niall lifted his head carefully over the animal's side. North of the carse, hot noon sun glinted off the archers' helmets. The second row filed in behind the first.

Shawn raised his head, too. "Men of Galloway, men of Inverness, men of the Highlands!" Edward Bruce roared above the fray from under his banner. "For your families, for your country, go now!" The English cavalry, those who had escaped the murder holes and caltrops, thundered across the field in a swirl of colorful trappings, horses decked in greens, reds, blues, and golds. Keith's cavalry pranced at the southern edge of the fray, straining for action. They didn't stand a chance against the larger warhorses.

The third row of bowmen locked in position. "Like a bloody high school choir!" Shawn muttered. The first row reached into their quivers, a deadly ballet.

Keith's arm rose. His cavalry bolted toward certain death under England's chargers. Hugh blazed through the chaos. His pony leaped a dead horse, dodged a knight's sword, Hugh slashing, hacking and bellowing. Robert turned, ghostly gray atop a ghostly pony in the thick of the battle. Bruce and Hugh skidded up next to each other, shouted for Keith, and within moments, the cavalry changed direction, charging north.

"The archers!" Shawn yelled. The first volley flew, a hailstorm of arrows into the schiltron. Men fell.

"Adam!" Niall shouted. Adam stumbled to his knee, pierced. His pike fell. Keith and Hugh charged from the south, kicking more dust into the chaos. The cavalry swarmed his and Niall's shelter, shaggy ponies, tartans whipping in the wild ride, wide eyes, muscled men, bloodied wounds, set jaws, long hair flying behind, all surrounded them, a nightmare kaleidoscope, and disappeared. They coughed on the dust, ducking low behind the dead horse and covering their heads. And when they looked again, the second row of archers had loosed its hailstorm.

Several archers saw the cavalry charge. They pointed, grabbed for weapons as the ponies stormed the ridge. Swords flashed for a murderous minute, two minutes, three, and Edward's deadly archers were no more.

Niall fell back, panting, shielded for the moment by the fallen horse. He'd done it! History said the archers destroyed the schiltrons.

But there was no time to grieve Adam or rejoice for Scotland. Battle swept over them; a trio of English foot soldiers lunged. Niall and Shawn leapt up, back to back, hemmed by the dead horse and Iohn's crimson-shrouded corpse. Exhausted from hours of battle, Shawn swung weakly, barely parrying the attack. His opponent's hair hung in dark, sweat-soaked spirals from beneath his helmet. His mouth twisted in effort, backing Shawn up. And suddenly, the enemy was down on the blood-stained bog, Niall's sword flashing in and out. Behind them lay Niall's two opponents. Shawn gaped. "I see why they wanted you...me... to train the men."

A corner of Niall's mouth quirked up. "Aye," he said. "Now we must get ye haeme."

Shawn snorted, scanning a mile of medieval blood and warriors. "How?" The bristling pikes of a schiltron unhorsed a knight. The animal reared, pawing against green trappings and whinnying. Men descended on the fallen knight, hacking, stabbing.

Trumpets screamed. In the east, a banner bearing Edward's three gold lions lurched from the field. A phalanx of England's nobility galloped away under it.

Shawn and Niall stared at each other in amazement as the English, thousands strong against the Scots, paused in mid-charge, milled uncertainly, and turned suddenly in a vicious tide running, scrambling, galloping away, in full retreat. Some pointed west, mouths open.

Shawn turned to see what inspired such dread. Scots burst from Coxet Hill, another thousand, waving banners and weapons and loosing skirling cries into the chaos.

Shawn broke into a grin, grabbing Niall's arm, pointing, shouting. "She did it! She did it!" He pumped a fist at the charging town folk, shouting "Hoo-ah!" Schiltrons began trotting in formation, chasing the retreating knights.

Niall laughed, shouting to the skies before looking closer.

And he and Shawn stared again at each other, and back at the sight: not only the entire Scots army, not only the thousand 'wee folk' with pitchforks and spades from Coxet Hill, but hundreds of reenactors had appeared before the English, and thousands of twenty-first century spectators in their bizarre clothes, roaring and cheering, behind them.

It was a sight that would inspire dread in the bravest troops in Christendom.

They swarmed Niall and Shawn, the fresh clean trappings on the reenactors' horses charging alongside battle-weary beasts that had died seven hundred years ago, women in bug-eyed sunglasses, men in flowered shirts chatting on cell phones, a knight giving them a fleeting panicked glance and kicking his mount into swift retreat.

Niall searched the melee. "There are your people!" He pointed. Scottish bobbies shoved toward them, through a multitude of real and false Scottish warriors. "Go!" Niall shouted.

Shawn leapt over the dead horse, yanking at the ring on his finger. It would be Amy's. As he ran, he saw a knight, one of the few remaining on horseback, charging across the bog. He turned to see what brave warrior the knight intended to fell. His eyes lit on a child, a child from Coxet Hill, strayed from safety.

He looked back, in disbelief: yes, the knight was charging a child! Then he saw Amy, thirty feet away. Their eyes met. His heart lifted. He could tell her! He could show her! The bobbies surged behind her, pointing, shouting his name. And time suspended as he saw his chance to run toward her, to break through to his own time. To show Amy and the world he had become a better man.

His head swung in slow motion. The knight closed in on the child, fair-skinned, red-haired, clutching a grubby blanket. Tears made white streaks down the child's dirty face.

"Go to your people!" Niall yelled. His eyes, too, locked on the child. He rose, but the knight was too close. Niall couldn't reach the child on time.

Shawn threw the ring to Amy, screaming, "Get your ring back! I'll be right there!" He threw himself, sword and shield raised, between the thundering stallion and the child. His sword pierced the horse's chest as it rolled over him. The knight's sword flashed down. Shawn saw Niall, with the precious split moment's respite, scoop the child off its feet and run.

* * *

"There they are! Both of them!" Amy screamed to the police. "Shawn!"

The reenactors swirled around them, blocking her view. A child cried. She saw him, scared and alone in the middle of the field, his hair bright red, his face dirty, clutching a filthy blanket, surrounded on all sides by reenactors. A horse veered toward him, surely going to rescue him. Shawn burst through the warriors, running toward the child.

The police pointed and ran. Amy ran. The reenactors shouted, waved them off. Shawn yelled—she couldn't make out his words—and threw something. Her reflexes kicked in and she caught it instinctively. The horse charged. Spectators screamed. Amy threw her hands up over her face. The horse skidded to a halt in billows of dust, whinnying. Hot gusts of horse breath snorted into her face. The man in heavy armor threw up his visor, revealing a pair of glasses. "What the hell are you doing!" he demanded. "What the bloody effing hell is going on here today!" His angry eyes dug deeper than any sword. "It's an effing wonder I didn't run you down!"

"The child, didn't you see the child?" Amy said. Her words came out in sobs and gasps.

"There was no kid, lady! Get the hell off my field! Is everyone crazy today!"

Amy ignored him, pushing around the horse, searching for Shawn and fighting panic.

Shawn was not there.

Niall was not there.

She fell numbly to her knees. Horses and warriors fought around her, dust rising and swirling around it all, and opened her hand. A heavy, gold, medieval ring, worthy of a king, lay in her palm.

* * *

Niall shoved the child into its mother's arms. She cried and clutched him, thanking Niall even as he turned and sprinted back. The bobbies were gone. Amy was gone. The tourists in Bermudas with their cameras were gone. The English lay dead or wounded on the field, or scrambled in full retreat back across the stream. He chased one down, bellowing, and ran him through, stabbing over and over. Here was one man who would never again kill his loved ones. He turned for more prey and saw the horse, bleeding and screaming in pain, fallen to the ground. Three feet from him lay Shawn, grimacing, clutching his side. Blood poured between his fingers.

* * *

"Aer ye mad!" Niall shouted over the cacophony. "Ye threw away yer chance!"

Shawn gasped, wincing. "No," he whispered. He grunted, looking down at the blood spreading thick and fast around his fingers.

"Water!" Niall shouted, looking frantically into the thinning ranks. "Help!" Hugh appeared beside him, staring at the two Nialls. Silently, he helped Niall lift Shawn and carry him up Coxet Hill. Niall winced at Shawn's moans. Blood flowed freely, staining Niall's shirt and tunic.

They laid him down. The child's mother rushed forth, tearing at her skirt for bandages. A boy ran with water. She lifted Shawn's head gently, tipping it between his lips. Hugh tightened bandages around his wound. Shawn grimaced, his face chalk white.

"Leave us," Niall commanded. Hugh silently obeyed, taking himself back to the last vestiges of battle.

Niall leaned close. "You had a good life," he whispered fiercely. "You had everything. D' ye understand you're trapped in 1314?"

* * *

The field cleared quickly. The dead and wounded rose, wiping brows in the summer sun, laughing, shaking hands with their enemies of moments before, and making plans to meet at the pub that evening. The police, the local constables, the orchestra, Conrad, Amy, Dana, Celine, Aaron, and Rob searched the battlefield. They asked questions. They showed photographs everywhere. Several reenactors remembered seeing him the night before, remembered his stunningly authentic performance on the harp.

Amy nodded, understanding. But it didn't help.

Conrad stopped her under the towering statue of Robert the Bruce, the statue commemorating Scotland's greatest victory against insurmountable odds. He gripped her arm, saying, "I saw two of him. I saw it with my own eyes. What is going on!"

"I told you," Amy said. "I *told* you it was Niall who came back from Glenmirril." She stared up at the statue. "That was Edward," she said faintly.

"Edward? What are you talking about?" Conrad spared a glance for the statue of Robert the Bruce. "Niall Campbell, heir to Glenmirril." He snorted. "That's impossible."

The search spread into the fields to the south, north toward St. Ninian's and the castle, and into the surrounding town. After three days, the police called it off. "He just couldn't leave the field that fast," the chief explained. "We're verra sorry. There's nothing more we can do."

* * *

Shawn's eyes fluttered open. Niall sat on one side of his great four-poster bed, Allene on the other, as they had for days now, cooling his fever, giving him water and broth, waiting for him to come around.

"Why did ye do it?" Niall asked. "Why did ye throw away your chance?"

Shawn felt light inside. He'd spent days weaving in and out of dreams and hallucinations. His father, in the car with the fatherless boy. Amy, begging and pleading with him to keep their baby. The child, crying under the on-coming hooves of the horse. The pain had subsided, and he seemed to float in a lighter, whiter space.

"I took the chance...." He drew in a long, painful breath and fell silent till they gave him some water. "Kleiner means less," he whispered.

"What?" Niall stared at Allene and back to Shawn. "What does that mean?"

Shawn closed his eyes, breathing deeply the scent of the bluebells Allene had brought him.

Coda

Inverness, Scotland, One Year Later

The green room filled with the orchestra, arriving in jeans and t-shirts. They nodded at each other, young and old, men and women, but said little. Singly or in small groups, they approached Amy, patting her arm—*good to see you again*—or hugging her—*it's great to be back.* They'd come for a return engagement to Inverness, the last place Shawn had played.

Conrad hugged her. He'd grown thinner. "Anytime you want to come back." He kissed her son, glanced at the pastries on the table, and left without touching one.

"It's like a wake," Amy whispered to Celine. They stood near the counter, where tea and coffee languished, ignored.

"It is," Celine replied. "It's been a year."

Amy bundled her son on her shoulder. A year ago, she had resigned her position with the orchestra, found students in Inverness, and shortly before giving birth, won a spot with Scotland's symphony.

"It's starting!" Peter called. Amy and Celine joined the others in front of a television. Amid shushes, quiet fell.

A bright-eyed reporter squinted in the sun; delicate blue blossoms rustled in the fields. The great statue of Robert the Bruce stood guard behind her, gazing out protectively over the country he'd saved. "It's almost a year since renowned musician, Shawn Kleiner, disappeared inexplicably, during the re-enactment of Scotland's greatest victory, the Battle of Bannockburn." A picture of Shawn filled the screen, holding his trombone, in full tuxedo. Even in this photograph, his eye shone with mischief. Someone patted Amy's back. She bit her lip. It hurt to look. Even now, a year later, it was a double pain, missing both Niall and Shawn, and the pain compounded by guilt for feeling faithless and fickle. The situation with Angus didn't help.

She'd spent every free minute, between students, rehearsals, and performances, scouring the internet, museums, archives of any sort, for any mention of Niall or Shawn.

"We have with us his friend and former colleague, Rob Carlson, who is leading the search effort." Sunlight danced in his blond hair. He swallowed, looking from right to left. Amy lowered her eyes. Seeing Rob brought a different pain—guilt for not loving him as he wished.

He'd argued, called, and e-mailed, begging her to come home. There came a sudden two weeks of silence, at the end of which he'd knocked on her door. "I'll find him for you," he said. He moved into his own home, and started the search, despite her protests.

"Come on, Amy!" he'd raged one particularly volatile night. "If you really believe this insane story that he's been sucked through a time void, why are *you* still here?"

She laid the crucifix and the ring on the table between them, swallowing tears. "I just need to be here where they were."

"There weren't two of them," Rob yelled, and slammed out of her house, blinking rapidly and swallowing hard.

"Mr. Carlson," the reporter asked, "how's the search going?"

He looked into the camera. "We're, um, following leads that he's been spotted in Aberdeen, but so far, there's been no trace. We have a toll, uh, toll free number where we can be contacted with, uh, information." He swallowed hard.

"Tell us about the events of last midsummer's day," the reporter said.

"He, um, spent the night in a castle ruin," Rob said. His eyes darted from side to side. "When we found him the next morning, he had injuries, severe infection, and amnesia, and for the next week, he behaved strangely. After the last concert, he went into the, uh, mountains and walked from there to the re-enactment of the Battle of Bannockburn. We saw him on the field, we tried to reach him, but a horse came between us, and then he was just...gone."

"The police have speculated that he deliberately walked away from his life," the reporter suggested. "Thousands of people do it every year. They do not want to be found. Is that possible?"

"No." Rob spoke with certainty. "Shawn had everything. Talent, money, fame." He stared directly into the camera. "He had a beautiful woman who loved him. He'd be insane to walk away from that."

The camera skimmed past the towering statue of Robert the Bruce astride his horse, back to the reporter. The breeze lifted her hair off her shoulders. "Who was Shawn Kleiner?" she asked. "And where did he go?"

Another picture of Shawn flashed on the screen. His long hair blew in the wind. He squinted, laughing, into the sun. The camera closed in again on Shawn's smiling face, the face of a man who loved life.

* * *

Rob let himself into her kitchen. "How did I do?" His eyes held hope. She hated herself for deflating it again.

"I'm not marrying you."

His face flushed. "I didn't ask."

"You made your feelings clear on television in front of everyone. You're not going to find him, Rob."

"And you are?" He snapped off the whining kettle. "Looking in museums and at reproductions of books that fell apart hundreds of years ago?" He slapped two black mugs on the counter, filling each. Twin tendrils of steam twisted toward the ceiling.

"I know what I saw, Rob. Why do you listen to a thousand strangers calling a toll free number but not me?"

"Because what you're saying is insane."

"Am I the only one who remembers Niall reading page after page saying the Scots lost? We went to a re-enactment of the Battle of the Pools, won by the English, and left a re-enactment of Bannockburn, the Scots' greatest victory."

"That's impossible, Amy. You know it is."

"I showed you the crucifix and ring." She sipped her cooling tea. "I showed you what Niall wrote. You verified it for yourself."

"It's a huge leap from 'Shawn researched a crucifix' to 'Shawn and his medieval twin made a daring leap across time.'"

Amy sighed. "I saw Shawn throw himself between a charging warhorse and a child. I *saw* it, Rob!"

Rob circled behind her, rubbing her shoulders, and laying his cheek on top of her head. She knew the look of grief that would be on his face. "It wasn't a real battle. And even if it was, you and I both know Shawn would never do a thing like that." She sat quietly, Rob's hands on her shoulders, seeing Shawn running straight at the armored horse, as if it was still happening. Rob spoke again. "It was his joke. Shawn means..."

She finished the sentence with him. "...self, and Kleiner means centered."

"He wore it like a badge of honor," Rob said.

They remained quiet for several minutes, before Amy spoke again. "People change. Sometimes they grow up and become who they really were. One of the German translations of Kleiner is 'less.' He finally did something selfless."

The End

The *Blue Bells Trilogy* continues with...

The Minstrel Boy
The Castle of Dromore

Learn more about the books
and the world of Shawn, Niall, Amy, and Allene,
at www.bluebellstrilogy.com
and www.bluebellstrilogy.com/blog

For more books from the Night Writers,
visit www.nightwritersbooks.com

11777743R0021

Made in the USA
Lexington, KY
01 November 2011